IMPENDING

FATE

BOOK III: THE SHATTERED TRIANGLE TRILOGY

WILLIAM P. MESSENGER

ISBN: 978-1-61296-955-8
PUBLISHED BY BLACK ROSE WRITING
www.blackrosewriting.com

Printed in the United States of America
Suggested Retail Price (SRP) $19.95

Impending Fate is printed in Traditional Arabic

I dedicate this book to the late

Archbishop George H. Niederauer

Before his rise to the upper echelons of the Catholic hierarchy, Niederauer was a college professor. He was the first person to tell me that I possessed the skill of narrative writing. This book is one result of that encouragement.

ACKNOWLEDGMENTS

In the course of this trilogy I have been fortunate to have the dedicated assistance of

Adolfo Batres ensured that all the elements of police activity were accurate, both within the Los Angeles Police Department and its interaction with agencies in Boston and Washington.

Perry Leiker, Taylor Lilly and Marilyne Sherwood once again committed hours of their time to read, correct and re-read the manuscript, thereby providing invaluable insight and direction.

Barbara Fandrich again lent her excellent editing skills guaranteeing integration in the storyline and a grammatically correct reading experience.

Frank Hicks opened the doors of the Writers Loft providing a place for quiet composition.

IMPENDING

FATE

PROLOGUE
APRIL 2003

I am an identical twin and inhabit an almost unique world. There are, after all, not that many of us. And although others might find us perplexing, we are not that different from singletons. Contrary to popular belief we do not act or respond in concert; there is no invisible strand of intuition enabling us to sense one another's feelings while separated by distances great or small; we don't even think alike. We just look alike.

As a child there were times I enjoyed being a twin. My brother and I were often the recipients of special attention. Indeed, we were cute boys and most of the time it was fun to watch adults fawn over us. In school we did not play any of the stereotypical games such as changing seats in the classroom. It was sufficient to watch our classmates and teachers struggle to tell us apart.

As we grew older our interests diverged. That much was to be expected. We were not the same person. But it was not until my sister-in-law and her children were murdered that I realized how different we had become.

On April 29, 2003, I met with my brother, Senator Giuseppe Lozano, in his Washington, D.C., office. It was one last, futile attempt to discover if there was anything we still had in common. When I left him I regretted even the facial similarities. He was no longer someone I wanted to mirror in physical appearance. Nor was he someone I wanted to possess in my heart. My name is Giovanni Lozano, a priest from the Archdiocese of Los Angeles. And my brother is a murderer.

CHAPTER 1

Secrecy. A critical element of childhood, it can often be a joy. The experience of entrusting another with our privileged information or our innermost thoughts is a test of friendship. It builds surety and speaks significantly about the value we place on those closest to us. Exchanging confidences continues into adulthood, but along the way it loses the innocence and fun of juvenility. Although still a test of faith, it frequently becomes burdensome with age.

In Catholic sacramental life, the seal of confession carries a gravity beyond even the deepest confidence, shrouding the priest in a secret solitude. Most of the time it is not difficult to maintain the privacy of the sacrament. It is a welcome safeguard that helps people develop the courage to change their lives, even to find healing and peace. When it is abused by either priest or penitent, the promise, the hope, the joy of forgiveness becomes onerous. Such was the case with my twin brother, Giuseppe.

I learned in the confessional that he was responsible for his family's murder. He did not pull the trigger, but he arranged for their deaths. As if that were not bad enough, he manipulated me, choosing to admit his action in a mockery of the sacrament. He knew full well that I would be bound to secrecy, and thus prevented from revealing the truth or even hinting at it with Lt. Tom Moran, a close friend and LAPD detective. But I also think Giuseppe is diabolical enough to know that this knowledge would weigh upon my psyche, perhaps hoping that it would incapacitate me. In that he was not far from the truth.

For two-and-a-half years, every waking day, I carried the strain of knowledge. That's one reason I went to see him. I wanted to believe that there was still some good in him, that I could reach the depth of his soul, his conscience. I was wrong and returned to Los Angeles convinced that my brother of almost fifty years was no more. He had become a stranger in the truest sense of the word. But this was a revelation I could not share with family or friends. My parents, my sister, and others believed Giuseppe to be a victim. And I was in no position to dispossess them of that belief.

•   •   •

I returned home late Tuesday night overwhelmed by my failure and the stark truth I now had to face. On Wednesday, April 30, I called Lt. Tom Moran and asked him to come over that evening for a drink. We had known each other from the age of six, and although I count some priests among my intimate friends, of everyone I know including family, Tom is closest to me. As a lieutenant in the Los Angeles Police Department, he was lead detective in investigating the murder of my brother's family. Like me, he happened upon the truth and, like me, was manipulated by Giuseppe in such a way that he was unable to publicly solve the case. Before visiting my brother in Washington I had not told Tom about my trip. Now I felt a need to share that experience and my deepening concerns.

When Tom arrived I already had his drink waiting. We are both scotch drinkers and over the years had become particularly fond of Pinch. Like other such evenings I was comfortably in the company of two old friends. There were two cozy chairs in the room. He chose the recliner, leaving the rocker to me.

"How's Emily?" I asked.

"As feisty as ever," he laughed. "Life's been good since we got back together."

"Well, from my perspective, between your transfer to the Counter Terrorism and Criminal Intelligence Bureau and your remarriage to Emily, you're calmer, more settled than you've been for a long time. It's good to see you more like your old self."

"One thing's certain, Gio. It's nice to have someone to go home to."

"Tom, I need to talk to you about Giuseppe. That's why I didn't ask you to bring Emily tonight. I just returned from Washington, D.C." I had told him nothing about my intentions during my recent absence, but the statement did not appear to raise any questions. I doubt he ever considered that I would go to see my brother and probably assumed that I had some church business in the capital. "I went to Washington specifically to see him."

I had known Tom all my life and thought I could predict every one of his reactions, but not this time. His expression did not register the surprise I expected. In fact it did not register anything at all. He just looked at me and asked why. The question was not quite accusatory, but still I felt ill at ease and had to tread cautiously. Once someone has made a confession, the priest is not allowed to bring up the subject matter even to the person who confessed. When I visited my brother I did exactly that, knowing that he would not report me to church authorities. But it would be something else entirely if I spoke about the confession to Tom.

"I can't put the murders out of my head," I continued. "I know this has weighed on you, also. But Giuseppe is my twin brother and I can't figure him out. I went to try to get him to say something to me, something that would help me finally bring this whole thing to a close."

"Gio, I've never thought of you as a simpleton, so tell me. How could you possibly think he would admit anything to you? I've reached the conclusion that your brother's a true psychopath. I think you know it, too." He paused briefly then said with determination, "You're not going to change him."

"Tom, I've always believed that no one is beyond the redemptive power of God. That idea has driven my priesthood for more than twenty years. I thought I could reach him." My voice trailed off betraying a certain resignation.

Tom's tone of voice was surprisingly gentle. "Did Giuseppe say anything at all?" he asked.

"Well, we talked about some things I can't share with you."

"You mean things like the confession?" He knew exactly what I meant. We both did. But by church law it had remained unspoken between us. Tom tried a few times to break my resolve, to convince me to violate the sacrament. This time was different. His question was almost more of a statement. And I appreciated that he was not trying once again to draw me into forbidden territory.

"Yes," I replied. "But he added nothing. He feels safe in knowing that anything he said to me that December will remain private. He did say one thing, though, that I can share. He claims he was not involved in Jean-Paul Lecuyer's murder."

Up to this point Tom had seemed somewhat disinterested in my visit with Giuseppe. Now, however, he was intrigued.

"Did you believe him?" he asked.

"I'm not sure I believe anything he says anymore. But he did point out that they had only met on two occasions when Jackson and Jean-Paul visited Washington. As Giuseppe says, there was no motive for him to kill Lecuyer."

"Yeah," Tom said. "That's the missing link right now. When I met with the Brussels police the only thing to go on was the modus operandi, single shots to the head or heart, a Glock 9mm left at the scene. Like the murders of Yolanda and the kids it was clearly professional. Also like theirs, no usable forensic evidence was left behind—no fingerprints, no DNA. A motive would be helpful, critical even. I have to admit, though, that even if one were to turn up it would be difficult to tie Giuseppe to Jean-Paul's death. But when you look at the matching M.O.—I just don't believe in those kinds of coincidences."

"Neither do I," I replied. "But we're dealing with a professional assassin. It stands to reason that he has done this before and will continue in the future. It's not inconceivable that he would have clients around the world."

"Are you trying to convince me or yourself?" Tom asked.

"I don't know. I'm just grasping and I don't know how much longer I can hold on. I've expended so much energy these last couple of years trying to contain my knowledge and mask my depression. If Giuseppe was not involved in Jean-Paul's death and that of his friends, then that's a ray of hope."

"Gio, I don't like the idea of you playing detective. It's beyond your skill set. Your talents lie elsewhere. I don't care if you talk to Giuseppe about Yolanda and the kids, but I want you to leave the Brussels killings alone. We may never know the why of those murders. Besides, it's not our business. It's someone else's problem. Let's suppose Giuseppe did have something to do with it. If you get too close, do you think you'll be safe? He has no qualms about eliminating people he thinks are in his way. Let the Belgian authorities handle their own case. As for Yolanda and the kids, we'll just never be able to prove what we both know. And since I'm not on the case anymore, I'm content to focus my attention on my new job and try to keep Los Angeles safe from terrorists.

"In my opinion you need to give up on your brother. I know you're not going to betray the sacrament and you know you can't change Giuseppe." He took a drink of scotch, swirled the glass in his hand, and said, "I'm worried about you, Gio. If you don't find a way to put this behind you, you're going to crack. I see the stress every time we get together. Emily's noticed it, too."

"Have you said anything to her?" I asked.

Of the many things I knew to be true of Tom one was that he was a fierce and loyal friend, another that he was an excellent detective. But that last characteristic also bred a unique skill for deception. His concern for me would not allow him to answer my question honestly. I did not know it at the time, but only one week before he had stoked his wife's journalistic curiosity by suggesting that the *Los Angeles Times* initiate its own investigation into the Lozano and Lecuyer murders. He shared with her what he had learned during the investigation, including Giuseppe's admission of guilt. However, he was not ready to reveal that to me. He chose, instead, to lie.

"So far, Gio, I've managed to deflect her comments. But she's bright— more so than either of us. She's seen how your parents and your sister have adjusted. Then she sees you. It's only a matter of time before she pieces things together. Nothing goes unnoticed with her."

He had a point. Emily had not pressed me about the murders since she came back into our lives, but she surely noticed a darkness in my mood. Maybe Tom was right. I should let it all go. How incomprehensible that the suggestion should come so easily while its execution remained impossible.

Tom continued. "Listen, Gio. I know better than anyone the tension you're under. You haven't really taken any time for yourself. For example, when was your last vacation? You and your friends enjoy Mexico so much, why not take a week and go to Puerto Vallarta?"

"Funny you should mention it," I replied. "Perry called the other day to suggest that very thing. He wants to go in August. Maybe I should. It's just so damn hot and humid down there during the summer."

"Then you can sweat your tension away," Tom suggested.

"Well, I have to let him know soon so he can arrange the flights. In the meantime I had to tell you about my trip to Washington. I just don't want any secrets between us."

It might have been my imagination but I thought I saw Tom briefly dart his eyes away as if trying to hide a reaction to that last comment, possibly the result of guilt since he had not told me the truth about his revelations to Emily. It was nearly imperceptible and now I know I was right. In any case I was glad I told him why I went to D.C. and what had transpired there. His response was measured and he left me with good advice. He was probably right regarding my brother, too. If I wanted to be honest with myself I had been inching toward the same conclusions for many months. But judging my brother for what he had become and forgetting what he had done were worlds apart. I said good night, and after Tom left, I prepared for bed.

CHAPTER 2

Tom returned home to find Emily still awake. As a reporter she was accustomed to late nights, especially when meeting a publication deadline. But she was not working. She was waiting. When they had remarried the previous year they made a pact. Unless one was traveling they would not retire to bed without the other. Occasionally the nights were quite long, but the wait was always filled with anticipation and going to bed together a joy.

Tom frequently wondered how he had missed all this the first time around. The facts were simple enough. He let his work take precedence over married life. But in truth they were both driven by their professions during their first marriage. Even if they had had the children Emily desired, she would not have sacrificed her career. Things were different now. Tom and Emily proved the songwriter Sammy Cahn correct: "Love *is* lovelier the second time around." In this marriage they made certain to set their priorities around each other.

As Tom walked in the door Emily was there to greet him.

"How was your visit with Gio?" she asked.

"I guess it was OK," Tom replied. "He wanted to talk about his asshole brother. You won't believe it but last week he went to Washington to see Giuseppe. He actually thought he could reach him—as if his brother still had some fundamental good inside him or even a soul worth saving."

"Tom, give Gio a break. It's not really that difficult to understand. He's driven by the depth and power of his faith." Then she gently added, "A faith you gave up a long time ago."

Emily had received a strong Catholic foundation from her parents, and although Tom and Giuseppe had surrendered that same faith to the powers of the world, Emily still believed.

"Perhaps he sees something you don't," she suggested.

"I'm sure. But there's nothing good left in Giuseppe. Of that much I am certain."

"Don't you think that's a little harsh?" she asked. "This whole thing with the murders has to be even harder for Giovanni than it is for you. It must have rattled his faith as well as his emotions. He needs room to work through everything, including to determine if there is still good in his brother. And being in Washington must have been difficult. I'm sure that in the capital Giuseppe elicits sympathy. He is seen as a victim."

"Come on, Emily. You went to see him. Don't tell me he fooled you."

"Yes, I went to see him. That was before you told me what he admitted to you about his family's murders. But it's not so much a matter of being fooled. Even if I had already known that he had his wife and children killed, I would have to admit that Giuseppe was as pleasant to me as ever. And it didn't seem artificial. Maybe Gio was hoping to reach that part of him."

"I still say there's nothing to reach," Tom insisted. "From my perspective Giuseppe has accomplished the not inconsiderable achievement of making the serial killer look tame. But you know, Emily," he mused, "I don't even think I hate him anymore. I don't want to give him that satisfaction."

"And that's exactly the difference between you and Giovanni," she replied. "Love and hate are two sides of the same coin. I think Gio still loves his brother—and also hates him. You don't do either."

Tom walked over to the bar to pour a drink. "You want one?" he asked. Emily just shook her head. After he had his drink in hand he continued. "The problem with Giuseppe's narrow and insular world view is that it is nearly impossible to determine who the next target will be. But I promise you, Em. He's not through killing."

"You're still assuming he had something to do with Jean-Paul's death. I know you have reason to be suspicious. But at this point, you don't have any evidence. And before you ask, I'm not being naïve. I've been around too long for that, and I have my misgivings, too. I've seen the same evils in my job that you have in yours. And I've seen them up close on a global scale. I'm not fooled by Giuseppe."

"But you give him the benefit of the doubt regarding Jean-Paul."

"No," she replied. "I just don't have enough information yet. A similar M.O. does not mean that Giuseppe was involved, especially given that the murders occurred on another continent. It merely raises questions that are as yet unanswered.

"I have a meeting with my editor, John Carroll, tomorrow," she continued. "I'm going to present your suggestion that the *Times* initiate its own investigation into the murders of Yolanda and the kids. However, given the sensitivity of the case—the fact that the victims were the family of a U.S. senator, the perceived failure of the LAPD, and what Giuseppe admitted to you—he'll want to discuss it with Puerner."

"What do you think Carroll's response will be?"

"I think he'll want to investigate. He's not one to shy away from controversy, no matter who is involved. But Puerner is the publisher and he's out of town right now." She paused to think for a moment, then continued. "Tom, I'm going to have to tell him about your meeting with Giuseppe and that he admitted to having his family killed. It's the grail of this murder case."

"I figured as much," he replied. "But, Em, you should let Carroll know how dangerous this case is. Giuseppe will not be able to manipulate a newspaper the way he did the police."

"Meaning?"

"Meaning his only refuge will be more violence."

"I still think you're overstating it," Emily said. "But I will tell him."

· · ·

Emily had established herself as a highly respected reporter during her career, first with the *Los Angeles Herald Examiner* and then with the *Los Angeles Times*. But her true value was not appreciated until 2000 when new management came to the paper. In April of that year John Carroll was made editor. He had been brought over from *The Baltimore Sun* after The Tribune Company purchased Times Mirror, which owned both the *Sun* and the *Los Angeles Times*. In the same leadership shakeup John Puerner was named publisher. Both men possessed unimpeachable journalistic credentials, but it was Carroll who set the direction for the newspaper. He brought with him a history of principled and uncompromising journalism and set about to raise the seriously deteriorating standards of the *Times*.

Carroll had familiarized himself with Emily's body of work and recognized that she sheltered greater potential, particularly in the area of investigative journalism, but he was not about to sacrifice her reporting skills. After his arrival at the *Times* he expanded her field of coverage and gave her frequent assignments in Afghanistan and Europe. His reorganization of the newspaper included doubling the investigative staff, and when war broke out in Iraq the *Los Angeles Times* was unrivaled in its coverage. Through it all Emily remained Carroll's prize overseas correspondent.

Emily and Tom awoke at five o'clock, showered, and had a quick breakfast. At that hour Emily could be in her office by six fifteen, which was perfect since the meeting was set for six thirty. May 1, 2003 was a mild day in Los Angeles. Although the temperature would eventually reach the mid-sixties, the early morning was quite cool and slightly breezy. The briskness only added to Emily's anticipation. She arrived on time, set a few things on her desk, poured a cup of coffee and went straight to Carroll's office.

As it turned out Emily was fortunate that Puerner was out of town. If the *Los Angeles Times* began an investigation of the Lozano murders, she wanted to be the primary reporter assigned to the case. The publisher's absence worked in her favor since Carroll had another assignment ready for her. She entered his office at six thirty in the morning. He welcomed her with a warm greeting. "Hello, Emily."

"Good morning, John," she replied.

"I see you already have your coffee. Give me a moment to pour myself a cup."

As he did so, Emily settled into a cloth-covered chair opposite him. Carroll had a habit of sitting behind his desk for most meetings. He was not excessively formal, nor was this custom a display of power. It was practical. Although he was noted for near perfect memory recall, he still took copious notes and as they began to speak had pen and paper at hand.

He smiled and said, "I know you have something important on your mind, Emily. So do I. But why don't you go first?"

She had rehearsed her presentation and proceeded without hesitation.

"John, I think the *Times* should initiate an investigation into the murders of Yolanda Lozano and her children." She paused and took a drink of coffee. In part she was being deliberate in her speech. But she was also waiting to see if there was any reaction. None was forthcoming. Carroll merely scribbled a note and waited for Emily to continue. "Actually, the suggestion comes from my husband. Tom seems to think that the paper can succeed where the LAPD could not."

Carroll continued to write. Emily could not tell if he was jotting down what she said or noting his own response, but she knew him well enough to know that he was intrigued. He also was no fool and understood how profound this suggestion was. As she paused again he looked up and asked, "Why does he think that?" He still revealed nothing of his own thoughts.

This was the moment of truth and Emily would have to tell everything her husband had shared with her.

"Tom knows who the killer is." Carroll merely cocked one eyebrow as she continued. "When he and I got back together last year he told me about the investigation and what he had learned. Every path led to one person— Giuseppe Lozano."

Carroll still appeared unfazed. Like any good reporter, he was driven by the adrenaline rush that accompanies a journalistic scoop, especially the surfacing of evidence that leads to explosive and exclusive copy. But this conversation was far too preliminary and it involved a sitting United States senator. There was a great deal at stake, including the paper's reputation. He knew this was not an impulsive suggestion. Still, he would need much more information. For the time being he would keep his own counsel.

"Emily, I arrived at the *Times* only a few months before the murders. The paper covered the police investigation very carefully and I followed the case as closely as anyone. From my recollection Lozano was not at the house and there was nothing to suggest he was involved. What is it you're *not* telling me?"

Pitching this kind of story was akin to a waltz. Emily was leading and each piece of data was a dance step. She glided smoothly through the information lest she stumble and lose her partner before the final note.

"Tom told me that the LAPD kept significant information from the press and out of the public eye. To tell you the truth, given all the reporters in this city and their contacts within the department, I was surprised there were no leaks."

"Yes," Carroll mused. "At the time it seemed as though the LAPD was withholding information. At first I thought the department was playing out a grudge against the *Times*. But the rest of the media also came up empty. No one was able to pry information from the police." He reached for his own cup of coffee and asked, "I suppose Tom told you what they held back from the public?"

"Not everything. I think he wants a commitment from you first. But I'll tell you why *I* think we should get involved." Emily kept her composure, but her natural instincts took over as she began to make her case. "There was evidence left at the crime scene. First of all the murder weapons were left behind in an obvious attempt to taunt the police. I think that's one reason they did not reveal that information. It was also clear that the murders were a professional hit. The only other piece of evidence was an accidental footprint in the flower garden. Neither of those facts were reported to the media. But there's more.

"The M.O. was repeated two more times, linking additional murders to the original crime. The police had only one suspect from the Lozano murders, Gary Bass. He was under surveillance but managed to evade the detectives and was found dead a day later. The police believed that if that information became public it would compromise their ability to apprehend the other assassin."

Carroll was carefully writing but interjected a question. "You said there were *two* additional killings. What was the second one?"

"Lozano's lawyer, Christopher Coker, was found dead on the street outside his house. In both of these incidents the weapons, the same make and model as the ones from the original murders, were left at the scene."

"And how does the senator figure into all this?"

Professionalism aside, Emily looked a bit forlorn. She had known Giuseppe a long time and had cared deeply for him and his family. There was sadness in her eyes as she continued.

"As I said before, the evidence all leads to Giuseppe. At first Tom thought he was being blackmailed by someone who set the murders in motion. As the investigation proceeded and the police dug deeper, Tom came to the conclusion that only one person could have been responsible. He confronted Giuseppe at the Pegasus Group headquarters, the electronics company he had founded. He admitted to having his family killed, but he did so in such a way that Tom could not use it as evidence. This has haunted my husband for three years, and he now thinks only the *Times* can bring Lozano down."

Carroll did not respond immediately. He stood up and went to the coffeemaker. "Would you like another cup?" he asked.

"I think I need it," Emily replied.

Carroll brought the coffeepot over, poured a cup for her and one for himself. Then he sat down and wrote a few more notes. For the time being Emily had decided not to address the fear and danger that so concerned her husband or the suggestion that Giuseppe would kill again. But her proposal had another condition.

"There's one more thing, John. I want this assignment. I want to break this case for the *Times*. Nobody on the paper knows the players better than I. And it will be easier for me to solicit information from the LAPD."

She realized that her closeness to Tom and Giuseppe's family was the strongest argument in favor of her getting the assignment. At the same time it was her greatest potential liability, just as it had been with her husband who had commandeered the police investigation. Yet she remained certain of her ability to sustain objectivity and not surrender to emotion. Carroll agreed.

"That part's a no-brainer, Emily. But I need to think about the whole story, including the timing. And I will have to discuss it with Puerner when he returns. He will need to back this if we're going after a U.S. senator. I'll also have more questions before we commit. In the meantime I have another pressing assignment for you."

"You want me back in Iraq?" she asked.

"No," he replied. "But the conflict there, as well as in Afghanistan, along with the assignment I have in mind, are additional reasons why we need to delay an investigation into the Lozano murders. When we break that story, it cannot be overshadowed by international events. And there are many right now. As you know, yesterday the Quartet on the Middle East announced a roadmap for peace—a new and ambitious attempt to end the Israeli–Palestinian conflict. I want you to fly out tomorrow and cover the plan."

She did not have to respond. As soon as he spoke those words he sighed and said, "I know, Emily. I can see it in your eyes. There have been so many other attempts at peace and they've all failed. Why should this one be any different? To tell you the truth I don't know that it will be. At least not if it is left to the politicians. That's where your unique skills come into play.

"In all your assignments you've managed to engender trust among the people on the street. That's what makes your writing so good. I want you to report on the reaction of everyday Jews and Palestinians. The future of peace lies with them. At some point they will have to band together and demand it from their leaders."

She opened her calendar, unsure how much time this assignment would require, and noted that there were no significant events coming up.

"John, thanks for meeting with me and for being open to my request. I'll finish up some work here, arrange a flight, and take the rest of the day off. Tom's going to be anxiously waiting to hear your response, but he'll understand your caution."

Emily stood up and returned to her desk confident that if the *Times* investigated the murders, she would be the reporter. Even if she were not being sent to the Middle East in the morning, she would have left work early. Her meeting with Carroll had not been merely business. There was a stronger emotional dimension than she wanted to admit. Whatever her objective abilities, she was personally vested in this story. Tom's revelation about the murders and Giuseppe's admission of guilt had energized *and* distressed her. In the meantime she had accomplished her goal for the day. The *Times* was onboard. Perhaps the best way for her to prepare would be by shifting attention to another world crisis and resting on a long trip to Tel Aviv.

CHAPTER 3

Shortly following WWII, the United States and the Soviet Union squared off in what would come to be known as the Cold War. No direct conflicts resulted between the two super powers, but for almost three generations they were engaged in proxy wars in Asia and Africa, and sparred for leverage in Latin America.

Although the establishment of Israel in 1948 was not an outcome of that emerging cold conflict, the arbitrary declaration by David Ben-Gurion and the "Jewish Agency for Palestine" that an Israeli State would begin operating in part of the Palestinian territory occasioned violent opposition from the neighboring Arab countries. Since that time the Middle East has been fraught with violence, Israel steadfastly defending its right to exist and some of its Arab neighbors calling for its destruction.

Over time this provided the United States and the Soviet Union another theatre in which to vie for influence. Many of the countries in the region have played the East-West dichotomy to their own advantage, shifting allegiance when deemed expedient. Perhaps no country has been more successful at this than Egypt. To this day the exceptions include the alliance between Russia (formerly the Soviet Union) and Syria, and the bond between the United States and Saudi Arabia, not to mention the bedrock U.S. support for Israel.

Among the many efforts to bring peace to the Middle East, only two have paid dividends. A 1979 peace treaty between Israel and Egypt was signed in Washington, D.C., and in 1994 Israel and Jordan met to sign a treaty at the Arabah border crossing. These achievements have, unfortunately, been overshadowed by continuing conflict between Israelis and Palestinians, fueled in no small part by the unrelenting obstinacy of their leaders. One has to wonder if those politicians, whose strongest appeal is their belligerence, would be out of a job in a world of peace.

.   .   .

Following decades of mistrust and violence President George W. Bush floated the concept of a roadmap for peace in 2002. The idea was rooted in a two-state solution, one for the Israelis and the other for the Palestinians. A draft was circulated among the Quartet on the Middle East (the United Nations, the United States, the European Union and Russia) with a final version announced on April 30, 2003, the day before Emily met with Carroll and he assigned her to cover this latest peace attempt.

On May 2 Emily took a morning flight to New York to meet with Susan Sachs, a correspondent at the *New York Times*. They had met in 1995, when they were both covering the assassination of Israeli Prime Minister Yitzhak Rabin, and quickly became friends. For almost a decade they covered the same terrain of the Middle East and Central Asia, and in the last couple of years had practically established residences in Afghanistan and Iraq. They were both invaluable to their respective papers because each possessed the ability to understand complex foreign cultures and write with clarity for American audiences. It was natural that each would be asked to cover the roadmap.

Emily's brain, always distinguishing between work and vacation, could never unite the two. In spite of a five-hour flight across country she neither slept nor rested, instead she spent the time pouring over her notes, recalling names, places and events on previous trips to Israel and the West Bank. Since the roadmap called for establishing two independent, viable and neighboring states, she replayed in her mind the history of the area since 1948.

The United Nations was formed at the conclusion of the Second World War and was, arguably, the most ambitious attempt ever to procure a peaceful planet and guarantee security for all. Regarding the Palestinians, in one year alone, 1948, the United Nations Security Council passed no less than twelve resolutions, and parts of three more, seeking an end to the hostilities between Israelis and Palestinians and a homeland for each.

On December 11, 1948, the larger UN General Assembly passed resolution 194, calling for refugees to return to their homes and defining the principles for peace and an end to the conflict. Ironically and unfortunately, although the resolution passed by a substantial majority, six Arab nations—Egypt, Iraq, Lebanon, Saudi Arabia, Syria and Yemen—all voted against. It has been, in part, the intransigence of these nations that has emboldened Israel to thumb its nose at United Nations' resolutions for nearly sixty years, trusting that it would be protected by the United States. After all, when UN General Assembly Resolution 273 passed on May 11, 1949, securing Israel's membership in the United Nations, these same Arab states along with Iran voted no. For over half a century the region has seemed destined to live in perpetual violence.

History is not only a compilation of dates and facts. It is a wellspring of unanswerable questions. Had the Arab states supported the U.N. efforts for peace and the membership of Israel, might the 1967 war have been averted? Might there already be two states existing side by side, their peoples living in peace? Cynics on both sides of the conflict, along with outside observers who trust neither the Israelis nor the Palestinians, find such musings naïve and pointless. Still, Emily wondered.

· · ·

Her plane landed in the late afternoon and she took a taxi to the New York Times Building in Manhattan. Susan was absorbed in her writing and did not even notice Emily walk into her office.

"Hello, Susan," Emily said.

She looked up and answered somewhat apologetically, "Oh, hello, Emily. I'm sorry I didn't see you come in. I had my head buried in work."

"Not to worry. I know what that's like and I don't want to interrupt."

"I'm almost finished," Susan replied. "Why don't you sit for a few minutes?"

Emily rolled her eyes and said, "That's what I've been doing for the last several hours. I think I'll just wander around and see if I can find someone to annoy. I'll meet you back here in a little while."

"OK," Susan replied.

Over the years Emily had become friends with many journalists around the world, and her presence at the *New York Times*, while unusual, was not distracting. Everyone was busy getting their articles, columns and reports ready for press. Emily greeted a few of them, but mostly just walked around aimlessly wishing she could have avoided this trip to Israel entirely. Not only was she convinced of its futility, but her mind wanted to focus elsewhere. Following her meeting with Carroll the previous day she felt ready to begin working on the murder investigation. Yet she knew it was far too premature at this point.

Emily made her way back to Susan's office just as she was finishing her work. "Still busy?" she asked.

"All done," Susan answered. "You're probably tired of flying, but we'd better get to the airport. We only have a couple of hours before we board."

"And then we'll be flying all night with only a short layover in Rome," Emily sighed. "By the way, I spoke with Daniele Mastrogiacomo this morning. He'll meet us at the airport; we'll have lunch and then fly on to Tel Aviv."

"That sounds great. It seems like ages since I've seen Daniele. It will be good to catch up."

Daniele Mastrogiacomo was a reporter for *La Repubblica*. The paper had only been founded in 1976, but by 1980 when he began working for the publication it was printing 180,000 copies and well on its way to becoming the most read newspaper in Italy. Certainly one reason for its success was a progressive agenda. However, bringing Mastrogiacomo onboard, with his expertise in international affairs, was sheer brilliance. Like both Emily and Susan, he was a premier war correspondent and the three of them were often embedded in the same conflict zones at the same time. They had a mutual respect and appreciation, and relied on one another to maintain some normalcy amidst the insanity of violence.

At 8:00 p.m. Emily and Susan boarded an Alitalia flight from JFK to Rome. Shortly after takeoff Emily recalled why she tried to avoid that carrier. Although most airline food is one step above hospital fare, Alitalia's is two steps below. And whatever hospitality Italians are known for on the ground does not extend to the skies. The flight attendants tend to toss the food onto passenger tray tables like skilled Las Vegas card dealers. The only redemption would have been if the expected hot food had been at least warm. It was not.

Emily made yet another mental note to not fly Alitalia again. Fortunately, the flight from Rome to Tel Aviv would be on Israel's El Al Airlines.

Arriving in Rome at quarter to eleven in the morning, Daniele was waiting for them. One of the luxuries of a layover in Italy is the food, and they had sufficient time for an almost leisurely lunch. Per Daniele's suggestion they dined at Capella, a small establishment on Via della Stelletta, around the corner from Casa del Clero. It was a small restaurant with a single waiter, unrivaled for its pizza. Daniele assured both women that the food was good, but by way of warning, explained that he had nicknamed the restaurant "Stinky's" due to the waiter's apparent aversion to showers.

In the middle of their meal he asked, "Well, what do the two of you think?"

Susan replied, "You were right about the waiter!" That brought out a laugh in all of them. Then she continued, "But you did a disservice to the food. It's beyond good. I don't think I've ever had a pizza this delicious, not even in New York."

"You're just starving due to the food on that Alitalia flight," Emily suggested, probably reflecting her own mood more than Susan's. "I don't expect an airline to provide handmade, brick-fired pizza. But you'd think an Italian airline could serve something more appetizing than a half-frozen, half-warmed dinner."

"You're too harsh," Susan replied. "It must be that laid back California style."

By this time they had finished lunch and needed to return to the airport. Thank God for Capella, Emily thought to herself. In what would amount to two days of travel, it was the only real food she had. They took an El Al flight from Rome to Tel Aviv arriving at 9:00 p.m.

• • •

Every journalist has a different approach toward investigating and reporting, especially on matters as potentially significant as the roadmap. Susan and Daniele gravitated toward the political establishment, while Emily played to her strengths, spending the days meeting with ordinary Jews and Palestinians.

On Sunday morning she joined Susan and Daniele for breakfast then took a taxi to the Old City.

Emily recalled the first time she was in Jerusalem and the fascination of walking through the Jaffa Gate. It still held the same excitement for her, much like the wonder people experience in that instant when *The Wizard of Oz* switches from black and white to color. However, that was accomplished through the alchemy of film, this was history in rewind—the conjuring of an ancient era. Passing through the gate Emily was transported into the world of Arabian Nights. The farther she wandered into the city the greater the expectation of running into Ali Baba himself. Not, of course, reciting an incantation to open the door of a cave. But perhaps he would be tending a shop, a merchant like his father. Once oriented to her surroundings, Emily's flights of fancy returned to earth.

On her first trip to Israel Emily met four brothers who owned a quality souvenir shop near the Dome of the Rock. They were Christian Arabs but only the youngest, Michael, went by a western name. He was about the same age as Emily and she had maintained a friendship with the brothers and visited their shop each time she was in Jerusalem. This time she was specifically interested in speaking with the oldest, Kadir. He was at the shop daily, but tended not to do the actual selling of merchandise, preferring to sit at a small table overlooking the store.

When she arrived she found Kadir sitting at his customary chair, dressed in thawb and keffiyeh, drinking Turkish coffee and smoking cigarettes, an authentic image for tourists snapping photos. Only the smoking of a hookah would have perfected the picture. The brothers were not given to an abundance of tradition or ceremony and they quickly surrounded Emily, each greeting her with a warm embrace. Then Kadir, knowing she was not there to purchase souvenirs, invited her to join him for coffee.

He poured her a cup, sat down, smiled and said, "My friend, always it is good to see you. You're here because of this new peace plan, what they call a 'roadmap,' no?"

There was no wariness in his speech. His smile and eyes conveyed nothing but gentility. All four brothers had a genuine affection for Emily and trusted her implicitly. They knew she was a fair reporter and that anything shared with her would be handled professionally.

"Yes, Kadir. That is why I am here."

"And you are still working for the *Los Angeles Times*?" he asked.

"Yes. My editor knows that the politicians will get extensive coverage by the rest of the media. He wants me to talk to regular people."

Kadir shook his head and said, "Emily, always you are . . . how do you say . . ." he closed his left eye, cocked his right eyebrow, scratched his head, "'the wily one,' no?" They both laughed.

She knew that he intended it as a compliment and replied, "Well, I'm not sure I would say it like that. But my editor thinks I have a way with people on the street."

"Ah, but here we are not on the street. My family, we are merchants and well-educated. Michael even went to university."

"True, but your life is more than this store. You live in East Jerusalem, and you know many people. You also know other merchants and I know you carefully study everyone who comes into your shop. And you talk to people. In America we have a phrase: 'You have your ear to the ground.'"

"Ah yes, I know this phrase," he said. "It is like a man who puts his ear on a rail track to hear if a train is coming, no?"

"Exactly. That's why I want to ask you what you think of the roadmap for peace."

It was direct, but over the years they had built up both respect and trust and Emily felt no need for circumspection.

Kadir was also direct. "This will not lead to peace." He waved his right hand, raised his shoulders and continued. "These plans come from outside Israel. The rest of the world—the Americans, the Europeans, the Russians—they all think they know our problems better than we do. They think they know how to solve them. But you know, my friend," he said pensively, "sometimes I think they do not want peace for us, but for themselves."

She thought for a moment. She did want to know the honest opinions of ordinary people. She decided to probe a little further. "Then tell me, Kadir. Why don't the people here seek peace?"

He shook his head again and sighed, "My dear Emily. You have been here many times and you see how we are. I have Israeli friends and I have Palestinian friends. I have friends who are Jews and Christians and Muslims. We live in peace with each other. The governments are standing in the way."

"That's too simple," she replied. "There are Arabs in the Knesset."

He paused, not sure how to respond. He lit another cigarette and said, "There are a few. But they are a minority just like we are and they have no power. As you say, my brothers and I, we live in East Jerusalem. We are Israeli citizens and we vote. But the government does not represent us." Emily started to speak, but Kadir continued. "Tell me, my friend, does your government represent the minorities in your country?"

This was supposed to be a conversation about the peace plan. Emily did not want to compare the problems in Israel to those in the United States. She quickly realized that her ready answers would not be good enough. The fact is, minorities rarely feel represented anywhere—even in the United States. There are always ways for the majority to manipulate the democratic process so that control remains in reliable hands.

Her response was measured. "The test of every democracy is how it governs the minority. I guess no government is perfect, not even my own."

Kadir gave out a hearty laugh and said, "My dear friend, do not be so defensive. In America you do not have to fight over land and identity the way we do. Your problems are different so I would not tell you how to fix them. The world has good intentions but the roadmap won't work. We have to do it ourselves and we need our own plan. When Yitzhak Rabin was prime minister we all had hope. Now, not so much. But come, I want to give you something new we have in the store. And you must speak with my brothers."

As they finished their coffee, Kadir escorted Emily through the shop. She took some time to speak with the younger brothers and agreed to join them for lunch the next day. Kadir showed her a variety of new items, then handed her a bronze and enamel cross.

"This should look good in your house, Emily. Thank you for visiting our humble shop and for our talk. I will see you tomorrow."

As Emily passed through various check points, as she mingled with citizens on the bus, with shopkeepers and their patrons, she was repeatedly met with smiles and a welcoming demeanor. Everyone she interviewed spoke of shared concerns, their words reflecting her conversation with Kadir and echoing a sincere hunger for peace. There were, of course, some people who sided with the government, but none who supported the roadmap. With little exception their expressions revealed no sparkle or expectation. In their eyes she saw only dejection and defeat.

Emily found herself drawn into a realm of darkness inhabited by a people fatigued from constant and unpredictable violence. She had spent time in active war zones where conflict seemed unending. This was something different. This land had come to embody Dante's City of Woe without the warning: "Abandon hope all ye who enter here." These were people living with broken spirits who, in spite of their own desires, did not seriously believe this peace process would end any differently than the others. She began to realize that even with the inspiration of their own gifted poets, Israelis and Palestinians were a people without hope, forever teetering on a precipice of warfare.

Each night Emily, Susan and Daniele would meet and share notes and impressions from the day's work. They all reached the same conclusion: the roadmap was ill-fated in spite of personal investment and leadership from the United States.

On Sunday, May 11, Secretary of State Colin Powell met with Palestinian Prime Minister Mahmoud Abbas. Abbas was eager to accept the plan as laid out, and expressed a deep desire to curb the terrorist groups among the Palestinians and uproot the violence. But he had two major concerns. First, his authority was constrained. Even though he was appointed by Palestinian President Yasser Arafat, their relationship was tenuous at best. Also, unlike the West Bank, his influence in the Gaza Strip was limited. For all practical purposes that area was controlled by Hamas. Its military wing, responsible for much of the violence against Israel, was unlikely to cease its attacks. Nonetheless Abbas was prepared to attempt to curb the violence.

Second, although he encouraged Israel to accept the plan unaltered, he feared that the Israelis would place conditions that would effectively dismantle the roadmap. As the Palestinian Foreign Minister Nabil Shaath stated, "You cannot say that the Palestinians must first do everything that is required, and then the Israelis will decide. That is what killed every peace agreement so far."

The following day, May 12, Powell met with Israeli Prime Minister Ariel Sharon. Like Abbas, he had concerns about the practicality of the roadmap. Israel continually faced attacks from Palestinians, mostly in the Gaza Strip, which shares borders with both Israel and Egypt. The night before Powell's meeting with Sharon, the Israeli Defense Force (IDF) killed two Palestinians in Rafah, in the southern Gaza Strip. The men had been in the process of planting bombs near Israeli forces.

In an honest and prescient exchange Sharon indicated that, although the idea of the roadmap was desirable, it was doomed from the beginning. The first phase called for Israel to freeze all new settlements in Palestinian territory. The international community had already determined that the settlements were illegal. Among its many condemnations are five separate UN Security Council Resolutions in 1979 and 1980 that passed unanimously, with only the United States abstaining. The use of abstentions rather than vetoes was intended to send a message to Israel. But taking advantage of the American Jewish lobby and knowing the importance of Israel to American security concerns, the Israeli government continued to ignore the international community.

Sharon made his opposition to the first phase of the roadmap very clear when he told Powell, "Our finest youth live there. They are already the third generation, contributing to the state and serving in elite army units. They return home and get married, so then they can't build a house and have children?" In a great non-sequitur of international dialogue Sharon continued, "What do you want, for a pregnant woman to have an abortion just because she is a settler?" In truth, he was reflecting the position of the right wing parties that formed the coalition government. Like Abbas, Sharon was at least willing to make some effort so the two leaders agreed to meet the following weekend.

What could have possessed the Quartet to imagine that either party would acquiesce now? They were attempting to be rational in a situation beyond reason. Had this been a traditional war, one side would have emerged the victor and each would have signed an armistice. Of course, such treaties can initially be one-sided and onerous. Still, following WWII the Axis countries repaired their relationships with the Allies. Japan resurfaced as a strong U.S. partner and Germany eventually became the economic center of a unified Europe. The Israelis and Palestinians, though, were not in a traditional war and the roadmap was not an armistice. This was terrorism and occupation, uncomfortably reminiscent of Judea in the first century when the Romans were the occupying forces and the Jews were considered terrorists.

Underlying the conflict is the broader reality of the Middle East. The entire region is fractured by ancient hatred and distrust, both ethnic and religious. Within individual countries, barbaric brutality keeps minorities in control, while among nations a cautious tension holds sway between Sunni and Shiite Muslims. Hostilities are kept in check, in part, because of mutual hatred for the Jews and opposition to the existence of Israel.

Overarching the conflict is an apparently insurmountable problem. There is no parity of power. The Israelis are militarily strong and well-funded, the Palestinians are not. In the absence of such a balance, Emily concluded that compromise with the hardliners on each side should not really be expected and would most likely prove impossible. To her, it seemed unlikely that the Palestinian leadership would ever be able to rein in the perpetrators of terror. And as she witnessed in Jerusalem and throughout the country, Orthodox Jewish leaders and their Israeli extremists will forever cling to a biblical myth of inherited land. No wonder then, that when Emily returned to Los Angeles she felt the same as the Israelis and Palestinians she had met on the streets. She also was without hope.

CHAPTER 4

On Wednesday, May 21, Giuseppe left his office early and headed home. As he walked in the door, the telephone was ringing. When he answered he heard Jackson on the other end.

"Sep, this is Jacks."

"I do recognize your voice," he said with amusement.

Jacks started to laugh. "I figured as much. I called your office, but they said you had already gone home."

"Yeah, I just felt I needed a break today. How are you doing, Jacks?" Giuseppe asked.

"I don't know," he replied. "The house is empty since Jean-Paul's death. Some days I think I'll be fine, but others are difficult to get through. Most of the time I'm unfocused. I don't sleep well and my work is substandard. My boss has been very understanding, but I don't know how long that can last."

"Jacks, that's not surprising. You haven't had any time for yourself. You went back to work immediately after the funeral. Why don't you take some time off?"

"That's actually why I'm calling. I'm going to take a week's vacation beginning this Friday and want to know if I can visit you."

"You know you're always welcome. You can spend the whole week here if you want."

"Thanks, Sep. I'd like that. I'll fly down on Friday. You don't have to meet me at the airport. I can take the Metro to your house."

"No way. I'll pick you up. Just let me know what time your plane arrives and I'll be there."

"That's not necessary, but thanks. I'll call you after I make a reservation."

"OK. I look forward to seeing you." With that he hung up and checked his calendar. There was nothing significant happening the following week. It would be business as usual in the legislature, thereby affording him plenty of time to spend with his friend.

•   •   •

On Friday afternoon Giuseppe left his office for Ronald Reagan National Airport at four o'clock. Jackson deplaned at four forty-five, and they met at baggage claim to pick up one piece of checked luggage. They went to the car and drove to Giuseppe's home. On the way Jackson started up a conversation about the Senate.

"Sep, I heard on the news that the Senate passed the tax-cut bill today."

"It's more than just tax cuts. It's really a jobs bill, an attempt to grow the economy, which, as you know, has been struggling since 9/11."

"I noticed that you didn't call to ask my opinion," Jacks said.

"I already know your opinion about taxes," Giuseppe replied.

"Then you only want to consult with me when I already agree with you." He did not intend it to sound so sullen. Giuseppe was quick to reassure him.

"Come on, Jacks. You know that's not true. I can't call you before every bill that comes up in the Senate. I asked you to be my advisor and let me know how ordinary people feel about important issues, but there is some legislation that we don't need to discuss."

"And you don't think taxes are important? You didn't want to know how the person on the street feels about tax breaks for the rich?"

"I told you, this legislation was not just about taxes. It was a jobs bill. And besides, it includes tax breaks across all income brackets."

"Sep, you're not talking to an uninformed constituent. I've spent my entire life in the financial world. This is an area I'm familiar with, and I think you'd want my advice even if our political affiliations are different. I would have appreciated the opportunity to tell you why tax breaks for the rich will never benefit the poor."

Giuseppe could tell that Jackson was disappointed and that he felt passionately about the issue. But he did not want to start the week's visit by

33

squabbling over government policy. Rather than arguing he chose a little honesty.

"Jacks, calm down and let me tell you something. Nobody in the Republican leadership believes that cutting tax rates for the wealthy will create jobs or grow the economy. Even Ronald Reagan did not really believe that when he first advocated supply-side economics. It's never worked and no serious economist or politician believes it ever will. Tax cuts are about shrinking the government. Do you remember when Reagan said that government is the problem? That has practically become a Republican mantra. If the government does not bring in enough revenue, it gets smaller. And when that occurs it can no longer control every aspect of our lives."

"Why would anyone who thinks that want to be in government? Why do you?" he asked.

"Some politicians want business to function unencumbered by excessive regulations. As for me, I don't happen to agree. I believe in government, and in the common good. And I'm not alone. Both Senator George Voinovich and I spoke out against the size of the cuts, in part because we both interpret history the same way. Specifically, we understand that what the United States accomplished after World War II was only possible because the government had grown in size and that was only possible because of a reasonably fair and progressive tax rate that was very high for upper-income brackets.

"Things are complicated in Congress today. Along with shrinking the government, tax breaks that benefit the wealthy keep the Republican Party well-funded and in power. Anyway, your point of view on tax cuts was well represented by the opposition. I didn't call you about the legislation because the tally was carefully calculated. It was a done deal with the vote dead-even, mostly along party lines, setting the stage for Vice President Dick Cheney to cast the tie-breaker. That's just the way the Senate is. In this instance I was not going to be the clog in the wheel. I could not vote against the bill. I have long-term goals and being a faithful and reliable member of my party is essential. If I want to cement my role in Republican politics, I have to be careful and choose my issues of opposition cautiously."

"You mean you have to find a way to manipulate the other senators," Jackson suggested.

"That's a crude but accurate description. For example, I questioned the legitimacy of war in Iraq and raised doubts about the so-called intelligence regarding Hussein's nuclear program and his possession of weapons of mass destruction. But when the vote was taken, I cast mine in favor of the resolution.

"Even on the tax question I wasn't completely silent. I expressed concerns about the efficacy and fairness of the cuts, but I did it in private conversations with other Republican senators. I'm a rich man and I don't need a tax cut. Neither does any other wealthy American. I also recognize that something grossly unfair is in play when millionaires receive tax breaks of almost $100,000 and the average family settles for benefits between $150 and $300. The various political cartoons, such as the one depicting a billionaire pissing on the masses, illustrate the reality of trickle-down economics. These tax cuts do not serve the common good. But voting against this bill was simply not conceivable. I still want to hear your opinion about legislation introduced in Congress, but mostly when there is room for me to maneuver."

Once they arrived at Giuseppe's home Jackson took his suitcase to his room and changed for dinner. Since he would be spending ten days in Washington and would not be working he offered to cook their meals. But on the first night, by Giuseppe's request, they went out to eat.

For many years Jackson and Jean-Paul had lived a very simple Bostonian life, rarely dining out or attending parties—certainly nothing near a high-powered Washington existence. Before being elected senator Giuseppe had never met Jean-Paul, and he had not seen Jackson in twenty years. As such it seemed understandable that he would want to impress both of them when they had visited D.C. the preceding year. But Jean-Paul was now gone and there was no need for any pretense. He made a reservation at Prime Rib, a well-known steakhouse frequented by many politicians.

They decided to take the Metro. On the way Giuseppe described the restaurant and its clientele. "You never know who you'll run into. All the nation's power players eat there. It's particularly popular on Friday nights among those who don't travel home for the weekend."

With resignation in his voice Jackson replied, "I didn't come to Washington to meet any politicians. I came to see you and get some rest."

"It's only one night," Giuseppe assured him. "And I'll make sure that we are not disturbed."

The meal was superb. In spite of being a steakhouse there were plenty of seafood and even vegetarian choices on the menu, thus pleasing almost every palate. And Giuseppe kept his promise. Although several members of Congress dined at Prime Rib that night, he only interrupted dinner once, when Senator Bill Frist walked by. Frist had assumed the role of majority leader after Trent Lott stepped down the previous December. His political tactics were alienating, even among some in his own party. However, that was of no concern to Giuseppe, who was playing a long political game and not about to distance himself from the most powerful Republican in the Senate. Prime Rib was always a busy establishment, and after dinner they both appreciated the contrasting atmosphere of a quiet home.

Once back at the house, Giuseppe offered Jackson his choice of after-dinner drinks and opened his humidor, displaying a collection of expensive, quality cigars. Just being away from Boston and the constant reminder of Jean-Paul's murder was a comfort for Jackson. And at the end of the evening it was time to retire to bed and hopefully some much needed sleep.

As they were about to go to their rooms, Jackson made an unexpected request.

"Sep, do you mind if I sleep in your bed tonight? Ever since Jean-Paul's death I spend most nights restlessly tossing, and even in the quiet of the night I am unable to find peace. I'm just not used to sleeping alone." He quickly added, "According to Jean-Paul I don't snore very much."

"I don't mind at all, Jacks. I can still remember what it was like after Yolanda died. It took me quite awhile to adjust. I also spent many sleepless nights, even though I was often exhausted from campaign work. However, I don't know if I snore."

"I'll take the chance," he replied. Then he went to his room to change into his pajamas.

Giuseppe had just left the bathroom when Jackson walked into the bedroom. As they each slid into bed Giuseppe turned out the lights. Whether it was the companionship of an old friend or just the comfort of knowing someone else shared the bed, Jackson quickly fell asleep.

Not so Giuseppe. He found himself unusually uncomfortable. As he lay awake his attention was consumed by a flood of contradictions. During the years of their estrangement, Giuseppe had willed himself to dismiss Jackson from memory. He was content with the life he and Yolanda had created and he loved his children. His romantic nights with his wife made it easy to forget about his friend from Boston. But that night, with Jackson beside him, he remembered. In their youth he had never been able to speak of his affection. Now his mind swirled in the emotion of a love that had been suppressed for decades.

His feelings were not all sexual. He would have been content merely to hold Jackson in his arms, an act that would have gone a long way toward quieting an unfulfilled love. But simple as that would have been, this was a time for restraint. Jackson had never been so vulnerable and Giuseppe decided to respect that. He turned to face the wall and eventually drifted off to sleep.

•　•　•

Jackson was still sleeping when Giuseppe awoke Saturday morning. He quietly slipped out of bed and went to the kitchen to prepare some food. Although not a particularly good cook, it was difficult to screw up breakfast. He put on a pot of coffee and heated up the frying pan. A few minutes later his friend wandered into the kitchen, awakened by the combined aromas of bacon and brew. He was still a little sleepy-eyed and had not even removed the crusty discharge that collects in the corners of the eyes. The important thing was that he looked rested, at least more so than the night before.

Giuseppe greeted him with a cup of espresso roast and said, "Good morning, Jacks. How did you sleep?"

"Surprisingly well," he replied. "God, it smells good in here."

"That's the bacon. In my opinion it's the perfect way to greet the day, at least on weekends. Most mornings I don't eat at home. If I don't have an early meeting, which frequently includes breakfast in the Senate dining room, I survive on coffee and Danish at the office. Now, how do you want your eggs?"

"Over easy, please. And while you do that I'll make the toast."

"Great. There's some bread in the refrigerator. You have your choice of sourdough or whole wheat. I'll have sourdough."

They settled down for a hot but simple meal. When they finished Jackson offered to clean the kitchen, but Giuseppe refused, insisting that he would have plenty of opportunity to wash dishes since they planned on eating at home during the week.

After showering they headed out to the heart of the capital and spent the day sauntering around the National Mall, occasionally visiting one of the museums. Mostly they just talked. Jackson had lost Jean-Paul through a murder eerily similar to the one that left Giuseppe childless and a widower, and he hoped that sharing their experiences would help him adjust and finally find peace. In the late afternoon they entered a subway station and headed back to the house.

Jackson had originally planned on cooking a typical Belgian dinner, but his emotions were still too raw. He promised one in the future, but not on this trip. Instead he decided to test his Italian culinary skills with spaghetti Bolognese, Caesar salad and garlic bread—just a plain, home-cooked meal. His personal touch was to make the sauce from scratch and hope that it measured up to Giuseppe's. That night they once again shared the same bed, this time each of them easily slipping into a sound slumber.

During the days that followed Giuseppe worked in his Senate office while Jackson toured museums and monuments. There was no significant legislation pending and no late meetings of any import. They were both free to spend the evenings together. It had been a calm, relaxing and quite enjoyable week. Since renewing their friendship three years before they had grown increasingly close, even more than they had been in graduate school. In that attachment each had come to know he could trust the other completely. They spent many hours reminiscing about their families, always returning to the murders that now bound them inextricably together. Giuseppe found himself feeling and expressing a tender compassion he hid from most people. On Friday their relationship took a turn.

Dinner was once again simple. Giuseppe had barbecued dry-aged steaks while Jackson baked potatoes, sautéed mushrooms and prepared a salad. Although neither was exhausted when they went to bed, Jackson seemed to have once again slipped into a quick sleep as he had done all week long. Or so Giuseppe thought. He listened to the gentle cadence of his friend's breathing. Not intending to wake him, he turned and placed his arm over Jackson's chest.

However, Jackson had not yet fallen asleep. He grasped Giuseppe's hand, held it for a moment, gently squeezed and then slowly slid it down under his shorts and between his legs. Giuseppe's senses heightened. His muscles tensed. Within moments he felt his heart begin to beat faster as he filled with anticipation. His fingers foraged for love in unfamiliar territory, yet he needed no map. Every inch of this wonderland had been burnished into his imagination over many a lonely night.

At first Jackson just lay there letting Giuseppe probe with expectation, each stroke of his fingers conjuring the explorer seeking treasures hidden deep in an untamed jungle. Then he moved his own hand between Giuseppe's legs and rested his head on his shoulder. He began to shake and said softly, "Sep."

"Jacks, you're trembling. Are you scared?"

"I don't know, maybe a little. I never foresaw this. I didn't think I would ever feel this way again." They had both grown quite hard by this time, their appendages rising with an excitement and fervor that they did not wish to temper and that would not be denied.

Giuseppe kissed Jackson's forehead and said, "I have always loved you, my friend. Let's get undressed." He pulled away for a moment and they each took off their clothes. When they embraced again it was if they were one. Warmed by each other's bodies, two hearts pulsating in rhythmic harmony, even climaxing came in sync. This was a love years in the making, driven by a powerful but subdued passion.

Afterward they lay for a while in each other's arms neither of them wanting to speak for fear that such sacred joy would descend into mere banality. But Jackson could not contain his confusion. He kissed Giuseppe's chest and nestled his head beneath his chin. "Sep, that was spectacular and you are beyond beautiful, but I'm a little overwhelmed. I did not anticipate this. And I feel a little guilty. Jean-Paul has only been dead for six weeks."

Giuseppe had to figure out a way to derail these thoughts, and quickly. He could not let Jackson wallow in feelings that might cause him to regret what they had done.

"Jacks, I think I know how you feel. You're the first person I've been with since Yolanda died two years ago. But I don't think length of time is the issue. We both lost someone we loved very much. The only difference is that you found someone new sooner than I did. This might not have been planned, but perhaps it wasn't an accident, either. We found each other. That's what matters. And I think Yolanda and Jean-Paul would both approve. I know they'd want us to be happy."

Jackson did not respond immediately. He just held Giuseppe tighter. He slid up so their eyes could meet. "You're a good friend, Sep. Better than I deserve."

"Shhh, Jacks. That's not true. If anything, I'm the one who should be awed. You've opened a whole new world for me. But we can talk about that later. I'm just glad you're here." They kissed again and fell asleep in each other's arms.

In the morning Giuseppe awakened first and his movements rustled Jackson from sleep. "Good morning, Jacks."

Jackson smiled and said, "Mmm, what a night! Too bad it had to end."

"You're kind of cute like this," Giuseppe replied. "But the sun has lit the sky and it is another day. Are you ready to get up?"

"No," Jackson insisted. Then as he pulled his friend close he laughingly said, "I don't ever want to get up again."

Giuseppe looked at him and suggested, "I guess we could stay here a little longer." No convincing was needed. They slipped under the covers and let passion have sway. This was not the lust of youth. It was truly a choreography of love. However, they did eventually rise, shower and eat.

Over morning coffee Giuseppe confessed, "I think you know that you're the first man I have ever been with. I had no idea what I was missing."

"I never figured you were so inclined," Jackson replied. "I must say, though, you seemed pretty comfortable for your first time. And, by the way, you were terrific!" He sent a winking smile across the table. "Tonight I'll show you how men do oral sex." At that they both laughed.

For Giuseppe the day seemed to drag. At least it could not pass quickly enough. Sunday Jackson would be returning to Boston and he was still a little uncertain if this new relationship could be sustained. When night descended he was ready.

As they prepared for bed Giuseppe suggested, "I guess pajamas are wholly superfluous. I don't think we'll be keeping them on anyway."

"I agree," Jackson replied.

They stripped, got into bed and snuggled next to each other. "Jacks, this morning you promised me something."

"I did indeed," he countered playfully. "And I have not forgotten." He proceeded to teach him how to make love in the proverbial sixty-nine position. Leading by example he was delighted that Giuseppe was such a quick study. Between moments of love and passion they chatted the night away, dreamily wondering what life would have been like had they done this while they were in graduate school.

In the morning Jackson began packing his bags. Giuseppe walked into the room and asked, "Do you mind taking the Metro to the airport?"

"Of course not. I imagine you've had a lot of work pile up at the office. It's not easy entertaining a houseguest for an entire week."

"It's not the work, Jacks. My life is not exactly private and being seen around town in the constant company of one person could cause skepticism."

"I understand. Some closets must remain closed. Do you want me to come back next weekend?"

Giuseppe smiled and answered with a long and passionate kiss.

"That's what I was hoping for," Jackson said. He smiled as he continued, "I left my toothbrush in the bathroom." Then he looked in Giuseppe's eyes and said, "Just so you know, I'm a bottom."

Giuseppe chuckled and said, "I don't really care. I just want you to come back soon. Call me when you get home."

Jackson left for the airport a very different person than the one who had arrived a week earlier—much more relaxed and even feeling a little peaceful. Giuseppe, on the other hand, was unsure how to handle the situation. It was what he wanted and he would not trade it for anything. But he had a shrewd and observant staff and he knew he would have to check his emotions on a daily basis lest he accidentally disclose the cynosure of his affection. That would now be difficult for he felt as though he were entering a second adolescence, emerging from the cocoon of childhood and seeing the whole world of sexuality for the first time.

CHAPTER 5

My brother's admission of being a murderer was unlike any confession I had experienced since my ordination to the priesthood. Although I had spent most of my life preaching forgiveness and reconciliation, Giuseppe's secret truth devastated me, its weight crushing any semblance of the peace that should accompany the mercy of God. Inspired by the words of the Prophet Jeremiah, I have always believed in God's unique approach to mercy and compassion. God simply forgets—so completely stripping our lives of sin that our transgressions fade from history. Indeed, in God's realm our sins never even existed.

If I was in need of humility, my brother's twisted use of the sacrament reminded me that I was not God. His disclosure that he had his family—my family—killed for political gain was something I could not forget, and something I did not want to forgive. I was a man at odds with my faith, my preaching, my God. The stress was becoming more and more unbearable. Within me raged a war I could not win and only hoped I would not lose. I engaged all aspects of my personality: the wit and wisdom of my intellect, the pain and suffering of my emotions, the commitment and strength of my character. All my energies were required to maintain balance lest I collapse in total defeat.

I tricked myself into sanity, pivoting between depression and denial, each path offering a different method of escape. Denial was only temporary, but I could control it and it proved very utilitarian. I marshaled profound forces to bury the murders in the back of my mind so that my attention could be consumed by pastoral responsibilities. And there were many of those.

Although St. Catherine was not a large parish, it was a busy one. And with the changes I had initiated over the years and the dedication of the people, it was a growing community. The parishioners had gradually come to recognize that it was not my church, it was theirs, and they willingly embraced ownership. Their need for priestly service increased and, despite the burden brought on by my brother's confession two-and-a-half years earlier, I could not shirk my responsibilities as pastor. I was often grateful for the demanding hours needed to minister to others. Still, I could feel the anxiety build. Nor was it unnoticed by my friends. I regularly spent my days off with a select group, but frequently felt alone even among them. They had learned to either discreetly question me or ignore my moods entirely.

Still, every day must end and that is when depression surfaced. In the dark and silent night the dead fought back. My sister-in-law and her children, refusing to be confined to unwelcome oblivion, would not be forgotten. They did not speak to me, nor was I haunted by restless spirits. But my soul found no peace. They needed me to remember because I knew the truth. I willingly allowed the dead to inhabit my memories and in the warmth of those recollections realized how gently seductive depression can be. With my nightly scotch in hand I also learned a deeper truth about depression—it does not necessarily cloud clarity. Through every emotional turn I was aware of and remembered precisely what had happened to my family. I knew who the killer was, but I was paralyzed by the rules of my church and despondent that the murderer would never be brought to justice.

With each rising of the sun the cycle replayed itself. I stepped into the shower where I kept a wooden stool. Many mornings I would sit for long periods, water cascading over my head, my eyes closed in an attempt to empty any thought from my mind. Sometimes I found myself lost in music, as some earworm took up residence in my brain, relentlessly bouncing from side to side in disturbing stereo. This was my way of allowing the night's depression to give way to the day's denial. I was certain this routine could not last and probably would have taken its toll long ago had I not possessed two treasured gifts: Regardless of the company I was in, my intellect enabled me to segue from one topic to another with uncommon ease, and when necessary my personality permitted me to feign interest in the midst of pure boredom. These two deceits protected me and in the process walled out others, even friends.

But at some point I would need to be rescued or risk losing my sanity altogether.

The previous year I had met a young woman named LaQueesha Williams. She was a prostitute, a single mom, and one of the most disarming people I had ever encountered. There was no pretense in her, and whenever I spoke with her I did not feel as though I had to be the priest. I was just myself, the man behind the collar. Though not Catholic, LaQueesha began frequently attending Sunday Mass, after which we lunched together at a nearby restaurant. Our friendship was a much-needed haven and I began coveting Sunday afternoons in anticipation of that meal.

On Sunday, July 13, LaQueesha was at the eleven o'clock Mass. When all the parishioners had left, she and I walked to La Barca restaurant just down the street from the church. On the way she asked, "Where were you last Sunday?"

"I thought I told you," I replied. "Every Fourth of July weekend, I go to Napa Valley for the Grgich Hills Wine Festival with Bill Messenger, Perry Leiker, Gilbert Cruz and Mario Lopez. Bill met Mike Grgich about ten years ago and is often asked to open the festivities with a blessing."

"How was the trip?"

"It was great, even though the temperature was almost 90 degrees. The festival takes place on estate property in Yountville where Mike Grgich used to live. After he built his new home in Calistoga, the winery took over the house and now uses it for staging events like this one. Each year the celebration includes similar activities, among them carnival-type games for the kids and a caricature artist. It opens with the singing of both the U.S. and Croatian national anthems and a Croatian dance group. Officially everything begins at eleven o'clock with the staff pouring all-you-can-drink wine and waiters weaving through the crowd serving a variety of hors d'oeuvres. That is followed by prayer and an extensive lunch. This year's meal included pork, turkey and lamb, which had been roasted in pits dug in the ground beside the house. Mike was born in Croatia, and in honor of his heritage, the formal name of the event is 'Annual Croatian Extravaganza Wine Club Festival Celebrating the Judgment of Paris.' You can see why we shorten the name."

"What's the Judgment of Paris?" she asked.

I smiled at her and commented, "You're not a wine drinker, are you?"

"Not really. I wouldn't know a good bottle from a bad one."

"Well, Mike Grgich is one of the people responsible for putting Napa on the map, as they say. In 1976 there was a blind tasting held in Paris pitting the best French wines against California's finest. Napa entries won top prize in both the white and red categories. At the time Mike was the winemaker for Chateau Montelena and the 1973 Chardonnay that he crafted won first place among white wines. In fact, its final score was higher than any other wine, white or red. After his Chardonnay was judged the best white wine in the world, Mike Grgich was catapulted to international fame."

"This might sound ignorant," she said, "but isn't taste a personal thing?"

"Oh, LaQueesha," I answered with emphasis. "Of course it is, but there are certain characteristics connoisseurs look for that elevate one wine above another in quality and desirability. Also, you don't know the French. They can be a bit haughty when it comes to wine—even more than they are about their language. After all, it had long been believed that the world's best wine producers were in France.

"To test that belief nine French judges gathered at the InterContinental Hotel in Paris. There were two additional tasters, an American and a Brit, but they were not on the judging panel and their ballots were not counted. All of the French were wine authorities which made the results of the tasting even more surprising. As they discovered, there is peril when blind tasting a national proprietary drink. The palate is freed from mental preconceptions and no one knows what the result will be. When the moderator announced the winners, one of the French judges, Odette Kahn, demanded her ballot be returned, embarrassed that she had given Stag's Leap Wine Cellars, one of the Napa entrants, the number one ranking among reds. Apparently Miss Kahn could not overcome her national pride.

"After the Paris tasting Mike teamed with Austin Hills of Hills Brothers Coffee fame and opened his own winery. They broke ground on July 4, 1977, and that's why the festival is always held on Independence Day weekend. After lunch I'll give you a couple bottles to take home, one red and one white."

"What if I don't like them?" she asked.

I laughed. "Then there's something wrong with you." But I continued more seriously. "LaQueesha, I can tell you some of the things to look for when you open a bottle and pour a glass, but the first maxim regarding wine is 'If you like it, it's good.' Who cares what somebody else thinks? There's a certain amount of pretension in the wine world, anyway. Just read some of the critics' reviews. They write about a particular wine having hints of tobacco, chocolate, pepper, lavender, dirt, shoe leather, etc. Unless they remember back to the age of two or three, how would they recognize the taste of dirt or shoe leather? Don't worry, though. I'm sure you'll like Grgich Hills."

By this time we had arrived at the restaurant. Surprisingly we did not have to wait long for a table or a server. After placing our order, LaQueesha said, "That was an interesting passage from the Prophet Amos this morning."

I looked at her with surprise. "I'm impressed. I don't think the average person pays that much attention to the readings, especially not that one. What did you find so interesting?"

"It was when God spoke to Amos and called him to be a prophet. It reminded me of you and the way you preach about peace and reconciliation. Your words are very challenging, especially in the current climate of war."

I did not know how to respond to that. Over the years people had said good things about me, but to my knowledge no one ever called me a prophet. And, of course, I had not been feeling very peaceful personally, nor was I conciliatory toward my brother. She must have had an inkling of what I was thinking and said, "I don't mean to embarrass you, Gio."

I had no intention of sharing any additional reflections and chose to run with her last comment. "I'm not embarrassed. It's just strange to hear you say that. Sometimes I wonder if there's something wrong with my preaching. I have believed in peace most of my life and don't really comprehend violence. I look at the gangs in our cities—here in L.A., across the United States, and in other countries. I see the ease with which they kill one another in their wanton disregard for human life.

"Then I look at politicians, how casually they speak of bombing another country, their willingness to march us off to war, and their deceptive attempt to justify it through the use of altruistic or humanitarian language.

"Something is amiss in today's world: the way people look at each other, and view human life. We are descending down a road of disregard, both in our own country and around the world. In our weakness we diminish the worth of others because they are different, whether it's the language they speak, or their politics, education, economic status . . . whatever. I don't even know if I'm making sense. I'm just spinning ideas here. But I don't see that my preaching makes much of a difference."

"Don't be absurd, Gio. You're not responsible for the gangs, the discord among people or the wars. The whole world is not going to change because of what you say on Sunday morning. But you do make a difference in people's lives. I hear the comments after church. The people in this parish love you." She smiled and continued, "I'd say that they worship you, but that would be a poor choice of words having just come from Mass."

I tried to dismiss her reflection. "It's just that I'm different from any priest they've ever known before."

"Why do you do that?" she asked.

"Do what?"

"That thing where you deflect compliments. It's irritating and it's not healthy. Can't you just appreciate it when people say nice things about you, perhaps even be happy? Or did they teach you that in the seminary?"

"I'm just being honest," I replied, probably too quickly and too defensively. "It doesn't require great skill to follow a pastor who couldn't relate to the congregation."

"You're not being honest, Giovanni." I looked up with surprise as she addressed me so formally and saw that she was deadly serious. "Maybe you can't always see the effect you have on people, but it's there. Take me, for example.

"When I was young my mother dragged me to church every Sunday and over the years I've heard a lot of preachers. I like your style, the way you speak so personally about things. You feel and you tell the truth. But mostly, I like the God you preach about. There's no hellfire language or threats of damnation because people have sinned. You accept everyone as they are and there's an easy way about you. But you're also complicated. I suspect the reason you don't condemn others is that you are aware of your own weaknesses and mistakes. That's a great gift. But as a result there are no simple solutions when you preach and you won't see any quick conversions.

"My mother asked me why I keep going to your church when I'm not even a Catholic. I think the reason is that on some level I'm finding God. In other churches the ministers tell you how to act, what to think and what to believe in. For them life is straightforward and reduced to rules. They make everything simple because they have all the answers. When I hear them I feel like a puppet. I don't want to be told what God wants, as if those ministers would even know. I want to think and find out for myself. After you preach I walk away with more questions than answers, but I'm processing and finding ways to change my life. And I regularly hear your parishioners say the same thing."

LaQueesha was encouraging me and I appreciated that. But I was aware that this conversation was not as spontaneous as she pretended. There was something enigmatic about the entire afternoon. It was not subterfuge on her part. That would have more accurately described me. Still, it was obvious that she had an agenda.

"Gio, our relationship is different from what you have with your parishioners. I see things they don't, and the more I get to know you the more I realize that you're in pain. I saw it that first night we met at McDonald's and it's never gone away. If anything, it seems to have gotten worse. Even when you're on the altar I often fear that you can't hold it together."

In some bizarre way she was doing the same thing with me that I tried to do with Giuseppe. But I did not want her inside my head and was uncomfortable on multiple levels, not the least being that her probing forced me to think about my brother. Although he and I are twins, I had come to see him as an unattractive person. For my own vanity's sake I had to admit that on the outside he was physically acceptable. But there was an internal ugliness that eluded the casual observer and even some of his closest friends. I saw the sundered soul, dislodged from any sense of humanity. And I wondered how he coped.

I had seen no particular signs of strain when I was in Washington, and I suspected that he had chosen simply to deny his own involvement in the murders. It was certainly a convenient approach. But it was also a cheap escape, opening a breach into an alternate universe untethered from any reality or personal responsibility. Not unlike me, he had no one he could turn to. I told myself that I would come to his aid if ever he asked, knowing full well that it was a safe prospect. He would never seek my help.

The chasm between us had grown so great that whatever wonder I had about him and his feelings did not translate to brotherly concern. Was I becoming like him? That unease was calmed by one major distinction. In my case I avoided speaking to others not from fear of prosecution or a lack of desire, but due to the burden of obligation. What could I now say to LaQueesha? She could almost see through me. Still, she was no exception to the rule of silence. If I were very careful, I might be able to distract her with a partial truth and minimize the risk.

"LaQueesha, you're right. I can't hold it together because I can't put it together. Some time ago I told you I thought I knew who murdered my family. Well, the truth is I *do* know. So does my brother, Giuseppe. We each have our own reasons for keeping silent and yet I went to see him five weeks ago hoping he would be willing to speak. Instead he upended everything I believe in. I walked out of his office convinced that Charles Dickens was wrong. For some people, including my brother, there are no better angels. There is only shadow. Sometimes I'm afraid of becoming like him."

She furled her brow, her expression turned to sadness, and simultaneously she sighed. But she said nothing. For a moment she closed her eyes as she measured her next words. Instead of countering what I said, she attempted to appeal to my heart.

"Gio, think about all the people in your life: your family, Tom and Emily, and your other friends. Don't they represent something better in human existence?"

"I used to think so. Now I'm not so certain. Maybe we're all just working our way through chaos. Maybe that's all life really is."

"Wow!" she exclaimed. "Such existential negativity does not become you. Neither does self-pity. Whatever else you are, you are not your brother. I cannot imagine what it must be like for you to bear the knowledge you possess, but it does not have to be crippling. Try believing in the God you preach about."

That stung. She had never been so blunt before and she might have been right. I had spent too much time wallowing and it got me nowhere. It only distanced me from everyone that mattered. At times I wished I were more like

Tom. His life also had been radically altered by the murders, but somehow he seemed less burdened. He had chosen to write off my brother and move on. Then again, he also had Emily.

Lunch with LaQueesha had been mildly therapeutic and I decided to reflect further on what she had said. In the meantime we headed back to the church. When we arrived I went into the rectory and retrieved two bottles of Grgich Hills wine, a Chardonnay and a Cabernet Sauvignon. Once again I assured her that she would enjoy them. As she left I thought, *That woman needs a new job. She has more to offer than turning tricks.*

Later that evening I called MaryAlice Johnson. I had met her in my last parish and over the years she and her husband, Morris, had become good friends of mine. MaryAlice grew up in a modestly middle-income family in Beaumont, Texas. Morris frequently joked with her that because she was light-skinned she could pass for white as a child and did not experience the prejudice that plagued most blacks. However, she vividly remembered the rioting that took place in her hometown in 1943.

Beaumont was one of several cities in the nation to experience rioting that year. The demands of war and a suddenly integrated defense industry drew mixed populations seeking employment, exacerbating the city's interracial fears. In what could have served as inspiration for *To Kill a Mockingbird*, a white woman in Beaumont claimed to have been raped by a black man. She was unable to identify a perpetrator and subsequently a mob of some four thousand whites rioted for three days. Black neighborhoods were destroyed and five people killed, yet no one was ever held accountable or prosecuted for those deaths.

MaryAlice and Morris made an innately handsome and elegant couple. She was the paradigm of a Spelman College graduate. Her carriage, the way she dressed and her manner of speech all radiated refinement. After moving to the West Coast she built a career in the Los Angeles County Department of Public Social Services, first as a counselor and then a department head. One time she had the difficult task of informing the singer Ella Fitzgerald that her request to adopt a child had been denied due to her exhausting touring schedule and long periods of absence from home.

Morris had always been more acutely aware of prejudice. During WWII he had been stationed in Naples, Italy, as a member of the Tuskegee Airmen, the famed corps of African-American military pilots. This elite group had been necessitated by the fact that the United States Armed Forces were still segregated in the 1940s. After the war he graduated from Harvard Law School becoming a distinguished Legal Aid Foundation defense attorney and a revered law professor.

MaryAlice answered the phone on the second ring. "Hello?"

"This is Gio," I said.

"Hello, darling," she replied. It was one of her affectionate names for me. "How are you?"

"I'm fine, thanks. I'm calling because I have a very special favor, but I don't want to ask over the phone. Are you free for lunch tomorrow?"

"No, I'm afraid not. I have a meeting. What about dinner? Morris wanted me to call you anyway. He's finishing one of his chili recipes."

"Which one?" I asked.

"The three-day chili. He wanted me to call you because he said he made it especially for you." That meant extra hot. Morris loved to cook and had been making chili for several years. He had a collection of more than fifty recipes from special cook-offs as well as from celebrities and other sources. He was always trying to see if he could overpower my taste buds. I really appreciated it, especially since he did not even eat it himself. The three-day chili was so named because it actually takes that long to make, with new ingredients added each morning.

"Sounds good to me," I replied. "But tell him I already know it won't be hot enough."

She just laughed and said, "That's between the two of you. He'll make something else for me."

I arrived at five o'clock. MaryAlice opened the door and said, "Hi, darling. I hope you're hungry; Morris has been slaving away and he's been fretting that it won't be spicy enough."

Just then Morris walked out of the kitchen. "Hello, Gio. I sure have missed you. You're looking good today."

"He always looks good," MaryAlice replied, almost snappingly. They had that interruptive give and take of an older couple that has been together for years. Anyone who did not know them could have mistaken it for a spat. But there was great affection and respect between them.

Morris responded sharply, "I know that. I'm just glad to see him. Gio, how have you been?"

"Busy, as usual," I said.

"Well, I hope you brought a good appetite. I put seven extra peppers in this pot. I even added habanero peppers this time."

"I'm ready to give it a go," I replied.

Morris turned to his wife and said, "MaryAlice, get him a scotch first." As she went to the liquor cabinet, he turned and assured me, "We still have some of that Pinch you brought over the last time." He himself only drank Smirnoff Vodka, carefully measured with water, and MaryAlice, although she liked scotch, only drank when I was there.

"Say, Gio. I have a religious question for you."

"Oh, let him be," MaryAlice said. "He just got here."

"I don't mean now. I mean after dinner. I just want to make sure I get to talk to him before he leaves." Morris rarely joined us at the table. He had a strict routine that began with eating a solo meal at three in the afternoon, then taking a short nap, waking up, watching a little TV, and calling his family and discussing religion, one of his favorite subjects. Occasionally he would call me on the phone just to ask a simple question hoping to resolve an argument with someone.

Morris was Baptist but respected my training and ministry. Although a highly educated man, he was not trained in religious studies and occasionally I would catch him off guard. I remember one time we were discussing an issue about the Book of Genesis. I explained that the first and second chapters were two separate creation stories, written from two different traditions within ancient Israel. He had never heard that before and went scurrying back to his resources. I do not think he found anything on the subject, since he never brought it up again.

Once the food was ready MaryAlice and I settled down to a good meal. Morris knew the chili would be too hot for her so he had barbecued brisket. As for me his creation was perfect. It was not as spicy as I expected but MaryAlice suggested that I exaggerate a little when he asked me about it so as not to hurt his feelings.

During dinner I explained why I had called. "I met this woman about two years ago. Her name is LaQueesha Williams, she lives with her mother, and is a single mom raising a son on her own. She needs a job. I know her pretty well now and I'm willing to vouch for her if you have a position open at DPSS."

"Couldn't you find her a job at the church?" she asked.

"We don't have anything available at St. Catherine. But even if I could find her employment at another parish, it would be a waste. There's something quite special about her. It's not just that she's thoughtful and genuinely cares about people. She also has amazing and insightful instincts. She would be perfect in social services. Nothing fazes her. She responds to everyone and each situation with acceptance and sensitivity. LaQueesha is exactly the type of person the government should be hiring."

"Does she have a degree?"

"No. She finished the first two years of college and then got sidetracked. But she'd be willing to go back if she got a job. She could attend night classes. And I have some friends who would help with her tuition and other educational expenses. I'd like to arrange for you to meet her. I promise she is someone you don't want to miss out on and would be worth pulling strings for." I smiled, and it suddenly dawned on me that I had not discussed this with LaQueesha. Still, I was fairly certain she would be open to the idea. I was not ready to reveal her occupation to MaryAlice. I am not sure it was my place, anyway. What I wanted right now was to test the waters.

"We're going through some restructuring in the department and we'll be looking for some new employees. She'd have to go through the normal procedures, but I'd just as soon hire someone you recommend. Why don't you set up a time for us to meet informally?"

"Thanks, MaryAlice. I'll do that soon."

After dinner I went to the garage to talk to Morris. As usual, it was not a lengthy conversation. He just wanted me to clarify something for him. I thanked him for the chili, underscoring that it was spicy. Although it could have been hotter, it was having an esophageal effect. When I returned home that night I felt pretty good about myself—I had visited with good friends and planted the seeds for improving LaQueesha's lot in life. If I retired to bed early I might even be liberated from the night's depression.

CHAPTER 6

One of my roles as a priest is helping people accept reality as it is while maintaining optimism about the future. It is not as simple a task as it sounds. We easily think of fantasies as the province of children. Some boys seek perpetual youth in visions of Neverland and many a girl imagines herself a princess as she slides her foot into a slipper. Cinderella and Peter Pan serve as companions for the young on quests to discover their place in a complex and often frightening world. The problem is that fairy tale characters are not real and for all the charming comfort they bring to childhood, children must grow up.

But adults are not immune to reverie and their fancies frequently whirl in reverse. Disenchanted with the way things really are, they are drawn by the imaginative allure of a yesteryear that never was. At the conclusion of Alan Jay Lerner and Frederick Loewe's retelling of the story of ancient England, King Arthur pleads with a young boy to never forget "that once there was a spot, for one brief shining moment, that was known as Camelot." Adults while away countless hours longing for nonexistent history, the good old days that persist only in unreliable memory. For grown-up myths, like the fables of youth, are mere illusion. When the curtain falls or the book is closed, reality rains like a relentless storm, leaving only the fool and the optimist to dream. It was difficult to decipher which was at play in the Middle East, but the peace envisioned in the roadmap was as likely to materialize as the knights of the roundtable.

The Second Intifada (Palestinian uprising) against Israel had begun in September 2000. It would claim the lives of thousands of Palestinians, hundreds of Israelis and dozens of foreigners, before its conclusion.

On June 29, 2003, two months after the announcement of the roadmap, three Palestinian groups—Fatah, Hamas and Islamic Jihad—declared a unilateral ceasefire against Israel. It was slated to last three months and during its first fifty days violence did diminish but was not entirely extinguished. Suicide bombings and Israeli defense actions continued. By the middle of August it was clear that peace had once again eluded the area and on the nineteenth a major suicide attack on a Jerusalem bus killed twenty-three people including seven children. Israel's response was swift and all those who plotted the bus attack were either captured or killed.

In September of 2003, Mahmoud Abbas resigned his post as prime minister of the Palestinian National Authority. Although he truly desired peace and an end to the violence, his was a commitment not shared by President Yasser Arafat. Abbas was left with no room to maneuver and a waning credibility. It seems that Alexander Pope may have been a little too poetic and certainly less than visionary when he penned the words, "Hope springs eternal." Then again, he was writing two-and-a-half centuries earlier in a vastly different culture.

Nowadays there are few places left on earth where hope remains a treasured commodity. Even in our churches and other houses of worship we sometimes simply seem to be spinning our wheels. So many people have given up, that what passes for prayerful expectation might better be described as desperation—voices crying out in vain to a God who no longer listens, a God who apparently abandoned them to tragedy and misfortune.

Such adversity creates a vacuum of authenticity, leaving whole populations ripe for manipulation. The concatenation of 9/11, the wars in Afghanistan and Iraq, and the continued unrest in Israel was true to form, and from one country to another there was no dearth of unscrupulous schemers. In Washington, D.C., two people rose above the rest. Empowered by the confluence of a fictional past and a forlorn future, my brother, Senator Giuseppe Lozano, and Vice President Dick Cheney each sought to shape the country and the world to his own design. Had they not both suffered from megalomania they might have made strong allies. As it turned out each was keen enough not to trust the other.

Giuseppe had only recently entered the world of elected politics and was on a different trajectory from that of the vice president. His election as a senator from California had been fairly easy. At the beginning of his campaign he was not well known in the northern part of the state. But he had no negatives to overcome. He was young and charismatic with a universal appeal, exactly the type of person people associate with the Golden State. Following his election he settled comfortably into the Washington lifestyle.

He had so mastered the art of superficiality that no staffer, colleague or acquaintance could possibly suspect the deep secret he buried inside, namely that he had his family murdered in his quest for political office. Nor did anyone have reason to conjecture about his future. As far as anyone knew he was laying the foundation for a long senatorial career. In his pursuit of the presidency he had two concerns. First, his relationship with Jackson was a liability, but for the time being he was certain he could keep that furtive. Secondly, he needed to harness all his skills as he sought to outmaneuver the vice president.

Cheney had the upper hand. For, as Giuseppe had learned earlier in the year, the vice president operated a shadow government, a group of people who helped him craft policy that he advanced in his efforts to control President Bush. He had already succeeded in forging a devil's accord between Bush and British Prime Minister Tony Blair. This led to a White House meeting on January 31, 2003, during which the two leaders secretly agreed to invade Iraq whether or not the United Nations Inspection Commission found weapons of mass destruction. U.N. Secretary General Kofi Annan appointed Swedish diplomat Hans Blix to lead the inspectors. On February 14 Blix reported to the Security Council that after seven hundred inspections, no weapons of mass destruction had been found in Iraq. Nonetheless, on March 20, two months after the clandestine agreement, the United States and Britain began the invasion.

Cheney had fabricated evidence, bartered an alliance between the U.S. and England, lied to the American people, and started a war. He had the world at his fingertips and should have been approaching satisfaction. Instead he was running headlong into the inconvenience of the Constitution. While he could circumvent certain of its provisions, he could not escape the presidential term limit. His control would hold only as long Bush was in office. For unlike Giuseppe he did not have the kind of personality that could sweep an electorate as large and diverse as the United States.

But Cheney was a savvy student of history and realized that regardless of its lifespan, all power is temporary, a veil before which he could cause the world to tremble but behind which he camouflaged a disturbing truth: smallness is not measured in height nor greatness determined by might. Like tyrants of all ages, Cheney could not accept that reality. He was convinced that he could be the exception. A little man, burdened with anxiety over life's futility and fearful of being forgotten among the world's six billion people, his character was easily corrupted by the pull of puissance. How ironic that he would be the power behind the downfall of Saddam Hussein. War became the tool for writing his own story, for emblazoning himself among the stars. It mattered not that his myth would be one of deceit, death and destruction. As the present faded into antiquity his would be a name remembered for countless generations, especially those mourning innumerable innocents.

This was a delusion beyond grandeur. On some level it was one he shared with Giuseppe. They both saw people purely as pawns. But where lay the greater evil? When measured in numbers Cheney was responsible for the deaths of tens of thousands of soldiers and scores of thousands of innocent civilians. When measured from the heart, Giuseppe had his own wife and children murdered for political gain. Both were driven by a craven thirst for power. Even after a lifetime commitment to my faith, I found nothing redemptive about either man.

•　•　•

For more than three months Jackson traveled to Washington almost every Friday, arriving at Giuseppe's home in the early evening and departing on Sunday afternoon. Occasionally they would reverse the itinerary, spending the weekend in Boston. Given that Giuseppe's neighborhood was quiet and somewhat exclusive these trysts raised no suspicions. The two were rarely seen together in public and usually entered or exited the house separately. Jackson kept a closet of clothes in D.C. so that his travels were less conspicuous. Only

Giuseppe answered the house phone, and when he needed to go to the office he used the subway, leaving the car for Jackson to do the grocery shopping. Once or twice they would go out to a nice dinner, usually in one of the suburbs of Maryland or Virginia. It was not an ideal arrangement, but there were few options if they wanted to be together.

Jackson was in Washington the weekend of September 5, 2003. He and Giuseppe spent a typically romantic Friday evening and night together. Very early Saturday morning he got up and went to the bathroom. As he came out, Giuseppe said, "Wait. Stop there for a moment."

Jackson paused by the door and asked, "What's wrong?"

"Nothing," Giuseppe replied. He had been lying on his side facing the bathroom, his head resting in one hand. He motioned with the other hand and said, "Turn around." Jackson turned his back as Giuseppe spun his hand in a circle saying, "No. I mean all the way around, one complete turn." Jackson obliged, and Giuseppe said, "Now just stand there. I want to look at you." He gazed at his friend and commented, "You know, Jacks. You're not bronze enough to be Adonis and you're not white enough to be Michelangelo's David. But you're hung better than either of them and I wouldn't mind having a sculpture of you in my garden."

Jackson folded his arms, leaned against the doorframe, crossed one leg over the other and asked mischievously, "Is that why you were chiseling me last night?" They both laughed.

"No, no. That, my love, was pure passion."

Jackson smiled and said, "You do realize that if you had a nude statue of me, especially in the backyard, our little secret would be out." He followed his comment with a wink.

"Well," Giuseppe replied. "It's only a fantasy, anyway. Still, it would be a nice way of keeping you here when you're in Boston."

Jackson did not move, but a quizzical expression crept across his face. "Sep, at times I wonder if I disappoint you."

Giuseppe looked at him incredulously and asked, "How can you possibly think that?"

"Well, we see each other every weekend and it's really great. But we don't talk much about the Senate. Sometimes you seek my opinion on a piece of legislation, but I rarely ask you anything about your work." He shrugged his shoulders and continued, "I just thought maybe it bothers you that I'm not politically involved."

"Ah. But you're involved with a politician," he commented with a wry smile.

Jackson could not help laughing as he replied, "Sep, that is so fucking corny."

Giuseppe gave one big sigh as he looked at Jackson and said, "That's enough talk and enough eye candy for now." He threw back the blankets and said, "Get back in here and let's continue where we left off."

Jackson needed no additional incentive and leapt into the bed, practically landing on top of Giuseppe. They proceeded to spend much of the morning making love. Eventually they got up, showered, dressed and fixed breakfast. When they finished eating they continued to sit at the dining room table drinking coffee.

"Jacks, I want to tell you something," Giuseppe said.

"I know," he replied. "You love me."

"No," Giuseppe answered with a half grimace of his mouth. "I mean, yes. Of course I do. But that's not it. I was thinking about what you said this morning, the part about your not being politically involved. Well, that may need to change." He looked straight into his eyes and continued, "I'm going to run for president."

Jackson had a stunned look on his face. "You decided that because of what I said this morning?"

"Don't be silly," Giuseppe responded. "I've been thinking about this for a while now." He waited for a reply, hoping it would be supportive. At first Jackson did not know what to say. In the three years since they had reconnected, especially during the last several months when they had been seeing each other, Giuseppe had never even hinted that he had such designs.

"Isn't it a little early? Bush still has another year and a half and will probably be reelected."

"I intend to run against him next year." His statement was pure matter of fact and delivered without hesitation.

Jackson did not know what to say. He started to run his fingers up and down his chin and over his lips. Giuseppe sat there patiently awaiting a response. Finally Jackson furrowed his brow and asked, "Why?"

"Would you believe me if I said I want to end the war?"

"Oh, I believe that, but your expression and voice tell me it's only a half-truth. What's the rest of the reason?"

Giuseppe considered Jackson a good test subject. If he was going to challenge Bush the following year, he had to have a compelling argument, especially starting this late in the electoral season. Bush had already declared his intent to seek reelection and there were no serious Republican contenders. Several Democrats had announced their candidacies, and although Senator John Kerry had done so only two days earlier, his exploratory committee had been laying that foundation for ten months.

Giuseppe had a few things going for him though, not the least of which was that Bush was extremely unpopular in California. Shortly after being sworn into the Senate, Giuseppe was invited to a private lunch at the White House during which the president asked for his help winning California in 2004. Now Giuseppe was about to rebuff Bush in a most blatant and public manner. He would be energized if he could sell the idea to Jackson.

"First of all, Jacks, I *am* opposed to the war. I know I voted for it, but what is unfolding in Iraq threatens to be an unending disaster. Bush is a fundamentally decent guy and when I met with him I found him to be very personable. But he's not a good commander-in-chief. He was able to sell the war, but I don't think he can end it. As you know by now there were no weapons of mass destruction, Saddam Hussein is still at large and security throughout the country is a mess. You get a feel for just how bad things really are by listening to Dick Cheney and Donald Rumsfeld talk about Iraq. They trip over each other trying to be the most bumptious person in the American government. Every word they speak screams misdirection and cover up. But your astuteness serves you well, Jacks. There is more behind my plan than opposition to the war. I've learned things that threaten the foundation of our government. Tell me. What do you know about the vice president?"

"Not much," Jackson answered. "Mostly that nobody seems to know where he is. He's always listed as being at some undisclosed location."

"I know where those places are and I've been to one of them. But his whereabouts is not the real issue. It's what he does when he's at those sites."

Giuseppe was about to cross a line from which he could not retreat. He did not question Jackson's allegiance, but he would be leading his friend into precarious territory. He went back into the kitchen to prepare more coffee. He spoke from the other room. "What I'm about to tell you can never leave this house. It's going to sound like science fiction, but I assure you it's very real, and I've never shared it with anyone else."

It did not take much to capture Jackson's attention. But this sounded very momentous and he was instantly rapt. He collected the dishes from the table, took them into the kitchen, then they both returned with the pot of coffee and sat down.

"When I built my electronics company, The Pegasus Group, our reputation centered on the computer microchip. We surpassed Intel and set a new standard for the industry, but that was based on technology that already existed. I wanted the company to do something truly spectacular, so I hired the best engineers and turned their imaginations loose.

"Our first real breakthrough was in developing impenetrable security systems that we installed for high-end clients, First Interstate Bank being our first. These are not like the ones you see in movies. Not even the combined skills of screenwriters, directors and special effects teams can break them. But our research and development department is way beyond anything that either the government or the military has.

"My team created a unique electronic device that we named 'the Silencer.' Its importance far exceeds protecting possessions and warding off burglars. When activated, it renders a particular space impervious to any kind of surveillance or recording. Somehow Cheney found out about it. He also knew I had one installed in my senate office. What he didn't know was that it was a prototype and the only one in existence."

"Then you don't have one here?" Jackson asked.

"Oh, I do now. That's why we're having this conversation in the house. Cheney asked me to procure three devices for him. I figured I might as well have a fourth made. I never envisioned the Silencer for widespread distribution and would have liked to have known the source of his information. However, that was the least of my concerns. What I learned about the vice president was very disturbing.

"Cheney invited me to a secret meeting, which turned out to be a gathering of people that can only be described as a shadow government. He has a genuine disdain for George W. Bush and a Hitlerian view of life."

"Who was there?" Jackson queried.

"The names of the attendees are not all that important. Suffice it to say they are all leading neocons, the intellectual and political force behind the movement. But I discovered something sinister that night. Cheney uses this group to control the country. They were the source of the false information that led us into war in the first place."

Jackson was clearly intrigued. This was as good as an Ian Fleming novel. And he had no trouble envisioning his newfound love as an American James Bond.

"Why would he invite you to the meeting?" he asked. "And why would he let you leave without securing your allegiance? You know too much now. That seems like a huge risk on his part."

"Not really," Giuseppe answered. "Cheney did invite me to join his cause. He thought that because I was new to politics I was also naive. However, I think his invitation was only half-hearted. I delivered three Silencers to him, but I have no intention of being part of his secret group."

"Aren't you worried for your safety? If he's as fascist as you suggest, he might consider you expendable."

"That would be too perilous, even for him. He might not be able to control the investigation into a senator's sudden and mysterious death and he could never be certain that I did not have some hidden information that would surface in case of just such an event.

"I'm more concerned about you, Jacks. That's why none of this can be repeated. I feel as though we are now caught in a vortex of secrecy." He shook his head and continued, "I don't know what Cheney's capable of given another term as vice president. That's why I have to run."

This was a lot for Jackson's mind to absorb. During their conversation he had drunk more cups of coffee than he usually consumed in three days.

"Sep, you know I'll support you. I'm just not sure you can win. People are definitely beginning to sour on the war, and Bush is sinking in popularity, but he has history on his side. No American president has ever been voted out of office during a time of war."

"I know that, Jacks. But financially we cannot afford to continue this fight. I've been speaking with Senator Voinovich. We agree about raising taxes to pay for the war. But we have not yet figured out what parts of the budget to target as a balance, and we don't have a lot of support from other Republican senators. The country is in a fiscal mess and Bush is in over his head. His personal history is a good indicator. On his own he was a failed businessman. His only genuine successes came either at taxpayers' expense or through the largess of wealthy friends. By contrast my businesses succeeded with no taxpayer assistance and no outside investments. There's a financial meltdown coming and I think I can steer the country clear. I also have some ideas about how to initiate a campaign run."

Giuseppe, who always drank more coffee than Jackson, poured one last cup.

"Jacks, right now I'm tired of talking about war, politics and especially the vice president. For the last several months, I find myself weighed down each time I think of Cheney and his escapades. Speaking about him makes the stress worse. Why don't we take a ride out to Great Falls, Virginia? We can spend a leisurely afternoon, stopping along the way, taking in the sights, and then have dinner at L'Auberge Chez François."

"That's a lovely idea," Jackson replied.

They washed the dishes and cleaned the kitchen. As they walked into the garage, Jackson commented, "I guess this morning's conversation was another part of being involved with a politician."

He laughed as Giuseppe punched him in the shoulder and replied, "Yeah. But you've already experienced the best part!"

"You won't get any argument from me," Jackson said.

CHAPTER 7

Emily had been waiting all summer to speak with her publisher, John Puerner, to discuss a potential *Los Angeles Times* investigation into the murder of Yolanda and her children. A meeting that also included the paper's editor, John Carroll, was finally set for Friday, September 12. When she arrived at work Emily went first to Carroll's office. She had already presented the concept to him at the end of April and was now prepared to defend it before Puerner.

"Good morning, John," she said.

"Hello, Emily. Are you ready?"

"I think so. What did you tell Puerner?"

"I told him you have an idea for a story that is potentially Pulitzer material, but that it was politically and legally sensitive. What does your husband think?"

"I told you, it was Tom's idea. But he doesn't want me take the story. He thinks it's too dangerous."

"I suspect you didn't tell him that you actually requested the assignment."

"No, I didn't. I want the appointment first. Then I'll tell him I volunteered."

"I've been thinking a lot about that, Emily. Tom's right. If what you told me is true, giving you this case is quite different from sending you to a war zone. Why do you want this so badly?"

"Because I'm privy to information that no one else can get. Not only were Tom and Giuseppe once friends, but I can speak to both of them. In the process I can safeguard my husband's reputation as a police officer while securing the confidentiality of my work as a journalist. I can also protect the integrity of the *Los Angeles Times*. Think about it, John. I'm the only person on this staff who can navigate the treacherous currents of this investigation."

If Puerner came on board then choosing which reporter to assign would be Carroll's call. With resignation he said, "I know you well enough to realize that I can't talk you out it."

"Well, it won't matter anyway," Emily replied, "unless Puerner gives us a green light."

"Then, let's go find out."

*   *   *

The offices of many newspaper publishers are extravagant and opulent, but not John Puerner's. He was a brilliant but down-to-earth man, secure in himself. Prior to his arrival at the *Times* he held executive positions at the *Chicago Tribune* and *Orlando Sentinel*. He needed to impress no one and was content with an unassuming office. Anyone who got as far as his door already knew they were at the center of power for Los Angeles's major publication.

After arriving at the *Times*, Puerner quickly immersed himself in the culture and history of Southern California. It was a technique he employed each time he was assigned to a new location. This enabled him to relate more comfortably in his new environs while seeming less like a transplant. He discovered that despite being more casual and laid back than the East Coast or the Midwest, the yesteryear of Los Angeles is every bit as rich and compelling. From the California missions, the haciendas and vast ranchos of the Old West, the oil, military and space industries and the hosting of two World Olympics, to the romance and stardom of Hollywood, this was the most exciting place he had ever lived.

As Carroll and Emily entered, Puerner stood and moved around his desk to greet them. "Hello, John. And welcome, Emily. Please sit down. Would either of you like coffee?" In a newspaper office that is a rhetorical question. Journalists survive by ingesting frequent infusions of caffeine. He poured some freshly brewed Tanzanian Peaberry, handed each of them a cup and in the process demonstrated his grasp of recent L.A. history.

"One of the great benefits of working in Los Angeles is the variety of coffee shops. Like most people I enjoy Starbucks, but it is so ubiquitous these days, with stores even on the East Coast, that it has lost some of its allure and luster. I had never heard of The Coffee Bean and Tea Leaf until I moved here. Did you two know that their ice-blended drinks predate Starbucks's now famous Frappuccino? Even though TCBTL is a smaller company it is every bit as good and has quickly become a personal favorite of mine. It's a good thing that when Starbucks moved into the Los Angeles market in the early '90s it was unable to purchase The Coffee Bean."

The two nodded in quiet agreement. This was so typical of Puerner. He always began his meetings with a relaxed touch, and when everybody was comfortable he cut to the chase. Just as they began to drink he abruptly turned to the point of the meeting. "Emily, John tells me you have an idea for a story."

"It's more than just a story, sir. It's an investigation into the Lozano family murders. Although it's not technically a cold case, the police are still at the dead-end they hit three years ago and are not actively investigating anymore."

"How does this involve us?"

"As you know my husband is Lt. Tom Moran. He was the lead detective on the case until his transfer out of the Robbery-Homicide Division. In fact, it was his suggestion that the *Times* do its own investigation."

"What does he think we can accomplish that the police could not?" Puerner asked.

"First of all, our methods are different and people are often more willing to speak to a reporter than to a detective. Also, Tom told me that there is information the police never shared with the press. He thinks we can use that to our advantage."

Puerner thought for a moment and asked Carroll, "John, I assume you agree with Emily or you would not both be here."

"I think it's a great opportunity for the paper," Carroll replied. "This goes beyond just scooping the other news outlets. This will exhibit the depth of the *Times*."

Puerner was capable of instantly processing information. But he had developed the habit of pausing in conversations as if mulling over what he had just heard. He let some seconds elapse and then said, "I have a couple of concerns. First of all, how do we get the information from Lt. Moran? Second, what makes him think we can amass enough evidence to solve the case if the police could not? And third, who do you suggest should be the reporter?"

Emily responded first. "Sir, my husband still has his original notes and he knows how to access the confidential information in the department. He can deliver. There is also an international angle that the LAPD has not pursued. Tom thinks that if we include that element in our investigation it will help us determine the truth. As for who should be assigned—"

"If I may, I'd like to answer that question," Carroll interjected. "I think Emily should be the reporter. She and I discussed this whole project at length before deciding to bring it to you. Right now she's not working on any major story, she's the best we have when it comes to international reporting, and as she just said that is an additional angle. Also, her husband may be more willing to share information with her than with someone else."

Puerner took out a cigarette, lit it, leaned back in his chair and thought for a moment. "There's something you're not telling me, maybe a couple of things. What is this international angle?"

"Back in April a similar set of murders occurred in Belgium," Emily replied.

"I remember the story, but how does that connect to the L.A. murders?" Puerner asked.

Carroll looked at Emily then back at Puerner and said, "It's not a matter of *how* they connect, it's a matter of *who*." He took a deep breath and continued, "There's reason to suspect that Senator Giuseppe Lozano is involved. So far no one knows that except a few people in the LAPD."

"And you think that's the reason they stopped investigating?" Puerner queried.

"No," Emily responded. "The LAPD would never roll over for a U.S. senator. My husband told me that he actually got a confession out of Lozano. But it's useless in a court of law."

"And what?" Puerner asked incredulously. "The senator's just going to confess to you?"

Emily dismissed his tone and said, "Lozano is an intelligent and very clever man. But Tom is convinced that if the *Times* pursues the international connection, tying those killings to the Lozano murders, we can trip up the senator and break the case."

Carroll spoke up. "I told you, John, this has Pulitzer written all over it. It's also a dream story for any newspaper."

"And if we're wrong," Puerner observed, "it has libel written all over it."

"Then we'd better not be wrong," Carroll said.

Puerner spun around in his chair and gazed out at the now familiar L.A. landscape. The morning sun was lighting the upper floors of the city's skyscrapers, casting massive shadows across the downtown freeways. Beneath him were millions of people in love with their automobiles: Vans, pickup trucks, motorcycles, sedans (both two door and four door), SUVs, sports cars. A colorful strip of metal streamed in from the distance, then disappeared behind the towering outlines of superstructures. Every motorized mode of transportation conceived in Detroit, Europe and Asia had come to Los Angeles. This was the world, moving at a snail's pace in rush-hour traffic. The muted hum from the streets below focused his thoughts.

Over the last three and a half years Puerner and Carroll had worked at the *Los Angeles Times* and forged a trusted bond. Together they had restored the newspaper's tattered reputation and rescued it from financial distress. Where would this investigation take them? To call it risky would be restrained understatement. Even the supermarket tabloids, famed for their yellow journalism, would shy away from accusing a United States senator of murdering his own family. But Puerner knew that Carroll had been examining all aspects of this case for months, in the process bringing to bear years of journalistic integrity. The fact that he came to this office now and brought Emily with him, meant that Carroll was morally convinced that this cause was just.

Puerner turned back around and said, "OK. I trust you, John, and I have confidence in you, Emily. Still, this is extremely delicate and high profile. I'd like frequent updates. When we start running with the story I want to be able to defend against any backlash."

As Carroll and Emily left Puerner's office, she was surprised at her feeling of relief. They talked a while longer about the details of the case as Emily knew them at the time. Carroll cautioned, "Let me see your plan once you've outlined it. I'll back you all the way on this, Emily."

"Thanks, John."

. . .

That evening Emily told Tom about the meeting. She could see the consternation in his face and knew the cause.

"Emily, why is it necessary for you to be the reporter?"

"Come on, Tom. You know I'm the right choice. My relationship with you, with Giuseppe, my international credentials, my communication skills, need I go on?" She attempted to mollify him with a kiss on the cheek. Then she stepped back, and with a slight smile and raised eyebrows proclaimed confidently, "I'm very good at my job. Besides, this is the story of a lifetime."

"And it's unsafe," Tom sternly said.

Emily did not want to dismiss his concerns or speak flippantly. Still, she stood her ground. "I've been in perilous situations before. I've been embedded with the military in battle zones and even been under fire. Sometimes we didn't know who to trust or where the next bullet was coming from. The truth is, life's dangerous for reporters." Then as a reminder she added, "And for police lieutenants."

"I know that, Emily. But this is different. I told you before that I don't think Giuseppe is through killing. I even warned Giovanni. I don't think either one of you is safe. At least not if you push Giuseppe too far."

"Are you sure you're not letting your personal feelings get in the way, just a little bit?" Emily asked.

"Maybe I am. But you did not see the expression on Giuseppe's face the day he admitted to me that he had his family killed. At least let me get Gavin de Becker to provide a couple of bodyguards for you."

"Absolutely not," Emily insisted. "There's no way that I can do my job with a couple of muscle men by my side."

"And if they're not there? What happens if Giuseppe's assassin pays you a visit? I don't like this at all, Emily."

From the time they got back together the previous year, Tom and Emily had not had one serious fight. Disagreements, of course, but nothing intense, and she did not want this to be the first. She had already witnessed the damage

Giuseppe had exacted in Tom's life and she would not allow their relationship to become another casualty.

"Tom, I'll discuss all my plans in detail with you. You'll know every place I go and everything I do. And I promise to listen carefully to your concerns. Just don't hinder me with bodyguards."

Tom realized that this would not be resolved in one night. Besides, Emily had not begun the investigation yet. There certainly would be additional opportunities to address his misgivings and possibly find other ways to protect her. In the meantime he addressed another concern.

"Em, Gio doesn't know about this yet. It's still early. Let me call and invite him over for a drink."

"That's a good idea. If he's free I'll prepare some light snacks."

* * * *

I had just finished a Friday night Mass and the telephone rang as I walked in the door. It was now eight o'clock and all I wanted to do was relax. But this was my private phone. I answered.

"Hey, Gio. This is Tom. Are you free to come over for a drink tonight? Emily and I need to talk to you."

I did not really feel like going out, but I had not seen them in a couple of weeks and I always enjoyed their company.

"Give me a half hour," I replied. "Do you want me to bring some scotch or a bottle of wine?"

"No, we have plenty here. I'll let Emily know you're coming."

"OK. See you in a bit."

On the way I wondered. It was not unusual for Tom to call and suggest getting together, even last minute. But there was something ominous in his voice that night. I knew that he and Emily were not having marital problems. For one thing he would have talked to me about it privately. Besides, it is not something we would discuss in a social setting and he did say there would be food and drinks at the house. I would find out soon enough.

When I arrived Emily answered the door as warmly and friendly as ever. "Hi, Gio. Come in. Tom's in the other room getting the drinks."

I kissed her and said, "Thanks, Em." As I entered she closed the door and sure enough Tom walked into the room right on cue, drinks in hand.

"Hey, Gio. Have a glass of Pinch."

"Thanks, Tom."

We sat down and Emily brought out some snacks. It was not a large spread, but included some of my favorite finger food: Taquitos and guacamole, deep-fried chicken wings and sausage rolls. Except for lacking any salad or vegetables, it would make quite a satisfactory dinner, and for me, it often did. It was quick and other than making fresh guacamole from scratch it required little effort.

Emily and Tom sat on the couch across from me. I swirled the scotch in my glass, looked at the two of them and said playfully, "My favorite couple, my favorite drink and some of my favorite food; what's up?"

Tom spoke first. "Emily's been given a special assignment for the *Times*."

I had no idea where the conversation was going and cautiously replied, "That's hardly a reason for this spontaneous invitation."

Tom continued, "Gio, the *Los Angeles Times* is going to investigate the murders of Yolanda and the kids."

I am rarely at a loss for words and I am not sure if I was then. But I did not immediately respond. For a few moments no one spoke. I guess they were giving me time to let the information sink in.

My thoughts were neither coherent nor sequential. The news jumbled images of my brother and the people he had killed: his wife, Yolanda, and their kids, Carmen, Gina and Leonardo; Giuseppe's lawyer, Christopher Coker. Then there was the murder of Jackson's partner, Jean-Paul Lecuyer. Almost simultaneously I realized that Tom had not told me the truth back in April. He had indeed shared what he knew of the murders with Emily. Of course, I was in no position to judge him for not admitting that. After all, I had not told him about my visiting Giuseppe in Washington until after I returned. I cannot quite describe my feelings on hearing the news other than to say that neither anger nor disappointment were among them.

After a few minutes I spoke, asking only, "Why? And why now?"

Emily answered. "Gio, ever since Tom and I got back together, even before we remarried, I could see that something bothered him. Both of you, in fact. It wasn't just that the two of you had been changed by the murders of

Yolanda and the kids. I sensed something in your interaction with each other, even with your family. And there was the not-so-subtle lack of any mention of Giuseppe's name. Last year when Tom went to Belgium he stopped in London to visit me and told me everything."

She paused, giving me a chance to reply. I did not. But I did finish my drink.

"Would you like another?" Tom asked.

"Just bring the bottle over," I said. I anticipated that one more would not be enough. I could feel hatred welling up, not for Tom or Emily, but for Giuseppe. It had been less than three years since I learned the truth about his wife and children, but I had kept so much information private that those three years seemed like an eternity.

Emily told me about her meetings with her editor and publisher, their decision to launch an investigation, and Carroll's selection of her as lead reporter. Tom shared his concerns for her safety, but was resigned to the fact that she would not give up the case. They outlined their strategy, including his plans to share with her information gathered in the original LAPD investigation. Until that night I had never had so comprehensive a discussion about the murders. Although suggesting it was a conversation might be an overstatement, for I remained as relentlessly reticent as ever.

At some point my attention began to slip out of focus, most likely the combined effects of the subject matter and the alcohol. I managed to bring the evening to a close, assuring Tom and Emily of my ability to drive home.

My spirit was restless as I prepared for bed. Deep inside I felt as if my body housed two tectonic plates in constant tension, each waiting for the other to shift ever so slightly, an unseen power capable of rupturing the surface for miles around. However, unlike those geologic forces, the stress inside me would not give. I had to maintain balance. Finally, after what seemed like hours, I drifted off to sleep.

CHAPTER 8

In spite of a somewhat restless night, I awoke on Saturday morning clear headed. Although Emily's freshly-purposed conversation from the previous night had originally disarmed me, it now began to make perfect sense. She was the only one in a position to expose my brother as a murderer.

I had long appreciated Emily's journalistic skill and sensitivity. She possessed the ability to identify the human interest in every narrative, no matter its import, without letting it descend into the fluff that defines local television news. But just as she was no ordinary reporter, this was no ordinary story. I understood, as did Tom, that she was placing herself in clear and present danger. After celebrating morning Mass, I called Tom and asked him to join me for breakfast. He and Emily had risen early and had already eaten, but he agreed to come over for coffee and arrived just as I finished preparing my own bacon and eggs.

"Hello, Tom." I handed him some coffee and said, "I hope you don't mind if I eat something. I just got in from church."

"Not at all," he replied. "You know, Gio, you look unusually bright this morning. I expected you to be either bleary eyed or nursing a hangover." We both smiled recalling the many days that began with one or both of us in just such a condition.

"Well, I admit I didn't sleep too soundly, but duty calls. Besides, my mind has been focused on last night's conversation. It was the first thing I thought about when my alarm went off."

"I'm not surprised," Tom replied. "We didn't give you any warning about the subject. You know, I really thought you'd react differently."

"How so?"

"I'm not sure. Maybe with a little anger. After all, I told you a couple of months ago that I had said nothing to Emily about the case. Last night you found that wasn't true."

"No. But that didn't really bother me. I suppose on some level I knew you would have talked to her about both the murders and the investigation. But I didn't expect the *Times* to get involved. That was a surprise."

"I'm sorry I lied," he said. I knew that to be the truth. We had been friends all our lives and I recognized his contrition. "But, Gio, I have not been able to let go of things any more than you have. Once Emily and I got back together I finally saw a way out." He paused for a moment and I could see the frustration in his face. "Ah, fuck it. For three years at every turn in this investigation, every time I thought it might get somewhere, I found another trap. Now, however, I'm afraid I might have been too clever by half. Getting the *Times* to do an investigation was my idea, not Emily's. It never even dawned on me that she would get the assignment. It turns out that the very reason I thought she would be disqualified is the reason she was selected; namely, she's my wife and since I have access to confidential information, so does she."

"And now you're concerned about her safety," I said understandingly.

"Yeah. And I told her so more than once." He took a long drink of coffee and continued, "Gio, I love her but she's as stubborn as ever. I don't know if she's deluding herself or simply doesn't realize how perilous the situation is, but she's committed to following through on this."

"What are you going to do?" I asked.

"I'm still trying to figure that out. I suggested getting her a couple of bodyguards, but you can imagine how that went over. Still, I do have one idea, but need your help to keep it secret."

I wanted to mock him for having lied to me months earlier. That would have been a natural bit of banter between us. But this was too serious and he was deeply worried.

"Of course," I replied. "What you tell me goes no further."

"I set up a meeting with Gavin de Becker. I'm going to ask him to have a couple of guys tail her when she's out of town. They're the best security outfit in the world and his men will be discreet and invisible."

"What about when she's in Los Angeles?"

"I think I can handle that. Most of her work here will be done at home, anyway. My personal notes are there and I'll bring department documents to the house. It's when she's traveling that she'll be most vulnerable."

I began to wonder how Emily would proceed.

"I suppose Emily will want to talk to me, too," I mused.

"I'm sure she will. By the way, Gio, she knows about the confession." I remained expressionless giving no hint of either annoyance or acknowledgment. "Let me rephrase that," Tom continued. "She knows what I know. And she realizes that you will not divulge anything you heard from Giuseppe that night. Still, she'll want to talk to you about other things. After all, you are brothers and you were there the night we found Yolanda and the kids. Plus, you'll provide an important human element to the backstory. Don't worry, though. Emily won't try to manipulate you."

I waved off the comment and replied, "I know that. She has more integrity than either of us."

I finished my breakfast and cleared the table. This provided a lull in the conversation, but I kept thinking. When I came back with more coffee I said, "Tom, Gavin de Becker is not going to come cheap. How can you afford to hire them, especially without letting Emily know?"

He shrugged and replied, "De Becker owes me a few favors, not the least being that he made a fortune providing security for Giuseppe after the murders. And that was at my insistence. He'll cut me a deal and I'll find a way."

"If you need any help, Tom, ask me." He was silent but nodded his head in agreement. I asked, "Are you going to tell de Becker that Giuseppe is a suspect?"

"Of course not. Letting anyone know, even de Becker, would compromise the story and put Emily at further risk. Besides, it isn't necessary. He knows the dangers of any murder investigation, especially one as sensational as this. He's also smart enough to eventually figure it out for himself, certainly once his operatives beginning sending in their reports. At this point the only people besides us who know the target of Emily's investigation are her editor and publisher. I think she should be allowed to reveal everything in her own time and in her own way."

As Tom got up to leave I said, "Keep me informed about Emily's progress, OK?"

"Of course, Gio. I wouldn't want you to have to wait and read about it in the newspaper!" He laughed at the reference to the countless people in literature who learn about stories only after seeing them in print.

On Sunday, September 14, I went to lunch with LaQueesha. I had not seen her for a few weeks and she said she had some important news. After Mass we sauntered over to our customary hangout, La Barca's, a block from the church. As we were walking down the street she said, "There's something different about you today. I noticed it even during Mass."

"Have I become that transparent?" I asked.

"Probably not to most people, but I told you before that I see you differently than your parishioners do."

"Well, I'm more interested in your news."

"That can wait until lunch," she insisted. "Tell me what's going on with you. What's this attitude of yours?"

I always thought I hid my feelings pretty well. Then again, she was unusually perceptive. Still, I had to keep my promise to Tom, and by extension to Emily. This was the biggest story of her career and I owed her the chance to break the case. Since LaQueesha did not know the truth about my brother, my reply could be circumspect.

"For the first time in almost three years I have reason to hope. There is a possibility that the murder of my sister-in-law and her kids might finally be solved."

She stopped abruptly, looked at me and asked, "Have the police reopened the case?"

"I can't say anything more, at least not right now. Nothing's guaranteed and there are other complications. But, as I said, for now there's hope."

"That doesn't tell me very much," she replied. "But, I know you well enough not to pry. I'm just glad to see you a little more calm, a little more relaxed."

La Barca was crowded and, since the restaurant does not take reservations, we had to wait for a table. Despite the fact that I was a regular customer and everyone knew I was a priest, the collar carried no clout when it came to being seated. I could not complain, though. Every time I went there one of the owners or cooks would make a special salsa, extra spicy, just for me.

After finally getting a table and placing our order I looked at LaQueesha and said, "Your turn. What's your big news?"

"A position opened up at the Department of Public Social Services and I have an interview this week." I smiled, but did not interrupt. "MaryAlice Johnson set it up and I think she's going to use her influence to help me get the job. It will also provide me the opportunity of taking night classes to finish my college degree and then pursue a master's or at least a certification in counseling. Of course, if you hadn't originally arranged a meeting between me and MaryAlice back in July, this wouldn't be happening now. I owe you a lot, Gio."

I deflected her gratitude. "I just happen to have had a connection, and thought you needed a break."

We were interrupted for a moment as the waiter brought our drinks, a Margarita for LaQueesha and a Rob Roy for me. After the waiter left she continued.

"It's more than that," she said. "I mean, why would you even care? I'm nobody."

I looked straight in her eyes and spoke with determination. "LaQueesha, whatever else you may be, you are not a nobody. There's something special, something unique about you. I saw it last year when we first met at that McDonald's on Hollywood Blvd. I keep many things private and am pretty skilled at projecting the image I want people to see. Even though we'd never met, you sat across the table and were able to see through my facade. That was more than just perception or a lucky guess. As I've gotten to know you better I've come to realize that you have a gift, a great insight into people. You're both charming and disarming. In the right job you can benefit a great many others. You deserve this opportunity, and so does your son."

"But I'm not even a member of your parish. St. Catherine's is a large church and you have a lot of people to be concerned about."

"And I am. However, my ministry is not restricted to Catholics and I'm not neglecting anyone. Besides, as often as you've gone to Mass over the last year you might as well be a parishioner." She flashed her charming smile suggesting a touch of levity, but did not respond.

"LaQueesha, you've heard me preach many times. My belief that everyone goes to heaven is rooted in many of the Bible's passages as well as church history and philosophy. It is also coupled with another belief. I don't think God cares what religion people belong to. Jesus ministered to non-Jews, to sinners and outcasts, and was soundly criticized for it. Don't you think the church should be doing the same thing?"

"Gio, you know I don't know any other priests. And everything I know about the Catholic Church I've learned from you. Still, I can't help thinking your bishop would not agree with you."

"Maybe not, but God doesn't belong to any religion. I remember a story about Mahatma Gandhi. He possessed a great knowledge of the Bible and frequently quoted Jesus. A missionary once asked him why he rejected becoming a Christian. He responded by saying, 'Oh, I don't reject your Christ. I love your Christ. It is just that so many of you Christians are so unlike your Christ.' On another occasion he said, 'I'd be a Christian were it not for the Christians.' Gandhi was a man of deep faith. How could anyone suggest that he was not pleasing to God, that he could not be saved because he was never baptized and did not accept Jesus as his Lord and Savior? If they're right, that is a God I don't need. Anyway, we were talking about you and your upcoming interview. Are you nervous?"

"Not really. MaryAlice has been wonderful and repeated that age-old advice of being myself. I'm just trying to not be overly optimistic."

"Well, I think it's exciting. I'm sure you'll do well in the interview and I know you'll be great in the job."

LaQueesha was not the only one who noticed a change in my demeanor. The following Tuesday I spent my day off with my regular priest friends. Having known one another for more than half our lives we knew when and how to push each other's buttons. Over the previous three years they had all proved remarkably sensitive and disciplined. They gave me space when I needed it and avoided prodding or criticizing me even when my sullenness threatened to dampen their own spirits.

Such is the nature of hope that I must have displayed a lightness of bearing, even though nothing drastic had changed by that Tuesday. We were meeting at Perry's and Tim, Gilbert and Bill were already there when I arrived. Gilbert was the first to question me.

"What happened to you? You look almost happy today."

The fact that they were priests did not change the rules of the church; the fact that they were friends had not altered the demands of my conscience. I constantly bore the co-burdens of murder and truth, all the while keeping my friends in the dark. Even now they would find no illumination in whatever light might be breaking on my personal horizon. But on this day I was able to provide better company.

"I don't know if I'm happy, Gilbert. But I'm in a better mood."

Had I told them what I said to LaQueesha, they might have pressed me for a little more information. But perhaps I could use her news as a cover. None of them had met her, but I had shared some of her story with them, omitting the fact that she had become a prostitute out of necessity.

"I learned on Sunday that my friend LaQueesha has a good chance of being hired by the Department of Social Services. This is just the opportunity she needs. She'll have a secure job and be able to pursue her education. It's positive news that, at least for the moment, gives me reason to be joyful."

Tim, who always seemed to get away with anything he said, however inappropriate, chimed in. "Does this mean we're all free to tell you when you're being a jerk?"

"Well, apparently you are," I replied. "Besides, I haven't noticed you holding back recently."

To the outsider the exchange could have sounded a little terse but it was merely friendly repartee. It fit my mood that morning and I felt like I fit in for the first time in months. Gilbert started to laugh and said, "Oh, yeah. Tim can say it but if I tried, you'd attack me."

"Come on, Gilbert," I replied. "You know that Tim only gets away with what I let him. Anyway, I'm feeling pretty good right now, and I'm glad to spend the day with you guys."

Perry suggested that we have lunch at La Adelita, a Mexican restaurant in Echo Park, renowned for its salsa and freshly made chips. It wasn't much of a surprise. We went at least two or three times a month. In the afternoon we went to see *Pirates of the Caribbean: The Curse of the Black Pearl.* I chose the film because I had long been a fan of Johnny Depp and had not been to the movies in months. Besides, all of us had fond memories of the Pirates of the Caribbean ride at Disneyland. It was an easy sell even though Tim had seen it a month earlier. Besides being thoroughly delightful, *Pirates* provided me with a much needed escape from reality.

After the movie we returned to Perry's parish for a barbecue. September is a warm month in Southern California, and since we were still enjoying daylight savings time the sun shone well into the evening hours. Before cooking we sat in the backyard, had a few drinks and just talked. Over the years we had occasionally discussed the upcoming Sunday scripture readings and shared subjects for preaching. As I think back on it, I am not sure we made much of an impression on each other. Our preaching styles were all quite different, with Gilbert's being the most radical, I might even suggest a bit bizarre.

He had always been a very visual person and employed many props during his Sunday sermons, often leaving the sanctuary to change clothes and return to deliver the homily as if he were in a stage play. They had become almost legendary from the time he came out of the sacristy wearing a diaper and sat down at a desk to write a letter to his dad on Fathers Day, to the times he dressed up as a chef, or airline steward or a bird watcher.

"Gilbert," Perry asked, "what crazy thing are you going to do at Mass this Sunday?"

"I haven't thought about it yet. I usually get those ideas the day before."

Bill just sat there, shook his head, and asked, "Why do you do that stuff? It's ridiculous. I just talk to my people."

Tim quickly came to Gilbert's defense. "Leave him alone, Bill. From what I hear people love it."

"Tim's right," I said. "There's a family that moved from my parish to Gilbert's about a year ago, but they also still come to St. Catherine's. Cynthia, one of the daughters, always tells me what Gilbert did at Mass. You have to admit, people do remember those things."

"My favorite," Perry said, "was the Ascension homily."

Gilbert never got defensive when people criticized him. He either ignored them or laughed. As soon as Perry spoke, Gilbert started to chuckle as if acknowledging that this particular homily was over the top. The Ascension of Jesus into heaven is a major event in the Christian faith and most priests treat it with the solemnity it deserves. Gilbert had a different approach. After reading the Gospel that Sunday he left the sanctuary, entered the sacristy and started throwing suitcases onto the floor in front of the altar.

"What the hell were you thinking of?" Bill asked.

Gilbert just shrugged and said, "I don't know. People pack suitcases when they leave." There was nothing left to do but laugh.

"You should have played 'Leaving on a Jet Plane' by Peter, Paul and Mary," Tim added.

By this time we were all ready to eat. Perry barbecued lightly seasoned steaks and corn on the cob and brought a salad out from the kitchen. After dinner I looked at my friends and realized that for the first time in months my spirit did not darken with the night sky. I began to feel confidence that my hope in Emily's abilities was not misplaced. But it would still be awhile before she could publish anything.

CHAPTER 9

Emily wasted no time delving into her new assignment. She remained at home and began to immerse herself in news coverage of the Lozano murders. She had already collected copies of *Los Angeles Times* articles, and like any good reporter had gathered information from other publications. She had also brought home archival footage from the television broadcasts.

On a daily basis Emily thanked God that she was in print news, for despite the large media market that is Los Angeles, the local TV newscasts are as useless as any in the nation. Bloated with sound bites and inane chatter between anchors, these programs had long ceased to be a source of valuable information, preferring to morph into what is euphemistically referred to as "infotainment," leaving in their wake a woefully uninformed public.

The nightly news on the major networks proved substantially better in general, especially covering major stories. But regarding the murders in Hancock Park none of the newscasts provided useful information. Emily found the entire episode depressing to relive. The deaths of Yolanda and her children were treated with little more seriousness than the occasional bear or coyote that wanders down the San Gabriel Mountains and into one of the local neighborhoods that continually encroach on the animals' domain.

Emily decided to initially focus her attention on newspaper accounts of the Lozano family murders since the event drew attention from major publications throughout the nation. In an attempt to broaden her research she did not start with the *Los Angeles Times*, instead scouring coverage from other sources. Since Giuseppe was in the middle of his senatorial race when his family was killed, every paper in California covered the investigation. The *Sacramento*

Bee, home newspaper for Giuseppe's Democratic opponent, Anthony Gottesman, the *San Francisco Chronicle*, and *San Diego Tribune* all sent reporters who seemed to camp out at LAPD headquarters. After examining their reports and comparing them to stories and updates carried in the *Los Angeles Times*, Emily was frustrated with what she had not learned. She came away with nothing more than she already knew. At that point she needed a long and serious conversation with her husband. He was the only person who could set her in the right direction, and given his intense hatred for Giuseppe, she knew he was willing to assist. But being an LAPD lieutenant, especially the one who had been lead detective on the case, she was not sure how much information he would be able to divulge.

• • •

Although I did not know it, earlier the same week I met with Tom and Emily Giuseppe was preparing to launch the next phase of his political career. It was an ambitious presidential run. He was entering the primary race late in the game and would therefore be a substantial underdog in challenging George W. Bush's reelection. But the president's poll numbers were plummeting and by September they were barely 50 percent, indicating an unanticipated vulnerability. Much of the country's dissatisfaction surrounded the hostilities in Iraq. It had become obvious that America was drawn into battle by prevarication and deceit. Regardless the source of the lies, Bush found himself the recipient of President Truman's declaration, "The buck stops here."

The American people were beginning to demand that Bush answer for a war that was failing in every respect. Nor was he helped by his May 1 arrival at the *USS Abraham Lincoln,* a *Nimitz*-class aircraft carrier docked in San Diego harbor. Alighting from an S-3 Viking in full military gear Bush posed with members of the ship's crew beneath a banner reading "Mission Accomplished." Over the summer that appearance had come to be seen for what it was—a cheap stunt. America was at war in Afghanistan, Osama Bin Laden remained at large, the U.S. found itself in the midst of another conflict with no end in sight, and its president was starring in his own personal action movie.

Giuseppe was still new to Washington, but he was a clever politician. He understood that by beginning so late in the season the odds of a successful primary campaign were stacked against him. Never one to back away from a challenge, this only further emboldened him. In his favor he could tap into a growing disquiet in the country, and he was popular back home in California. As the largest state in the Union, it provided a powerful platform from which to catapult his candidacy. Besides, running for president was only a matter of timing. If not this election, than the next. Either way he planned on winning. Still, he realized that he would need a carefully crafted and highly organized campaign. And he would need a few known Republicans to support him from the outset.

Over the years, from business to games of chance, Giuseppe had parlayed the manipulation of others into a string of victories. For him the political theatre was just a larger card table and he knew that politics and poker have one thing in common: when you hold the high hand, you do not need to bluff. What differentiates the two is that in politics you let the other person know you have the cards. The trick is deciding whom to play against—who is sufficiently vulnerable to advance your own agenda, wittingly or un. Giuseppe did not need to wander the halls of Congress like a down-on-his-luck riverboat gambler in search of a mark. Like any good, calculating politician he knew that the game is won before it even begins, and he arrived in Washington ready to play, awaiting only the right moment, one that came rather quickly.

Giuseppe had been elected to the U.S. Senate in 2000 and kept his own counsel regarding his higher aspirations. In that same election Darrel Issa was chosen to represent California's forty-eighth district in the House of Representatives. But he had a dark and cynical past that allowed Giuseppe to pounce with a deft and envious alacrity.

In June of 2001 he extended Issa an invitation to a private lunch. In deference to Issa's Middle Eastern heritage, and as a means of disarming his prey, they shared a sumptuous variety of Lebanese fare in Giuseppe's Senate office.

During their meeting he engaged in a forthright exercise of blackmail, informing Issa that he had proof of his illegal and iniquitous past. If true, the charges could crush Issa's career in its infancy. So far he had skirted some of these same allegations due to lack of evidence, which left him wondering if Giuseppe could have been bluffing. But wariness attaches to the heart of corruption and trust does not come easily to the Mafia Don, the drug lord or the arsonist. No one becomes as nefarious as Issa without recognizing when he is outmatched. Bluff or not, he simply did not possess Giuseppe's level of gamesmanship and was in no position to risk his future.

On the surface his acquiescence was simple enough. In exchange for silence Giuseppe merely requested an ally in the House of Representatives. In actuality he was seeking a dupe and made this intention condescendingly clear—a peregrine circling a pigeon. Although insulted and incensed, Issa had little choice. As the British are wont to say, Giuseppe had him by the short and curlies, and Issa found reluctant surrender better than outright defeat.

Giuseppe's cunning superiority was validated by the fact that he did not overplay his hand. In the intervening two years he made only one demand of Issa and that was to vote against the war in Iraq. It was a safe request since the resolution was guaranteed passage. Now, however, he was prepared to put everything on the line. The House of Representatives had been on a month-long recess and only returned to session on September 3. Giuseppe invited Issa to a meeting on Monday, September 8, this time without the pretense of a lavish lunch. He was in the reception room when Issa arrived and extended a warm welcome.

"Hello, Darrel. How was your vacation?"

Recalling their meeting two years earlier, Issa had reason to be cautious. Nor was he overcome with warm feelings for his host. Nonetheless, he replied forthrightly, "Fine, thank you. I spent much of the time relaxing with my wife and son."

With a deliberate casualness Giuseppe said, "Let's go into my office and have some coffee."

Issa entered first, looked around, and after Giuseppe closed the door asked, "No food this time?" He was not trying to sound sardonic. He was attempting to assert an aura of equality. Giuseppe, of course, knew that there was no parity in the room and could afford a little magnanimity. He chose to ignore the comment and poured two cups of coffee. When they sat down he directly addressed Issa's feelings.

"Darrell, I know you felt ambushed during our previous meeting here. I'm not going to apologize. I had my reasons. I would, however, like to point out that since that time I have asked practically nothing of you. As it happened, there was only that one issue of the war in which I required you to vote a specific way. The fact is, our positions on most other legislation have been very much in sync. Now, however, I have a major request."

Issa did not even pretend to control his facial features. His eyes narrowed to mere slits and the corners of his mouth curled with suspicion. Even his posture shifted as if preparing to summon unseen forces to his defense. Internally, Giuseppe could not help laughing but he was easily bored by boorishness and mental deficiency. Before him was a man only pretending to project power. And it was quite a feeble attempt at that. Two years before he had pierced Issa's facade, revealing the grand theft thug behind the wheel of a stolen car, the bully strutting the streets with a concealed gun, the arsonist awaiting cover of darkness. Giuseppe took a sip of coffee and broke the brief silence.

"I intend to challenge Bush for the presidency." He stated this with the confidence of a fait accompli. Issa was momentarily bewildered by the arrogance and bristled as Giuseppe continued. "I have quietly been forming a team for a while now. And I want your support. You're liked in your district and you're fairly well-known in California."

"You've got to be out of your mind," Issa replied.

"Not in the least. Bush's popularity is in decline. Most of the country thinks he lied about the weapons of mass destruction in Iraq. We have long passed the 'Mission Accomplished' speech and the war is going badly. To top it off, Osama bin Laden is still at large. Maybe Bush can beat Kerry. But the truth is I don't want either of them in the White House."

Issa objected. "You don't have enough time to mount a primary campaign and I have been a staunch supporter of the president in the House of Representatives."

Poor Issa. He still did not understand. This was not an open discussion. Giuseppe invited him to the office to give him a directive. Perhaps Issa was still smarting from the last time they were in that room. He certainly carried a grudge.

Giuseppe continued, "Don't worry about how much time I have. I told you I've had a team working on this. What I need from you is an endorsement. In fact, I want you beside me when I make the announcement."

"And what do I say to the president?"

"I don't care what you say. Tell him it's a political game and you're merely playing the odds. He knows he has no chance of winning California, and your endorsing me will have no effect on his supporters. Tell him you're positioning yourself for another run at the Senate and you need to curry favor with the people in your home state. Tell him whatever you want, but I expect you to stand with me."

Issa had already been emasculated by Giuseppe, so any vigorous objection would have been mere bluster. And yet, he felt a need to put up some protest. He straightened in his chair and drew upon what little self-respect he still possessed.

"I'm a United States congressman. I was elected to serve the people of my district, not you and your delusions of grandeur."

It was pathetic, but it was the best he could do. Giuseppe restrained himself. He already held Issa in immense disdain, and this feeble, self-righteous gesture did nothing to free him of that contempt. Had he been more compassionate he would have truly pitied Darrell. But politics is not for the weak.

"You're right, Darrell. You were elected to serve the people of your district. But remember, you were elected on pretense. There's no way in hell you would have won if the people knew what I know about you."

"You can't blackmail me," Issa said. He had raised the tenor of his voice, but was unconvincing.

"Of course I can," Giuseppe replied, almost laughingly. "I already did. If you were going to take a stand, you would have done it two years ago. I owned you the moment you walked out of my office. Now I need an answer to my request."

Issa rose to his feet and prepared to leave. Giuseppe stopped him. Picking up a folder on his desk he asked, "Darrell, aren't you forgetting about this?"

Issa knew Giuseppe was holding documents that detailed his criminal past. He was in the same bind that he was two years earlier. But before he could respond, Giuseppe continued, "Darrell, this is my last request. You do this and I hand over everything I have on you."

"I know blackmailers," he replied. "They always keep a copy."

"You've read too many crime novels. This is reality. And I'm not stupid enough to hold the actual files in front of you. Don't worry, though. They're safe—for now." Then, in his most contemptuous tone of voice, he said, "Look, Darrell. At the risk of bursting your bubble, after this election I really don't have any more use for you. That means I don't need these documents, either. I'll willingly hand them over to you."

Issa had never felt so abject. Giuseppe could almost see his mental gyrations but he had left little room for maneuvering. Shaving just a little off his contempt, he said, "Darrell, you were sufficiently secretive and deceitful that you managed to win two terms in the House. I know you can sell this. But I'm going to need an answer. I'll give you until Friday."

With a personality shift reminiscent of Jekyll and Hyde Giuseppe invited Issa to the door and warmly shook his hand.

"Thank you for stopping by, Darrell. I'll speak with you later in the week."

Anyone else might have felt smug, but not Giuseppe. Issa was beneath him and besting him hardly deserved a claim of victory. He closed the door knowing that one more pawn was in place.

CHAPTER 10

Giuseppe had secretly been planning to launch his presidential campaign for some time. He had lined up support from several trusted business leaders but had approached few elected officials. He knew that the vast majority of Republicans would back President Bush in his reelection bid, and Democrats would be looking for someone from their own party. But there would be time to line up politicians after he formally announced his campaign. For the time being Giuseppe was content to put pressure on Darrell Issa who, although not absolutely necessary, would bring modest name recognition and support in the San Diego region. He would also open the door to additional financial resources. However, with or without him Giuseppe was prepared. In truth, asking Issa's support was mostly an opportunity to up the stakes in the psychological game he had been playing over the last two years.

Giuseppe had been an intelligent child. He was never precocious, but he was intuitive and observant. One of the lessons he learned in his youth is that bullies are universally the same. They pick on others to mask their own insecurity and feelings of inadequacy. But it is an illusion that causes them to wither when confronted by integrity or genuine strength. Nothing defined Issa's life more accurately than that playground nemesis, the bully. It was the reason Giuseppe took such perverse pleasure in subduing him, even though the conquest was unfulfilling. However, he was about finished with that particular game.

As was to be expected, Issa cowered before Giuseppe's extortion and called him on Friday, September 12.

"Senator Lozano, this is Representative Issa."

What a totally unnecessary engagement in formality! Giuseppe knew who was on the phone. Clearly there never was and never would be a friendship between them. But Giuseppe was as relaxed as ever.

"Hello, Darrell. Do you have an answer for me?"

"First, I want your assurance that if I agree to join your campaign you will give me the files, both the originals and all copies."

"I give you my word," Giuseppe replied. "Once we know the outcome of the election, whether I win or not, I'll turn them over to you. I also promise I will ask no more favors."

Issa did not trust Giuseppe, but he had brought this on himself—the culmination of a life of crime.

"When are you announcing your campaign?" he inquired.

"As a matter of fact, I just decided with my staff today. I'm calling a press conference for next Friday, the nineteenth. I'll need you in Los Angeles. I'll make the announcement from my home in Hancock Park. The exact time is not yet determined, but it will be in the afternoon. That way the evening news can carry the story. Bill Morgan will once again serve as my campaign manager and I'll have him call you with all the details."

"Very well," Issa replied.

"And Darrell," Giuseppe quickly added, "thank you."

There was no reply, just the clicking sound of someone hanging up the phone.

⋅ ⋅ ⋅

Giuseppe had told no one in Los Angeles about his plans. I would not have expected him to share them with me or Tom or Emily. But he had not even told our family. I guess he wanted to take everyone by surprise. Even had she known, Emily would not have rushed her research. She was a conscientious reporter and built her reputation on integrity. She developed a meticulous plan for this investigation.

Emily spent the week between September 13 and 19 piecing together newspaper accounts. She outlined a timetable from the killings to the funeral to the election, and on to the murder of Jean-Paul Lecuyer. For that last item she had obtained copies of two Belgian newspapers, *Le Soir* and *La Libre*

Belgique, both of which had reported the murder, albeit with scant details. The compiled material was thin. A few California reporters tried to enhance their work with human-interest angles, including information about Hancock Park, but they provided no real depth to the events. Not surprisingly, her best resource was her own newspaper. Still, through all her research no suspect surfaced in the general press. At that point she knew she needed evidence that was not public.

Friday morning Emily and Tom shared a quick breakfast of granola-cluster cereal and yogurt. And, of course, coffee. Their normal routine was to read both the *Los Angeles Times* and the *New York Times* as they ate. This Friday Emily had other concerns.

"Tom, I've put all the newspaper accounts in order. I carefully combed through every detail, but there's a lot missing. I'm ready to factor in the police reports now and I need to know what you held back from the public."

"I've already been working on that, Emily. I gathered all my personal notes and will leave them with you today. They contain the most important information that was withheld from the media, information that links the Lozano murders with those of Bass and Coker. They also include my conversations with Miguel Moreno from Interpol headquarters in Lyon, France, and my meeting with Chief Inspector Briek Dusmet in Brussels where Lecuyer was killed. From all that I think you'll be able to create a trail tying each of the killings inescapably to Giuseppe. He clearly did not pull the triggers, but he is the common link.

"Unfortunately, I wasn't able to record the conversation in his office when Giuseppe admitted to having his family murdered. Everything I have only gets you to the circumstantial, which means you're going to need more than my notes. I've decided to copy internal LAPD documents—detailed information from all the crime scenes, including photos."

"Won't that put you at risk, Tom?"

"Perhaps a little, but I considered that when I first told you back in April that the *Times* should investigate. I knew then that whether or not you got the assignment I would have to compromise my position with the department."

For a moment Tom's gaze and attention drifted away. She knew his moods better than anyone, but not his every thought. She watched his expression alternate from concern to exhaustion to consternation. Eventually he refocused.

"Emily, I'm tired. I've been on the force for over twenty-five years, and nothing has affected me like this case. I intend to do whatever is necessary to bring that bastard to justice. But I'm afraid that even with all the documents from the department, you're going to need your best skills as a reporter. My greatest concern now is for you and your safety."

She knew this train of thought would inevitably lead to the issue of her security and another discussion of bodyguards. It was a conversation she did not want to have.

"Tom, I won't be going anywhere for a while. Let's see where things are in another week or two. Maybe I won't need to travel at all."

He heaved a sigh of resignation, left the table, and came back with a box of his personal notes from the investigation.

"This is everything I have, Emily. It's depressing stuff."

"I'm already there, Tom. I have been ever since you told me about Giuseppe."

He kissed her goodbye and headed off to work. After she cleared the table she settled down to read.

At 9:00 a.m. the telephone rang. Emily answered, "Hello?"

On the other end was her editor, John Carroll. "Emily, did you know that Senator Lozano is in town?"

"No."

"Well, I think you should come into the office. He's called a news conference for one o'clock this afternoon."

"What's it about?"

"I have no idea, but it will take place at his home in Hancock Park. Ordinarily I would remain in the office and let one of our reporters handle it. In fact I am sending a reporter, but given the special assignment you're working on I think we should also go."

"OK. I'll come in about noon and we can drive together."

Emily hung up and immediately called Tom, relating her conversation with Carroll. Tom had not heard anything yet, but was seemingly uninterested.

. . .

Tom called me right after Emily hung up.

"Hello?" I answered.

"Gio, your brother is in town and has called a news conference for this afternoon at his home."

"Actually, I was just going to call you. I spoke with my sister a few minutes ago. Nobody seems to have known that he was coming home this weekend and no one knows what's on his mind. He asked the family to be there and she wants me to go."

"Are you?" Tom asked.

"I don't know. I have steadfastly tried to avoid him over the last three years. I think it's taking a toll on the rest of the family. So far the only one who has asked me about it is Bianca, and yet I know Mom and Dad are also affected. Those few times Giuseppe and I have been together at family functions we don't talk. Neither of us tries to make it too obvious and we're both pretty good at pretending, but Bianca's noticed. I think even her kids have.

"Over the last couple of weeks I've begun to place all my hope in Emily, trusting that she can finally bring this nightmare to an end. But then, I can't imagine what the truth will do to the family, either. I think I have to go this afternoon, Tom. It'll make my parents feel good and will satisfy my curiosity."

"Well, just so you know, Emily will be there. She called me and said that Carroll asked her to go with him. I'm not going. I'm content to wait and find out later."

When I arrived at my brother's house there were approximately twenty members of the press on the front lawn. The local television stations and affiliates of the networks were represented along with a half-dozen camera crews. I quickly spotted Emily. She was with her editor and another reporter. I made my way through the crowd.

"Hello, Emily."

"Gio, what are you doing here?"

"I wonder that myself. Tom called me after you he talked to you, but Bianca had already told me. She didn't know what was going on. Do you?"

"I haven't a clue," she said. "But I guess we'll find out soon enough."

She turned to Carroll and asked, "John, do you know the senator's brother, Fr. Giovanni Lozano?"

"No, I don't. And if you hadn't told me I would have sworn this is the senator, himself." Then, addressing me, he continued, "I knew you were twins, but seeing you in person is uncanny."

There were days in my youth when I would have regarded that comment as a compliment. But that was a lifetime ago. There was no particular warmth in Carroll's acknowledgement of the resemblance between Giuseppe and me. Instead there was an unspoken recognition between the two of us. We both knew what Emily was investigating. Before me was another man weighed down by my brother's darkness.

The door of the house opened and Giuseppe exited with my parents, my sister, and Darrell Issa. Looking at them it seemed such an odd assemblage. My parents and Bianca moved off the steps and into the crowd. Giuseppe stepped up to a microphone, while Issa stood behind him.

"Good afternoon and thank you all for coming. I would like to begin with a few remarks. Three years ago, when I was elected to the Unites States Senate, I promised to bring a new direction to Washington. I thought the country was on the wrong track after eight years of President Clinton. However, everything changed after the 9/11 terrorist attacks. No one in the country was prepared for that, and I supported President Bush as he sent American troops into Afghanistan, specifically targeting Osama Bin Laden. However, since that time I think we have once again lost our way. Our leaders lost their focus and as a result we are now engaged in an ill-advised war in Iraq, while Osama Bin Laden remains at large. Contrary to the shifting narratives we have been fed by the Bush Administration, Iraq was not involved in the 9/11 attacks, it did not pose a threat to the United States or our allies, and Saddam Hussein possessed no weapons of mass destruction.

"I lived through the Vietnam War and watched as more than 58,000 American soldiers died, another 150,000 were wounded and upwards of 2,000,000 Vietnamese civilians were killed. Like many of you, I lost friends and classmates in that conflict. I want to state categorically that America cannot afford, either in terms of money or lives, another Vietnam.

"Before and immediately after the invasion of Iraq, Defense Secretary Donald Rumsfeld promised a swift road to victory and the deployment of minimal troops. We have already been in that country longer than he projected and there is no end in sight. Given that Iraq is almost three times the size of the Republic of Vietnam, it seems clear to me that President Bush was wrong in suggesting that our mission is accomplished. We are most likely entering into another quagmire. For this reason, more than any other, I am declaring my candidacy for president of the United States."

Some news crews had already taken pictures, but this last comment caused a flurry of clicking from the cameras.

"I am happy to have with me this afternoon Representative Darrell Issa from northern San Diego County. As the Bush Administration inched us closer to invasion, Darrell demonstrated a cooler head and clearer vision and courageously voted against the war. I am honored to have his support in this quest. Now I will take a few questions."

As the reporters jockeyed for attention I turned to Emily and said, "Tell Tom I'm coming over tonight after dinner."

I moved toward my family and greeted them. They were in a pleasant state of shock, although I suspect Emily was a little less excited than my parents. Like many an immigrant before them, neither my mom nor my dad ever dreamed that one of their kids could grow up to be president of the United States. They also did not really know who their son was. I saw them swept up in the thrill of the moment and was in no position to disabuse them of that joy.

Bianca had known for a long time that there was some kind of problem between Giuseppe and me. She cautiously asked, "What do you think, Gio?"

I did not want to respond too quickly and pretended to ponder for a moment. "I don't think he's ready. He needs more experience. But we'll see." Then I made an acceptable excuse to leave and returned to my parish.

Later that evening I went to see Tom and Emily. What reliable friends! They had a drink waiting for me when I arrived. We sat down in the living room enveloped by a pall of disbelief.

"Who wants to react first?" Emily asked.

My unrest was palpable and I spoke quickly. "Emily, we're running out of time. You've got to find a way to bring him down. You have to succeed where Tom failed." He looked over at me somewhat askew and I quickly continued, "I didn't mean it the way it sounded, Tom."

"I know," he replied. "Besides, I feel the same way you do. The truth is I did fail."

Ever the steady hand, Emily said, "Look guys, that was depressing today, but you're overreacting. This is not a television crime drama. In the real world murders don't get solved in an hour."

Tom interjected a note of fatalism. "And some never do."

"This can't be one of those cases," I added.

"You two need to calm down," Emily replied.

I exhaled a huge sigh and said, "I'm tired. Today's announcement was not just out of the blue. It was a mockery of everything that has happened, everything that we've been through over the last three years." I threw open my hands to emphasize my bewilderment. "It's as if we're chasing the horizon. We never get closer to the end. I don't know how much longer I can keep putting up a front. You're the last hope, Emily."

She always exhibited such a calm demeanor. I am fairly certain she was as concerned and maybe even as rattled as I was. But one would never know it.

She laughed as she said, "Gio, you make me sound like Obi-Wan Kenobi! I have some ideas and I'm working on a plan. But I don't want to share it yet." She smiled and continued, "Besides, it's not as if he'll be president tomorrow. We have a long way to go before the election. I'm not convinced that he'll even get through the primaries. I'll have a better idea of what I want to do in a week or two. Until then, nothing's really changed."

I stayed for about an hour more and we all tried to relax. Listening to music, we changed the subject to less stressful matters. Being with Tom and Emily was probably the best thing for me that night, but eventually I had to return home. I was still processing this latest turn of events when I finally drifted off to a much-needed sleep.

CHAPTER 11

My brother's presidential campaign announcement brought him the attention he craved. For me it was a source of unwanted scrutiny. Few people were aware of the emotional distance between us. As a result no one, save Tom, knew the disgust domiciled within my heart. All Sunday long parishioners inquired about my thoughts regarding the campaign. It came up at lunch with LaQueesha and again on Tuesday with my priest friends. Almost robotically I cycled through variations of the same theme: He's not sufficiently seasoned; I think he needs more national exposure; it's a little too soon. Although I ordinarily enjoy the give and take of conversation, each of these queries proved an unwelcome intrusion. Giuseppe was the one subject I did not and could not talk about. Even speaking with Tom and Emily had its limitations. And now that she was actively engaged in her own investigation, I exercised additional discretion so as not to compromise her journalistic objectivity.

On the Monday following the campaign announcement, Tom began gathering information by accessing some files through the department's internal computer systems. Most of the initial reports were archived at the Records and Identification Division. R&I provides 24-hour, seven-days-a-week support for the entire Los Angeles Police Department. The chief clerk was Penny Cervantes, a middle-aged woman who proudly traced her family heritage back to the days when California was still part of Mexico, before becoming the thirty-first state in the Union. She had spent her entire career working in R&I and over the years she and Tom had cultivated a friendly relationship. Unlike many other officers who were perfunctory in their dealings with her, he was always personable and took time to ask about her family.

Although the Lozano murder case was unsolved, it was not being actively pursued and was technically still open. Tom was no longer in the Robbery-Homicide Division, and yet there was nothing out of the ordinary when he walked into R&I on Monday afternoon.

Mrs. Cervantes looked up from her desk.

"Hello, Lieutenant," she said smiling. "It's good to see you again."

Tom smiled back and said, "Same here, Penny. How's your daughter?"

"Which one?" she asked.

"Linda. The one with the baby. If I remember, the baby's name is Miguel, right?"

"You have a good memory, Detective, but he's not exactly a baby anymore. He's almost four years old."

"Already? And I'll bet you've spoiled him rotten."

"Guilty as charged," she answered with not a hint of remorse.

"Well, I guess you're allowed some slack, especially given that he's the first grandchild."

"I have a recent picture here on my desk." She handed it to him and asked, "What do you think?"

They had known each long enough that Tom did not feel imposed upon. Their friendship aside, his answer would have been the same. "He's adorable, Penny. Congratulations."

"Thank you. Now tell me. What brings you here today?"

He blithely shrugged his shoulders and said, "It's the Lozano murders. There may be a new lead and I want to go through some of the evidence."

"You know where the files are," she said. As he passed through the door she added, "And thanks for the little chat."

"Always a pleasure," Tom replied.

R&I houses public records and there was not much there that Emily had not already poured over in newspaper articles. There were reports of the murders of Yolanda and the kids, of Gary Bass and Christopher Coker but nothing that connected them. The files detailed none of the murders. There was no mention of the single shot deaths or of the weapons left at each of the scenes. There was nothing about Bass being a suspect in the Lozano murders, and although the documents noted that Coker was Giuseppe's lawyer, that fact had received minimal play in the media. He had been killed only two-and-a-half months after Yolanda and the kids, but absent the particulars there was no reason to make an association. Even the progress reports that were filed every ninety days were unenlightening. Nonetheless, Tom copied everything. Fully aware that they were only summaries, he was certain that Emily would be able use them to string together a compelling narrative. At the very least they outlined the timeframe. The most important reports were kept at the RHD and to access those he would need help.

• • •

Tom had spent eight outstanding years in the Robbery-Homicide Division, all of them as a lieutenant. But by the end of 2002 his career nearly ground to a halt due to his inability to solve the Lozano murder case. The two detectives who had worked with him, Gary Wharton and Philip Rose, had been transferred to other divisions and Tom saw no advancement in his own future. His former captain, however, had been promoted to commander, and it was he who enlisted Tom for his current position at the Counter Terrorism and Criminal Intelligence Bureau. Although it had been almost a year since he had been transferred, Tom had maintained good relations with some of the staff.

His next stop was to see Jermaine Ulises Jordan, a senior management analyst at RHD. He was a man not nearly as imposing as his name, standing five foot ten inches tall with curly brown hair and hazel eyes. He wore black-rimmed glasses to correct a vision strained from too many years of reading police reports. Among coworkers and friends he was known simply by his initials, JUJ (pronounced "judge"). The nickname bolstered his claim of being predestined for a law and order career.

Tom entered his office and said, "Hey, Juj. Can I steal a few minutes of your time?"

"Sure, Tom. Come in and have a seat. I haven't seen you for quite awhile. What's on your mind?"

Tom closed the door and sat down opposite Jordan's desk. "I have a favor to ask of you."

"Anything you want, Tom."

"This is above and beyond, Juj."

Jordan perked up at that. He knew Tom to be an upstanding detective, perhaps bending the law a little, but never breaking it. "Go on," he encouraged.

"First," Tom said. "I have to make sure this stays just between the two of us."

"Confidentiality is one of my specialties," he replied with a smile of assurance.

"Juj, the *Los Angeles Times* has assigned my wife, Emily, to do an investigation of the Lozano murders."

"What do they think she'll discover that we didn't?"

"It's not so much a question of her uncovering new evidence. When I was heading the LAPD investigation we kept a lot of information from the press. There are reports on file here that tie the Lozano murders to the Bass and Coker killings. The public does not know that. There was also a murder in Brussels earlier this year that I think is connected. That information I have in my personal notes at home. But there's more.

"I've always thought that Giuseppe Lozano was somehow involved. Initially I suspected that he was being blackmailed by the killer. Later I became convinced that he also had to be behind each of the Los Angeles killings. That was something I was never able to prove. And I have reason to believe that he was involved in the shooting in Belgium. If Emily links all these murders and the *Times* publishes her stories it might be possible to force Senator Lozano's hand."

"What exactly do you want from me?" Jordan asked.

"I need copies of all the files you have at RHD for each of the murders. I've already been to R&I, but those records are public and don't provide much insight. What I need is right here."

Jordan hesitated, struggling with ethical qualms of providing confidential department information to the media.

Tom looked at him intently and said, "Juj, this is important. Three days ago Lozano announced his intention to run for the presidency. I know he's guilty and I'm sure Emily can help prove it. But I can't do this without you."

Jordan had a reputation for integrity and discretion, and was not given to reckless decision making. But he was also an exceptional listener with a mind that processed information quickly. He realized, from what Tom said, that Emily had already begun investigating, that the RHD reports were critical, and that time was of the essence. He had a fervent commitment to truth, but more importantly, he trusted Tom. Still, he needed a few minutes.

"Tom, I'm going to get a cup of coffee. Would you like one?"

"No, thanks, Juj."

Jordan went to the lunch room. When he returned, he closed the door again and said, "Give me until Wednesday. I'll have everything you want. The original files will stay here, but I'll give you copies."

Tom stood up to leave. As they shook hands, he simply said, "Thanks, Juj."

Jordan replied, "I'm happy to help, but this had better work."

• • •

On Wednesday evening Tom brought Emily all the reports that were in the LAPD files. She had already sketched out the course of events in the Los Angeles investigations from the murders of Yolanda and the kids, the lost surveillance and killing of Gary Bass, the discovery of Christopher Coker's body, and the confrontation between Tom and Giuseppe.

As he handed her the folders Tom said, "Emily, this is everything from the department. But I have to warn you, it also includes photos from all the crime scenes."

She was unconcerned and mildly dismissive. "Tom, I've reported from the center of international conflicts and I've seen gruesome pictures before."

Even as she spoke, Emily knew that this would be different—at least in regard to the photos from Hancock Park. She had never known the children. She and Tom had ended their first marriage the year before Carmen was born. But she and Yolanda were once close, and until recently, she considered Giuseppe a friend. Despite being a seasoned reporter, this would be personal.

As she studied each murder she was struck by a stunning absence of the macabre. This was not the way shootings are depicted in film or on television. There was practically no blood and each victim displayed a different expression. Leonardo had been asleep and even in death he looked as if he could have been dreaming. Gina had been sitting on her bed listening to music and texting with friends. Although she looked up before being shot, her face was blank. A flicker of surprise could be seen in Carmen's eyes. She had just walked into her mother's room to ask a question, but she was shot instantaneously and barely had time to react to the presence of strangers. Yolanda's countenance, however, showed signs of terror and panic. She alone had spoken with the assassins. Although she did not see the bullet coming, it was clear that she knew that she and her children were all in peril.

As Emily moved on to the other murders she noticed a remarkable similarity. Each killing was clean, and like the previous scenes essentially bloodless. Bass was the only victim who knew his assailant and that recognition was evident. He was not smiling, but there was a discernible trust in his eyes. As it turned out that was completely misplaced. On the other hand, Coker never knew what hit him. He was simply oblivious.

Emily moved the photos of Yolanda and Coker and placed them directly in front of her, then sat for a long time. Ignoring everything else, she gave her attention to those two images. She studied the carefree countenance of Coker, a man out for an evening stroll unaware that the approaching stranger was death. Each time she closed her eyes she could see only Yolanda's expression of fear. Emily felt a brief, but recurring chill and knew full well that this investigation was fraught with danger and that Tom was probably right about providing her with protection. She certainly did not want to walk nonchalantly to her own death. On the other hand, bodyguards would hinder her freedom of movement. For the time being Emily decided to keep these reflections to herself.

CHAPTER 12

Emily worked tirelessly over the next couple of weeks. She outlined a series of feature articles creating a fascinating narrative that detailed each of the murders with the inclusion of evidence previously withheld by the police. This was the kind of story reporters dream of. Not just the opportunity to bring down a U.S. senator. After all, Washington, D.C., had long been rife with its share of corrupt politicians. This was far more enticing. Emily was facing a cloak and dagger adventure right out of fiction.

On the positive side, there was a built-in human interest angle. Yolanda was a beloved high-school teacher with three innocent children. More sympathetic victims would be difficult to find. On top of that the police could uncover no apparent motive for their murders. Gary Bass, given his former run-ins with the law and his shady, enigmatic lifestyle, was a tailor made assassin. Christopher Coker contributed a world of intrigue. As a lawyer with only two clients, Giuseppe and his company, the Pegasus Group, he provided an indispensable link to the original murder scene and to Giuseppe himself. He knew that a secret file had been stolen from the Lozano house that first night. Then he had flown to the Cayman Islands two days later and deposited an envelope in a safe deposit box in a bank where my brother maintained an offshore account. The two men had spoken on the telephone only hours before Coker's own death. And finally, the M.O. for all the murders was the same, right down to the guns left at each scene.

There were also negatives. Bass was only a suspect when he died. He had never been proven to be a killer. And Coker's murder, while obviously suspicious, supplied no useful forensic evidence. Worst of all, despite the fact that everything pointed to Giuseppe's being involved, he could not have personally committed the murders. Powerful circumstantial evidence pointed to his involvement and even possible guilt, but it was not adequate for arrest. Regardless of her personal conviction, Emily would never make accusations on the amount of data she had. And even if she did the *Los Angeles Times* would not expose itself to possible libel charges without more substantive information. For the time being she would have to be content with exposing the formerly secret police files.

Emily studied her approach, taking stock of every piece of evidence. The missing link was staring back at her, and she realized that she needed to do what her husband could not—connect the murder of Jean-Paul Lecuyer in Brussels to all the Los Angeles killings. To accomplish that would require more than police work. What was needed was a set of people skills that they do not teach at any academy or school of journalism. And she would have to manage this with a cloud hanging overhead; namely, there was still an unknown assassin at large.

• • •

Whenever possible Tom and Emily prepared their meals together, so when he returned home on Monday, October 6, at his normal time, he was surprised to find one of his favorite dinners almost ready. He had long held the belief that there are few foods as satisfying as fried chicken. It entices several senses simultaneously. The aroma fills the nostrils with anticipation, the sizzling sound reverberates through the ears, creating an almost greedy hunger, the mouth begins to water even before the first bite, and a soothing warmth envelopes the entire body. But, of course, that is the whole point behind comfort food.

Tom walked into the kitchen, came up behind Emily, pulled her close and kissed her on the cheek. "Hello, dear. What's all this?"

"I just thought we were overdue for this meal and if I waited until you got home it would take too long."

"It only takes twenty minutes," he replied. "It's not as if you're cooking for an army."

"I just thought it would be nice to have it ready. I've been at home all day, every day. This was an easy and welcome diversion from my work."

He turned her to face him and asked skeptically, "Em, are you up to something?"

"Don't be silly," she said.

As she did so, she demurely cast her eyes downward with a less-than-convincing innocence. Tom had never met a woman who could flirt so effectively with a mere glance. Each time she did he felt transported into some classic romantic film. Though he never tired of it, he knew her routine well.

"Now I *know* you're up to something," he mused.

"Let's talk over dinner," she replied. "The potatoes should be done. Would you mind mashing them?"

"Of course not."

Emily had already prepared the salad and heated creamed corn for a vegetable. When he finished with the potatoes, Tom set the table and opened a bottle of wine. Then they sat down to eat. As with many other foods, the first bite of chicken is the best.

"This is delicious, honey."

"Thanks, dear."

Initially their conversation centered on international affairs. On Sunday Israel had launched an air strike against an alleged Islamic Jihad training camp in Syria, the first such incursion in almost twenty years. It was retribution for a suicide bombing the day before in Haifa. Hanadi Jaradat detonated a bomb in the Maxim Restaurant killing herself, nineteen bystanders and wounding another fifty-five. This act was apparently in retaliation for the killing of her brother and cousin by Israeli forces in June. Emily shared the hopelessness she frequently heard on her trips to Israel. Many Israelis and Palestinians she spoke with expressed frustration with the never-ending cycle of violence. Fewer and fewer of them believed that they would ever see peace. Both Tom and Emily knew that this conversation was both a distraction and a delaying tactic.

Tom looked at his wife and with some apprehension in his voice asked, "Emily, what's going on? I can see something's bothering you."

Emily knew she could not continue to hold off the moment of truth.

"I've figured out how I want to approach my reporting on this case—how to write the articles and in which order. The first several will almost write themselves. But there's a missing link, and it's the same one you confronted. I need to find a way to tie Lecuyer's murder to the others."

She knew he would not like her next statement, but it was unavoidable.

"I need to go to Belgium to examine the murder scene, to get a feel for it. I want to describe the scene from a journalist's viewpoint and talk about the other people who were killed that night. According to your notes you considered them collateral damage. But they will be of interest to my readers. I'm also going to have to meet with Jackson in Boston. We both know he's the real key. But I still have no idea why."

"You know I can't protect you if you travel, Emily."

"You're not protecting me now," she retorted.

"So far I haven't had to. Only a handful of people know what you're doing. Once you start publishing articles, that'll change. Everyone will know, including Giuseppe. I already told you he's not finished killing. Let me—"

She cut him off. "Don't even ask, Tom. I can't do my job with bodyguards."

"We don't have to decide this now," he said. "Can we at least discuss it after the first couple of articles come out?"

"Well," she replied, "one of the things we're trying to do is force Giuseppe's hand. Maybe he'll do something before I travel."

"I just don't want him to do something to you. I'm not going to lose you again, Em."

Emily thought back to when they married—the first time. There had always been such deep affection between them. She never doubted his feelings for her. Even their divorce was not predicated on any lack of love. But since they got back together and remarried the previous year, his commitment and devotion were boundless.

"You're right, Tom. We don't have to decide this now. And I promise we'll have an open and serious discussion before I do any travel."

They cleared the table, washed the dishes, and retired to the bedroom with no intention of sleeping. Sex between the two of them had always been both passionate and tender. That night Tom held on to her as if she were falling from a cliff. For her part, Emily was secure in the knowledge that he would never let go.

CHAPTER 13

Monday afternoon, October 13, my telephone rang. On the other end was my sister, Bianca.

"Gio, I just got off the phone with Mom. Dad's on his way to the hospital."

"What happened?" I asked.

"The paramedics said it was a stroke. They're taking him to Huntington Memorial."

My parents, Luciano and Carmela Lozano, had moved our family to Pasadena in 1960 to the same neighborhood where the Moran family lived. Tom, Giuseppe, and I were all six years old at the time and quickly became friends. Our families developed a close relationship in our childhood that had lasted for more than forty years with our parents taking turns hosting various holiday gatherings. They continued to live in the same houses where we all grew up, less than ten minutes away from the hospital, especially by ambulance.

"I'll meet you there," I said.

"Gio, I'm going out the door right now. Would you please call Sep?"

In any other family that would have been a normal request. I hoped that the crisis would disguise my delayed response. It did not.

"Of course, Bianca. I'll call him now before I leave."

Aware of my hesitation she said, "Gio, I don't pretend to know what's going on with you and Sep, but this is not the time. Call him." Her response was firm. This was the big sister I grew up with, and despite the fact that speaking with Giuseppe was the last thing I wanted to do, I knew she was right. I dialed my brother's number in Washington.

He answered, "Hello."

"This is Giovanni," I said dispassionately. I had not talked to him since our meeting back in July, and that had not gone well. Hearing from me must have come as a surprise. In my mind I imagined a slight smirk on his face. If true there was no betrayal in his voice. In fact, in the self-centered universe he inhabited he acted as if we still had something in common.

"What's up?" he casually asked.

I had to contain my dislike for him and put the family emergency first. "I just got off the phone with Bianca. Dad's in the hospital. I'm heading over there now."

"What's wrong?" he asked. I had neither the energy nor the desire to discern his tone of voice or engage him any extended conversation.

"Bianca said it might be a stroke. But since Dad hates hospitals, whatever happened, it's serious. Can you fly home? I think Mom needs all of us."

"I'll take the first flight I can get," he replied. "I don't suppose you'll pick me up."

"No, I won't. You can rent a car or take a cab. It will be at least seven or eight hours before you can get to L.A., anyway. You might want to phone Bianca when you arrive to see if we're at the hospital. I'll let everyone know you're coming."

With that I hung up the phone and headed out the door.

Weekday rush-hour traffic begins to snarl the freeways of Southern California at about two in the afternoon, continuing well into the evening. Fortunately there are a dozen different routes between downtown Los Angeles and Pasadena, most of them under-appreciated by all but the native born. I skirted the freeway system, zigzagging from Adams to Figueroa to Temple to Broadway to Huntington Drive. Twenty-three minutes after leaving St. Catherine's I was parking at Huntington Memorial Hospital. My mother and sister were in the emergency entrance waiting room. As I kissed both of them I could not recall the last time I saw my mom so worried. She had already been crying and when I entered she immediately started again.

I looked at Bianca and asked, "How's Dad?"

"It was definitely a stroke. So far that's all the doctors have said. He's still in the ER, but they'll move him to the Intensive Care Unit once the tests are complete. Did you call Sep?"

"Yes. He'll fly out as soon as he can. Wait here a minute. I'm going to check with the doctor about anointing Dad."

I had been in many emergency rooms but only once at Huntington Memorial. I was called to anoint a middle-aged woman who had collapsed while shopping. Her first X-rays detected nothing. When I arrived she was alert and seemed reasonably fine. But she was short of breath and a little weak. A second set of X-rays revealed a spot on the back of her lungs. It had been difficult to find and turned out to be cancer. She was dead within a month. That was a memory I did not need to recall.

My dad was unconscious when I walked in, hooked up to a ventilator with various wires connected to machines that monitored his vital signs. The doctor was attending to another patient, but the nurse came by and told me he was stable for the moment. I asked if my mother and sister could join me while I anointed him. She consented, providing it was quick.

I went back to the waiting room, then brought my mom and sister to my father's side. The prayers for the Sacrament of the Anointing of the Sick include various options. I chose a shortened version and concluded with the prayer for those in extreme danger of death. Afterward, the nurse brought a chair for my mom. She stayed at my dad's bedside while Bianca and I went outside to talk.

"What did Mom tell you?" I asked. "What happened?"

"She said Dad had become confused and didn't seem to understand certain things. He kept asking her where he was and had trouble seeing the clock in front of him. He just couldn't focus. But she really became worried when he started getting dizzy and had problems breathing. Gio, I don't know if we got him here in time. What did the doctor tell you?"

"I didn't see him, only the nurse. And all she said was that Dad was stable."

"What do you think?"

"I'm not a doctor, Bianca. I've been in a lot of hospitals, and I've seen people with strokes." I paused for a moment, looked away, and took a deep breath. "I don't think this looks good."

She started to cry. As I held her in my arms she said, "Gio, you have to be strong for Mom." That seemed simple enough. Similar suggestions are often made at a time of death. But Bianca had no idea of the emotional ledge I was standing on.

We stood there a few minutes. Finally I said, "Go in the room and sit with Mom. I need to make a few calls."

"You should call Tom first," she said.

"I know."

Having known each other all our lives, my dad was a second father to Tom as his was to me. I knew he would want to be with us, but there was nothing to do at that moment. For the time being I wanted to minimize the number of people at the hospital and ease the stress on my mother.

He was still at work when I called. "Tom, Dad had a stroke and is in the hospital."

"Oh my God," he exclaimed. "Which one is he in?"

"Huntington."

"I'll be right over," he said.

"Wait, Tom. He's in the emergency room and stable. They'll probably move him to intensive care shortly. Why don't you go home and tell Emily, and I'll stop by the house later."

"Gio—"

I cut him off. "Tom, I'd rather have you here tomorrow morning. Giuseppe's coming home and I don't want to face him alone. No one in the family knows what we do. I'll call you when I leave the hospital."

A few hours later my father was moved to intensive care. There was nothing we could do but wait. About nine o'clock we left the hospital. My mom did not want to leave, but I insisted she try to get some rest. Bianca took her home while I went to Tom and Emily's.

When I arrived Emily gave me a kiss and a warm hug.

"How's your dad?" she asked.

"Not very good, I'm afraid."

"Oh, Gio." With those two words Emily conveyed such deep love and compassion, reaffirming what I had always known—Tom was a very lucky man.

We sat down and he made a shaker of martinis.

"Did you have anything to eat?" Emily asked.

"I didn't even think about it," I replied.

"We just ate a little while ago and there's plenty left over. Let me go warm it up."

"Thanks, Em."

As she heated up the meal and set out a plate, Tom and I just sat across from each other, speaking not a word. In the quiet we could read each other's thoughts and neither of us was thinking about my father. The silence was broken when Emily called me to the table. I sat down to roast beef, garlic mashed potatoes, gravy, and peas. Like every meal at their house it was delicious.

"Emily, this is magnificent," I said.

"Thank you, Gio, but it's just simple food."

"Let me get some wine," Tom suggested. He came back with a bottle of Charles Shaw Cabernet Sauvignon. This label is one of more than sixty that are owned by the Bronco Wine Company, founded by Fred Franzia. Most of the labels are held in abeyance and called into service as marketing purposes dictate. The Charles Shaw label was activated following a particularly large surplus of grapes, and in 2002 Trader Joe's markets began selling it for $1.99 a bottle. Although quite drinkable and certainly priced for everyday use, it is often frequently mocked by the public because of its low cost.

"I see somebody's been to Trader Joe's," I said. Then I shook my head. "I can't believe it. My father's lying in the hospital and you're serving me 'Two-Buck Chuck'!" That was the popular, if disparaging, moniker. We all laughed enjoying a brief, but much needed, respite from tension and worry.

"Gio," Emily said, "maybe I should put the investigation on hold."

She looked at Tom and I could tell that they had already discussed this before my arrival. My response was quick and definitive. "No."

"Don't you want to at least think about it?" she asked.

"Em, what you're doing is bigger than this crisis. It's bigger than my family. There will always be something, some excuse to pause. But if you do that Giuseppe will never face justice."

"Speaking of whom, what time is he arriving?" Tom interjected.

"I don't know. He didn't call me back with flight details, but I imagine it will be sometime in the morning. If I don't get a call from the hospital tonight, I'll go back at seven."

"I'll meet you there," he said.

"Thanks, Tom. As long as I have to see him, it will be good to have you with me."

We talked for a while. I told them about my mom and sister and how they seemed to be holding up so far. We didn't talk about Emily's work and, in fact, we didn't mention my brother's name again that night.

. . .

Giuseppe was able to get an early morning flight out of Washington on Tuesday morning and arrived at LAX at 8:00 a.m. He took a taxi directly to Huntington Memorial. My mom, my sister, Tom, and I had all arrived early and were sitting in the ICU family room. Bianca's husband, Edward, remained home with their children. As soon as my brother walked in Mom began to cry again. To his credit, he seemed almost tender as he embraced her. But I no longer trusted anything he said or did.

He looked at me and asked, "Did you anoint him?"

What an asshole—playing the good son in front of the family! I knew he couldn't care less about the sacrament. I found his pretense and even his very presence disturbing. Tom surreptitiously brushed against me—a gentle reminder to keep my emotions in check. "Yes," I answered, "yesterday afternoon."

Giuseppe sat beside our mother, put his arm around her, and drew her close. I assumed he had to dig deep to draw on such compassion. And yet it didn't seem artificial. For a moment I saw the brother of my childhood. I saw the good I went searching for when I visited him in July and wondered what had happened. How could he have turned out the way he did? I think I was actually dazed for a moment, the way people are often beguiled by some charismatic and disarming stranger. Fortunately, reality quickly dispelled my confusion. The person in front of me was indeed a stranger, but not of the charming variety. He was a man of darkness and deceit whose veil of grace had all the permanence of a winter coat.

Bianca suggested that we go into the room. The nurses were kind enough to let all five of us enter together, but only for a few minutes. Dad's condition had not improved overnight and he lay unconscious. We flanked the bed, Bianca, myself and Tom on one side, my mom and Giuseppe on the other. Like so many others in similar circumstances, my mom was convinced that my dad could hear her speak.

"Papa, I'm here. We're all here—Bianca, Giovanni, Giuseppe, and Tom. We love you, Papa. Please wake up." She did not wail or cry aloud, but neither could she hold back her tears or still her shoulders.

Since I had anointed him the day before I did not bring the oils with me. But Bianca wanted to pray. Being a priest, I suppose I should have been the one to suggest that. Then again, it was just one more thing I could blame on Giuseppe. When I was around him I did not think of God.

We surrounded my father. My mom and sister each took one of dad's hands and then we formed a circle. I was grateful that Tom was there, since he completed the link across the bed and I did not have to hold my brother's hand during the prayer. The very concept was incongruous, almost repugnant.

Bianca had suggested praying and she took the lead, beseeching God for the healing power of his Spirit to restore our father to health. Her words were as much for Mom as for Dad. I don't really think she expected him to recover. But such prayers are also intended to give us strength, whatever might happen. I was grateful for what she said and knew that one way or another God was listening.

Tom had to go to work so I walked him out to his car. He expressed his sorrow about my dad, concern for my mom and commiserated with me about my brother. Throughout the day my mother remained at my father's side. My sister, brother, and I all rotated in and out of the room, at least one of us always staying with her.

In the waiting room, Bianca took turns sitting with either Giuseppe or me. Judging from the conversations we had she was attempting the role of mediator. To her credit, she was keenly aware that internal family strife could benefit neither of our parents. That tension had never been vocalized but I suppose her concern indicated that speech was wholly superfluous. She could see the strain tensing between us in both our eyes and body postures.

At one point Bianca and I were reminiscing about our childhood and adolescence. Those were good days in our family. Everyone was close. Even in college and early adulthood, when our interests began to significantly diverge, there was little tension in our relationships.

"I'm going to get some coffee, Bianca. Would you like anything?"

"Not right now, thanks."

I went to the cafeteria, afraid that it would be as weak as the colored drink that most restaurants pass off as coffee these days. Although it was not as strong as I prefer, it was surprisingly flavorful. When I returned I sat down opposite Bianca.

"Gio, I need to talk to you about something."

My defenses tightened. I just knew where this conversation was going.

"A few minutes ago we were talking about all the good times we shared as a family. We haven't had those for quite awhile now. I've been thinking about this a lot, long before Dad's stroke. Everything changed after the deaths of Yolanda, Carmen, Gina and Leonardo. I didn't notice it at first, not for several weeks. In fact, I guess it was not until Christmas. I've never asked you or Giuseppe about it. But I want you to tell me now."

There had been times in the past three years that I wished I could have let my anger explode. I don't mean in violence. My own temperament and my religious beliefs had led me to the conclusion that violence is never the answer. It is the reason I have so fervently opposed both capital punishment and war. I truly believe in the mercy of God and in his call to forgive. But when it came to my brother I could not find that inside myself. I was like a pressure cooker with no one to tap the release valve. The thought of just screaming at someone appealed to me even though I realized that such an emotional outburst would inevitably be directed at the wrong person. I also knew that yelling at Giuseppe would only feed his narcissism.

I had been telling myself that although he and I are twins, we are only alike on the outside. In truth, I suspect we share other traits. I do not think I am as deceitful, but I can certainly misdirect a conversation as easily as he.

"Bianca, don't you think he should have dropped out of the senate race after the murders?"

I was successful. She squinted her eyes and shook her head. "Are you kidding me?" she asked. "That's the problem?"

"Of course not. It goes much deeper. But think about it. How much did he grieve? Right after the funeral he was back in the race as energetic as ever."

"Gio, this was not a primary. It was the general election. He was committed to the entire state. If he dropped out Gottesman would have won. That might have been good for Gottesman's supporters, but what about Giuseppe's?"

"I get all that, Bianca. But I watched him carefully as he continued his campaign. I did not see a man who was devastated by death. Both then and now I question the depth of his love for Yolanda and the kids."

That last statement gave pause to the conversation. When she spoke again it was with a touch of accusation. "You don't sound much like a priest . . . or a brother. What gives you the right to question his love?"

That might have stung if I had not known more than I could share.

"Gio, this has been going on for three years. If you really feel that way, then you owe it to your brother to talk it out. You also owe it to Mom and Dad. Do you think they haven't noticed a distance between the two of you? And now that I mention it, let's throw Tom in the mix. The two of you have obviously remained close, but he is also isolated from Giuseppe. Dad's only a few feet away right now, possibly on his death bed. At least talk to your brother."

It sounded so simple coming from her. But talking would accomplish nothing if he would not admit his guilt. I had no intention of going out of my way, but we were taking turns at Dad's bedside. There had already been times when he and I were alone. Although we had only exchanged superficial words, a real conversation was inescapable. After lunch it occurred.

•   •   •

I decided to give it my best shot but could not disguise my detachment. I looked at him and said, "I'm glad you're here, Sep."

"Really?" he asked. Naturally, he misunderstood me.

"I'm not speaking for myself. I told you on the phone that Mom needs all of us. It would be much harder for her if you were not here, especially if Dad does not pull through."

"Do you think he will?"

"No," I answered. "And that means we'll have to spend even more time together."

I did not disguise the resignation, the defeat, in my voice. Nor did he react. Instead, he shifted the focus of our conversation.

"Bianca has been trying to broker a peace between us." He spoke with such a casual disregard. I averted his stare, not even trying to hide my disgust. "And I can tell from your expression that you have not told her anything."

I looked directly into his eyes. "I'm not free to discuss what I know with anyone."

"You haven't told Tom?" he asked.

"You know I haven't."

"But he told you what I said to him," he suggested.

"Yes." I was beginning to feel exasperated. I could see no purpose in this conversation. "Why are we playing this game?" I asked. "You know what I think of you. Bianca's efforts notwithstanding, there will be no reconciliation between us. I'm content to leave you in God's hands."

"Yes. And I'm sure I'm going to hell. Oh! Wait. You don't believe in hell, do you?"

"I'm beginning to change my mind," I said. That was not true, but he seemed to bring out the worst in me. And I would not allow myself to be bested by him in conversation. Three years of secrecy was taking its toll. "I suppose if Dad dies you'll ride his death to victory, too," I said.

He was unfazed. Missing the whole point he said, "I would have won the election anyway."

I stood up and said, "Well, at least this time you won't be able to take credit for the death." Then I left the room.

I thought of the rest of the family. Speaking with Giuseppe was not a good idea. It had accomplished nothing positive. To the contrary, it only intensified my negative feelings and amplified the distance between us. If my father did die, it would be that much more difficult for me to help my family grieve.

That same afternoon Bianca's husband, Edward, brought the boys to the hospital after school. Tuesday, October 14, would be forever burned in their memories. It was the last time they saw their grandfather alive. Dad died the next morning.

CHAPTER 14

News of my father's death on Wednesday spread quickly. By evening there were many friends stopping by Mother's house to offer condolences. While my sister, her family, and my brother all stayed with my mom, I met with my support group at our usual gathering place in San Marino, the home of Dr. Brian Henderson and his wife, Judy. Although collectively we numbered eight, someone would occasionally be missing. That night was not even one of our regularly scheduled meetings, but out of respect for my father and concern for my needs, everyone made a point to be present—Brian and Judy, Sr. Barbara Nixon, four of my priest friends, Bill Messenger, Perry Leiker, Tim McGowan, Gilbert Cruz, and myself. The bonds among us varied from person to person, but I knew why it was called a support group. No community had ever sustained me as much as they did that night.

After the greetings, hugs, and kisses we settled in to pray. Barbara led us by acknowledging God's presence and invoking his spirit of peace upon my family and me. Then I retold the events of my father's last days: his stroke, his loss of consciousness, the peculiar peace that accompanied his demise and my own disquiet at having been denied a final goodbye. And yet I was grateful that he did not suffer endless pain.

Over the years all seven of these people had come to know my parents, and each shared a memory of a way in which my dad had touched their lives. Some of the stories I had forgotten, some I never knew. It was comforting to see how this simple man, unknown to most of the world, had achieved greatness among my friends. So it was that in their company I began to think of and plan the funeral.

Of course we would bury my father from St. Catherine Church where I was pastor. Bill was pastor at the university, just a few blocks from my parish, and he offered to arrange for students to provide the music. I had been to the USC Catholic Center and it was overloaded with talented musicians, many of whom were in the music school. We discussed different ways that my support group could be involved.

Tim asked, "Who do you want to preach? It might be difficult for you."

I remembered when Bill's father died several years earlier. Perry preached at that service. But I do not think it was any more facile for him. We were all so close it was as if we shared parents. I decided not to pass this particular baton.

"You're right, Tim. It will not be easy, but I went through this three years ago when Yolanda and her children were buried. I think I can handle it."

Brian was a good host and while we were discussing the funeral plans he opened the bar. I do not know how long the rest of them stayed, but I left at nine o'clock, first stopping by to check on my mom and sister, then heading home for some much needed sleep.

Brian was a good friend of Dr. Sathyavagiswaran, the Los Angeles County Chief Medical Examiner–Coroner. With his assistance my father's body received priority treatment and was released to McCormick Mortuary on Friday, October 17. The funeral was scheduled for the following Monday.

• • •

FUNERAL

My father was relatively young when he died, in his early seventies, but there was a natural cycle to his life. It did not end by accident or act of violence. As such his funeral lacked the drama that accompanied my family's previous foray into death. Even though my brother had announced his run for the presidency, nationally he was still an unknown quantity, and this celebration was simpler than the one three years earlier. To begin with, St. Catherine is a much smaller church than St. Vincent. Additionally, Cardinal Mahony was not in attendance, represented instead by a regional bishop, Edward Clark. And unlike the last time, when every media outlet was present, there were no television cameras and only a couple of journalists were scattered throughout the congregation. Far from being an event, at its core this was primarily a family gathering.

My mother, sister, and I—even my brother—drew upon friends for support. Tom, Emily, and Tom's parents sat with our family. I was gratified to see a number of other close friends: Barbara Nixon, Brian and Judy Henderson, LaQueesha Williams, Morris and MaryAlice Johnson. Morris was a surprise. He had become such a recluse that he only left his house to play golf once a week and attend the Baptist Church once a month. Giuseppe's campaign manager and his Senate staff were present, and his friend Jackson had flown in from Boston. In the sanctuary were about two dozen priests in a touching display of solidarity.

The service began at ten in the morning on October 20. The first part of Mass is called the Liturgy of the Word. It includes readings from the scriptures and a homily. There are many suggested passages for a funeral. I chose two that focused on the kingdom of God.

Revelation 21:1–5a, 6b–7

Then I saw a new heaven and a new earth. The former heaven and the former earth had passed away, and the sea was no more. I also saw the holy city, a new Jerusalem, coming down out of heaven from God, prepared as a bride adorned for her husband. I heard a loud voice from the throne saying, "Behold, God's dwelling is with the human race. He will dwell with them and they will be his people and God himself will always be with them as their God. He will wipe every tear from their eyes, and there shall be no more death or mourning, wailing or pain, for the old order has passed away."

The one who sat on the throne said, "Behold, I make all things new." I am the Alpha and the Omega, the beginning and the end. To the thirsty I will give a gift from the spring of life-giving water. The victors will inherit these gifts, and I shall be their God, and they will be my people.

Matthew 5:1–12a

When he saw the crowds, Jesus went up the mountain, and after he had sat down, his disciples came to him. He began to teach them, saying:

"Blessed are the poor in spirit, for theirs is the kingdom of heaven.

Blessed are they who mourn, for they will be comforted.

Blessed are the meek, for they will inherit the land.

Blessed are they who hunger and thirst for righteousness, for they will be satisfied.

Blessed are the merciful, for they will be shown mercy.

Blessed are the clean of heart, for they will see God.

Blessed are the peacemakers, for they will be called children of God.

Blessed are they who are persecuted for the sake of righteousness, for theirs is the kingdom of heaven.

Blessed are you when they insult you and persecute you and utter every kind of evil against you falsely because of me. Rejoice and be glad, for your reward will be great in heaven."

Homily

My preferred place from which to preach has always been the center aisle. Without notes or an imposing pulpit, I feel more connected to the congregation. Even at funerals the coffin becomes a bond that unites priest and people. But on this occasion I was afraid of being exposed. The people closest to the front would be able to see into my eyes, possibly reading beyond my words. As I scanned the assembly I would need to take great care not to let my gaze settle upon Giuseppe, lest anyone sense tension or discord.

I walked to the head of my father's casket and began. "Many times I have stood before congregations to mourn the loss and celebrate the life of a loved one. Occasionally I have wished that I could prove that there is a resurrection. Maybe that would make it easier for people to accept death. Of course, that is merely an academic question. We cannot prove that there is a resurrection any more than we can prove that there is a God. We believe . . . deeply . . . and for good reason. Many of us have inherited faith from our families, a faith that is rooted in our cultures and traditions. Others among us have had experiences during prayer that can only be described as the presence of God. But none of that is proof. Like all peoples and every generation before us we are left to wonder what happens after we die.

"For some people the answer is nothing; we simply dissolve into some kind of cosmic dust and become part of an ever-expanding universe, vast beyond our comprehension. Others believe that we are reincarnated until our life experience is perfected and we reach some state of Nirvana. But we, as Christians, have a very different understanding.

"Each one of us is a unique person. What differentiates us from one another is not our bodies, not the way we look or even the sound of our voices. Those are merely tools we use to identify each other. There is something else that we cannot see. We describe it with various names; most commonly we use words like soul or spirit. But whatever it may be called, that is what distinguishes us from every person who has ever lived. That is what makes human death different—from each other and from other forms of life.

"All living things experience a cycle of existence that has a beginning and an end. We look at a withered plant and know that no amount of water will bring it back. We see an animal stilled by a lack of breath and know that its life is over. Scientists can even identify stars and galaxies that burned out millennia ago, so far distant that we still see their light, and yet they are dead. For human beings, however, our life never truly ends. Our spirits never die. That may sound fine as an expression of faith. But is it reasonable to believe in resurrection? The two readings today suggest that the answer is yes.

"In the first reading from the Book of Revelation we heard the statement: "God's dwelling place is with the human race." That is powerful, but the testimony continues, "He will dwell with them and they will be his people and God himself with always be with them as their God." Beneath those words lies a profound faith—God cannot be understood without us. Yes, he existed before time began. But he needed the human race in order to really be God. And we need him in order to really be human. That divine dwelling among us is the foundation for the resurrection. Our bodies are only temporary shells and they eventually die. But the oneness with our creator has no end. In the resurrection each of us continues to live with God.

"Jesus expresses a similar idea in the second reading. This section occurs early in Matthew's Gospel at the beginning of the Sermon on the Mount. It is a popular passage known as 'The Beatitudes' and many people are able to quote it from memory. But I suspect the vast majority of Christians do not understand the Beatitudes. Many people see them as temporary problems that are rectified in eternal life. We may suffer now, but it will be better in the resurrection. That, however, is contrary to everything that Jesus is, contrary to the very reason he came into the world.

"We might better understand the Beatitudes by noting that the first and the eighth bookend or frame the rest. In the first Beatitude Jesus states, 'Blessed are the poor in spirit for theirs is the kingdom of heaven.' Note that he says, theirs *is* the kingdom of heaven, not theirs **will be**. Jesus came to establish God's kingdom on earth. It is not delineated by territorial boundaries, by political or economic systems, nor by any of the myriad ways that we divide and separate ourselves. It is defined by acknowledging God's presence, the same God who makes his dwelling place among us. And that kingdom embraces all people.

"Between the first and last Beatitudes Jesus offers six other blessings that appear more temporal in nature. Of special note is the second, 'Blessed are they who mourn for they will be comforted.' I believe what Jesus says, but right now I don't feel it. There is an emptiness in my heart that will not be banished today. I spent this past weekend with my family but there was no joy in being together. The sound of my father's laughter has been muted and none of us will ever again feel his embrace. That is much harder to bear than any physical pain. Death has once again cast its pall, dredging up memories of another funeral three years ago when we buried four other members of our family."

Making every effort I was able to look past Giuseppe and control my emotions. I remembered Bianca telling me that I needed to be strong for Mom. So I was.

"For a long time after that funeral sorrow lurked about our house waiting to pounce on any semblance of joy. Eventually light dispelled the darkness and hope conquered doubt. There was no defining moment, no light switch of revelation. Gradually we became aware that even in grief God is with us.

"That is the whole point of this kingdom that Jesus came to establish. If it appears somewhat transitory, that is because we are imperfect, our lives incomplete. We are both saints and sinners. Sometimes our choices distance us from God, at other times they bring us closer. While alive on this earth we move in and out of the kingdom. But in the resurrection there is perfection and the kingdom is complete. We live forever in God's presence.

"When I think of my father, I remember his commitment to faith and to family. I treasure not only the memory of who he was but what he taught me of God. From my father I learned to love and to forgive. I learned to be a man of peace.

"For me there is no doubt that God dwelt with my dad. And there is no doubt that my father now dwells with him."

Although I believed everything I said in the homily, I feared that some of my words might have rung hollow for I felt neither love nor forgiveness nor peace toward my brother. Fortunately, only three other people knew that: Tom, Emily, and Giuseppe himself. For everyone else in the church, especially my mom and my sister, I hoped that the homily would be consoling.

When the funeral Mass was over, we drove to Holy Cross Cemetery to inter my father in the same section where Yolanda, Carmen, Gina, and Leonardo had been buried three years earlier.

•　•　•

Following the graveside service everyone returned to St. Catherine Parish for a reception. The pastoral council had organized a simple but extensive spread of whole wheat and Kaiser rolls; slices of turkey, beef, and ham; a variety of pasta and green salads; and water, beer, and wine. Some Filipino women also donated their own ethnic food. After all, thin slices of meat on bread might be tasty, but cold cuts cannot compete with lumpia and pancit. They were the first to be devoured.

Most everyone mixed and mingled with ease. Only Emily was overtaken by duty. What made her such a consummate reporter was her ability to be dispassionate and objective even in the most emotionally charged environments. She was able to do what neither Tom nor I could—have a pleasant conversation with my brother. Giuseppe had no idea of her current assignment and unwittingly introduced her to Jackson.

"Emily," he said, "this is Jackson Carver, a friend of mine from Boston." He turned to his friend and said, "Emily is a topnotch reporter for the *Los Angeles Times* and the wife of Lt. Tom Moran."

Jackson extended his hand and said, "It's a pleasure to meet you."

"Thank you," she replied.

At that moment Giuseppe was called away by Bianca.

Emily said to Jackson, "I've heard your name before. Didn't the two of you attend Harvard together?" That was a cocktail party question, but she made it sound convincingly innocent.

"Yes," he answered. "Then after we graduated I remained in Boston while he came back and built a business career in Los Angeles."

"And now he's a United States Senator," she added.

Jackson looked across the room toward Giuseppe and mused, "I was surprised by that career choice. Back in school he exhibited no interest in politics whatsoever. Still, he seems to be doing a good job in Washington."

"Yes, he does," she agreed. "The last time I was in the capital I stopped by to see him and he was definitely in his element. But with all of his family in California I'm glad he has a friend on the East Coast. Do the two of you keep in contact?"

Emily had a style of speech that engendered confidence even as she gently probed for information. Jackson did not feel as if he were being scrutinized. On the other hand he was not about to volunteer unnecessary information. If his intimate relationship with Giuseppe taught him anything, it was to be careful.

"We see each other occasionally, and talk by phone whenever he needs to ask my opinion. He refers to me as one of his advisors."

"Does he listen?" They both laughed at the question.

"Well, sometimes." Then he added, "I'm not a Republican."

"Neither am I—or my husband or anyone else in Sep's family. Sometimes I feel as if we've all abandoned him."

"I doubt he thinks that," Jackson replied. "At least he's never suggested that to me. You know, Emily, you're the first person I've ever heard call him 'Sep.' It's quite endearing."

Tom had met Jackson three years before while investigating the murder of Yolanda and her children. From across the room he thought Jackson looked a little more aged, undoubtedly the result of Jean-Paul's death back in April. He went over to interrupt their conversation. "Emily, Gio wants to introduce you to some people." Then he looked at Jackson and asked, "Do you mind?"

"Not at all. I think I'll go get another glass of wine."

"I'm glad to have met you," she said.

"The pleasure was mine. The next time you're in Boston please give me a call."

As they walked away Tom put his arm around Emily's waist. Jackson was impressed by how natural it was, and how public. He wondered if he and Giuseppe would ever be able to express such affection openly. For the time being he was content with life behind closed doors.

•　•　•

Giuseppe had been staying with Mom since his arrival in Los Angeles the previous Thursday. Monday night, following the funeral and the day's activities, he decided to stay at the LAX Hilton on the pretense that he had an early flight to Washington. While that was technically true, what he really wanted was a private rendezvous. His staff had all returned to the capital that afternoon and Jackson, who was on a more restricted budget, was booked just around the corner at Four Points by Sheraton.

This early in his presidential run the press was not particularly interested in Giuseppe's choice of hotels. Nonetheless, separate accommodations were a precautionary step. In order to minimize the risk of being seen together, at least to avoid anyone noticing where they spent the night, Giuseppe went out for an evening walk that brought him to Four Points where he headed straight to Jackson's room without drawing any attention.

He knocked on the door and Jackson let him in, then closed and latched it again before they kissed. In the warmth of that embrace Giuseppe finally freed the emotions he had so stoically controlled over the weekend.

"Jacks, this is the first opportunity I've had to tell you how grateful I am that you're here."

"Of course I'm here. I couldn't leave you alone at this time."

Giuseppe let out a grunting noise. "Hmh. Funny you should use that word. I feel so alone with my family. I mean, I love them, but there's a distance. They don't really know who I am. You do. And when you and I are together I can be myself."

With all the duplicity that so accurately characterized my brother, there was more than an element of truth in his statement. I had spent a few years as a prison chaplain and met many coldhearted criminals. At least everyone in the system saw them that way. But beneath their hardened exteriors I came to know human beings who were lost in their isolation, real people who needed someone to care for them. Those experiences taught me that no one can survive completely alone. Beyond the physical, Jackson provided my brother with something no one else could. Although I suspect the honesty was not entirely reciprocal.

The next morning they had breakfast together in Jackson's hotel room. Neither wanted to discuss the obvious: Their time together would be limited and of necessity far more furtive. As the primary election season heated up, much of Giuseppe's life would be on display in the media. They felt mutual and competing desires play out in their hearts, both wanting Giuseppe to win the nomination, and both wanting to be together. If he lost the race, their first wish would be denied and the second a given. If he won, however, it would be nearly impossible to fulfill their love. But that was a conversation for another day. They flew back to the East Coast on separate airplanes to separate cities, each holding on to the same memory of another magical night.

CHAPTER 15

Over the years I had prayed with many families as they struggled with death, and in the process learned that each of us grieves in our own way. I knew that the sorrow my family experienced would come in waves, and that it would be most difficult for my mom. October 21, the day after the funeral, was my usual day off, but instead of relaxing with my other friends, I tended to my mother and sister. Both of them held up fairly well during the services, undoubtedly due to a combination of adrenaline and a deep outpouring of support, but the funeral was now over and there would be fewer friends around. My sister kept her children home an extra day and my mother took comfort in their presence. Whether part of her own grieving, or something else, my father's death emboldened Bianca to challenge me on our family ties.

In the early afternoon the two of us went to Lacy Park in the heart of San Marino, only a few minutes' drive from our family home. Like almost every aspect of life in that city, the park is highly regulated, particularly in regard to boisterous activity. That makes it an ideal location for an otherwise intimidating conversation. We found a pleasant place to sit and she began.

"Gio, for the last couple of years there has been a quiet tension between you and Sep. I haven't said much because I remember what it was like when we were kids. The two of you could remain angry at each other for weeks at a time. I used to think it was some strange symbiotic result of being identical twins. It seemed counterintuitive at the time because the bond between the two of you should have lent itself to an easy reconciliation. Eventually you always forgave and healed. Things are different now. What's happened between you guys?"

For two years I had felt like the Artful Dodger in Charles Dickens's *Oliver Twist*. Much as he escaped the reach of the law after pickpocketing people on the street, I managed to evade moments of truth with my sister, successfully deflecting her expressions of concern. But whereas the Dodger always seemed to find another alley leading to freedom, I finally felt cornered—trapped between the love of God guaranteed in the confessional and the love of my sister sitting beside me. Unknown to her we were sitting beneath an arch of animus. For a moment I said nothing, wondering if there existed one more excuse I might conjure up. When I spoke, my words were carefully measured and honest. She would have noticed any untruth.

"Look, sis, I have spent years ministering to people in need. Most of the time it has been a pleasure—rejoicing at a birth, a baptism, a wedding, or some other joyous occasion. At other times ministry has been trying—supporting people as they adjust to divorce or death or battle any number of life's problems. But all of it has been gratifying."

"Then why haven't you done the same for your brother?"

"That's just it. I tried. What I discovered was that he neither needed nor wanted me. I told you last week that I questioned his feelings for Yolanda and the kids." I took a deep breath, sighed, and on the trailing wisps of that exhale said, "I wonder if he cares about anyone."

She looked at me and asked sarcastically, "You're upset with Sep because he didn't *need* you?"

"No, Bianca. I'm upset with him because he didn't need *anyone*."

"Gio, when we were growing up I thought both of you were self-centered, but this is beyond belief. You're making this about you and your feelings. He lost his wife and children."

Closing my eyes and clenching, I remained silent. I had managed to focus her attention on me and my apparent lack of sensitivity, and was even willing to bear the accompanying scorn. At least she would have no reason to suspect that a more profound secret lay within me. When I did reply I stayed on that same track.

"You're partly right, Bianca. I know I can't feel what he does, but I was hurting, too, and needed to be needed—especially by my twin brother. We spent a lot of time together between the murders and the funeral. But then . . . nothing."

"Gio, be realistic. There were only a few weeks left before the election and he had to finish his campaign."

I waved my hands and said, "I get that. But it doesn't explain everything. From my perspective he treated the death of his family like a man walking through a revolving door, taking only half a revolution for grief, then exiting unchanged."

"You don't have the right to make that judgment," she said sternly. "Even if you're right, and I'm not granting that, how can you assume that he hasn't suffered like the rest of us—especially if, as you claim, he did not take sufficient time to mourn?"

"It's a feeling. Besides, I spoke with him, just as you asked me to. He's not the brother we grew up with, Bianca. He's changed."

She half laughed and said, "I thought I was supposed to be the dramatic one in the family. But you've got me beat."

"Well," I replied, "I'm not laughing. And I'm not just being dramatic. But on the off chance that I could be wrong, I'll keep an open mind. OK?"

She sat silently and turned her gaze skyward. It was a clear October afternoon. Rains had not yet come to Southern California; still, the air was crisp and cool. She stood up, tucked her arms together, and hunched in the chill.

"Gio, I know you and I know when a conversation is over. Let's go home and see how Mom's doing. I hope the kids did not drive her crazy today."

"I'm sure she was grateful to have them around."

"One more thing," she added. "Now that Dad's gone, try to pretend a little harder for Mom's sake."

She had no idea the task she was asking, but I knew how to begin the pretense. I dug deep and masked my response with my most sincere and promising tone of voice. "I'll try."

On the way home we passed "The Hat," world famous for its pastrami. We decided to pick up some sandwiches, fries, and onion rings. That would avoid any cooking or fuss in the kitchen. Besides, Mom was very partial to pastrami. After dinner I decided to stop by Tom and Emily's house.

•　•　•

Tom opened the door and welcomed me with a warm embrace. Emily came over, gave me a hug and a kiss and asked, "How is the family doing, especially your mother and sister?"

"I think Mom's worn out from the funeral. And although Bianca might be tired, she's focused her attention on Giuseppe and me. The two of us went to Lacy Park for a private conversation this afternoon. That's one of the reasons I came by tonight.

"You asked me last week if you should delay the investigation and I said no. Now I'm thinking that not only should you continue, but you should move quickly and I want to help."

Tom cut in. "I thought you wanted to stay out of it in order to safeguard Emily's objectivity."

"I'm not going to compromise her integrity or reveal anything I shouldn't. But I have to do something."

"What did you have in mind?" Emily asked.

That was just the opening I needed. "Once word gets out about your investigation, whether in a published article or unexpected leak, Giuseppe will know and that will put him on alert."

"So what?" Tom asked. "You're not a detective or a reporter."

"No, I'm not. But If I know your strategy I can help to anticipate Giuseppe's responses. Maybe we can stay a step ahead of him for a change. At least I'll feel like I'm contributing."

They looked at each other as they mulled over my suggestion. I could tell that neither one was particularly keen on the idea. I pressed forward.

"Emily, I know you want to interview Jackson. How do you think Giuseppe will react to that? Not one of us really knows him anymore. The three of us need to be in on this together."

There was no tension in the room, but we had entered a world of uncertainty, for trying to foresee my brother's actions was like searching for a path on the other side of the rabbit hole. His personality had blended the fury of both the Queen of Hearts and the Red Queen, making him a more dangerous obstacle than anything Alice had ever encountered.

Tom said, "Why don't I fix us all a drink?"

"I don't need a drink, Tom," I emphatically replied. "I want to know your plans and I want in."

Tom started to speak, but Emily stopped him.

"It wouldn't hurt to go over the outline," she suggested.

She went into the other room to get her notes. While she was gone Tom said, "I'm gonna have a drink even if you're not." Then he went to the bar. Our go-to drink was scotch, but when the mood struck him, he made great martinis. That night in deference to his wife's British heritage he selected Beefeater London Gin, added barely a splash of dry vermouth, then finished it off with olives. "Are you sure you won't have one?"

I always thought that if Tom ever quit the LAPD he would make a good bartender. Between his personality and his mixology skills he could have converted Mahatma Gandhi into a drinker. "I might as well," I answered. "But no amount of alcohol will temper my resolve tonight." As he brought me my drink I said, "Look, Tom, I know you're still concerned about Emily's safety—"

He cut me off. "Whatever you're thinking, Gio, there's no way you can protect her. But there may be a way you can help with the investigation."

Just then she returned, looked at the two of us, and said, "I see Tom talked you into that martini."

He handed her a glass. "I took the liberty of fixing you one, also."

"Thanks, sweetheart. Now let's get to work."

Emily laid out her plans, explaining that the first article would need to recreate interest. Since the murders of Yolanda and her children were now three years old, publication of photos from the crime scene would awaken memories and generate fresh concern among the *Times'* readers.

"What photos do you plan on using?" I asked. If my expression did not give away my concern, the hesitation in my voice certainly did.

"Don't worry, Gio. They won't be graphic. I would never print pictures of the bodies. But the other forensic shots—the house, the guns on the coffee table, the open safe in the bedroom, the footprint in the flower bed—they are essential, especially given the lapse of time since the murders took place."

I leaned back, closed my eyes and sighed. Tom and Emily, respecting the moment, said nothing. They gave me room for solitude and in the quiet I could not help but think of the effect this would have on my family. Over the years I discovered that truth rarely journeys alone. Whether by intent or happenstance, pain piggybacks on its travels, and one way or another Giuseppe needed to be brought to justice.

My next words came from a place halfway between question and statement. "I suppose these photos will include the chalk outlines."

"Yes," Emily replied. Her response was both honest and sensitive. There was no other way to reignite the curiosity and concern of the city and of *Los Angeles Times* readers nationwide. My family's agony would be unavoidable collateral. I knew that and pressed on.

"What comes after that first article?" I asked.

"I want to develop an engaging narrative," she answered. "I've been dissecting all the information Tom gave me, focusing on how to present the material that the LAPD never released to the public. Even though most of it is new, it's contained in a lengthy and boring police process that cannot sustain the average reader. However, a newspaper investigation and exposé is in a different world and chronicling the events as they actually unfolded might make a more compelling read. For example, the second article could be about the secret file that went missing from the bedroom safe the night of the murders. That would introduce Christopher Coker and his overseas trip two days later. It won't be necessary to prove that he secreted the document into Giuseppe's safe deposit box in the Cayman Islands. It will be enough just to raise suspicion. Nothing sells like a conspiracy theory."

"Emily will have no trouble stringing the story together," Tom said. "But we still have to find a connection to the Lecuyer killing in Brussels. How do we get to Jackson before Giuseppe does?"

"Well," I said, "obviously, all the evidence has to be in place before the first article is ever printed. Emily, since you have everything else I think you should meet with Jackson next week."

"And your brother?" she asked.

"The sooner you go to Boston, the better—before he gets wind of anything. I'm not sure how close they are, but they will certainly talk afterward."

"Yeah," Tom replied. Looking at his wife he continued, "Once Giuseppe knows what you're doing your safety will be in jeopardy."

We all understood what he was implying. But she remained adamant. There would be no bodyguards. For the moment there was another practical concern.

"Emily," I said, "as soon as you try to set up a meeting with Jackson he's going to let Giuseppe know."

"Maybe not," she replied. "When I met him at the funeral, he told me to contact him the next time I was in Boston. I can fly out there pretending that I'm on assignment, and call him unexpectedly. He'll have no reason to be apprehensive."

"And if he happens to speak with Giuseppe before you meet?" Tom asked.

"I got a good read on him yesterday. He's too innocent to be skeptical."

With effortless sarcasm I replied, "That's probably why they're friends."

"Don't worry, you guys. I can make it all seem natural. Of course, eventually Giuseppe will know."

Tom looked at me and said, "Well, Gio. You wanted in on the action. It seems to me that you're the one who's going to have to confront your brother."

That was not what I wanted to hear or had in mind, but he was right. The last several days had been so long and exhausting that I had not been thinking clearly. Exposing Giuseppe was not a mission from some spy drama. There certainly was danger to be had, but it was not laced with thrill or excitement. And yet I did not regret my decision to be a part of it. As I drove home I thought of Tom and Emily and contemplated our impending fate. We were all on the same ship heading into treacherous waters. I trusted both of them with my life, but I felt more comfortable knowing that I was helping to chart the course. And if that included facing my brother again, so be it.

CHAPTER 16

Despite its obvious permanence, death is one of life's temporary distractions, with family and friends momentarily numbed by loss. With little heed to human pain, the world spins on, our place forgotten. Not even the assassination of a president or prime minister can halt the passage of time. So it is that work intrudes on grief and loved ones slip into memory.

After a week of tending to my family, I was grateful to return to pastoral duties. My busy schedule occupied my time, turning what would have been hours of bereavement into productivity. In the process of relieving some sorrow it also brought joy. On Friday afternoon, October 24, I was in my office when my secretary put through an unexpected phone call. It was my friend LaQueesha.

"Hello," I said.

"Gio, I know this is short notice, but would you be available for a celebration dinner tomorrow night?"

"I think I could arrange that," I answered. "What are we celebrating and where would you like to go?"

"I'd like you to come here and have dinner with my family. And I'll tell you the reason tomorrow."

In the two years we had known each other I had never been to her home nor had I met either her mother or her son.

"I'd love to. I can be free by six thirty, if that works for you."

"Perfect," she said. She gave me her address, which was about five miles from my parish.

At six fifteen Saturday evening I arrived at the Williams's residence, an unassuming two-bedroom home on South Bronson Ave in the Leimert Park district of Los Angeles. The front yard was small, but well cared for. It had been planted years before with Zoysia grass and the lawn had developed into a lush carpet of green. In various parts of Los Angeles one can find houses painted in loud, if not garish colors. Not so in Leimert Park. The residents tend toward softer, quieter hues. LaQueesha's home was painted bluish-gray, with the trim and front door a cumulus white.

I knocked and her son Tyriq rushed to answer. He was eight years old and like many a child his age took great delight in welcoming a new visitor. He had tight, curly black hair, brown eyes, and a chocolate complexion. As cute as he was for his age, his looks hinted at a handsome future. He had his mother's smile and would most likely become a charmer in adolescence and a beguiler in young adulthood.

LaQueesha's mother, Roberta, was five feet six inches tall. Graced by time she dressed with such care that one would be hard-pressed to guess her age with any precision and most people would think her younger than the forty-eight years she actually was. Mothers and fathers base the names of their children on many criteria, always hoping the choice will bond with the child's personality. LaQueesha's grandparents had apparently mastered the art, for standing before me that night was a woman as stylish and dignified as her name. Her hair was auburn and, like many women of her generation, she forsook natural curls for generous waves. But it was her charisma that won over admirers.

After the introductions we sat in the living room visiting—LaQueesha and her mother both expressing condolences on the loss of my father; I commenting on the loveliness of their home. Tyriq fidgeted for a few minutes, but after he demonstrated his manners he was allowed to go to his room where toys rescued him from the boredom of adult conversation.

LaQueesha had prepared a luscious dinner. I do not know whether she was aware of it, but the salad was one of my favorites: mixed spring lettuce, Bartlett pears, walnuts, blue cheese crumbles, and pear juice for dressing. This was followed by a tender roast beef, new potatoes, and carrots. For dessert, Roberta had baked what I later learned was her signature apple pie.

LaQueesha waited until our dinner conversation to share her latest news.

"Gio—" she began, but was quickly interrupted by her mother.

"LaQueesha, that's no way to address a minister."

"It's all right, Mrs. Williams," I assured her. "We have been on a first-name basis for a long time."

"Well, this is new to me. Where I come from no one would call a pastor by his first name." She turned to her grandson and said, "Tyriq, when you speak to him you say, 'Reverend.'"

"Mama, they go by 'Father,'" LaQueesha interjected.

"OK, then," Roberta responded. She looked at me and said, "It's not that I'm very formal, but I've never been on a first-name basis with a minister."

"Mrs. Williams, you feel free to call me whatever you want." I tried to ease things by adding, "It'll be better than what some of my friends say." Fortunately, she had a good sense of humor and a welcome laugh.

She turned to her daughter and said, "Go on, baby, tell him the news."

LaQueesha's face lit up as she said, "I got the job at the county Department of Public Services."

"That's wonderful," I said. "When did this happen?"

"I heard last Friday, but that was only three days after your father died, and I didn't think it was the right time to tell you."

"When do you start?"

"In a couple of weeks." She looked at her mom, then back to me and said, "But I already quit my other job."

I could see peace in her eyes and relief in Roberta's. Tyriq, on the other hand, had no idea what his mother did for a living. All he knew was that she loved him and worked nights to make his life better.

I never judged LaQueesha; I never felt I had a right to. She was a prostitute because she had little choice. The first night we met, at McDonald's on Hollywood Blvd., she told me what she did and that it was out of necessity, to take care of her son. That deserved admiration, not condemnation. Still, I was pleased that a better future lay in store for her.

During dinner Roberta shared stories of growing up in Atlanta and of hearing Dr. Martin Luther King Jr. speak on various occasions. Her parents were staunch believers in equality and her father had worked closely with several civil rights leaders. When she was eight years old they took her to the August 1963 March on Washington. Separated in age by only a year, her life seemed so much more exciting than mine. Los Angeles also had its share of racism and segregation, even a fair amount of violence, but most of the attention during the civil rights movement centered on the South and Roberta's memories were captivating. As if that were not enough, she was the only person I had ever met who had heard Mahalia Jackson sing live. I looked at the clock and realized how quickly its hands had swept by.

Tyriq's bedtime was eight thirty and even though he was approaching adolescence, his mother always spent time with him before he fell asleep. In part this was her way of compensating for spending nights on the streets. If he needed anything in the wee hours, he had only his grandmother to turn to. But LaQueesha's nightly action was rooted in more than a sense of guilt. Her gentle and tender love shone through all her interactions with her son. When he was younger she would read to him. In more recent years she would sit beside his bed as they checked his homework and talked about what would happen the next day. She always kissed him good night before leaving him to his sleep. She was not sure how many years were left for this routine. Tyriq was fast approaching the age when it would seem too childish and perhaps even a bit embarrassing.

When they left the dining room, LaQueesha's mother brought out a pot of coffee. As she poured me a cup she said, "Thank you for what you did for my daughter."

"All I did was make a connection, Mrs. Williams—"

"Please," she interrupted, "call me Roberta."

"Very well, Roberta. Then you call me Giovanni or Gio. But what I started to say is that all I did was make a connection for her. She did the rest herself."

She sat back down. In her eyes I saw a combination of gratitude and puzzlement.

"I've never met a Catholic priest before, and I have to admit you're not what I expected."

I started to laugh. "I get that a lot."

"I'm serious," she continued. "I never understood why LaQueesha started going to your church or why she continued. But I see it now. You've been a good friend to her, and for that I thank you."

"Did she ever tell you how we met?"

"Yes, she said you bought her some food at McDonald's one night. Must have been Providence."

"Or just an accident," I replied.

"You mean an act of kindness," she prodded. "You're a priest, Giovanni."

I tilted my head and raised an eyebrow. "Well, whatever it was, I saw something in her. I listened as she told her story and saw a woman who was trapped, not just in her work, either. As we continued to talk I could see a gift caged inside her. To be honest, I really wanted to be left alone that night. I certainly didn't want to talk to anybody. But she knew something was bothering me and somehow she drew me out. At first I tried to deflect her questions, then suddenly I found myself telling her about my family tragedy."

"She's always been like that. Everybody tells her their problems. She's a good listener."

"Yes, she is. I was fascinated when we first met, but grew even more impressed as we became friends. You've raised a remarkable daughter, Roberta."

"Thank you. She and Tyriq are my life."

LaQueesha walked back into the dining room, poured herself some coffee, lifted the pot and asked, "Would you like more?"

"Yes, please. After your mom."

"Not for me," Roberta said. "I only have one cup after dinner."

LaQueesha sat down and smiled. "I see you two are getting along just fine."

"Yes, we are," her mother replied.

I looked at them and said, "You know the two of you are a lot alike. You're both very easy to talk to."

"We've had many years of practicing on each other," LaQueesha replied. Then she winked at her mother and continued, "It's not always been so easy."

"Maybe not," I said, "but that skill is going to serve you well in your new job. This is such great news. And for me it is a welcome change from the last few weeks."

She probably thought I was referring to my father's death, which I was. But I was also thinking about my brother's presidential campaign. LaQueesha, like everyone else, was in the dark as to my real concerns about him. They had all been willing to believe that my reservations were tied to his inexperience. I was content with that, trusting that Emily would eventually expose the truth.

The evening had been a delight and passed quickly, but I had an early Mass on Sunday morning. At nine thirty I said my goodbyes to LaQueesha and Roberta, thanked them for a wonderful dinner, and promised a return visit.

•   •   •

Giuseppe had flown back to the East Coast the morning after the funeral but did not stay long in Washington. His campaign had already begun to open field offices in Iowa and New Hampshire, the states with the earliest voting in the primary season. Between his lack of name recognition and Iowa's moderately conservative makeup, winning the caucuses there would be a long shot. He had a better chance in the New Hampshire primary, due mainly to a slightly more liberal leaning electorate. But win or lose both states were essential to making himself known nationally.

My relationship with my brother had so deteriorated by the time he moved to Washington that I did not even attend his swearing-in ceremony and in the subsequent years paid little attention to his career. He had never spoken with me about a desire for higher office, yet when he announced his presidential run I was surprised at how natural it seemed. It was one thing for him to represent his home state of California in the United States Senate. But presenting himself to unfamiliar audiences all across the nation did not seem to fit his profile. In this one respect I had misjudged him. Clearly he enjoyed the excitement of national politics and took to the spotlight of public speaking better than I expected. And yet, fulfilling one's desires often comes with a downside. Giuseppe's latest quixotic adventure would significantly alter his new found love life. He would need to find a way to shore it up.

During his campaign for the senate Giuseppe had kept his home off limits to political activity. He held no meetings there and was accessible by phone only in an emergency. He sought to intensify those same rules for his new quest, thus ensuring a privacy unmolested by the press. When he returned to Washington following the funeral he refused to do any campaigning that following weekend. He needed those days, or at least the nights, to be with Jackson.

Friday, October 24, was typical of their recurring rendezvous. Jackson arrived by plane in the afternoon, took the Metro to Georgetown, let himself into the house with his own key, and was there when Giuseppe returned from the office. They greeted each other with a kiss and an embrace that lasted a little longer than usual. As Jackson stepped back he could tell that his friend wanted more.

He smiled and said, "Sep, we were just together a few nights ago in Los Angeles and we have the whole weekend. I'm taking Monday off so that I can stay here Sunday night."

Giuseppe looked at him longingly and exclaimed, "It's not my fault that you're so sexy! Besides, our time is likely to be limited over the next several months. We should take advantage of every moment."

"We will," Jackson replied. He gently tapped his friend's shoulder and continued, "But, as you can tell from the smell of bacon, I already started cooking. Let's eat first."

Their meal consisted of Caesar salad alongside fettuccini carbonara and garlic bread. Simple to fix and easy to clean up, it left the rest of the evening free for leisure. After eating they relaxed for a while in the living room, smoking Cuban cigars and drinking twenty-year-old Castarède Bas Armagnac. They talked about Giuseppe's family and his father's death.

"How's your mom holding up?" Jackson asked.

"So far she seems OK. My sister's spending a lot of time with her and I've called her each day. She's a strong woman and she'll get through it."

Jackson dipped the unlit end of his cigar into the armagnac to absorb the flavor, taking those moments to think. Then he took a long draw on the cigar. When he continued it was with caution.

"Sep, last week was only the second time I've seen your brother. In both cases it was at a family funeral. Last Monday I met him and we spoke for a few moments. Besides being a good preacher, he seems like a good person. Yet you never speak about him. Why not?"

This was a conversation Giuseppe had firmly avoided over the last couple of years. He did not answer immediately, choosing instead to imitate Jackson's actions with the cigar. Then he looked up and said, "It's complicated."

"Come on, Sep. That line is reserved for movies."

"I'm serious," Giuseppe continued. "Giovanni and I obviously have a history. Even before my wife and children were killed our relationship was strained. After their deaths we grew closer, but it did not last."

"What happened?"

"For one thing he was upset that I did not drop out of the Senate race. He thought it indicated that I did not love my family. But that was not true. I thought that he, of all people, would realize that life goes on. Besides, I owed it to the citizens of California. My opponent and I had different views on how to represent the state and I did not want to entrust its future to him."

Giuseppe had been honing his political skills among his colleagues and this deflection came more easily than he thought. There was just enough truth in what he said to make it sound sincere and convincing.

"And you're content to leave it at that?" Jackson asked.

"What I'm content with is letting Giovanni be. He'll come around in his own time. You're right about him being a good priest. He's also stubborn and a little judgmental. But I don't really want to talk about him. Right now I'm interested in us."

"Talk about complicated!" Jackson replied. "I've been thinking about what will happen as this campaign heats up. That's the reason I'm staying over on Sunday. I don't think we're going to have many more nights together."

"We can find a way," Giuseppe assured him.

With the wisdom and sensitivity of a parent explaining puberty, Jackson replied, "Things are going to change, Sep. I work on weekdays and you'll be campaigning on weekends. Even during respites you'll be under much closer scrutiny. Someone will surely notice if I keep frequenting this house and you can't exactly skip off to Boston on a whim. Maybe, just maybe, you could get away with being a gay senator. You are, after all, from California. But this country is not ready for a gay president."

"What are you saying?" Giuseppe asked. "Do you want to call it quits?"

"Of course not. I'm trying to be realistic."

Giuseppe had been so caught up in his own ambition that he had not given this scenario serious thought. He was like the teenager swept up in the emotion of intimacy, myopically disengaged from reality, who thinks he can have it all.

Jackson continued, "I support you and if you want to be president I hope you win. But it will be much easier for us to be together if you lose."

Giuseppe shrugged his shoulders and said, "I don't really have much chance of winning anyway. I'm hoping to gain some traction for the next election when I won't have to challenge an incumbent president."

"And in the meantime? What do we do?"

"I don't know. This whole national exposure and demand on my time is new to me. But there has to be a way. I don't want to lose you."

"Nor I you," Jackson replied.

Giuseppe chuckled and said, "You know, Jacks, the people of Iowa and New Hampshire might just solve the problem for us." He put out what remained of his cigar, finished his armagnac, stood up and said, "It's time for bed."

That night and, indeed, the rest of the weekend, was more passionate than usual, as if each lover were desperate to cling to a dissolving dream. On Monday morning, after breakfast, Giuseppe left for his office. A few hours later Jackson returned to Boston.

CHAPTER 17

I had great confidence in Emily. There was a reason she was a prized reporter at the *Los Angeles Times*. Yet within me an uncomfortable truth gnawed at every attempt to find relaxation or peace. Whatever her skills, she was confronting an evil previously not encountered even in the midst of war, an adversary sprung from the pages of Goethe or Milton. I had finally come to agree with Tom and I now saw Giuseppe for what he was—a man veiled with the cloak of Beelzebub, capable of wielding the most fiendish of forces. In more than twenty years of being a priest I had never had my faith so shaken, not just because of what my brother had done to our family, but the way in which he sacramentally ambushed me in the confessional. I began to doubt the power of good and its ability to conquer evil. In my worry and confusion I had questions.

What if Emily did not succeed? What did I have to offer in our quest for justice? How could I right the horrific wrongs perpetrated by my brother? What was I prepared to do? What was I willing to risk?

The choice before me was rather stark. As Tom had so accurately noted, I was neither a reporter nor a detective. I was the holder of a secret truth, unable to leverage it to my advantage. Even if I were motivated by love I would not have been able to reduce my dilemma to the convenience of situational ethics for I held a knowledge that rightfully belonged to God, entrusted to me only as his servant. But I was not driven by love. In moments of truth I knew that vengeance and retribution had invaded my heart, two perfectly logical human reactions to an evil that I had rejected in both word and deed my entire adult life. Drawing upon the example and the command of Jesus I had always been able to forgive personal injury and offense. This was something different. Three years of turmoil had brought me to the breaking point. If Emily failed I only had one play, only one contribution, and prudence suggested that I be prepared for a decision I hoped to never make.

•CHAPTER•

I requested a meeting with Cardinal Roger Mahony, the archbishop of Los Angeles. He was neither my spiritual director nor advisor, but he was my immediate superior. We set a time of 7:00 p.m. on Thursday, October 30, and not wanting to meet with him at his office he graciously invited me to his residence.

The original "Mother Church" for the Los Angeles Archdiocese was St. Vibiana Cathedral. Shortly after it was completed in 1876 it was deemed too small for the burgeoning population of the city. Bishop Thomas Conaty received approval from Pope Pius X to build a new cathedral but economic problems in the early 1900s prevented its construction. By 1945 the Catholic population of Los Angeles had increased by nearly tenfold, renewing calls for a new building. The Holy See consented to a project proposed by Archbishop John Cantwell in 1945 but he died in 1947, and his successor, Archbishop James McIntyre, saw another way to address the now exploding Catholic population of the area. He redirected the money to the building of churches and schools throughout the four counties that, at the time, comprised the archdiocese.

In 1994 the Northridge earthquake with a magnitude of 6.7 struck Southern California. Centered in the San Fernando Valley community of Reseda, the ground shook for a distance of over two hundred miles, and the thrusting of the earth severely damaged St. Vibiana's. The cost of repairing the structure was disproportionate to its design, capacity, and ability to serve an archdiocese numbering more than four million people. As a result Cardinal Roger Mahony announced his intention to build a new principal church for the archdiocese. Eventually land was purchased diagonally across from the Los Angeles County Music Center, and the Cathedral of Our Lady of the Angels was constructed. The dedication Mass was held on September 2, 2002.

The cathedral complex includes a plaza, conference center, and residence for the archbishop and other priests but the cornerstone is the church itself. Spanish architect José Rafael Moneo succeeded in creating a worship environment unrivaled in the southland. Looking toward the altar from the back of the center aisle one stands in awe of the divine, much like Moses before the burning bush. Massive, though artfully designed, tapestries line the walls inviting worshipper and visitor alike to embark on a journey to God. The cathedral conjures biblical images of the Holy of Holies but unlike in ancient Israel, all are welcome to enter this truly sacred space.

At the core of Catholic life is what theologian Michael J. Himes calls the sacramental principle. To paraphrase, "If something is true everywhere and all the time, it must be celebrated sometime somewhere." We do not build churches because that is where we find God. Rather because God is to be found everywhere, we build houses of worship to remind us of his presence. Today, towering alongside a busy freeway and overlooking the city's downtown, the Cathedral of Our Lady of the Angels proclaims to all passersby, "You are in the presence of God."

Although the church and plaza were built on a palatial scale befitting the enormity of the City of Los Angeles, the rectory is modest and far from ostentatious. It is a plain box structure adjoining the conference center on the opposite side of the plaza from the cathedral. Mahony did not easily succumb to opulence and the interior of his living quarters reflected an elegance rooted in simplicity. When I arrived he met me at the door and escorted me to his sitting room.

Like the rest of the residence, this room is simple. It is spacious and designed for entertaining more than just a few guests simultaneously with several couches and chairs organized into a social area. The walls, flooring and furnishings complement each other in rich earth tones. That evening one item stood out from the rest. Every bishop and cardinal in the Catholic Church wears a zucchetto or skull cap—purple for bishops and archbishops, red for cardinals. Mahony keeps a duplicate of his in a glass case with a miniature one for his pet cat, Miguel. I suppose everyone is entitled to a little silliness now and then.

A meeting with the cardinal is quite a bit different from one with my friend Tom. Mahony's first suggestion was not to offer me a drink, although that evening I could have used one.

"Sit anywhere you'd like, Giovanni."

I chose one of the couches in the center of the room and Mahony's reaction reminded me that in certain circumstances he could be quite personable. He knew I had something serious on my mind and that sitting across such a large room with a vast distance between us would not be conducive to confidential conversation. As such he selected a chair next to the couch, creating just enough space for comfortable dialogue.

"Giovanni, I know we do not see each other very often, but I want to thank you for all the wonderful work you do at St. Catherine's."

This was vintage Mahony. Listening to his public speaking one soon discovered that his two favorite words in the English language were "wonderful" and "helpful" and yet I did not feel in the least manipulated. He did appreciate my work as a pastor; it made his job as archbishop easier. As archbishop, Mahony had a tendency toward micro–management, but when things were running smoothly, he generally left people alone. Not hearing from the cardinal was an indication that a priest was doing a good job.

"Thank you, Roger," I replied, "I like the parish a lot. The people are very supportive and generous with their time and commitment to the church. It's a good place to be."

"I was sorry to hear about your father," he said, "and wish I could have been at the funeral, but I was in Rome at the time."

"I understand and I appreciate your concern. Besides, Bishop Clark was present, which I'm sure made my mother happy. I also shared with her the note of condolence and sympathy you sent."

"You and your family have been through a lot, Giovanni. I've been around a long time and have seen many calamities. It could not have been easy for you to cope these last three years. Murder is no ordinary death but losing an entire family, as you did, is nothing short of tragic. I thought you should have taken a short leave of absence."

"Roger, I appreciated your suggestion at the time, but life goes on and staying busy proved good for me. I had the encouragement and support of my friends and Lt. Tom Moran kept me apprised of the police investigation. I don't think time off would have served any purpose or been particularly beneficial."

"Speaking of the investigation," he replied, "it seems as if the police have given up. There have not been any media reports for a long time so I presume they still have no suspects."

"Actually, the murder of my sister-in-law and her children is why I came to see you tonight. And it's one of the reasons I wanted to meet here instead of the Archdiocesan Catholic Center. This is all very difficult for me and there are just too many people around your office."

I tilted my head up, closed my eyes, and took a deep breath. This conversation was not going to be an easy one. Before me was an intellectually astute man more than capable of reading between the lines. Like a thief whose only approach to a prized jewel is to nimbly traverse a series of crisscrossing infrared light beams, I was about to engage a narrative in which one ill-chosen word could trip an alarm. I decided to begin with an upfront statement of fact.

"Roger, I'm in a dilemma. I know who killed Yolanda, my nieces, and my nephew."

If I expected a reaction, one was not forthcoming. Mahony was content to let me do the speaking, at least for now.

"The problem," I continued, "is that I learned of it through the confessional."

That seemed to get his attention. He ever so slightly shifted in his seat and his eyes took on an intense stare.

"As you know, Lt. Tom Moran and I are lifelong friends. When he was in charge of the murder investigation I watched him diligently struggle to uncover evidence. But he didn't succeed. Along the way, in my capacity as a priest, I learned who the murderer was."

I chose those words carefully in order to guard against any possibility that he might guess that my brother was the guilty party. Such a conclusion was unlikely at this point, since everyone knew that Giuseppe was not at home the night of the murders and could not have pulled the triggers himself. Thus I preserved a little room for maneuvering.

I continued, "There were times I wished I could have shared that information with family—my parents, my brother or sister. There were other times I wanted desperately to tell Tom. But I have been a priest for over twenty years and I'm committed to the obligations of my faith. All this time I have remained silent."

With compassionate caution he asked, "Why are you here tonight, Giovanni?" He did not know the answer to that question and in truth, I was not sure of the answer either.

"Roger, like you I've heard thousands of confessions, some of them quite troubling. Yet it has been fairly easy to forget, or at least to compartmentalize them. This one is different. It is my first and last thought of every day, the only respite coming in the brief hours of sleep." I paused for a moment. This was the closest I had come to telling anyone about the fateful night when Giuseppe told me that he had his family killed. Mahony remained still, calmly and intently listening. "I believe in the sacraments and in the love and peace that accompanies the confession of sin. But what should be a blessing from God has become a curse. I feel lost at sea, tossed by powerful currents, and barely buoyed by the love of God. I just don't know how long I can continue to swim against this tide."

Mahony saw strain in my expression and heard stress in my voice. His response was not immediate but it was thoughtful. After a brief pause he said, "Maybe this would be a good time for a sabbatical."

"That would just give me more time to think," I replied.

"Or time to pray," he suggested.

"I'd just be praying about what I'm thinking. No. I don't see where that would help at all, not in this situation. I don't need a sabbatical."

"What do you need then?"

"I need to figure out what to do with the knowledge I possess."

"You already know the answer to that," he said. "The seal of confession…"

I interrupted him. "Roger, I know the theology and the teaching of the church. Why do you think I've kept quiet so long? But this was not a normal confession. The sacrament was deliberated abused in order to guarantee my silence."

Mahony nodded his head in agreement.

"That seems obvious," he replied. "But intentions of the penitent aside—"

I interrupted again with a laugh. "Penitent? That's rich! This person was not seeking forgiveness, nor was there any remorse. I don't see why I should be bound by the rules in this case."

"It's not a question of regulations. This is about the core of our faith, about who we are as a church. We have to preserve the sacraments even if others abuse them. Are you sure you're not being pulled by vengeance? It would be perfectly understandable."

"Roger, I assure you this is not about vengeance. I know the web it weaves. I've seen its death and destruction before. If I merely wanted to get even, I would kill the murderer and would relish the satisfaction. This is about justice, about preventing more deaths."

"You're obviously holding back," he replied.

"That's because I'm not free. I'm here because I've been thinking of breaking my silence, of speaking what I know about the murders of my family."

Mahony's response was calm, but firm. "That would not be helpful."

"Perhaps not to you, but it would relieve me of this terrible burden."

"And what would it do to the faith of the church? You don't want to see anyone else killed. OK, I understand that. But if you violate the seal, you violate peoples' faith in the sacraments. Why should they believe that you or any other priest will keep their confessions secret in the future? I can't let you do that."

"Excuse me, Roger. I may have misled you. I did not come here to ask your permission or even your advice."

That did not come out the way I intended and he bristled at those words. I tried to backtrack a little.

"I'm sorry. Let me rephrase that. I honestly don't know what I'm going to do and tonight is a matter of courtesy. I have no intention at this time of revealing anything heard in that confession. Should I so choose, the reasons will be obvious. However, given the import and magnitude of the event you would be pressed by the media and placed in a very awkward situation, forced to condemn my action, while fully aware that both options, silence and speech, served a higher good. I think it only fair that you be prepared. And I know what the repercussions would be for me. As I said, I don't intend to break the seal of the sacrament. More than anything else, Roger, I need your prayers."

That last comment tapped into his own priestly ministry. Whether or not I soothed his concerns, he seemed willing to trust me. He certainly realized that little could be achieved by further discussion that night.

"Then let's pray right now," he replied.

Mahony took a few moments for silence. When he spoke again it was to invoke the spirit of God, asking for the gifts of wisdom and courage. Recalling God's constant presence in our lives and his unlimited blessings, he specifically asked that I find justice and peace through love. After praying together, I thanked him for his time and returned home.

Preparing for bed I considered what had been accomplished that night. The most obvious thing was that Cardinal Mahony had been alerted to a potential crisis for the church. For me, personally, a line was now crossed. In retrospect, my decision to work with Tom and Emily on the investigation may have been a bit rash. But I believed Tom when he said that Giuseppe was not through killing. What if my silence enabled more death? What if Emily were to be killed trying to uncover the truth about my brother? More than anything else, my love for her and concern for her safety necessitated my meeting with Mahony.

I closed my eyes and tried to see my life from outside my body. For three years I had stood motionless in front of a door that represented a darkness of soul, held in suspended animation by the conflict raging within. If I opened the door, my priestly ministry was over; if I did not, I feared the malevolence that had come to define my brother. Love and hate, good and evil were all to be found on each side of the door.

When I opened my eyes again, in the stillness of my room, I realized that my conversation with Mahony was the first real step I had taken in a long time. Now I was prepared for any eventuality. I did not know what would come next, but I had stretched out my arm and placed my hand around the doorknob.

CHAPTER 18

Giuseppe's campaign for the presidency kept him busy, cutting into his private time, thus providing Emily a variety of options for meeting with Jackson. Her plan was to establish a comfortable rapport, convey new details of the murders of Yolanda and her children, delicately discuss the death of Jean-Paul Lecuyer and sow seeds of doubt about Giuseppe—all in one sitting. She would have preferred the luxury of a two- or three-day interview, but realized that would not be possible because Jackson would almost certainly contact my brother after she left. She would need to draw upon a range of journalistic skills honed over years of reporting from battle zones, corrupt capitals, strife-torn cities, and epicenters of disaster.

After verifying the senator's scheduled appearances in Iowa and New Hampshire, Emily chose the weekend of October 31 to fly to Massachusetts. She and Tom had also reached a temporary compromise on the security issue. He would accompany her to the East Coast and stay at the hotel while she met with Jackson, whom she would interview at his home. She would not even call him until after arriving in Boston. This plan was a bit impractical, since there was no guarantee that he would be in town. However, it left little risk of putting her in danger that weekend or in the immediate weeks to follow.

The flight out of Los Angeles was uneventful. The Transportation Security Administration, which had been established following the 9/11 terrorist attacks, had made flying a nightmare for the average traveler. In larger airports such as Los Angeles, long lines snaked through the terminals as passengers and carry-on luggage were screened for safety. Being a lieutenant on the LAPD has advantages, though. Tom, using his Los Angeles Police identification and a special ID granted by the TSA, was able to skip the security check. Unfortunately, it was a privilege not extended to spouses and Emily was subjected to the same scrutiny as any other passenger. Nonetheless they were able to board without incident or delay. The plane left Los Angeles International Airport at 8:20 a.m. and arrived at Boston's Logan Airport at 5:00 p.m.

People who move to California from the East Coast often speak in paradox about West Coast weather. They marvel at the consistent sunshine and moderate temperatures, but bemoan the lack of seasons. Since it is fair to assume that no one laments the absence of snow covering a front porch or driveway, the complaint seems to center on the foliage of fall. In the West, with relatively few hickory, birch, or maple trees dotting the landscape, the season unfolds without the flaming hues of the rainbow lighting the branches of the forests. Evergreens dominate the canopy of the state, their autumn leaves turning to neither red nor gold. But nature, unrestricted by the human calendar, offers seasonal tradeoffs. While in the northern hemisphere the almanac heralds the arrival of winter on December 21, October weather on the Eastern Seaboard can be as brutal as January. Tom and Emily were greeted at Logan Airport with a temperature in the low forties and a wind chill factor reducing it another ten degrees. They shielded themselves in heavy coats, expressing shared preference for a warm climate over colorful leaves.

It had been a long time since either of them had been to Boston, and given that Emily was fully prepared for her meeting with Jackson, she and Tom opted for a relaxing weekend away from the bustling tourism of America's colonial past. They made reservations at the Winthrop Arms Hotel about five miles outside downtown Boston. Despite being nearly eighty years old it has remained one of the North Shore's lesser known establishments—quiet, elegant, and unassuming. Along with its signature chicken pot pie, the in-house restaurant offers a wide range of fresh seafood and meat dishes capable of pleasing every palate. On Saturday morning Emily was ready to go to work. Keeping her fingers crossed she called Jackson at nine thirty.

He answered, "Hello?"

"Jackson, this is Emily Moran. We met in Los Angeles at Luciano Lozano's funeral."

"Yes, I remember. What a surprise! Don't tell me you're in Boston," he said half-jokingly.

"As a matter of fact, I am," she replied. "And I remembered that you told me to call you."

"How long will you be in town?" he asked.

"I leave tomorrow and I realize this is totally out of the blue, but do you happen to have any free time today?" She regretted the necessity of withholding the true purpose of her visit, but decided it could be rectified later.

"I don't have any specific plans. We could meet someplace or you would be welcome to come to my home."

"I would enjoy that," she assured. "I'm staying at the Winthrop Arms Hotel but I rented a car, so transportation is not an issue. Where do you live?"

"My home is in the South End. I have a condo on Wellington Street just off Columbus Avenue."

"I know the area well," she replied. "I've been to meetings at Northeastern University and I've attended many concerts at Symphony Hall."

"I'm within walking distance of both," he answered. "Would you like to come by for lunch?"

Emily's purpose was not that casual and trying to interview Jackson over a meal would prove awkward.

"I can't make it for lunch, would two o'clock work for you?" she asked.

"That would be fine. I look forward to seeing you again." Then he gave her his address and hung up.

.   .   .

Emily parked her car a short distance from Jackson's home and proceeded on foot. She had always been amazed at the walkability of Boston, especially here in the South End. On previous trips she had taken in performances by the Boston Symphony Orchestra, had numerous occasions to visit the university, and had also attended Mass at Holy Cross Cathedral, only blocks from Jackson's house. Never had there been need for an automobile.

This particularly diverse part of the city includes a variety of culturally distinct immigrants from as far away as Europe, the Middle East, and Latin

America. Its population is well-educated and industrious and the area is both family and gay friendly. As she walked along, Emily easily imagined Jackson and Jean-Paul strolling together on their way to dinner or a local bar. She pictured them spending a Sunday afternoon at one of the many boutiques or art galleries, possibly even snuggling beside each other on a park or library bench. For people desiring a quiet, undisturbed life, few places can equal the South End. On a warmer day she might have been tempted to saunter a little longer. But it was cold that Saturday and her mission did not allow for such a luxury.

She walked along Columbus then turned onto Wellington. Like many of the other streets in the South End it was lined with row houses, creating a charm typical of the Northeast and reminiscent of parts of London where she'd spent her childhood. She found his home—a red-brick, bow-front house with gray limestone trim and dark brown shutters around the windows. She ascended the stairs and rang the bell.

Jackson quickly opened the door and greeted her. He was casually but impeccably dressed, wearing tan and white deck shoes, beige trousers, a cream-colored shirt, and a dark grey Nehru jacket. He had begun to let his beard grow, but kept it short and sharply trimmed. Emily found him far more striking in this ensemble than in the suit he had worn to the funeral. Charm aside, he cut a stylish and elegant figure that was magnetic in any social setting. This was Eastern midlife preppiness at its best, and she was duly impressed.

"Hello, Emily. Welcome to my home. May I take your coat?"

"Thank you, Jackson."

"Please, call me Jacks."

"Very well," she said.

Emily looked around the living room. Fortunately it was not decorated with the Colonial furnishings so trite and typical of Northeastern hotels and tourist attractions. In a home setting such a style is pretentious at best and boring at worst. This room was subtle, subdued, and surprisingly eclectic. The flooring was classic gunstock oak, the walls and trim were painted in a bold Lead Gray, and crown molding offset a white ceiling. Mactan stone coffee and end tables with smoked beveled glass tops perfectly accented a dark gray throw rug. The entire sitting area was framed with matching charcoal sofa and two loveseats. This was a home decorated with care and attention to detail.

"This is quite lovely!" Emily exclaimed as she glanced around.

"Thank you," Jackson replied. "I certainly think so, although I can't take the credit. My partner, Jean-Paul, had an artistic flare." He gestured as if embracing everything and said, "This was all his idea. In fact, he decorated every room in the house. Each one is different, but they all bear his unmistakable style."

Emily walked over to the mantle and commented on the portrait hanging above. "I presume he is the one with you in this photo."

"Yes, a good friend of ours, Walter Erickson, owns a studio and took that about eight years ago. I thought it would look good in the bedroom, but Jean-Paul insisted on putting it here. He wanted our guests to appreciate Walter's talents. Besides, he used to joke that we saw enough of each other in the bedroom." Emily laughed.

"It's a beautiful photo," she said. "Jean-Paul was a very handsome man, Jacks." She looked back at him and said, "You made a truly attractive couple."

"Thank you, Emily. We were together for nearly twenty years. He looks almost the same in that picture as he did the day we met. Of course, I might be a bit biased." With a wistful smile he continued, "The house is empty without him. But it is filled with treasured memories." He took a long, deep breath through his nostrils and said, "Sometimes I feel as though I can smell his presence, as if he's still here with me. But when I go to bed at night reality sets in and I know I'm alone."

"How long has it been since he died?"

"Six and a half months," he answered.

"That's a very short time. Not nearly long enough to swallow years of memories."

Jackson looked longingly up at the photo as if resisting the pull of nostalgia. Changing the subject he asked, "Emily, would you like some coffee or tea?"

"Coffee, please, if it's not too much trouble."

"Not at all, I assure you. Give me three minutes and I'll have some freshly brewed, just like a restaurant." Then with impish confidence he smiled and added, "Only with more flavor."

When he went into the kitchen, Emily perused more pictures of Jackson and Jean-Paul. There were photos of the two of them on vacation in major tourist spots in Europe: the Tower of London, the Brandenburg Gate, the Eiffel Tower, among many others. Captured in each image was a tender affection between the two men; an invitation for observers to glimpse cherished moments of love.

But there was also another presence in the house. Separate pictures were grouped together: one set on top of a demilune table against the side wall, the other set on a sofa table behind the couch. They were of Jackson and Giuseppe. There were a few photos taken at the National Mall in Washington, others from places Emily did not recognize, and one of the two of them having dinner in a restaurant. Jackson walked into the room as she was looking at them. He was carrying a tray with a pot of coffee and two cups.

"I guess I don't have to identify the person in those photos," he said.

"No," she answered. "I'm quite familiar with him." Her tone of voice was very non-committal, raising no concerns.

As they sat down, Jackson poured the coffee and handed a cup to Emily.

"Thank you," she said. "Jacks, I was thinking. We didn't have a lot of time to talk when we met in Los Angeles a couple weeks ago."

"No, we didn't," he replied. "But then the environment was not conducive, either."

"That's true. There were too many people milling around during the reception. And even if we had found a quiet corner table, we would have been conspicuously out of place."

Emily tasted the coffee and said, "This is quite delicious. Where is it from?"

"I buy all my coffees from Barrington, a company in western Massachusetts. Their dark roasts are rich, balanced, and never bitter. This particular brew is French. Of course, that only refers to the style of roast, not the origin of the beans. These particular coffee beans come from Costa Rica, from the Doca estate next to the Poas Volcano."

"You sound like a salesman."

Jackson laughed. "I guess I do. On one of our trips around the state Jean-Paul and I stopped at a coffee shop in North Hampton that was serving Barrington. It was the best coffee I had ever tasted and I was quickly hooked. Since then I've been spreading the 'good news,' as your friend Giovanni might say."

Emily smiled and shook her head saying, "It's a different kind of good news, Jacks, but I admit the coffee is great."

"For me the story gets even better," he continued. "I understand that Barrington plans to open a cafe next year in Fort Point. You can guess where I'll spend most of my weekend mornings after that."

Emily needed to move this conversation to more pertinent matters. She put her cup down on the table and looked at Jackson. "Jacks, this trip is not really spontaneous."

That revelation did not seem to concern him. He just waited for her to continue.

"I'm on assignment for the *Los Angeles Times,* and if you don't mind, I would like to ask you some questions."

Emily was very personable and engaging, so much so that even her last statement did not alarm him. He seemed more puzzled than leery.

"I'm perfectly willing, Emily, but isn't this a little cloak and dagger? Why didn't you just call ahead of time?"

She seized on his imagery. "Because it *is* cloak and dagger." That got his attention. "I couldn't call you," she continued, "because I didn't want you to alert Giuseppe to my visit."

"Why not?" he asked.

She was prepared for that query, but not ready to answer it. Instead, she proceeded with her own question. "Tell me, Jacks. What do you know about the death of Giuseppe's family?"

"Not much, mostly what I read in the papers. He and I were close friends when we attended Harvard but we had a falling out and had not been in contact for years. The murders made headlines across the nation three years ago and when I read the story I remembered better times. I felt compassion for him and went to the funeral to show my support. Why do you ask?"

"Because that's the story I'm investigating. As you know, the police have been unable to solve the case and the *Times* decided to do its own inquiry." She took another drink of coffee and said, "I got the assignment."

"Why didn't you want Giuseppe to know?"

Now she was ready. She had already decided that the best way to lead Jackson was to play the angle the police originally pursued.

"You probably know that my husband, Tom, was the lead detective on the case for the LAPD. From the very beginning they suspected that someone was blackmailing Giuseppe. If that were true he might have said something to you. I couldn't risk the two of you having a conversation ahead of time and him possibly thwarting our meeting."

Jackson was no fool. He began to feel a little wary but displayed no caution in either facial expression or speech. "I spent the entire day after the funeral with him and he said nothing about any blackmail. We used most of the time to catch up on lost years, twenty of them, and when he talked about his family he never mentioned the murders or any kind of extortion. Of course, the investigation had just begun. But even since then he hasn't said anything."

Emily had a non-threatening style when interviewing people, gently gaining their trust and carefully leading them to the information she needed. This conversation was no different. She certainly did not want to push too hard.

"Jacks, in the beginning the police were quite cautious and kept most of their investigation under wraps, including the fact that there were two murderers. That much they knew from a video tape. They didn't have much more to go on, so they shared very little with the media. They didn't want to compromise their case or tip off either of the killers. In the end that ploy failed since neither of them made any mistakes."

"I didn't even know they had suspects," Jackson said.

"They had one and were watching him carefully. But he managed to slip their surveillance and was shot by the second assassin whom they had not identified."

"How did they know he was killed by his partner?"

"The modus operandi was the same—a single shot through the heart and a Glock 9mm left at the scene. The fact that he was a suspect meant this could not have happened by chance."

That made Jackson a little uncomfortable. Whoever had killed Jean-Paul in Brussels used the same M.O., but it could not possibly have been the same person. There was no connection. Noticing that both cups were empty, Jackson refilled them.

"I still don't know why you want to talk to me," he said. "I don't know anything. If what you assume about Giuseppe is true, he's kept it to himself.

But I have to tell you, Emily, I've seen him many times since he moved to Washington. He doesn't seem to be on guard against anyone. I don't see how I can help."

So far everything was proceeding according to plan but she was quickly approaching the crux of the conversation. She only had this one opportunity and intended to imply without accusing; to let Jackson, on his own, draw the same conclusions she had.

"My husband is no longer on the case. In fact, he's been moved to a different division of the LAPD. But he managed to get copies of the evidence the police kept secret. I'd like to share some of it with you. Maybe something will jog your memory about an offhand comment Giuseppe made, or perhaps you will think of some question to ask him yourself the next time you speak."

Emily had brought with her an attaché case which contained the photos from the Los Angeles murders. She would either hook him or lose him on those. For her purposes that afternoon the rest of the evidence did not really matter.

"Jacks, I want to show you some of that evidence. These are police photos taken at the scene of the murders. They won't appear in the paper, but I want to share them with you. However, they're graphic and will be difficult to look at."

When she began developing her story outline, Emily had promised that she would not publish pictures of the bodies. However, showing them to Jackson was another matter. It was crucial to opening his eyes.

Emily set out the first one and said, "When the police entered the house, the first thing they saw were these two guns on the coffee table. They're both Glock 9mm and untraceable."

She surreptitiously stole a glance at Jackson's reaction. She was looking for some hint of recognition but he remained stoic. Even with her experience he was hard to read. At this point she moved more quickly, laying out each photo as she spoke.

"These are the painful ones, Jacks. They're of Giuseppe's family and are not for publication, but I need to show them to you. The first body they discovered was Carmen's. She was in the upstairs hallway. As they proceeded down the corridor they looked into the bedrooms. Leonardo was on his bed, apparently asleep when he was shot. Gina had been reading and texting on her phone. And finally, Yolanda was found lying on her bed, face up."

She stopped speaking to give him time to process. No one could have looked at those pictures without being moved. But Emily was seeking something more revealing.

Jackson was not given to hysteria, tending to let his feelings simmer before expressing them. He sat still, processing the information in the photos and understood why Emily would not publish them in the *Times*—the exhibits of lifeless innocence were quite disturbing. For him it drove home the similarity between these deaths and that of Jean-Paul and his friends in Brussels. He wondered where she was going with this. Maybe he should just ask.

"Emily, I can see the parallel between these murders and Jean-Paul's. Are you suggesting they are also linked? Even if Giuseppe had been being blackmailed there's no relation. They had only met a couple of times and were not really friends. At best they were acquaintances and had no business dealings. I don't see where Jean-Paul would have presented any leverage for someone to use against Giuseppe."

Emily had not known about the intimate relationship between Jackson and Giuseppe, but like Tom she was convinced the deaths were somehow related. What was missing, what had always been missing, was a motive. The best she could do for the moment was raise questions and suggest that Giuseppe was involved in the murders that took place in Belgium.

"Jacks, I'm sorry to dredge up the memory of Jean-Paul's death. I know it's painful, but as a reporter I don't believe in coincidences. If he had died any other way I would not press this issue. I probably wouldn't even be here. The circumstances of his death are too similar to the ones in Los Angeles—each victim killed by a single shot and a Glock 9mm left at the scene. The only people, besides the killer, who provide a connection between the two sets of murders are you and Giuseppe. Since you never even met Yolanda or her children, that leaves him. I'm just trying to find the link and that's why I'm asking you to try and remember anything he might have said to you that would help."

Jackson's mind whirled with confusion. The facts were indisputable. The problem was interpreting them. He knew Giuseppe better than she and had seen a side of him that no one else had. He believed that Emily, like the police before her, was on the wrong track regarding blackmail, but he began to fear that there might be something else going on and that Giuseppe was somehow involved in each of the murders. Yet despite the similar M.O.'s, the motives could not have been the same. He wanted to avoid making any rash judgments. But he had already become apprehensive. Why was she really here? They were both intelligent people. All this talk about the Lozano murders, including the police photos, was merely a ruse.

He looked directly into her eyes and said, "Emily, I appreciate your gentle and sensitive style, but give me a candid answer. Do you think Giuseppe was involved in Jean-Paul's death? And please don't use the pretense of blackmail."

She had hoped to avoid such a direct confrontation. All she wanted to do was plant a seed of doubt. But he asked for honesty. "Yes, I do," she replied. "I admit I don't know how he's connected. But I believe he is."

Emily had no idea what Jackson was thinking but could tell that he was bothered. She regretted this turn in the conversation and the forthrightness it demanded, fearing that Jackson might consider it more of a stratagem than an interview. It was also very unlike her. Then again, her objectivity, like that of her husband, was somewhat compromised. The truth was that this situation required a more direct approach. She continued, "I don't really know you, Jacks, and I never met Jean-Paul. But I know Giuseppe, and he won't level with me. To be honest, the blackmail angle doesn't work for me, either. It just doesn't make any sense. So I was hoping you could give me something else to go on."

At this point, Jackson really needed her to leave. She had done more than sow a little doubt. His inner self started twisting and turning in a series of contradictions. The muscles in his upper back constricted and his jaw tensed while within his stomach a witch's brew of turmoil and despair began to bubble. He had to exercise every bit of fortitude to control himself.

"Emily, I don't know what to say. Giuseppe never said a word and it would have been safe with me. Of course, I wasn't investigating the case and, as you pointed out, I had no association with his family. I assure you he has said nothing." Then as soberly and adroitly as possible he added, "But I promise I'll talk to him about it."

Emily had long ago learned to tell when an interview was over. She gathered the photos and returned them to her case. She knew Giuseppe was guilty even if she still lacked the evidence. She was also a compassionate person, and had to impress that truth on Jackson before leaving.

"Jacks, I can only try to imagine how difficult this has been for you. I'm sorry about everything that's happened, including the way I set up this meeting. I don't usually work like that, I just didn't know what else to do in this case. I really am trying to help and I want you to know that you can call me anytime."

Emily was not sure how much had been accomplished that afternoon. She did not walk away with any new information, but Jackson was no longer unwitting. Whether or not he held the key to unlocking the Lozano family murders, she left him to confront the fact that somehow Giuseppe was involved in Jean-Paul's death.

As Emily left his house, Jackson could not close the door fast enough. He rushed to his room, changed into gym clothes and went for a run. He had friends who prayed as they jogged. It was part of their spiritual discipline and he respected that. But he was not among them. First of all, he was at best an agnostic. More importantly, though, this was not a jog. As soon as he stepped out the door he leapt to the sidewalk with the speed of a raptor swooping up prey and with equal swiftness sped down the street in a dead run. He didn't pray. He processed. He raced along the twisting and turning roads of the South End with no set destination. His mind was a jumble of denial, questions, and fear.

Emily was wrong. It was impossible to conceive of Giuseppe having his own family killed for political gain, or any other reason. He loved Yolanda, Carmen, Gina, and Leonardo. Jackson had watched him grieve at their funeral three years earlier, and more recently witnessed loneliness and sorrow vex his dreams. He spoke frequently about his wife and children, every word tinged with anguish and tender longing. A devoted husband and loving father, he would have given his own life to save theirs.

Emily was wrong. There was no way that Giuseppe could have been involved in Jean-Paul's death. The senator he knew was a man of integrity and honor, and Jackson's faith and trust in him were absolute. They were friends who had shared catastrophe and love, whose lives had been wrecked by an evil far beyond their comprehension or control. The circumstances of their personal tragedies were mere coincidence and there was no need to explain away the similarity. If there were any connection, the police would have discovered it long ago.

Emily was wrong. It was Jackson who had renewed a long-lost friendship with Giuseppe and had willingly accepted a role as advisor to the new senator. It was he who introduced Jean-Paul to his friend, then watched him open his home, extending a warm hospitality. This man was kind and generous. He was not a manipulator. *But what if she were right?*

He remembered being in Washington a year earlier while Jean-Paul was visiting his ailing mother in Brussels. Giuseppe made an unexpected, intimate advance one evening. It was not overtly sexual and at the time seemed more driven by loneliness than desire. Jackson, though flattered, had no problem resisting and explained why the friendship could not take that turn. For his part, Giuseppe was embarrassed and apologetic. Nothing further happened or was even hinted at until after Jean-Paul's death.

Jackson began to feel sick. He had no idea how long he had been running, but night had long ago consumed the Boston sky. He found his way home and entered the house. Despite the cold weather he was dripping with perspiration, unsure if it was the result of strenuous exercise or nerves. Regardless, he was in desperate need of a shower during which he replayed the thoughts that had preoccupied him during his run. But it was the question that continued to press forward and assert itself. *What if she were right?*

Jackson toweled himself dry then stood nude in front of the mirror. He had a handsome face and, although in his forties, had maintained an acceptable physique, weighing little more than he did in college. With no thread or stitch to hide behind, he was left to plumb beneath the surface as questions materialized one after another. *What if Emily were right? . . . Could Giuseppe really have been involved in Jean-Paul's murder? . . . Why? . . . What was to be gained? . . .* Then the most disturbing question of all: *Was he, himself, the prize?*

He stared past his own image wondering what had become of the man inside the skin. He had always been trusting but never thought himself naïve. On the other hand, he had been manipulated in the past. He was not a man driven by sex for its own sake. Even in his youth his encounters were never superficial. They were always about the relationship. This was no exception. He and Giuseppe had made love for the first time only five months prior, but a friendship had been firmly established long before that. Besides, the idea of sleeping in the same bed was his and it was proffered with no hidden agenda. It was about companionship in a time of mourning and Giuseppe was there for him. What emerged over the next several months was completely unexpected. But was something subconscious going on? Had he been so disoriented by Jean-Paul's death that he allowed himself to fall in love with a murderer? Before Emily's visit he'd had no reason to suspect his friend.

He looked at his naked body and thought of the hours he and Giuseppe had spent making love and of the even longer hours just lying next to each other. That time was so satisfying and fulfilling—much as it had been with Jean-Paul. He was genuinely happy for only the second time in his life. This could not have been the result of some savage scheme. At least that's what he wanted to believe.

But he also knew that Giuseppe never did anything by accident. If his goal was for them to be together, Jean-Paul would have to die. Then they would both be free. Given time and under the right circumstances, the pieces would fall into place on their own, for there was no one else Jackson would turn to for comfort. Giuseppe knew him so well. The question was why he did not know himself better. Maybe Emily was right. If so, everything he knew about Giuseppe, every element of their relationship was a lie.

Jackson suddenly realized that he was still naked but it was no longer something to celebrate or revel in. As if falling from Eden, he was ashamed, his body seeking some frond for cover. Yet unlike his human progenitor, he felt no guilt. His innocence had been stolen, not given away. He put on a black and gray terrycloth robe and a pair of slippers, then went into the living room and poured a drink. He knew he would not be able to sleep, but he was also tired of thinking. Fortunately, he could rely on the television to provide some mind-numbing distraction. Eventually he fell asleep in his chair.

CHAPTER 19

Tom had remained at the Winthrop Arms Hotel anxiously awaiting Emily's return. When she entered their room she did not look like a reporter who had just scooped a story. Her expression was one of serious concern.

"I gather things did not go so well," he said, expressing a consternation of his own.

"I don't really know. Jackson heard what I had to say but I'm not sure how it registered with him. He doesn't inhabit the same world you and I do, Tom. He's a very sensitive and trusting man, not exactly unsophisticated, but far from corrupted. It's rare to find such a level of innocence and trust in a person our age. It's further complicated by the fact that over the last few years he and Giuseppe have become close friends. In fact, it was rather eerie.

"Jackson and Jean-Paul had been together for some twenty years, yet Giuseppe's unmistakable presence permeated the home. Semi-romantic pictures of the two of them had been artfully set about the living room. I'm afraid I may have done Jackson irreparable harm this afternoon."

"Isn't he better off knowing the truth?"

"Of course he is. In the long run. But that doesn't make what I did any easier. I watched as his life was upended by my questions and innuendos. Although he didn't say or reveal much I could tell that his entire world was being shattered before my eyes. I was not proud to be a journalist today."

"Don't be so hard on yourself, Emily. Sometimes investigations just don't go the way we want."

"I know that. But this was different. During our conversation he pressed me to admit my suspicions about Giuseppe being involved in Jean-Paul's death. I couldn't get a complete read on Jackson, but I got the clear impression that he was holding something back."

"You don't think Giuseppe would have confessed to him, do you?"

"No. He didn't seem to know much about the murders of Yolanda and the kids, and Giuseppe certainly would not have admitted to having Jean-Paul killed."

"Then what?" Tom asked.

"I'm not sure. The light in his eyes dimmed as if his mind were suddenly overwhelmed by darkness, his visage conveying an unspoken riposte. He politely, yet abruptly, brought the discussion to a close. I've never had a meeting end quite like that, not even when interviewing politicians in times of crisis. He knows, or at least suspects something, but did not tell me."

Tom walked over to Emily. Her encounter with Jackson had dashed any hopes he harbored for an amorous evening, but he still drew her close, his embrace defending her against approaching melancholy. He gazed into her eyes and was struck, as he often had been, at how her compassion and empathy seemed antithetical to her career and to her skill as a reporter. Unlike so many of her colleagues, she had not become jaded by the crises of modern life or the vagaries of the human spirit. Still, she was not immune to disappointment or discouragement and in his arms found comfort and surety.

Emily was not known for erratic swings of temperament. Occasionally she would withdraw so as to process information, but this was something entirely different. For the rest of the evening and throughout the next day, including the return flight to Los Angeles, she remained in a crepuscular state of mind. Even the reliable sparkle in her eyes was reduced to a flicker, at best. More than anything that she said, this unfamiliar disposition convinced Tom that she was distressed by her meeting with Jackson. As a result he kept the conversation light, steering clear of any discussion of the murders or the investigation, allowing her to bring up these subjects in her own time.

Early Sunday evening they landed at LAX. After settling in at the house Tom said, "I think I'll go over to see Giovanni."

"Give him my love. I'll be waiting when you get back." He kissed her goodbye and headed out the door.

•　•　•

The church secretary had already closed the office and gone home by the time Tom arrived. I let him in and as we went to the living room, I asked, "How was the trip?"

"You mean, how was Emily's meeting with Jackson?"

"Of course I do. Asking 'How was the trip' or 'How was the flight' is a mere pleasantry and as meaningless as asking someone how they are. It's a conversation starter. So, tell me. How did the meeting go?"

"I'm not sure. When Emily returned to the hotel she was in a strange mood, different from anything I've ever seen. So far she's said very little about it. I think she's worried, Gio."

"About what?" I asked.

"Mostly about Jackson. She thinks the interview may have been too much for him. I'm guessing her questions left him feeling betrayed."

"By Giuseppe?"

"Who else?" he replied. He proceeded to relay to me what Emily told him, including the bit about the pictures.

I went to the bar to pour us a drink. "You want a scotch?"

"I don't think so." He walked over to the stereo, turned the volume up a little and asked, "Do you have any good wine to go along with this jazz?"

I laughed, threw open my arms and said, "I'm a priest, for God's sake. Of course I have good wine. How about a Cab?"

He thought for a moment and said, "No. I think I'd prefer a Malbec or a Syrah tonight." Intrigued by the music he asked, "Isn't that Sarah Vaughan singing?"

"Yup. The album is "In the City of Lights." It was her last recorded concert, an appearance she made in Paris just a few years before she died."

"I'm not familiar with it, but I like what I hear."

"I could listen to Sarah all night long," I said. "And frequently do." Then I opened the wine cooler and retrieved a bottle. "Here's a 2001 single vineyard Malbec from Argentina called Afinicados. It's from Terrazas de Los Andes Winery."

"You're the expert," he said.

"Not this time," I replied. "I've never heard of this winery. I received the bottle as a gift from some friends who recently traveled to South America. Tonight is as good a time as any to try it."

"OK with me," he replied.

I uncorked the wine, took out two glasses and began to pour.

"You know, Gio," Tom continued, "Emily's experience this weekend has me thinking. None of us really knows Jackson. We may be expecting too much from him."

"You're right," I said. "I met him at Dad's funeral a few weeks ago, but that was a very brief encounter."

I handed him one of the glasses. He raised his in a toast and said, "Here's to defeating your brother."

I laughed and said, "Geez, Tom, we're not knights preparing for a morning joust."

"No, but we are engaged in battle—in fact a war. And a deadly one at that." Then, as an afterthought he added, "It's also one we can still lose."

"Unfortunately, on that point you're right," I said shaking my head. As we walked toward our chairs I took a sip of wine and observed, "Hmm . . . . This isn't bad. It might be a little young. But it has good body and a rich flavor. Definitely quaffable." Tom just rolled his eyes at my description. He often said that I should write for the back of wine and whisky bottles.

We sat opposite each other, a glass-top coffee table between us, and listened as Sarah spun her way through a captivating rendition of Gershwin's "Fascinating Rhythm." When the song was finished I asked, "Do you remember when Giuseppe was in graduate school and we visited him in Boston?"

"Yeah," Tom answered.

"As I recall, Jackson was having an affair with his own therapist at the time, which really bothered Giuseppe. When he confronted him about it they had a falling out and we ended up not even meeting Jackson. After that trip his name never came up again." I paused, placed my fingers under my chin and tilted it up to look toward the ceiling for a moment. Then I mused, "Until the funeral of Yolanda and the kids."

"Until then," he echoed.

I took a drink, and pensively gazed at the ceiling for several long moments.

"Tom, I know we're on the right track in this investigation. We're both certain that Giuseppe had his family killed and that he was somehow involved in Jean-Paul's death. But when it comes to the murders in Brussels we keep tripping over the same obstacle—a motive. What you told me about Emily has me thinking again about that trip years ago. Do you think it could have something to do with his friendship with Jackson?"

"Where are you going with this?" Tom asked.

"I'm just wondering. In trying to develop a chain of events we keep speaking of a missing link between the murders in Los Angeles and Brussels. Suppose there is no link and that they are not connected."

"But we know Giuseppe was involved," he protested.

"Because of the M.O. That and the fact that Giuseppe knew Jean-Paul. But what if the murders themselves were completely unrelated, unconnected to any specific event or common motive?"

"Meaning?" he asked.

"Something Emily said. That her interview might have been too much for Jackson, that he felt betrayed, that he was holding something back. According to her it seemed deeply personal and that makes me recall our trip to Boston. What if instead of trying to link the two sets of murders, we focus on the Brussels' killings as simply a matter of Jean-Paul being in Giuseppe's way."

Tom was momentarily stunned. "You've got to be kidding!" he exclaimed.

"Nope. No pun intended, but I'm deadly serious. What's so surprising about it anyway? If a man could have his wife and children murdered to secure an election, he is certainly capable of eliminating someone who stands between him and a love interest. I know it's been over twenty years. But in hindsight, don't you think that Giuseppe's reaction back in graduate school was a bit strange, maybe even over the top? Why did he care so much that Jackson was having an affair with Helen? They were both adults and could sleep with anyone they wanted to."

"Because she was Jackson's therapist."

"Exactly. And who better to manipulate someone, especially someone so naive, than a therapist?" I raised my right hand, extended my index finger and said, "Unless the manipulator is Giuseppe. Suppose he and Helen had the same interest in Jackson."

"Then why the twenty-year disconnect?" Tom asked.

"Because things didn't go as Giuseppe planned. Remember how depressed he was after their argument. Helen proved to be a better controller than he was. The meeting between Jackson and Giuseppe ended badly, as did the friendship. They both had to get on with their lives."

Tom held out his glass and said, "You'd better pour me some more wine."

Between our two glasses I drained the bottle.

"Think about it," I said. "Maybe Giuseppe wanted Jackson for himself."

Tom sat alert and aghast. Despite being a superb detective, the idea had never occurred to him. "Gio, we all grew up together. There's never been any reason to suspect your brother of being gay."

"We didn't think he was a murderer either. And nobody kills without reason. While the demise of Giuseppe's family was driven by political motives, every other attempt to explain Jean-Paul's death has come up empty. If Emily's interview with Jackson left him as uneasy as you say, then maybe something's been going on and he suspects the truth. She did, after all, bluntly admit that she thinks Giuseppe was involved in Jean-Paul's death."

"I don't know." Tom shook his head in reply.

"Let's look at it logically and chronologically. Jackson shows up when Giuseppe's family is killed and they reconnect—a long lost friendship reborn. Giuseppe returns the favor after Jean-Paul is killed, a seemingly innocent gesture. Except that he orchestrated Jean-Paul's death. Then something more intimate and physical develops between them. It's at least an angle worth investigating."

"It sounds like a plot from some novel," Tom replied. "God help him if you're right, though." He looked at me intently and continued. "Everyone is disposable in your brother's world. If your assumption is correct, then we are venturing into far more dangerous territory." He took another drink of wine and said, "Gio, don't say anything about this to Emily. She's been very adamant about not allowing me to hire security. In spite of this she's not going to change her mind and I don't want her to get distracted."

"I won't say a word, but you can't keep her in the dark for long. This is her job and her story. Besides, she'll be pissed if she finds out you're hiding information, even if it's only conjecture."

"I know that. I just need a few days. I'll call some friends in D.C. and see what I can find out, then I'll tell her myself."

On Tuesday morning Tom received a phone call.

"This is Captain Jack Gorman."

What an asshole! Tom thought to himself. The "captain" introduction was totally unnecessary and even a bit snide. Tom knew his rank. They had known each other for years but were never on friendly terms, not even when they were stationed together at Wilshire Division. Of the many reasons Tom appreciated being appointed to Robbery-Homicide—among them being that it was prestigious and a good career builder—not having to work with Gorman was a real plus. That, however, was not the end of it.

The night Yolanda and her children were killed Tom had been at a local bar less than two miles away and reached the house within minutes of hearing the news. Shortly afterward Gorman, who was still working Wilshire, arrived. The two men immediately clashed over jurisdiction. Although the murders occurred within Wilshire Division territory, Tom knew that the prominence of the crime would require that RHD take over the case and do the investigation. Subsequently, Gorman delighted in the fact that Tom had never been able to officially solve the case. When he was appointed to RHD and made captain he saw reason to look down on the lowly lieutenant.

"What can I do for you?" Tom asked.

"I understand that you've been messing around with the Lozano murder investigation."

"What investigation?" Tom asked almost laughingly. "Your detectives aren't doing shit."

"That's not the point and you know it. You're not in RHD anymore and you don't have any business being involved. You had your chance and you fucked it up."

That was, of course, not entirely true. Tom had figured out who was responsible for the murders and even got a confession. But the circumstances were such that he could not use it as evidence. For three years Giuseppe had gotten away with the perfect crime. Still, Tom was not about to share that information with Gorman. Besides, he felt no need to defend himself. Instead, he decided to pose a question of his own.

In an almost innocent tone of voice Tom asked, "What makes you think I'm still looking into the Lozano murders?"

"Don't fuck with me, Moran. I've had a detective working on this case. He found files out of order, dug around a bit, and discovered that our idiot analyst, Jordan, made copies for you."

Gorman operated from personal bias. He always had. As a result he could accept certain facts but was never able to recognize the truth behind them. Tom, who always thought quickly on his feet, was not about to jeopardize Emily's work. Still, he did not have to be overtly deceptive in his answer. It was simple, honest, and only mildly misleading. "I'm not investigating the case. In fact, I'm quite happy with my current assignment in counterterrorism and intelligence. I was putting some of my personal notes in order the other day and when I came to the Lozano case I realized that there was some information missing. This is important to me, personally, and I want to have a complete file of my own."

"That doesn't change the fact that you have no right to that information. If it wasn't in your notes already you can't just waltz in here and take copies."

"I don't know why you're so upset, Jack." He knew that using Gorman's first name would piss him off, but Tom could not care less. "I didn't remove any physical documents from RHD. I only have copies."

"I want them back," Gorman replied.

"You forget something, Jack. I don't answer to you and I don't give a shit what you want. If you're this concerned, maybe you should run a tighter division." He regretted that last comment as soon as he said it. Jordan had done him a huge favor. And in all honesty, RHD ran smoothly under Gorman. On the other hand it was true that even though a disparity of rank existed between the two of them, Gorman being a captain and Tom only a lieutenant, there was no chain of command linking them.

"This isn't over, Moran. I'm sending this to Internal Affairs. You'll be sitting before a board of rights with no backup from command staff. We'll see if you're still so fucking cocky then." With that he hung up.

When Tom returned home that night Emily noticed his mood.

"What's wrong, honey?"

Tom kissed her and asked, "How long before you print your first article on the murders?"

"I'm working on it now. Why?"

"I'm just wondering. I ran into a problem today."

"Was it something about the case?"

"Yeah. Specifically the files I gave you. I got a call from Jack Gorman. I've always despised that guy and the feeling's mutual. He's a real kiss-ass if ever there was one but for him it worked. He got a promotion to captain and he's in charge of RHD. Somehow he found out about the department documents that I brought home. He wants me to return them. Of course, that's not going to happen. It wouldn't matter anyway. I never trusted Gorman and I know that even if I gave in to his demands he's not going to let this go."

"What can he do?" Emily asked.

"On his own he can't do much. As I told him on the phone, I don't answer to him. But he has friends in the department and he could create some problems. I just want this whole thing behind us."

Tom still had not told Emily about my musings regarding Giuseppe and Jackson. That could wait for now.

CHAPTER 20

In the media world, the legs of the most salacious and sensational news stories are only as long as the public's attention span. In the absence of material developments people tend to lose interest. Such had been the case for the murder of my brother's family. Contrary to what Captain Gorman told Tom on the telephone, the police were not actively investigating, and as their inquiry waned, so did popular passion. The only people who still seemed to care were Tom, Emily, and myself. Each of us in our own way was privy to information no one else possessed and undoubtedly that drove our zeal and desire for justice. But the *Los Angeles Times* had another agenda.

Emily's story represented a potential increase in readership and with it a surge in circulation. The *Times*, fully prepared to exploit any newfound interest in the murders, scheduled the lead article to run on Sunday, November 9, 2003. Even if this did not result in new subscriptions the choice at least guaranteed additional attention for the length of the series.

I had been so obsessed with the idea of exposing my brother that I almost ignored the impact it would have on the rest of my family. All my pertinent conversations about the murders, the investigation, and subsequent suspicions had been limited to Tom and Emily, and even then I was so restricted by the demands of my church that I mostly listened. Where possible I offered to help, but with all previous avenues having led to dead-ends I pinned my remaining hopes on Emily. The night before the first story was published I had dinner with my mother and my sister's family. After finishing our meal we sent the children off to play.

Since my brother-in-law, Edward, maintained a wonderful liquor collection, he suggested that we share a dessert wine. The rest of us sat in the living room while he went to the cellar and retrieved a 1968 Caves Messias Port. After we each had a glass in hand I began.

"My coming over tonight was not impromptu. I have something important to share with all of you." Long ago they had each learned to expect the unexpected from me and my statement raised no eyebrows. "For several weeks Emily has been on special assignment for the *Los Angeles Times*. She's developing a series about the murders of Yolanda and the children. It starts tomorrow."

Bianca started to respond. I knew she was about to ask why I had not said something sooner. I quickly continued, "It was Tom's suggestion that the *Times* initiate its own probe into their deaths. Like the rest of us he has been frustrated with the inability of the LAPD to solve the crime. He feels as if he personally failed our family."

As I took a breath, Bianca managed to voice her question. "I still don't understand. Why couldn't you have told us?"

How was I going to answer? This late at night I had no concerns about anyone speaking to Giuseppe. He was in a time zone three hours ahead of California. And yet I did not want to undermine Emily's carefully crafted series of articles.

"I'm telling you now," I replied. "Let me continue. There is significant information that the LAPD withheld during Tom's investigation and although getting the *Times* involved was his idea, he was not happy that his wife received the assignment. Most people don't know that there were at least two additional people killed who were also connected to the death of Yolanda and the children. Tom believes there is still a great deal of danger for anyone looking into the murders. Over the last couple of months he has done everything possible to secure Emily's safety. Part of that was limiting the number of people who knew about her work. That's why I couldn't say anything to all of you before. But now that the first article is about to be published I want you to be prepared."

"What's in it?" Edward asked.

"Some of the information previously withheld, including photos from the murder scene." Both my mother and sister winced at the thought. I tried to soothe them. "You know Emily. She'll be sensitive. She won't show pictures of the bodies."

"Have you seen them?" my sister asked.

"Yes, and they were not easy to look at. Emily will spare all of you that."

My mom asked, "What about Giuseppe? Have you said anything to him?"

I wished she hadn't raised that question. I prize truthfulness, yet lied with a deceptive ease. Perhaps it's a gene I share with my twin. At any rate I looked at my mother and without expression assured her, "Yes, I already told him."

I could feel hate flowing within me and wanted to say so much more. For the truth that was yet to be revealed was far worse than what they would read in the Sunday paper. It would be better for them if I were the one to divulge Giuseppe's dark past. But I was still bound by my faith, nor did I wish to sabotage Emily's hard work. There would be time in the coming days to further discuss this matter so I steered the conversation away from the upcoming news to more mundane and less stressful topics.

After finishing our drinks I said, "Tomorrow will be a difficult day for all of us. I imagine I will be inundated with questions from well-intentioned parishioners. Besides, I'm feeling a bit tired and can hear my bed beckoning. I'll stop by in the afternoon." With that I took my leave.

• • •

I rose early the next morning and retrieved the newspaper from the front porch. Bold block letters proclaimed "**New Evidence in MURDER OF SENATOR'S FAMILY**." Like many a headline it was misleading—though only slightly so. The evidence presented in the article was not new, merely previously unreleased. Immediately clear from reading the piece was that the gamble to devote time and resources into investigating the murders would pay significant dividends for the *Times*. Emily's skillful writing was captivating, and with a promise of enticing elements in future installments, it ensured continued public interest for the length of the series.

The inclusion of the crime scene photos all but guaranteed turmoil within the police department over the unauthorized dissemination of its internal files. This, in turn, suggested additional ancillary stories about the LAPD itself.

Indeed, the *Los Angeles Times* was prepared to surf an enviable journalistic wave.

Despite my meetings with Tom and Emily over the preceding weeks I was disheartened by the morning paper. I put on the best possible face as parishioners and friends commented and sought my reaction throughout the day. But seeing everything in print was significantly different from discussing it. Given the effect the story had on me, I was glad that I had braced my family. This was all new to them and it would have been unfair to catch them by surprise.

For her part, Emily was not prepared to rest. Although she had enough information to run a series of articles hinting at Giuseppe's guilt, it would mostly be by inference. She was still hoping for some revelation from Jackson. Like I did with my mother and sister, she called Jackson on Saturday to forewarn him that the first article would appear in the next day's paper.

No one called Giuseppe. There was neither a desire nor a need. Television, satellites and other technology have been shrinking our world for decades creating instantaneous access to events around the world. He would know as soon as the paper was off the press. Besides, he did not deserve to be notified.

. . .

The week before the first article came out was a complicated one for Jackson. Although not Emily's intention, she left him in a state of emotional turmoil following their meeting. In order to process the information she had shared he needed to distance himself from my brother. Giuseppe was kept fairly busy with campaign activities but the state of New Hampshire borders Massachusetts and it would be too easy for them to meet.

Jackson decided to take a week off from work and visit Jean-Paul's mother in Brussels. Her disease was incurable and her son's murder only brought her own death closer. Traveling to Belgium, however, was not the ideal solution to his problems, since people are accessible by telephone the world over. But at least he would not have to see Giuseppe in person.

He returned home on Saturday afternoon and received Emily's phone call. Since she was not sure that he would easily find a copy of the *Los Angeles*

Times in Boston, she detailed the substance of the story. There was nothing in it that they had not previously discussed, nonetheless it unleashed fears and insecurities that he had been tamping down throughout the week.

Giuseppe, unaware of the impending article in the *Times*, called him late Saturday night. Jackson answered and, of course, recognized the voice on the other end.

"Jacks, this is Sep." They had spoken by phone but had not seen each other for more than a week. "I've really missed you, my friend. How was the trip to Brussels?"

Still overwhelmed and disconcerted by Emily's visit he tried to disguise any mistrust in his response. "The trip was fine and I had a good visit with Jean-Paul's mother. But she is not doing well. I don't think she's going to last long and I'm worried about her."

"I'm sorry to hear that," Giuseppe replied.

Jackson believed him even though he was still processing what Emily had said the previous weekend. She suggested that my brother inhabited a very narrow world, one that revolved only around himself. Jackson listened as Giuseppe spoke and heard the voice of a man oblivious to the reality that was about to explode around him. But within his heart, he heard the sounds of love and compassion and found it difficult to surrender those feelings. The man on the phone was not the man Emily had described.

"Jacks, I have a campaign event tomorrow afternoon, after which I'm heading back to Washington. If you're free I'd like to stop in Boston." Then in his most seductive tone of voice added, "Maybe even spend the night."

Jackson could feel the pull of sexual desire as fibers vibrated in various parts of his body. His back and midsection sprung to life and he twitched in his efforts to calm them. The anticipation was simply too exciting. He had come to love Giuseppe very deeply and although Emily had cast a large net of doubt around my brother, it was just that—doubt. Jackson wanted to believe that just being in my brother's arms could prove Emily wrong. Hearing Giuseppe's voice was simply too tantalizing to resist and aroused feelings he could not and did not want to deny. Cordless telephone still in hand, he moved to look at a picture of the two of them in Washington and imagined their next night together.

"I'll be home all day," Jackson answered. Then almost dreamily he continued, "Come over whenever you can."

•   •   •

November 9 was unlike any other Sunday. The *Los Angeles Times* article was picked up by news wires across the country and quickly became the nation's hottest topic, especially among the Washington elite. How it would affect my brother's campaign in the long run was unclear. There was nothing reported that even remotely intimated his involvement in the murders. But it hit him and his staff like a bolt of lightning, threatening to adumbrate the positive reception he was garnering in Iowa and New Hampshire. For the moment, though, he could count on the good will and understanding of the American people. The story also provided cover for him to cancel all events that day. He flew to Boston and arrived at Jackson's house at eleven in the morning.

Whatever negative things might be said about Giuseppe, no one could deny his charisma. Jackson opened the door and was immediately struck with delight and joy at seeing his friend. The uncertainties that Emily had planted a week earlier easily faded as they looked in each other's eyes and then embraced. Jackson's arms encircled his friend, his tight embrace expressing a promise of support. When he stepped back he realized that there was no way the man in front of him could be a murderer. Although glad to see each other they could not escape the serious atmosphere resulting from the story in the Sunday newspaper. He was surprised and relieved that Giuseppe was alone.

"How did you get away from the media?" Jackson asked.

"I had a car waiting at the airport," he replied. "Everyone thought I was heading straight back to Washington. I imagine they're camped outside my door as we speak."

"No one knows you're here?"

Giuseppe smiled, shook his head, and answered, "Not even my campaign manager."

"Sep, I can't imagine what you're going through, but I want you to know that I'm here for you."

"Thanks, Jacks. This has come as quite a surprise to me. I don't know what the *Los Angeles Times* hopes to accomplish. If Tom, marshaling all the forces of the LAPD, could not solve the mystery, then I doubt Emily will either. It appears as if they are pooling their resources and working on this together, even though the story carries only her byline."

Jackson looked at Giuseppe. He had never seen him so forlorn—not even at any of the funerals they had both attended. And yet he was not defeated. A figurative expression was embodied before Jackson's eyes as if he could actually see the wheels turning inside Giuseppe's head.

"Would you like something to drink?" Jackson asked.

"Do you have any vodka?"

"I have an unopened bottle of Van Hoo."

Giuseppe wrinkled his nose and said, "I've never heard of it."

"It was a gift I received in Brussels. I brought it back yesterday."

"I thought Belgians were famous for their beer."

"They are. But they also make good vodka. Van Hoo is the oldest distillery in Belgium, dating back to 1740. This is a favorite in the Lecuyer family. I think you'll like it." He poured each of them a glass and said, "I recommend having it neat."

Each took a sip and Giuseppe said, "You were right. This is quite good."

They sat for a few moments in silence. It was more reflective than awkward, but eventually Giuseppe spoke. "Jacks, I'm not going to be able to spend the night. Even if I don't meet with the press this evening, it will be difficult to explain my not arriving home until the morning."

With a little disappointment in his voice he said, "I understand, Sep."

They had become so close over the last several months that they could read each other's thoughts. Jackson spoke for both of them.

"Do you remember Marvin Gaye's hit single 'Sexual Healing'?"

"Are you suggesting what I think you are?" Giuseppe impishly inquired.

Jackson tilted his head, gave a wry smile, and replied, "It may be a while before we can be together again."

Neither needed convincing from the other. They put down their drinks, stood up and had not yet left the living room when passion got the better of them. Their lips locked in an intense kiss as they pulled off each other's shirts and trousers. They made it to the bed and for the next twenty minutes needed no words to pass the time. Warmed by each other's bodies they surrendered to a love that had been consuming them for months.

Afterward they lay together listening to the gentle cadence of one another's breathing. Giuseppe appeared outwardly calm. They both did, but Jackson was unsettled within, unsure what he should do next. Whatever else he had to be honest. It was his nature. Finally he rolled over onto his side and looked at Giuseppe.

"Sep, everything will be fine. But you need to be cautious of Tom and Emily. I don't trust them."

"Why not?"

"She came to see me last weekend."

Giuseppe's body remained still but he turned his head to peer into Jackson's eyes, his own look steely and cold, and asked warily, "What did she want?"

"She said she was on assignment investigating your family's murder. At first it seemed innocent enough. She was following the same line of thinking that her husband had and thought maybe you knew something about the killer. Perhaps you were being blackmailed by someone. She wondered if you had said anything to me."

"That's absurd," Giuseppe replied.

"I thought so, too."

Jackson's response was guileless. He was almost enthusiastically in agreement with his friend. But something in Giuseppe's response caused him discomfort. He suddenly wished he had not begun this conversation. But since he had, he would see it through.

"She said more, Sep, a lot more."

"Tell me," he encouraged.

"I didn't know much about your family's death or the investigation. According to her there were two other murders that were never reported in the news. One of the people killed was your attorney."

"That's true, but I never saw any connection. Coker was a good lawyer and certainly would have told me if there was anything going on."

"She claims that all the murders had the same M.O."

Giuseppe was ever the master manipulator, but even he knew they were in threatening territory. He decided to continue to play innocent.

"That doesn't prove anything, Jacks. There are only so many ways to kill. I'm sure there are many murders with similar M.O.'s."

Jackson pressed on carefully. "She said the other person killed was a suspect in the murders of your family."

With impeccable incredulity Giuseppe said, "There were no reports of any suspects."

Despite how close they had become, despite the fact that they were lying naked next to each other Jackson could not fully dispel the doubt Emily created and he didn't know whether or not he was being played. A week before he had been dragged through the whole scenario by Emily and it left him devastated. Now he didn't know if he was being led by my brother or where it might lead him. The previous weekend he questioned himself, wondering if his naiveté had allowed him to fall in love with a murderer. Now he wondered if that same innocence was at work in this conversation. He chose to trust Giuseppe over Emily. If this were to be his Waterloo it would be the result of gullibility and love.

Jackson returned to a reclining position on his back not wanting to look at Giuseppe as he said, "She also talked about Jean–Paul's murder."

Giuseppe had already anticipated this. He looked at the ceiling, his mind racing ahead of the conversation as fast as possible and asked, "Why?"

"It started as a result of the M.O. She claims not to believe in coincidences."

"Did she suggest some kind of connection? Because I don't see it. He didn't know my wife, my children, my lawyer."

"I told Emily the same thing. Her answer was that *I* was the link. She believes that you had something to do with Jean–Paul's death." He turned his head toward Giuseppe and said, "It unnerved me, Sep. And I feel guilty."

In his mind Giuseppe had not scripted this part. "Why should you feel guilty?" he asked. "She was the one who made the accusation."

"Because I didn't go to Brussels just to see Jean–Paul's mother. I went to get away from everything, even you. I needed time to think. Emily created so much doubt and uncertainty."

"About us?" Giuseppe asked.

"Yes," he responded forthrightly. "But even more about you." Then, with a bit of trepidation he continued. "Tell me, Sep. Why did we become lovers?"

"Come on, Jacks. That's like asking why the sky is blue. There's a reason but only scientists care what it is." It was his turn to roll on his side. As he did so he noticed that every inch of Jackson was sexy. He put his hand on Jackson's chest. There was not much hair, just enough to tug slightly. His lips barely parted with a loving smile as he said, "I told you before that I have always loved you. But no one can force love in return. So why did we fall in love? It's like the sky being blue. We just did."

"And if Jean-Paul had lived? Would we still have fallen in love?"

This was what Jackson really wanted to know. He needed reassurance. Giuseppe possessed nearly every interpersonal skill set and wielded them to perfection. He looked at his friend. His eyes gently softened into a glance of pure devotion and he replied, "No, Jacks. If Jean-Paul had lived we would not be together." As if anticipating his thoughts, Giuseppe eliminated the need for the next question. "My love would have gone unrequited and I would have been content knowing that you were happy."

Their bodies may have physically merged but in every significant way they were on parallel trajectories: Jackson a tender, tranquil spirit open to all of life's experiences, Giuseppe a scheming, self-absorbed, soulless psychopath.

"I knew Emily was wrong about you," Jackson said. "I feel ashamed that I doubted you."

"Don't be." He slid his hand down between Jackson's legs and kissed him. "It's not your fault. It's not really her's, either." He sat up on the side of the bed, his back to Jackson. "Tom's behind this. He can't handle failure." As Giuseppe got up and started to dress he continued his monologue. "When Tom's investigation led nowhere he turned his sights on me. With paranoid delusion he sees my hand in everything. He dragged you into this and tried to sully our relationship. I'll find a way to take care of it."

Jackson also rose and got dressed.

"Do you really have to leave?" he asked. "We could make love a couple more times." He grinned and said, "I have it in me."

Giuseppe laughed and said, "I have to get back to Washington. Not only will the press be waiting, but we don't know what Tom's up to. Irrespective of our love, the world would see this as a compromising situation and we can't risk that. Caution will have to dictate our activities for the time being. The next time you come to Washington you'd better stay in a hotel. We can meet in my office or a public restaurant."

"It doesn't sound like much fun."

"No, it doesn't. But it will make you appear more like an advisor and keep conjecture at bay."

They walked to the door. Before opening it they shared a long, passionate kiss, knowing it would be some time before they could do that again.

The flight between Boston and Washington, D.C., was only an hour, yet it was time enough for Giuseppe to contemplate his future. He was used to controlling life and so far that ability had served him well. From his point of view he had no equals and from business to politics he bowed to no one. His arrogant superiority was not without some justification. After all, he had bested both Tom and me, thwarting all our efforts to bring him to justice. Nor did he fear Emily and the *Los Angeles Times*. Still, her series would pose new challenges for him.

During the original police investigation Giuseppe anticipated every move, easily remaining several steps ahead of Tom. This new development was unexpected. He knew that Tom would confide in Emily, but even that had posed no threat. His concern now was for Jackson, a man he had come to love but a man of innocence who could be manipulated by both him and Emily. This was going to be an opportunity for Giuseppe to prove that his own powers of persuasion were greater than hers.

CHAPTER 21

I was anxious for the Sunday morning to end. It seemed like everyone had read the newspaper before going to church, and answering the queries of parishioners was more stressful than I had anticipated. As soon as the final Mass was concluded and the church emptied, I called Tom and Emily to say I was coming over. When I arrived she opened the door and welcomed me as warmly as ever. I greeted Tom and we all went into the living room.

"Emily, do you have any coffee?" I asked.

"I brewed a fresh pot right after you called. It's in the kitchen."

She went into the other room while Tom and I sat down not knowing who should start the conversation. I did.

"It's been an emotional morning, Tom, and I needed to get away."

"That bad, huh?"

"Yeah. We've been living with this for so long that I didn't expect it to take such a toll. Everyone means well, but it has been nonstop today, both in terms of the questions and my emotions."

Emily returned with the coffee, poured a cup for each of us, and sat down.

"Gio," she said. "You already look exhausted and it's only one o'clock in the afternoon. I'm glad you're here."

"I really didn't have any place else to go," I replied. "You're the only ones who know as much as I do, and the only two people I can truly trust."

"Speaking of which," Tom interjected. "I think you should tell Emily what we discussed after she and I returned from Boston."

It would have been nice had he made that suggestion in private or in some way forewarned me. I don't like being caught off guard. But I also knew he was right. Emily was trying to construct a convoluted puzzle and my musings were a critical piece. I suddenly wished I had requested something stronger than coffee.

"Emily, I've figured out the motive for Jean-Paul's murder and how it connects to Giuseppe. Or at least, I think I have. I believe he and Jackson are in a relationship and I don't mean just friends. I think it's sexual."

Emily listened attentively but did not react. Looking at neither Tom nor me, she transfixed her eyes on the wall behind us as if momentarily transported to another place and time. Within moments she returned to the present conversation displaying neither surprise nor astonishment. Her countenance conveyed the calm gratification of the investigative journalist, equivalent to the satisfaction of the mathematician who has laboriously locked multiple calculations in place, and realizing that the formula works, finishes it off with a final stroke of punctuation.

"You're not shocked by the idea that Giuseppe is gay?" Tom asked.

"No," she replied. "Sexual orientation is not a choice. It's a discovery. Some, I suppose the lucky ones, recognize it early. For others it can be a long, drawn out, and even painful process. Maybe it just took longer for Giuseppe. That's not what concerns me.

"I was thinking back to my meeting with Jackson. He was a difficult person for me to read and did not reveal much. Whatever he was thinking, he kept it to himself. Additionally, he demonstrated little reaction to anything I said that day, although he seemed more than a little bothered when I expressed the belief that Giuseppe was somehow involved in Jean-Paul's death. He also brought the conversation to an abrupt end. Your misgivings, Gio, might explain a lot.

"Suppose they are involved and imagine further that Jackson is in love. He is a very sweet and innocent guy. By contrast, there is no depth or integrity in Giuseppe. Such an imbalance would never be able to stand but I may have inadvertently caused it to teeter over prematurely."

"Look, Em," I replied, "you exposed Jackson to a devastating truth. But whether or not he believes you and how he reacts is beyond your control."

"The reason I brought it up today," Tom chimed in, "is that your series in the *Los Angeles Times* might not be enough to expose Giuseppe. Also, I asked some friends on the D.C. police force—the Metropolitan Police

Department—to do a little investigating for me. I just thought I should be upfront about that. It might come in handy for you, Em."

She looked at him and said, "I hope you're not proposing what I think you are. I'm not going to drag Jackson into the story."

"Of course not," Tom replied. "I'm not suggesting that you slide into tabloid journalism. Besides, we don't have any evidence yet. But you're clever. You can hint at the subject without ever mentioning Jackson's name."

"Come on, Tom," I said. "That still sounds like something for a gossip column." I turned to Emily and continued, "When I talked about this with Tom a couple weeks ago, it had nothing to do with you, the paper, or your story. I've seen a lot of things in ministry. I've seen what people do for love and it is not always good. An affair between Jackson and Giuseppe is the only comprehensible motive I can imagine for Jean-Paul's death."

"Do you think they were involved before the murder?" Tom asked.

"That I don't know," I replied.

Emily offered her opinion. "I don't think so. Jackson's not the type. There's a gentle goodness to him that runs counter to betrayal. When I was in his house Jean-Paul's presence permeated the home, the imprint of his memory everywhere. If you're right, Gio, Jean-Paul's murder was a means to an end for Giuseppe. What's more, I may have left Jackson feeling a bit distrustful. There was something unsettling about his demeanor toward the end of our conversation. But his misgivings seem not to have risen to a conscious level. I'm not going to write about it, but I think I need to talk to him again."

"Maybe I should speak with him," I proposed. "We don't know each other. But as a priest and Giuseppe's brother, I can be a little more surreptitious."

"No, Gio," Emily said firmly. "First, I've already established a rapport with Jackson. Second, and even more importantly, your suggestion sounds a little too manipulative. I realize we're all involved in this investigation, but do we really want to devolve into the same kind of deceit that defines Giuseppe? The person you need to speak with is your brother. He thinks he's outsmarted the two of you, and now probably me. He has no idea about this latest development in your thought."

"You're right, Emily. But I'm not ready to confront Giuseppe just yet. When the time comes I'll know it and hopefully I'll be ready." I finished my coffee, thanked them, and said, "Mom is with Bianca's family today and I think I'd better go see how they're all doing."

As I headed to my sister's house I was struck by one of the oddities surrounding this case. Throughout the morning I had been deluged with questions about the murders and it was with enervated emotions that I sought refuge in the company of friends. Yet the entire time I was with Tom and Emily all we did was talk about the murders. I realized that day, as I had on many other occasions, that there's something comforting and energizing about being with them. For despite the subject of our conversation I left with my spirits lifted high. I felt we were finally approaching a conclusion.

• •

The success of Emily's story was beyond expectation for the *Times*. Throughout the city it was as if people had awakened to a sensational series of new murders and they couldn't get enough. Everywhere I went—the gas station, the store, even the local Starbucks—I overheard people discussing my family. In the nation's capital elected officials from the president to members of congress expressed sentiments of sympathy and concern toward my brother as the *Times* article disinterred emotions that had barely been laid to rest.

Emily's tantalizing promise of printing more previously unpublished evidence, created the greatest fallout at the Los Angeles Police Department. Within hours of the paper hitting the streets, reporters and journalists from all the city's media thronged Parker Center, the headquarters for the LAPD, demanding answers and questioning the competency of the department. They wanted to know why the public was only now hearing of this evidence, why it had been kept secret, why it was revealed by the *Los Angeles Times* and in particular, what the department had been doing for three years.

Media relations might have been caught off guard, but not the Internal Affairs Group. Captain Jack Gorman was not given to idle threats. Five days before the story broke he followed through on his warning to Tom and formally requested an IAG investigation.

188

Internal Affairs Group, originally a bureau of its own, had been subsumed by the Professional Standards Bureau, and as the investigative arm of the Chief of Police is charged with preserving and safeguarding the integrity and reputation of the department, its commanding officer reporting directly to the chief. Although Tom's removal of evidence was not a criminal activity, it represented a potential violation of policy and procedures and, as such, would fall under the purview of IAG. Depending on the alleged infraction a typical probe and subsequent discipline can take weeks. Priority is frequently given to complaints brought forward by senior officials, such as Gorman, especially when the offender is another high-ranking officer. Ultimately, the chief decides what administrative action is appropriate.

At the time of Gorman's request Tom's activities were still very much an internal LAPD problem. No one knew of the impending series in the *Times*. But due to Tom's rank and the source of the accusation, IAG gave the complaint immediate precedence. The issues were not very complicated, the facts were not in dispute nor were they likely to require a lengthy review. Everything was in motion before the weekend and Jermaine Ulises Jordan had already been interviewed. Nonetheless all hell broke loose on Sunday.

William J. Bratton had been Chief of the LAPD for just over a year, having been appointed on October 28, 2002. Previously, he had carved out a daunting reputation providing successful leadership as Chief of the New York City Transit Police, Boston Police Commissioner, and New York City Police Commissioner. He brought to Los Angeles a rather direct, some might say brash, East Coast style of communication and control. Even had he been raised in the laid back mode of California living, he would have been livid over the *Los Angeles Times* article. No police chief can tolerate the dissemination of confidential files to the media. He had already been informed that IAG was investigating Tom's activity. On Sunday he spoke with Deputy Chief Connie Marting, commanding officer of the Professional Standards Bureau, to request that the investigation be further expedited.

• • •

Within the LAPD, like any other ambition-driven institution, gossip can be difficult to control. By Monday afternoon Commander Erick Haskell, Tom's former captain at Robbery-Homicide Division, had heard about IAG's inquiry and called him into his office.

The door was open. Tom knocked and said, "Hey, Erick."

Haskell looked up and said, "Ah, Tom. Come in, close the door, and sit down." He obliged. Then the commander raised his eyebrows, tilted and gently shook his head in a knowing way as he said, "The *Los Angeles Times* has caused quite a stir around here. And in case you haven't heard yet, Internal Affairs is investigating you."

"I'm not surprised," Tom replied, brushing off the news. "Gorman's pissed-off at me and said he was going to IAG. He was upset that I copied some files from Robbery-Homicide."

"What were you thinking?" Haskell asked.

"I was thinking that we have several murders that have not been solved in three years and you and I both know who's responsible—a fucking senator who wants to be president."

"That's not really the point, Tom. We have protocols to follow."

Tom rolled his eyes and replied, "And just where did all those protocols get us? Nowhere. When you and I were at RHD we actually worked on the case, but since Gorman took over they haven't done shit. Besides, there's more. You and I never discussed the murders in Belgium earlier this year."

"No, we didn't. We've had our hands full here, and it wasn't our case, anyway."

"Well, I'm pretty sure that Lozano was responsible for those killings, too." His voice was more certain and authoritative than his words.

"Tom, you've always been a good detective and your instincts have served you well. I also know that you have long suspected Senator Lozano of being involved in the murder of his family. But don't you think you've let your emotions cloud your judgment?"

"No. I certainly have emotions about the deaths in Hancock Park. Yolanda was a friend of mine and I had known her children since birth. But as far as my job was concerned, I followed the clues, just as I always have. What I discovered in Brussels only convinced me more. But the authorities over there uncovered even less usable evidence than we did. I finally decided I had to do something."

"This time you may have gone too far. You put your career on the line. The chief is really pissed and there's going to be a Board of Rights hearing."

Tom knew what Haskell was trying to say. The truth was that the real problem was not the chief. It was Gorman. Tom's transgression, while serious, would not usually lead to a Board of Rights. That was all Gorman.

The command staff of the LAPD is separated from the rest of the officers. Beginning with the level of captain right on up to deputy chief, they are no longer considered rank and file. As such, they operate under different guidelines than those who are doing real police work, such as officers on patrol or even detectives. Many superiors target people they don't like, willingly trying to make their lives miserable. In that regard, the LAPD is not much different from other hierarchical institutions such as the military and even the church. People with power tend to abuse their authority, lording it over others.

Within the upper stratum of the LAPD it is common for the command staff to do each other favors even if it means conspiring against other officers. No one excelled at this kind of exploitation better than Gorman. He was friends with Jefferson Yandell, IAG commander, and solicited his assistance in bringing Tom before a Board of Rights. In his own way Haskell was trying to tip Tom off to the dangers ahead.

"Tom, we've known each other a long time and I'll do what I can to help you through this. I can be a character witness and testify to your exemplary work, especially when you were at RHD. But I'm afraid Gorman might be more influential than I. As you have so aptly described him in the past, he's a kiss–ass. If he has his sights set on you, your future is anything but secure. If not this problem, he'll find another."

"It was worth it, Erick. Giuseppe Lozano is a smug son of a bitch. He headed off to Washington practically daring me to bring him to justice. This was the only way I could do it. Whatever the outcome, I'm OK with it."

"And involving your wife?" Haskell asked. "Was that wise? If Lozano's as dangerous as you suggest then haven't you put her in peril?"

"She and I talked about that at length, but she is not worried. First of all, she's not going to accuse Lozano outright. She's hoping the publicity will cause him to slip up. Also, he can't be certain how much she knows and it would be far too suspicious if anything happened to her. Of course, I'm still concerned, especially if this ploy doesn't work." He smiled and continued, "Then again I may be looking at a suspension, so I'll have time to protect her myself."

Haskell was not amused. "A Board of Rights is not a laughing matter, Tom, especially in this case. Bratton's only been chief for a year and your actions have made him and the department look bad. I don't know what decision the board will come to, but he's gonna demand some kind of accountability. He needs to save face before the mayor and the commission."

"I realize that, Erick, but I've already crossed that bridge. I fully expect a suspension, but it doesn't matter. I did what was necessary. And I'm rather proud I did it on Gorman's watch. I've never seen him so upset." Haskell ignored that comment, even though he agreed with Tom. Neither one of them had any respect for Gorman. Tom continued, "Even if I lose before the board, I win."

"It's not like you to be unprepared, Tom, so I imagine you anticipated the fallout. Do you know how you're going to defend yourself at the hearing?"

"I'm not," he replied matter-of-factly. Then he took a deep breath and continued, "Look, Erick. I considered the various contingencies and I knew what I was getting into. I intend to rely upon the truth and the need for the facts to be out in the open. With any luck I'll win over the civilian member of the board but probably not the two LAPD officers. That's why I fully expect to be suspended."

"Tom, we've known each other a long time. I think you've made a big mistake especially with a new chief. No one knows what Bratton will be like. I just don't see how this turns out good for you."

"If it brings down Lozano, it will be good no matter the cost. Anyway, it's too late now. But thanks for your concern, Erick." He got up to leave and laughingly said, "I have to get some work done while I still have a job."

Haskell's concern turned out to be prescient. On Monday afternoon Tom was called into his captain's office and was served notice that a Board of Rights hearing would be convened on Friday, November 14.

CHAPTER 22

Giuseppe had two copies of the *Los Angeles Times* delivered to Washington each day, one to his office and the other to his home. He expected another article on Monday morning, but the *Times* had decided to space the series with one appearing every three or four days. It was a business decision. If each article generated sufficient interest, then daily conversations would center around a real political drama—the Lozano saga—instead of the latest episode of Aaron Sorkin's fictional *West Wing.*

Despite the hiatus in Emily's writing, Giuseppe read the morning paper with interest. He was, after all a senator from the state of California and staying informed about events affecting his constituents was critical to his job. Besides which, Los Angeles was his home city. He sat in his kitchen drinking coffee and eating banana walnut muffins as he flipped the pages of the newspaper. The house was empty, but not the front yard. The previous afternoon, following his visit with Jackson in Boston, Giuseppe returned home to find a bevy of reporters and cameramen camped out on his lawn. Although in no position to criticize the sensitivity of others, he was nonetheless amazed to see how little was on display in the media.

He was pummeled with questions that he was unable to answer. There were the typical *"How do you feel?"* and *"What do you think?"* questions that are as inane as the person asking them. He had become so skilled at public relations that he showed no reaction to the more probing queries, such as *"Where were you this afternoon?"* and *"Why did it take so long for you to return to Washington today?"* He did his best to silence reporters for the evening by promising a statement the next day. A few had congregated again by 6:30 a.m. When he opened the door to retrieve the paper, he assured them that no statement would be forthcoming until he had met with his staff. Then he went back into the house to have his breakfast.

Giuseppe's campaign manager, Bill Morgan, and his speechwriter worked together Sunday evening and had a draft ready for him when he entered his Senate office Monday morning. Even though neither knew the truth about Giuseppe they saw an opportunity for him to play the victim and chastise the LAPD. Due to the number of reporters in attendance, Giuseppe addressed them, and the cameras, from the front steps of the capitol.

"I want to thank you all for coming today, and providing a collective environment in which to respond to your questions. As you can imagine this is painful and complicated and I do not wish to spend the day talking to one reporter after another.

"Three years ago my family was devastated by death. As I sought to serve the state of California, my wife and three children were wrenched from life in a cold, calculated murder. For the first few days I found myself adrift, uncertain if I should continue or withdraw. But quitting the race would not have been my wife's desire, nor would it have brought my family back, so I drew upon her strength to continue my run for office.

"Whether this heinous act was the endeavor of some nefarious forces seeking to derail my campaign or the work of some other evil, the Los Angeles Police Department was charged with solving the crime. This they were unable to do despite having one of their best lieutenants as lead detective.

"Yesterday the *Los Angeles Times* began a series of articles revealing information that the LAPD withheld from the public, including the fact that there were two murder suspects, one of whom was gunned down only weeks later. At this point I know no more than the rest of you, but so far the reporting suggests ineptitude on the part of the investigators.

"It is my fervent hope that this exposé will bring forth the tangible results that have so far eluded the police and I am grateful to the *Times* for its commitment to pursue the truth. The rest of my family and I have had to live with this terrible atrocity for far too long. In my opinion it's time, past time in fact, for the police to do their job. That's all I wish to say at this moment, but I am willing to take just a few questions."

Every television station in Los Angeles carried the press conference live, making it possible for me to watch from my living room. It was amazing stagecraft. Giuseppe was so suave and adept at deception that without knowledge of the truth no one could suspect that he was lying. To the outside world he came across as the victim grieved by assassins, aggrieved by the police. I saw only his typical, arrogant self. That should have depressed me. Instead it offered another flicker of hope. He was so cocksure of himself that I thought Emily really could cause him to slip up. Her work was not yet finished. She had been giving serious thought to our discussion on Sunday and decided to contact Jackson. Although not a conversation she desired to have by telephone, she also realized that another flight to Boston would be too ominous. She settled on a call.

• • •

Wednesday, November 12, the front page of the *Los Angeles Times* carried the following headline: "**SUSPECT IN LOZANO MURDERS SHOT DEAD IN MAC ARTHUR PARK**." Emily was chronicling her stories in the same order that the events occurred; in the process exposing the inside world of police work. She and her editor decided to devote an entire day's story to each of the other deaths, those of Gary Bass and Christopher Coker. On Wednesday she detailed information on Bass, including his criminal history and deceptively quiet lifestyle. In the lead story on Sunday Emily had already made a case for the murders being carried out by professionals and emphasized that same efficiency again on Wednesday, contrasting what appeared to be Bass's insignificant existence—a man bereft of family or friends—with his work as a hired gun. Although unable to tie him to any murders beyond the Lozano family, that one connection was sufficient in drama to be believable and to maintain interest among *Times* subscribers.

Throughout the official police investigation there had been no mention of any suspects. When Bass was found dead it made little news in the media since no one knew anything about him. No one stepped forward to claim his body. He was just another nondescript bum lying on the shores of MacArthur Park, an all too common occurrence in Los Angeles.

On Wednesday morning Bass's name was resurrected and his story woven into the popular imagination. Los Angeles, having already experienced political assassination, cemented its position among the likes of Washington, D.C., New Delhi, Dallas, and Memphis. Although unknown in life, in death Bass joined the ranks of John Wilkes Booth, Nathuram Godse, Lee Harvey Oswald, James Earl Ray, and Sirhan Sirhan. With his picture in the newspaper and a gripping story written about his life and death, ordinary citizens fueled the myth, for Bass's murder unleashed a foible in human nature—the need to be important. At the time of his death he had been manager of the Men's Wearhouse store in Glendale. People who had never darkened the establishment's door were suddenly his regular clients; neighbors who never even saw Bass claimed to speak with him regularly on walks around the block; and others insisted that they recognized him as a frequent patron of local restaurants. All of this despite his solitary, hermetic existence.

Emily's narratives were gripping, placing each reader in the thick of the drama. Jackson, of course, was no ordinary reader. His interest was intensified by the death of Jean-Paul, his relationship with Giuseppe, and his recent conversation with Emily. When the phone rang Wednesday evening he was not entirely surprised to hear her voice on the other end.

"Hello," he answered.

This did not seem an appropriate time for her to address him by his nickname.

"Jackson, this is Emily," she said. "Do you have some time to talk?"

"Sure. I was just sitting here relaxing. What can I do for you?"

Emily often referred to these moments as the Bell Paradox—the false intimacy created by the telephone that enables the human voice to traverse thousands of miles in a split second. Regardless, its warmth cannot compete with a soft look or gentle touch. Even in anger its stridency pales when compared with a face-to-face confrontation. In an optimal situation Emily would have chosen to sit in Jackson's presence for this conversation. That luxury, however, was not available to them.

"Jackson, are you following my series in the *Los Angeles Times*?"

"Of course I am. I'm now getting a copy daily and this morning I read the second installment. You're a good writer, Emily, but it's a tough story. I know Giuseppe is having a hard time with it. I talk to him each day. And if you saw his news conference on Monday you can understand."

"I did see it," she replied. "But that's not why I'm calling. I need to ask you about something in particular. And for me, even as a journalist, it's uncomfortable."

"Relax, Emily. You can talk to me about anything. I imagine it has to do with Giuseppe."

"Yes, but it's also personal. My husband has put a lot on the line for this investigation and I owe it to him to follow through on all leads. Still, I promise that anything you say tonight is off the record. I will use it only to shape my own understanding."

"You make it sound almost sinister, Emily."

"That really depends on how you respond. As I was building the story I spoke frequently with Giovanni. The other day he suggested something that I had not considered, but which I need clarified." She took a moment to draw a little courage, then continued. "Giovanni thinks that you and Giuseppe are having an affair."

His momentary silence was all the verification she needed. Jackson always knew that despite efforts to conceal their relationship the secret would someday become known. Like so many people in love they let feelings cloud their judgment. It was foolish to think they could contain it until Giuseppe had been elected president. Still, they were exceedingly discreet. They also lived on opposite sides of the country. Jackson decided to deflect with a question before an admission.

"Why does he think that?"

"Jackson, I don't want to trade questions with you. But the answer to yours lies in another. Were the two of you involved before Jean-Paul died?"

He was suddenly as startled as when a crack of thunder shatters a dream. Her insinuation was pointed and resurfaced feelings he had experienced during their previous meeting. It also answered his query.

He sat in another momentary silence and began to entertain a conspiracy theory. It was obvious that Emily, Tom, and I all believed Giuseppe was involved in Jean-Paul's murder. But now it appeared as though we were looking for a way to frame him. Emily's question was a no-win. No matter how he answered, his response would be twisted to support a preconceived determination of Giuseppe's guilt. And that was something he could not accept.

"Emily, I don't mind talking about myself. I've been open about my sexuality for most of my life and I'm quite content with the person I am. But I'm not a fool. I know what you're up to and let me tell you that I'm not comfortable talking about Giuseppe in such a manner. He is a friend. That's all I intend to say. If you want to know more, then you'll have to ask him."

"That's fair enough. But you should know not only was Gary Bass mysteriously murdered, so was Giuseppe's lawyer, Christopher Coker. That will come out in the next article. What I'm not ready to print was that Giuseppe knew Tom was investigating both of those men."

"So now you're suggesting that he was involved in those murders, too? You're unreal, Emily."

"Jackson, I'm just looking for the truth. The dead deserve that much."

Jackson had enough of this conversation.

"If you don't mind," he said, "I'm three hours ahead of you and would like to get some sleep."

"Not at all, Jackson. Thanks for your time."

But he did not go to sleep. He immediately called Giuseppe in Washington and relayed his conversation with Emily, during which he also expressed his frustration, even anger, at her implications. For his part Giuseppe mostly listened, reassuring Jackson of his love while professing innocence and disbelief. He saved his reactions for after the phone call.

Over the years Giuseppe had grown masterful in his control of people and events. Jean-Paul's murder was a necessary manipulation, for if there was one real thing in his life it was his love for Jackson. But secreting away the truth was beginning to take its toll and the possibility of being exposed created genuine turmoil within, especially now that Emily was poking around his private life. His agitation displayed itself in unusual quirks. He fidgeted in his chair, and his muscles twitched involuntarily as energy pulsated through his bones. Even his mind was unfocused. He periodically stood up and walked about the room trying to regain some kind of discipline and perspective. His body was beginning to reflect his life. He saw everything slipping from his grasp and felt invaded by outside forces.

He was hounded daily by an incessantly present press corps but his ability to manage the media was the least of his concerns. Thoughts that he had kept neatly compartmentalized collided simultaneously in his mind, creating frightening visions. He could foresee his popularity plummeting, his quest for the presidency fading, accompanied by a potential arrest and jail sentence, the rejection of his family, even the loss of love from Jackson.

This was a world of his own making in which he had spent years isolating himself and insulating his feelings. Now he was beginning to discover that the chasm between *being* alone and *feeling* alone is not so vast and he did not know what to do. He closed and squinted his eyes, then squeezed his shoulder blades together as if calling forth some super power. But he was no Hulk and there was no inner strength to rescue him. Attempting to calm his emotions, he sat with his spine erect against the back of his chair, relaxed his muscles and unfurled his brow. What if this were just his imagination run wild? What if it were not? Either way he would have to do what he always did and calculate an avenue of escape.

Following her telephone exchange with Jackson, Emily immediately spoke with Tom and then called me to convey her version of the conversation. It became increasingly evident that I was running out of time. I would need to speak with my brother sooner, rather than later. Unlike Emily contacting Jackson by telephone, I would need to be in Giuseppe's presence in order to properly express everything I had to say. I phoned him late Wednesday night and somewhat surprisingly he agreed to schedule a meeting in Washington on Saturday afternoon.

•   •   •

On Friday morning, November 14, Tom found himself on the fifth floor of the Bradbury Building in downtown Los Angeles for a Board of Rights hearing. As is always the case, two LAPD officers and one civilian constituted the members.

Tom had drawn four slips from a hopper containing the names of all current command-level personnel. From those he chose two. It is a random process providing the accused officer with some level of objectivity. He selected Captain Dolores Moreno and Commander Andrew Reynolds. He knew neither of them.

A certain amount of equity also imbues the selection of the civilian representative. The Police Commission had provided the names of three members: David S. Cunningham III, Rich Joseph Caruso, and Rose Ochi. The department advocate eliminated Cunningham. Caruso had spearheaded the committee to select the new chief of police, and Tom was not entirely convinced that he would be impartial. He thus excluded Caruso, leaving Rose Ochi to complete the board. He would need two of the three to win.

Emily and I had talked Tom into presenting at least a mild defense. My friend Morris T. Johnson, both a lawyer and law professor, had a prestigious career with the Legal Aid Foundation and willingly agreed to represent him. Tom was right about one thing: Since he had no intentions of challenging the evidence, there was not much defense to be made. The only hope was that the board would see the necessity of his actions and recommend a light reprimand.

Ordinarily an LAPD Board of Rights hearing is public. Since this case involved a sitting U.S. senator and presidential candidate, as well as confidential police files, the board opted to keep it closed.

The LAPD advocate was Detective Robert Lewis. He began the hearing by calling Detective Philip Newton who testified to discovering misfiled confidential documents regarding the Lozano murders. Since he was the only person working on the case he took his concerns to Captain Jack Gorman who, when called before the board, testified to tracing the files back to an RHD analyst, Jermaine Jordan. Gorman also claimed to have confronted Tom by telephone and that he not only did not deny the charges, but was subordinate in his tone of voice. Johnson, Tom's counsel, asked no questions of either witness.

Jermaine Ulises Jordan, complying with the demands of a subpoena, reluctantly took the stand. Gorman had already testified to what Jordan told him and unlike in a court of law, hearsay evidence is permissible at a Board of Rights hearing. Jordan's testimony was crucial for another reason—he was the only one who could connect Tom personally and directly to the documents. He had no choice but to appear and under the rules governing these hearings, no witness or accused can invoke the Fifth Amendment or refuse to answer questions.

After being sworn, Lewis began a brief interrogation.

"Mr. Jordan, you are a senior management analyst at Robbery-Homicide Division. Is that correct?"

"Yes, sir."

"On September 22 of this year, did Lt. Tom Moran visit you in your office?"

"Yes."

"Will you please tell us what he asked you to do, specifically in terms of the Lozano murder files?"

Jordan was clearly uncomfortable and looked at Tom with regret before answering.

"He asked me to make copies of all the reports and give them to him."

"And did you?" Lewis asked.

"Yes."

"Thank you. That's all."

When Tom met with Johnson in preparation for the hearing, they agreed that the evidence was incontrovertible and decided not to challenge it. Instead, they determined that the best approach would be to present a compelling need for violating department policy. Morris Johnson was a consummate lawyer and master of courtroom theatre and even though there was no jury to impress he still placed value in humanizing the proceedings. Whereas he did not cross-examine the first two witnesses, he rose to question Jordan.

"Your full name is Jermaine Ulises Jordan, but how do most people in the department address you?"

He smiled and said, "They use the initials from my three names and call me 'Juj.'"

"I see." Johnson smiled back, saying, "The department's version of onomatopoeia. Tell me, did Lt. Moran say why he wanted the files?"

"He claimed that the senator was behind the murders both of his own family and two other people connected to the investigation. He also said he was building a case against him."

"But," Johnson pressed, "Lt. Moran was no longer in RHD and it was no longer his case. Correct?"

"Yes, sir."

"Did he say why he needed the files?"

"He said that his wife was investigating the murders for the *Los Angeles Times*."

"Let me underscore," Johnson said. "Lt. Moran told you he wanted internal, confidential files from a case that was no longer assigned to him, so that his wife could publish the information in the newspaper. Do you mind telling us why you agreed to help him, considering you were putting your own career in jeopardy?"

"I've been in the department a long time and I've seen a lot of cases go cold. This one was different. Tom, I mean Lt. Moran, was going to resurrect it and I saw a chance to help. He said there were two other murders connected to the investigation and that there was reason to suspect Senator Lozano in all of them. It was his opinion that publishing information in the *Times* might bring the case to a conclusion."

"I see," Johnson replied.

Jordan continued, "But there is another, more important reason that I copied the files. I did it because the lieutenant is a good detective and I believe in him."

"Thank you. I have no further questions."

Jordan stepped down and left the room. His testimony was no more damaging to Tom than had been expected nor was it particularly helpful. Given that the defense did not contest the allegations, Lewis rested his case.

Confronted by overwhelming evidence, Johnson planned on a simple defense. He first called Erick Haskell to the stand.

"Commander Haskell, how long have you known Lt. Moran?"

"I've known *of* him the better part of twenty years."

"In what capacity?"

"I had heard good things when he worked the Wilshire Division. Then he was hired at RHD where I was captain and we worked together for almost a decade. During that time I came to know him very well."

"How would you describe him?"

"Lt. Moran is one of the best detectives I know. He's thorough, dedicated, and what's more he has integrity. Unfortunately, as we've seen in recent department scandals, that can't be said for everyone."

"You have confidence in him and would recommend him, is that right?"

"Absolutely," Haskell replied. "I trust him implicitly and supported his transfer to the Counter Terrorism and Criminal Intelligence Bureau, his current assignment."

"Thank you, Commander."

Lewis realized that he would not be able to impeach Haskell's testimony. He also knew that it was not critical to the case. Nonetheless he wanted to cast just a shadow of doubt. He stood up and asked, "Commander, would you say that you are biased in Lt. Moran's favor?"

"I think it is more accurate to say that over several years he earned my trust."

"Have you ever known the lieutenant to bend the rules?"

"We all bend the rules. If you're asking more than that, I can only say that while under my command I never knew him to break them."

There was no need for Lewis to pursue this line. He was saving his big guns for later. "Thank you, Commander. That's all."

If Tom were to win over a majority of the board it would have to be through his own testimony. He stepped forward, was sworn in, and Johnson began.

"Lieutenant, the facts in this case are not in dispute. Can you justify your actions to this board?"

"I think so," Tom answered. "When the Lozano family was murdered I headed the investigation. At some point I began to suspect and eventually discovered that Giuseppe Lozano was responsible, not only for the deaths of his wife and children, but also the murders of Gary Bass and Christopher Coker. I did not have useable evidence, however, and he was never apprehended. Earlier this year I learned of similar murders in Belgium and came to believe he was responsible for those, also. Realizing that he is a psychopath it seemed that the only way to force his hand was to publish the LAPD files in the *Los Angeles Times*."

"Why not take your concerns to Detective Newton?" Johnson asked.

"I didn't, and still don't, have proof."

"Then how can you be so sure?"

"Because Lozano admitted it to me. But it's his word against mine."

"You still could have discussed it with RHD."

"For what purpose? Nothing I said would have helped. The case was cold. In fact it was in danger of freezing over. Captain Gorman and Detective Newton certainly were not going to release the documents. I thought that if confidential files were made public an aura of suspicion would begin to engulf Lozano, he might make a mistake, and some proof might emerge."

"And this was worth risking your career?"

"You're not the first person to ask me that," Tom replied. "But my answer has not changed. I'm committed to doing whatever is necessary in order to bring Lozano to justice."

There was not much more that Johnson could elicit. Assuming that the board believed Tom, he had at least made his case and justified his actions. Even Detective Lewis had to admit that. But he had a responsibility to the process and would not let Tom's testimony go unchallenged. Besides, he was also friends with Gorman. This was an opportunity to tarnish Tom's reputation. He rose.

"Lt. Moran, if I understand you correctly, you admit to having removed confidential police records and turning them over to the press. Is that correct?"

"Yes."

"And your defense is that you acted out of some misguided sense of altruism."

"I wouldn't call it altruistic or misguided. The people simply have a right to know the truth."

"A truth you cannot even prove," Lewis emphasized.

"Not as yet."

"Lieutenant, from the outset didn't you, in fact, hijack this case from the Wilshire Division?"

"No, I did not."

"We have witnesses who heard you and Captain Gorman vociferously arguing over jurisdiction."

"On the night of the murder I immediately recognized the severity of the situation. Lozano was a prominent politician and the murders of his wife and children had significant implications for the state of California and even the nation. It was simply beyond the scope of the Wilshire Division."

"But Captain Gorman assured you that night that he was capable of handling it."

"First of all, he was only a lieutenant at the time." Then with obvious disdain for Gorman he continued, "And to be perfectly honest with you, there is not a lot that he is capable of handling. After he took over RHD he effectively gave up on this case completely."

"And you took that personally," Lewis prodded.

"I took the case personally from the beginning. I grew up with the Lozano family. The senator's brother, Giovanni, is my best friend and I cared for Yolanda and her children. I even cared for Giuseppe until I found out he was a murderer. It concerned me that nothing was being done about these killings."

"So this became your responsibility . . . *How,* exactly?"

"Because I know the truth."

"Oh, yes. The truth—one that only you know. Still, you couldn't solve the case when you were in charge of it."

"Not as far as the courts are concerned. But I was standing in Lozano's office when he admitted to having his family killed."

"Where is your proof? Where are your witnesses?" Lewis asked.

"I tried to tape the conversation. I had a small recorder in my pocket, but he had developed some kind of electronic device that prevented it from registering any sounds."

Lewis started to laugh mockingly.

"You want us to believe that a newly elected United States senator admitted having his family killed, but that he told you while standing under a cone of silence?"

"I didn't call it a cone of silence."

"It doesn't matter what you call it. It's still absurd. Aren't you really just covering up for your own ineptitude?"

Tom could feel animosity building inside. He began to think this whole hearing was a wasted exercise. "I'm not covering up for anything," he answered. "I did my job and followed the evidence as I always have. In this case it led to only one person, Giuseppe Lozano. But he beat the system."

"Hmm," Lewis responded. "Let me ask you about something else. Earlier you mentioned some murders in Brussels and claimed that they were also connected to the senator. Can you explain that?"

"I received a call from Lt. Miguel Moreno, the chief U.S. INTERPOL liaison stationed in Lyon, France. He noticed the similarity between the murders in Belgium and the Lozano family killings and suggested that I go to Brussels to meet with the authorities there."

"Which you did," Lewis stated. "Tell me, is it part of your job to travel the globe investigating crimes that occur in other jurisdictions?"

"I went to examine the similarities between those murders and the ones in Los Angeles, to see if I could pick up any additional clues."

"And you concluded the senator was involved."

"Yes," Tom answered.

"And once again you have no proof. Is that correct?"

"Yes."

Lewis paused very briefly to let that admission sink in. Then he continued, "Was this an official trip sanctioned by the department?"

Tom was beginning to get exasperated. He rolled his eyes and sighed as he responded, "No." Then he asserted, "But it was necessary so I used vacation time. Real life murder investigations are not neat and simple like they are in the movies or on television. They require hard work and sometimes call for extraordinary measures."

"Such as leaking confidential files to the press?" Lewis asked.

Tom had had enough.

"I don't need to justify myself to you," he said.

Matching his frustration Lewis reminded him, "You have to justify yourself to this board and to the chief." He paused before continuing although he knew what he would say next. "You know what I think, Lieutenant? I think you're a rogue cop."

"I don't give a shit what you think," Tom replied.

Lewis continued, "Weren't you just covering you own ass? You botched a high-profile murder investigation, targeted a popular politician, concocted a bizarre science fiction story to excuse your failure, invaded a foreign jurisdiction on some wild fantasy and when none of that succeeded you decided to violate police policies and procedures by releasing confidential, internal documents to the local press, the reporter being your own wife."

"I already told you it was a case of extraordinary measures."

"Setting aside for a moment the total impropriety and ethical issues of feeding confidential files to your wife, did it not cross your mind that letting her publish this information in the *Los Angeles Times* would undermine the public's confidence in the LAPD, make the department look bad, and embarrass the chief?"

"Let me make something clear," Tom replied. "We have six unsolved murders here in Los Angeles that are all connected and all leading to one man. There are three more murders in Belgium that point to the same man. It is my intention to get Senator Lozano no matter what the cost, preferably before he is elected president."

"Lieutenant Moran, I admire that you came here this morning and freely admitted to all the charges. It makes the board's decision so much easier." Then, in an attempt to goad Tom, Lewis continued, "You do realize, however, that there is always the possibility you won't be 'getting' the senator as a member of the LAPD?"

Tom stood up and said, "You know what? You're right. We finally agree on something more than just facts. I don't need this fucking shit from you or anyone else. I've put in my years. The board can tell the chief what it wants and he can do whatever he wants. I quit. And you, Detective Lewis? You should try being a real cop someday."

With that Tom walked out of the room and out of the LAPD.

CHAPTER 23

When Tom walked out of the Board of Rights hearing he felt an unexpected relief. He had just ended his career in law enforcement, but had no regrets, realizing that he was now free to pursue his own agenda and go after Giuseppe with no interference from or accountability to the LAPD.

Emily and I waited at their house for the results of the hearing, during which we talked more about her conversation with Jackson.

"Did you ever suspect your brother was gay growing up?" she asked.

"Never. And I've been trying to avoid the temptation of claiming clarity in hindsight. But it wouldn't have mattered anyway. I have long considered the traditional mores about homosexuality untenable and find myself at odds with the official position of the Catholic Church and even more so with the extremist proclamations of the evangelical churches. Jesus said nothing about it one way or the other—that alone should give pause to the vociferous outcry in some modern Christian churches.

"The truth is, Emily, that I didn't see any clues. Tom, Giuseppe, and I were very close when we were young, for the most part all through high school. And among the three of us Giuseppe was the biggest player, certainly the one with the most girlfriends."

"You know that doesn't mean anything," she said in a gentle tone of voice. Had our roles been reversed, those same words coming from my lips would have sounded patronizing. And although her speech did carry a certain conviction, that was not Emily's style. "Sometimes having a lot of girlfriends is just a cover."

"I know that. I've counseled men who grew up in the closet either because they couldn't accept themselves or were afraid other people wouldn't accept them. Still, Giuseppe and I are twins and I should have noticed something."

"Based on what?" she asked. "When I met you we were all in our twenties. I saw no indications, not even anything subtle. And that was a few years after the events with Jackson in graduate school."

"Still," I replied, "until the murders, and what we've learned since, I always thought he and Yolanda had a good marriage."

"Maybe they did, at least for a while. I think that what I said the other day is correct. It just took Giuseppe a long time to discover who he is."

"Emily, I couldn't care less about my brother's sexual orientation—except that he had Jean-Paul killed in order to be with Jackson. But being blind to the darkness within him disturbs me."

"Come on, Gio. Giuseppe is a master illusionist who believes his own hype. He has always been popular and knows how to sell himself. He's played the state of California for fools and now he's playing the nation. Why should you be any different than the rest of us?"

Emily was always so attuned to her environment. Regardless the circumstances, she was sensitive to the feelings of others and found multiple ways of expressing sympathy. She perceived that there was a struggle within me far beyond my ability to articulate.

"Gio, even after everything we've shared, all the conversations we've had, I still can't imagine what it's like for you to go through all of this."

"One thing's certain, Emily. I couldn't have done it without you and Tom. Your support means a lot to me." The words trailed off despite the sincerity of my feelings. Needless to say, she noticed.

"What is it, Gio?" she asked.

"I can't stop thinking about the dark side of Giuseppe. It's changing me, Emily. It's like a black hole, a vortex of evil, and I can't break free of its pull."

Just then Tom walked in the door. Emily greeted him with a kiss and as he wrapped her in his arms I took great personal delight. These close friends of mine were a couple very much in love. It made me wonder if Giuseppe ever truly had the same feelings for Yolanda. In the last three years he had become so different from the brother I grew up with. Indeed, he was the great unknown in my life.

Tom looked at his watch and said, "It's five o'clock somewhere. Let's have a drink. We need to celebrate."

Assuming his remarks indicated a positive outcome from the morning's hearing Emily asked, "What happened with the board?"

Tom brushed her question aside saying, "After I pour the scotch." When we each had a glass in hand he raised his in a toast. "Here's to a free man."

"What are you talking about?" I asked.

"I resigned from the force." He spoke almost as if he thought we anticipated this outcome.

"You can't be serious," Emily replied.

"Oh yes, I am," he answered. "Some hot-shot detective was making the case for the department and it was obvious to me that he was just a mouthpiece for Jack Gorman. I figured that he was going to press the board for more than a simple suspension. So I quit."

"You don't think you overreacted just a bit?" I asked.

"No, Gio. You had to be there. You know what it's like to look into someone's eyes and know what they're thinking. Well, I could tell the outcome was not going to be good. By resigning I placed my future securely in my own hands. I leave with my reputation and my pension." Then he lifted his glass again. "To freedom," he said.

Emily did not voice displeasure, but neither did she raise her glass or join in the toast. She did take a slow sip of scotch, peering at her husband as she did so, then said, "It's not like you to be so impulsive, Tom." Trying not to sound too accusatory she asked, "Did you plan this before you went before the board?"

"Not really," he replied. "But I knew it was a possibility. Look, the entire hearing was Gorman's idea. I suspected what I'd be up against and went in prepared."

"And you said nothing to me?"

"I was afraid you might try to talk me out of it."

"I see," she said somewhat knowingly.

"No, you don't, Emily. The other day I told Gio we are engaged in a war with Giuseppe that we can still lose. One way or the other I had to win this skirmish with the department. From here on in, I'm unencumbered by the rules. What I do as a private citizen will hold up in court, even if I break the law doing it."

"I don't like this," I said. "Before you walked in I was telling Emily that all these murders and what we've learned about Giuseppe is changing me. And not for the better. Sometimes I feel as if I'm in the grip of some evil and can't break free. There's no reason for both of us to lose ourselves."

Emily voiced her agreement. "When you were a young cop, Tom, you were almost sucked into a world of deceit and corruption. You managed to escape it back then and I don't want to see you go there now."

This was an expected turn of events and none of us knew exactly how to respond to each other. It was as if we were all talking at cross purposes.

I tried to focus on our common goal. "Tom, if we're going to beat Giuseppe, win the war as you call it, we need to stand on principle. This is not a 'fight fire with fire' situation."

Emily added, "Whether you're a cop or not, you're a good and decent man."

"You two are so dramatic," Tom said with a laugh. "And way too serious. I'm not losing myself or setting out to break any laws. I'm just saying that I have a freedom, a flexibility I did not have as a cop. By the way, Gio, I'm going to Washington with you tomorrow."

"To meet with Giuseppe?" I asked.

"No. That's your job. I want to do some sleuthing." He smiled and said, "Now there's a word I couldn't use as a cop. I think I'm going to enjoy this new life."

Emily merely sighed. We were all experienced enough to know when we could not change something—or each other. In this case, the damage was done. Tom had resigned from the police force and would have to set about making a new career for himself. But I doubted it would be as easy as he implied.

As I left their home I suspected there would be more discussion between them. Emily would support Tom but she was not happy at that moment.

• • •

Tom and I took a redeye flight from Los Angeles to Washington so as to maximize our time in the nation's capital. Once we reached cruising altitude the flight attendants began beverage service. Tom ordered a couple of scotches for us and as we drank we discussed our plans for the next day.

"What do you expect to get out of Giuseppe?" he asked.

"I'm not really sure. We know everything we need to about the murders of Yolanda and the kids, of Bass and Coker. He won't tell us anything more. But I want to pursue the death of Jean-Paul and I intend to use Jackson as leverage. It's a fair guess that he told Giuseppe about Emily's visit and phone call, so I've lost the element of surprise. But I might be able to make him sufficiently uneasy and cut through his arrogant veneer."

"You're not looking for a conscience, are you?"

"Nothing so dramatic as that. The best I can hope for is to make him uncomfortable. I think it's the only way he'll slip up."

"You know, Gio, for the last three years we've been on a long road. As I look around, the bricks have lost their luster, the city before us no longer glistens green and the wizard we seek is dark and evil. But he is not all-powerful and it has fallen on us to pull back the veil."

"Tom, I'm too tired right now. I want to rest on the flight." I leaned my head back against the seat, turned my face toward the window, and fell asleep.

We shared a room at the Watergate Hotel. It was a convenient location since I would meet with my brother in his Senate office. In Tom's mind its history also held out a promise of poetic justice, having been the beginning of the end for President Richard Nixon. Of course that was pure fancy. We were not investigating anything connected to the hotel, and whatever Nixon's personal demons may have been, he was not as evil as Giuseppe.

After checking into the Watergate and having breakfast, Tom set out for the D. C. Police Headquarters and then on to Georgetown. He was a little disappointed in his fellow officers from Washington. They had turned up nothing of value regarding Giuseppe. Tom suspected they did not try very hard. To be fair, D.C. has an overworked police department and asking them to investigate a sitting U.S. senator who is running for president, based on nothing but conjecture, was not very realistic. Tom decided to canvass Giuseppe's neighborhood while I met with him in his office.

My brother was waiting outside the Hart Senate Office Building when I arrived. That was just as well. Given our identical looks it would have been difficult to explain my lack of credentials as I passed through various security checkpoints. There were only a few people wandering the halls that Saturday and I enjoyed the surprise they displayed at seeing Giuseppe and me together. It was reminiscent of a much happier time when, as children, everyone had difficulty telling us apart. Walking toward his office it was surprisingly easy to pretend good feelings as we greeted passersby. Behind closed doors, though, there was only tension.

Giuseppe had grown quite content in his new environs. He was formally hospitable but his manners were tinged with something nebulous and difficult to pinpoint. Clearly he thought himself superior to me. It was evident in his tone of voice as he asked, "Would you like a drink or a cigar?"

"No, thanks," I replied. "Maybe just some water." It was important for my purposes that I maintain a professional attitude.

He invited me to sit, then retrieved two bottles of cold water from the executive refrigerator beside his desk, handed one to me, selected a chair opposite mine, and sat down.

"Well, Gio, I suppose you're here to talk about the *Los Angeles Times'* articles." He spoke with such a confident ease, as if his sense of superiority were divinely bestowed.

"Not just the articles," I replied. "I want to talk to you about integrity and justice."

I was glad he did not laugh outright. There was no need. He closed one eye and curled the side of his mouth in a condescending grin.

"I said everything I wanted to in confession three years ago."

"What about what you didn't say?" I asked.

"Meaning?"

"There were other deaths associated with the case, too." I said that somewhat perfunctorily, neither expecting nor getting any reaction. "You know, Giuseppe, you never offered an explanation for the murders of Yolanda and the kids. Why not tell me now? How could you have your family killed just to win an election?"

"Are you really that naive Giovanni? Life is short and purpose-driven and during that brief time everyone is expendable."

"Are you serious?" I asked. "We grew up in the same family, had the same training, and were exposed to the same values. How could you have ended up with such a fatalistic and dismissive philosophy of life?"

"You're the priest. You tell me. Sometimes sacrifices have to be made. Or do you just skip over the parts of the Bible you don't like?"

"The Bible?" I asked, having no idea where he was going with this.

"Yes. You say you believe in a God of love, but nobody complains about him asking Abraham to offer up Isaac or Jephthah killing his daughter in gratitude for a successful battle. Hell, Giovanni, you even believe in a God who sacrificed his own son, letting him be executed like a criminal. For what?"

I had heard people ridicule religion before, even mock the Christian faith, but this was something different and I hardly knew how to respond. I walked into this conversation with a carefully planned script but was beginning to think my brother had already read it and was rewriting as we spoke. Although I tried not to be drawn into his web, I was stunned.

"Are you really placing yourself on the same level as God?" I asked.

"I don't believe in God. But if he exists, I like the way he thinks."

Not only was I sitting in front of a man I no longer recognized, but he had no grasp of human dignity and would be impervious to entreaties on my part. I think I realized for the first time how isolated the world of religion can be. On a daily basis I dealt with people of varying degrees of faith: some deeply committed to God, some looking for meaning in their lives, others seeking redemption. But this stranger represented a very different reality. He could have just as easily been Stalin or Mao or any of the world's many despots. I was on the wrong track in this conversation. There was no moral depth to appeal to and so I needed to put him on the defensive.

"Giuseppe, I know about you and Jackson."

Completely unfazed he asked, "What do you know? Jackson is one of my advisors, someone outside the political system. He has been ever since I came to Washington."

"I know that the two of you are sexually involved."

"Really? Even if that were true what difference does it make? What could it possibly matter to you?"

I shifted slightly in my chair and leaned to the left, resting my chin in my hand. I looked at him intently and said, "Because I know that you had Jean-Paul killed, and I'm pretty sure the reason was that he stood between you and Jackson."

Giuseppe sighed and proffered his same tired denial. "I told you before that I had nothing to do with his death. I think you and Tom are both guilty of the gambler's fallacy."

"What are you talking about?" I asked.

"It's a mathematical and psychological concept—the tendency to see patterns where none exists, as in a coin toss or roll of the dice. The fallacy suggests that if a coin toss results in heads five times in a row, it must end up tails on the sixth. You are making a biased judgment that I had Jean-Paul killed because I admitted to you that I was responsible for my family's murder. The two are not linked and the death of my family is not predictive."

"You really think that you have a piercing intellect, don't you . . . that you've outmaneuvered us all?"

"Either that or you expect me to go to confession again, maybe even admit to having someone else killed?" I ignored his accompanying smirk.

"That was a mistake I won't repeat," I answered. "I'll never again hear your confession. You should know, Giuseppe, that I didn't walk in here to bluff. Tom and Emily and I have set a plan in motion. While you and I are in your office, Tom is interviewing your neighbors, and Emily has already spoken to Jackson."

"I don't know what Tom expects to discover and I'm not worried. As for Emily, I saw Jacks last Sunday and he told me about her visit. Then he called me Wednesday night after their telephone conversation. I must say, Giovanni, the three of you have been busy. But I've known Jackson a long time and he trusts me."

"That's his mistake," I replied. I could sense my frustration growing and continued, "You should know, Giuseppe, that we're not finished yet. No matter what Tom finds out today, I intend to talk to Jackson myself. And, in case you forgot, I can be just as persuasive as you." That actually was a bluff. And he knew it. Getting through to Jackson would require more than just a little convincing from a familiar face. Still, I decided to press on.

"My impression is that Jackson is a somewhat innocent and sweet guy. I think I can get him to see the real you. Emily planted seeds of doubt about Jean-Paul's death and proving you orchestrated it will still be difficult. But that's only a secondary goal. We don't need to prove that you had him murdered."

"Meaning what?" he asked.

"I just want to water the seeds, make Jackson a little uncomfortable, a little more unsure of himself and of you. I think he'll crack under the pressure and admit the affair. What I'm seeking now is to unmask your relationship and bring your candidacy to an end. I doubt that you really love Jackson. But whether you do or not, America's not ready for a gay president."

"So then," he replied, "we really are twins. Ruthlessness is in our blood."

"No. I don't want to hurt Jackson. But I can't sit back and watch you get elected president, either."

"Admit it, Giovanni. You want revenge."

"Against you? Absolutely. But I also want justice for Yolanda and Carmen, Gina and Leonardo. I loved them and they deserve to have you pay for what you did."

Giuseppe did not even flinch at the sound of their names. His gaze intensified as if his only concern was plotting his next move. When he next spoke his voice was cold, calculating.

"I have to give you credit, Giovanni—you, Tom, Emily. You're all passionate. But you've set your goals a little high. Do you really think I don't have plans for every contingency?" His arrogance was unbelievably offensive. "I've been manipulating you and Tom from the beginning. I admit I was initially caught off guard when you brought Emily into this. But I recovered quickly. It does not matter what your next move is. You can't win this."

"What happened to you, Sep?" His familiar nickname, which I had steadfastly avoided using for three years, slipped absentmindedly from my lips. The icy anger that had driven me through the conversation subsided into a helpless depression. "At what point did you turn into this soulless monster?"

"That's such a relative question, Giovanni. We merely view the world differently. From my perspective I evolved, whereas you are trapped in ancient myths of good and evil."

"And you prefer the company of tyrants?" I asked.

"Not exactly. Your language, like your worldview, is too narrow, too absolute. Most of the 'tyrants' as you call them have made the mistake of strong-arming people rather than cajoling them."

"You mean deceiving," I corrected.

"No, Giovanni. People need a leader, someone who can provide inspiration and direction. There may be such a thing as mass hallucination, but there is no collective vision. That is why Plato described the philosopher king as the best form of government."

"So now you want to be a king?"

"Wrong again," he answered patronizingly. "I have a better appreciation of democracy than Plato did, mainly because I think America got it fundamentally right. We don't need a king. We need a president who is not beholden to a party and we need parties that are driven by more than their own self-interest."

I began to wonder if he was totally delusional. It was not that I disagreed with him. It was his hypocrisy. Everything he did was to advance his own agenda—personally and professionally. He was in no position to either lecture or lead. I was not going to let him distract me from my purpose.

"Giuseppe, I did not come here to discuss your views on politics. I came to warn you. Your career is over."

He started to laugh and said, "Oh, Giovanni, you amuse me. What are you going to do? Your Catholic faith has you tongue-tied. You're no threat to me."

"It's not what I'm going to do," I replied, "not exactly. I told you I'm going to talk to Jackson. When I'm finished, he'll do the rest."

"Listen, Gio." He had not called me by that name for a long time. Still, there was no affection in it. "You don't know Jackson. The bond between us is unbreakable. Have at it, though, and do your best. And something else . . ."

"What?" I asked.

"I'm bored and I have other things to do. I wasn't all that interested in seeing you today. But I set aside the time because you asked. I had no idea you were going to come in and try to threaten me. Now, as you know, I'm in a campaign and need to get back to work. So, have a good flight home." It might have been my imagination, but despite his rudeness and typical arrogance, there was a soupçon of caution. He stood up, opened the door, and waited for me to leave.

As I exited his office and the Hart Building I wondered if I had achieved my goal. My intent was to put him off his game, distract him enough that he would make a mistake. At least I had put him on notice.

I had agreed to meet Tom later that afternoon at a restaurant where we would share the day's activities over a meal. We were both on a much tighter budget than Giuseppe, but we were in Washington, D.C. For me that meant having crab cakes. Tom, on the other hand, was very much the meat and potatoes kind of detective. We figured we could afford dinner at the Old Ebbitt Grill where the food is as great as its reputation. And given that it originated in the 1800s as a saloon, we were both quite at home.

I arrived at the restaurant first and took the liberty of ordering an eighteen-year-old Glenlivet scotch for each of us—neat. I sipped mine slowly and he walked in about ten minutes later.

"How did the sleuthing go?" I asked.

"It was not a very productive afternoon, Gio," he replied. "I may have to retract some of my criticisms of the D.C. police."

"You got nothing?"

"Nothing compromising. But I think I know why your brother lives in Georgetown instead of the city like so many other politicians. In the rich suburbs people don't seem to give a shit what their neighbors do. They don't even know each other. I went to every home on Thirty-Third Street. Some didn't know that Giuseppe lived there until he entered the primary race. Others didn't find out until the media hounded him following the first *Times* article. Only one woman had ever seen Jackson at Giuseppe's house. That was only three or four times in the last six months. It didn't raise any suspicions."

"Was she sure it was Jackson? Did you show her a picture?"

"Christ, Gio, of course I did. Who's the detective here anyway?" His wry smile reminded me that when it came to police work we were in his ballpark. "She was pretty sure it was Jackson. But it doesn't matter. Even if her identification holds up, she only saw him a couple of times and there was nothing out of the ordinary. Face it. Giuseppe was way too cautious. Like everything else he covered his tracks."

He had downed his drink quickly so as not to fall behind. We ordered a second round and he said hopefully, "I trust you fared better than I did."

"Not much, I'm afraid. Needless to say, Giuseppe admitted nothing. Then again that's not why I went to see him. I was surprised by one thing, though. He didn't seem bothered when I told him we knew about his sexual relationship with Jackson. In fact, it was almost as if he expected me to say that."

"How can that be?" Tom asked. "From everything we know and what little I discovered today, it's clear he's gone to great lengths to conceal their affair."

"I don't know. I just know he didn't care."

I filled him in on the rest of the conversation including Giuseppe's musings about political philosophy and my frustration with his unmitigated arrogance.

"Gio," Tom said, "I know he's your brother, but what a fucking asshole."

"Hey, you get no argument from me on that point," I replied.

We ordered a bottle of wine along with dinner. Or in our case, I guess food is always the complement to what we are drinking.

"When are you going to speak with Jackson?" Tom asked.

"I don't know yet. I just wish that we weren't always eating Giuseppe's dust. I'd like to get out in front for a change."

We finished dinner and decided to move to the bar in order to experience the full ambience of this legendary saloon. The next morning we took a flight back to Los Angeles.

CHAPTER 24

The *Los Angeles Times's* saga heated up on Sunday, November 16, with the headline "**SENATOR LOZANO'S LAWYER MURDERED DURING POLICE PROBE**." If Tom had not already resigned from the police department, and if Chief Bratton were in the process of deciding his fate, this might have sealed it. Emily used the contents of Tom's personal notes and internal police files to draw a straight line from the Lozano family murders to that of Coker. She linked her third story to the night of September 21, 2000, when Yolanda, Carmen, Gina, and Leonardo were all killed.

A file had gone missing from a safe in the master bedroom. Only Giuseppe, Yolanda, and Coker had the combination. According to my brother, the file contained the detailed schematics for a missile guidance system, the critical element being the computer chip design. The crime scene indicated that Yolanda had been forced to open the safe, but it appeared that the killers had not rifled through its contents, instead forcing her to retrieve the specific document.

Even in a case as personal as this one Emily did her best to present her material with objectivity. She reported on Coker's flight to Grand Cayman September 23, two days after the murders. Although planned in July it certainly raised a question of propriety. Why was the trip not postponed? Did Coker know something about the missing file? Then there was the coincidence of Coker's own death only hours after speaking with Giuseppe. Emily left her readers speculating. Could the police have been correct about blackmail as a motive? Or was something more sinister at play? And if so, who was behind it? She did not directly connect Giuseppe, but she had certainly turned up the heat.

•　　•　　•

While the city of Los Angeles was raptly following Emily's narrative, Tom started his Sunday with another effort at engaging outside assistance. As he had done with his counterparts in D.C., he called a friend in the Boston Police Department, a detective by the name of Diego Rivera. He was a few years Tom's junior, but they became friends while taking training at the FBI National Academy in Washington, D.C., in the early eighties. It was at that same training when they both met NYPD detective Lt. Miguel Moreno. Unlike Moreno who left New York and joined the U.S. Marshals Service, Tom and Diego remained with their respective departments. Rivera was energetic and talented. Best of all, he was discreet. Without revealing too much information Tom claimed to be working on a case that might be connected to Jean-Paul's death in Brussels. Since he and Jackson had lived together in Boston for seventeen years, Tom asked Rivera to interview some of their neighbors. If anything were amiss in the last several months, it might have been noticed. He said nothing about Giuseppe.

This was a long shot and Tom knew it. Since Giuseppe had been so careful in Washington he was not likely to have made a mistake in a less affluent neighborhood in a distant city. Also, when Emily had visited Jackson she saw no pictures of him and Giuseppe together anywhere in the Boston area. Still, things were moving quickly now and we needed something before the *Los Angeles Times* articles faded from the public's attention.

Tuesday, November 18, was my regular day off. A reliable constant in my life, it meant getting together with my priest friends. Sometimes we joked that it was more than a constant. It was a rut. This particular week Tim McGowan did not join us. But Perry Leiker, Gilbert Cruz, and I met up with Bill Messenger at the USC Catholic Center. We were in the parking lot of La Adelita Mexican Restaurant when the doors opened at eleven. After lunch we went to see *The Matrix Revolutions*. The final installment in the *Matrix* trilogy, it had been released on November 5. Since we were in the middle of

221

the week, some thirteen days after its opening, there was only a modest crowd at the cinema.

Following the movie our lack of Tuesday creativity found us in Tower Records on Sunset Boulevard. For Perry and Bill that meant checking out the latest classical releases, especially offerings from Neville Marriner and The Academy of St. Martin-in-the-Fields. I spent my time in the jazz and vocal section looking for re-releases of some of the great artists. Among my favorites were Nat King Cole, Sarah Vaughan, Ella Fitzgerald, Louis Armstrong, Carmen McCrae, and Dinah Washington.

In retrospect Gilbert may have been the smartest among us. Nobody had much money and he decided to keep his. If not reading a book in the car, he could be found in a corner of the store purchasing nothing, simply enjoying the soulful sounds of Motown. He prided himself on his ability to identify all the artists whose voices were coming through the speakers: the Miracles, the Supremes, the Temptations, the Marvelettes, pretty much anyone ever signed to the label. After far too much time in Tower Records we went out for drinks and dinner.

I returned home about ten that night and had several messages waiting for me from Tom. That was not only unusual, they were all marked "urgent." I called right away.

"Where the hell have you been?" he asked.

"It's my day off, Tom. I was with the guys. What's up?"

"Detective Rivera from the Boston PD called a couple of hours ago."

"You have some news already?" I asked.

"Yeah," he replied. "And it's not good. Jackson's dead."

"What the fuck!" I exclaimed. I quickly sat down in the nearest chair as Tom continued.

"It gets better, Gio. He was murdered."

"Son of a bitch." I didn't even know Jackson, but tears began welling up in my eyes. I don't know if it was shock, anger, depression, or a combination of all three, but I couldn't control my emotions. I was suddenly overwhelmed by an inescapable sense of defeat and could feel the energy drain instantly from every part of my being. Eventually I managed to muster a simple question. "What happened?"

"You can already guess the M.O.," Tom replied. "Jackson's death mirrors that of Coker's three years ago. Apparently he went out for a walk around eight o'clock. He was shot once through the heart and a Glock 9mm pistol was left at the scene."

I leaned back in my chair, closed my eyes, and dispassionately asked, "And my brother?"

"His ass is covered, as usual. He was at a meeting with a half-dozen senators. His business card was found in Jackson's wallet and since Giuseppe's pretty well known these days, Rivera called and gave him the news."

"Except it wasn't news," I observed.

"You know that and I know that," Tom replied.

For a few moments there was just silence on the line. I was trying to absorb the information. Tom knew me well enough to sense what I was going through and waited patiently for me to speak. "How's Emily?" I asked.

"She's pretty upset right now. She thinks she pushed Jackson too hard."

"It wasn't suicide," I replied.

"No, but she knew he would call Giuseppe and she thinks that put him in danger."

"Shit, Tom, just knowing my brother puts a person in danger. Besides I probably made things worse when I met with him the other day. I let him know that Jackson was the weak link in his defense. But when it comes right down to it, only one person is to blame—Giuseppe."

"Gio, why don't you come over and have a scotch? None of us is going to sleep for a while anyway."

"Thanks, Tom, but I don't feel like going anywhere tonight. I need to think." I took a deep breath and said, "We have to end this before anybody else gets killed."

"I hope you're not going to do anything rash," he said. I could hear the consternation, almost fear, in his voice.

"Of course not. But he is my brother."

"That doesn't make you responsible for him."

"I know that," I replied. "But we're not just brothers. We're twins and I should know him better. It makes me wonder. Did I overplay my hand last Saturday? I told Giuseppe that we were about to end his career."

"That is our plan," Tom assured me.

"Yeah. So I wonder—would Jackson still be alive if I hadn't promised to use him as a trump card?"

"For God's sake, Gio, you're overthinking this. Still, we've known each other all our lives and I know when you need space and when you need to be alone. Why don't you get some rest now? We can talk tomorrow."

"All right," I replied. "I'll call you in the morning. Good night, Tom. And give my love to Emily."

"Good night, Gio."

Over the next several hours I was rescued by neither rest nor sleep. I instinctively understood that even a stiff drink would not relieve the troubles of my mind. I allowed myself to succumb to the perennial, and usually unanswerable, questions.

Who was this man walking around with my face? Standing next to each other, even some of our friends could not tell us apart. As children we enjoyed role-playing characters from books and movies. But at forty-nine I now felt haunted by the imagination of the French novelist Alexandre Dumas. I had become the "Man in the Iron Mask," the difference between fiction and reality being that I knew I had an evil twin ascending the rungs of power. Despite our DNA, I no longer knew my brother.

What had happened to Giuseppe? Ours was a happy childhood and typical adolescence. Our parents guaranteed us advantages they themselves did not have, such as a college education. They supported our goals and aspirations. They kept us close as a family even after my brother and sister married and I entered the priesthood. There had been no tragedies in his adult life. Now, at the very core of his being, he was a changed man.

When did Giuseppe change? Everyone grows and develops over time, and his evolution into someone driven by ambition and financial success was evident. That was not abnormal. But he had always been a man who loved. In the twenty years that he and Yolanda were married they brought three sweet and beautiful children into the world. They were a happy family. Somewhere along the line he surrendered that love for what—power?

Why did Giuseppe become a killer? That was the hardest question of all. There is no evidence that he would have lost his senate race if Yolanda and the kids had lived. But maybe their deaths had nothing to do with the election. His subsequent actions raised the specter that he had long been fighting other demons. In the intervening years since his family's murders, I came to realize that he'd lost the battles and the war.

I closed my eyes and sat for a long while, exhausted but unable to sleep. I didn't even have the energy to get up and fix a drink, not that I needed one. In the absence of satisfactory answers to my questions, my mind began to play tricks and I feared that just asking them was a subconscious way to defend Giuseppe. That was not the case, of course. There was no way I could ever justify what my brother had done. Nor would I try.

Eventually I fell asleep in the chair, not waking until the rays of the morning sun lighted the room. My first thought of the day was the same as the last one of the night. Could it be that my brother had always been a psychopath and no one ever knew it?

●　　●　　●

Tom did not wait for me to call. At ten o'clock my phone rang.

"Good morning, Gio. Did you get any sleep last night?"

"Not much," I replied. "How about you?"

"I went to bed about midnight, but it was not a very restful sleep. I know you said you would call this morning, but I just finished a long conversation with Detective Rivera from Boston."

"What did he want now?" I asked.

"When he told me of Jackson's death I said nothing about Giuseppe. But Rivera's no fool. He's a very intelligent cop with a bright future. The fact that the murder took place only a couple of days after I asked him to talk to Jackson's neighbors did not go unnoticed. Much of the Boston media, like outlets around the country, reported on Emily's articles in the *Los Angeles Times*. Rivera has started to assemble the puzzle. He realizes that Jackson and Coker were killed in identical fashion and he wants to know what we know."

"Everything he needs is in Emily's articles," I suggested.

"He thinks I'm holding something back. Obviously I can't tell him about the confessions. What Giuseppe told you is secret, what he told me, or at the least the way he did it, is unbelievable. So far I don't think Rivera has connected Giuseppe to Jean-Paul. But that's only a matter of time."

"Then what did you say to him?" I asked.

"I must be getting old, Gio. I gave him advice."

We both started to chuckle.

"Well, we've each certainly aged over the last three years. But I don't know why either one of us is laughing. It's not really funny."

"It's that release of tension that people always talk about," he said.

"Tell me, Tom. What was your advice?"

"Now that I think of it, it was kind of foolish. I told him to do something no decent cop can—just forget about the case. Without mentioning your brother I acknowledged that it had to be the same killer, and I assured him that this assassin makes no mistakes."

We both knew that to be true, but Tom probably appreciated the reality more than anyone. He had seen a lot of crimes and too many murders. More often than not the perpetrator is apprehended. This was different. He had never encountered a professional like this one. There would be no loose ends.

Tom continued, "I reminded him that there is no statute of limitations for murder. Maybe eventually evidence would surface, but it wouldn't be now. I didn't convince him, though. I've known Rivera for more than fifteen years. He's tenacious."

"Then he'll discover that you're right in his own time," I said.

"It's not that simple, Gio. Look what happened to us. Rivera has a bright future, and I don't want to see his career sidelined because of Giuseppe."

"I think I might be able to help with that. But first I have to call my brother."

"What are you planning?" he asked.

"Actually, it's something I've been thinking about for a long time. Giuseppe has always been a couple steps ahead because he knows us so well."

"Yeah," he said somewhat skeptically.

"Suppose I do something completely out of character, something he would never conceive in his wildest imagination?"

"I'm afraid to ask what you have in mind."

"I'll tell you tonight over dinner. Why don't you and Emily come here around seven thirty?"

"OK. See you tonight."

•

November is a mostly cool month in Los Angeles, and that Wednesday evening was far too cold for a barbecue. Since the other priests had their dinner at six o'clock, the kitchen and dining room were free for me and my guests. I fixed a simple meal: a mixed green salad, pork chops, and sweet peas and rice flavored with butter and garlic. Of course, given that the three of us were together we began with the evening with drinks. Tom and I shared some Glenlivet Archive, a truly classic twenty-one-year-old scotch. Emily, however, decided to limit herself to wine so I opened a 1995 Silver Oak Cabernet Sauvignon from Napa Valley. I wanted to toast Jackson, but that struck me as being a bit macabre. Instead we just started drinking.

"OK, Gio," Tom said. "We're here. Tell us what you were thinking about this morning."

"I want to call a press conference."

"For what?" Tom asked.

"Let me back up a minute," I said. "I want to phone Giuseppe and tell him that I'm setting up a press conference. I want to play a bluff—of sorts."

"What kind of bluff?" Tom asked apprehensively.

"Giuseppe knows that I will not reveal anything he might have said in a confession. But that doesn't mean that I can't make a public statement that I know he had his family killed. I don't have to explain how I know. Just the fact that I, his twin brother and a priest, is the one saying it will carry weight. I certainly have nothing to gain by falsely accusing him."

"I don't like this," Emily said. "You know what your brother's like. This is too risky, especially if you alert him ahead of time."

I inhaled a deep breath, heaved a sigh, and responded, "I've already anticipated all the objections the two of you will raise. Yes, I'm taking a chance. But while all gambles are unnecessary, some risks are unavoidable."

Tom almost spit out his drink when he heard me say that and probably would have spoken if he hadn't started coughing. That left an opening for Emily.

"You're quite cleaver, Gio. You always have been. But this is not a game or a school debate. I'm uncomfortable with you matching wits against your brother."

"Isn't that what we've been doing for the last several weeks?" I asked.

"No," she replied. "We have not been trying to outsmart Giuseppe. We have been trying to get Giuseppe to outsmart himself."

"For God's sake," Tom interjected. "Do the two of you have to speak in riddles?"

We just ignored him and moved to the table to begin eating while the meal was still hot. As Emily and Tom were dishing up I poured each of us some wine. Then I sat down and we continued our discussion.

"Listen," I said. "We've been operating under the assumption that putting pressure on Giuseppe, through direct confrontation, newspaper articles, and innuendo would create some unease and cause him to make a mistake. But he wasn't afraid of us. The only thing we accomplished was to get Jackson killed. I want to instill real fear in him. That's where he'll slip up."

"I don't know," Emily replied. "This leaves me feeling uneasy. Your brother is too unpredictable these days, too irrational."

"Actually, I think he's super-rational and that may be what makes my plan work."

"How so?" Tom asked.

"He's cold, calculating," I answered. "The last time I talked to him he said he has a plan for every contingency. But that's only for the things he can predict. He admitted that involving Emily had initially caught him unaware. And although he adjusted to that reality, it gave me a glimpse into his weakness. He can't plan for things he doesn't know will happen. Nobody can do that."

"Then why alert him to the press conference ahead of time?" Emily asked.

I should have found it easy to answer that question. I was sitting with two of my most trusted friends. They were among a handful of people I could share my innermost feelings with. But the previous night I came to realize that for years I had not been entirely honest with myself. Now I found it difficult to bare my thoughts even to them. Still, these friends deserved the truth.

"It's the twin in me," I replied.

"What do you mean?" Tom asked.

"Giuseppe and I are not entirely different. I've been telling myself that our value systems are so disparate, that we possess such different ambitions, that nothing alike remains except our looks. But that's not true. On some deep level we share arrogance. He thinks that no one is a match for him. I think I am."

To make my point I poured the last of the wine, lifted and tilted my glass toward them, drained it, then set it down with a clear air of confidence and determination. They looked at each other worriedly.

Emily tried to assure me. "The two of you are not the same, Gio. You're not a psychopath."

"No, I'm not. I have a conscience. But there are things about him that I understand. I have an ego equal to his and a need to prove it."

"To whom?" Tom asked.

"Hold that thought," I said, then went to retrieve another bottle of wine. After decanting it and pouring a little in each of our glasses I sat back down.

"I need to prove it to him." I leaned toward Tom and said, "You've known us since we were six. He and I took such diverse paths in adulthood that we never had to live in each other's shadow. Still, he was far more accomplished than I. And over the years he found subtle ways of letting me know it—not just that he'd achieved more than I had, but that he was superior."

"So now you want to live out some sibling rivalry, to win some childish game?" he asked.

"It's not about winning. It's about conquering. And it's not childish. He put us, all of us, in a very grown-up situation of life and death. You two answered the challenge and put your careers on the line. It's time for me to do the same thing. Besides, it's the only play we have left."

CHAPTER 25

If Detective Rivera of the Boston PD suspected Tom of holding back information, his conjecture was verified by the *Los Angeles Times*. On Thursday morning the city awoke to the headline: "**DEATHS IN BELGIUM LINKED TO LOZANO MURDERS**."

To write her previous article Emily had relied heavily on Tom's notes ending it with uncertainties about Coker's trip to Grand Cayman, the missing file, the possibility of blackmail, and his own mysterious death. Those questions were built upon innuendo and were intended to fuel speculation as her writing mimicked Tom's narration of the events and the investigation.

In Emily's newest installment in the series she detailed information about the murders of Jean-Paul Lecuyer and his friends in Belgium earlier in the year. They occurred on Sunday, April 13, in the capital city, Brussels. These killings were marked by the same mystery as all the Los Angeles murders: One precision 9mm shot through the heart or head for each victim and an untraceable Glock handgun left at the scene.

As Emily noted that similarity she also took the first clear steps toward connecting Giuseppe to the murders. For this article she was careful not to imply his guilt, content merely to raise more questions. The takeaway for the readers was that other than the assassin, only Giuseppe could be linked with the victims.

. . .

Los Angeles is in the Pacific Time Zone, three hours behind Washington. That same Thursday morning I rose at five and took a quick shower. I wanted to call my brother early in his day, and that conversation would require me to be fresh and alert. Coffee brewed in the kitchen while I showered and was ready by the time I dressed. Without scripting the entire talk, I knew what I wanted to say to him. As such I was as prepared as possible for what would be yet another agonizing discussion with Giuseppe. He answered the phone on the second ring.

"Hello," he said.

At that early an hour and perhaps because the day was predicted to be one of nearly perfect weather, I had an immediate, visceral reaction to the sound of his voice. But I had to keep all emotions under tight control.

There was no need to identify myself. It didn't matter anyway. He gave me no opportunity. As soon as I said, "Giuseppe," he cut me off.

"Well, if it isn't my dear brother!"

I had grown quite accustomed to his condescension and dismissive tone of voice. Ever since his confession three years before he had acted as if he owned me. For that I was partly to blame. During that time I had been paralyzed by the demands of my Catholic faith and the secrecy surrounding the Sacrament of Reconciliation. I could talk to no one. There were a couple of brief excursions into that forbidden territory, but they were limited to conversations only with my brother. I was willing to bend the rule that far because he was in no position to object.

I repeated his name, attempting to make clear that I was in no mood for his nonsense. "Giuseppe, I heard about Jackson." My voice carried with it an unmistakable ring of accusation.

I paused for a few moments but he said nothing. I knew they had been in a relationship, a sexual one, but had no idea how close they really were. After what had happened to his wife and children, I wondered if he could truly love anyone.

I recalled the fateful night of September 21, 2000. Giuseppe and I sat on the living room couch, the bodies of Yolanda, Carmen, Gina, and Leonardo lifelessly lying upstairs. I held him in my arms as we both dissolved in tears. At the time he appeared as genuinely distraught as I.

Three months after the murders I learned that he had contracted to have his family killed. When he confessed this evil to me, he was not the same person I sat beside the night of the murders. And yet he was exactly the same. Not even Robert Lewis Stevenson who created the duality of Jekyll and Hyde could have dreamed up a character as twisted as my twin brother.

Now I found myself speaking with him about yet another murder and this one required no confession for me to identify the responsible party. This was just the latest in a litany of deaths all orchestrated to serve his delusional designs—his self-centered thirst for power, glory, legacy. Who knows what desires and drives inhabit such a mind?

Giuseppe did not break his silence so I repeated my statement. "I heard about Jackson. Do you have nothing to say about your friend, about his death? Let me rephrase that. Have you nothing to say about his murder?"

This time he answered, but his speech was not laced with hostility or arrogance or condescension. Neither did I hear remorse or even a hint of sorrow or sadness. Giuseppe sounded distant, emotionless; not quite cold or unfocused. In fact, quite the opposite. It was as if his mind had transported him to Boston, perhaps to Jackson's home, as if he might be conjuring the image of his dead friend.

"I guess there's no harm in admitting that you were right about Jackson and me. We were lovers. But it was not the tawdry or superficial affair you implied in our last conversation. You're a good priest, Giovanni, but you've been wrong about me on a number of things."

I was not easily disoriented in discussion. But Giuseppe was beginning to sound like someone from an alternate universe. Was he about to justify his actions? I decided to root him firmly in our reality.

"Are you suggesting I was wrong about all the murders?"

For once Giuseppe needed to exercise caution. What if I were taping this conversation? The Silencer that he was so proud of did not work over telephone lines. It would not render a recording on my end inoperable. He spoke with care.

"What you know about the murders, you know. What you surmise may be inaccurate."

"That's pretty safe and noncommittal, Giuseppe. What are you afraid of? This conversation is between the two of us only. I'm not making a recording, if that's what concerns you. Please, feel free to speak openly."

We had grown far apart over the last several years. Despite that fact, if he was certain about anything, it was that I never lied to him.

"OK, Giovanni," he replied. "I trust you."

I almost wanted to choke when I heard those words. I didn't care if he trusted me or not. I was more interested in his knowing that I was serious than in knowing that I spoke truthfully.

"Giuseppe, I already know about Yolanda and the kids. Am I wrong about the other murders?"

"No."

That was too quick, too easy. It was a good thing that I had not planned or composed this dialogue. The script would already have been discarded.

"Then tell me, in what way am I wrong about you?"

"First let me share an observation. I said you're a good priest. But I get the impression that you divorce the present from the past. Maybe it has something to do with your idea of forgiveness. I don't know. But you don't seem to grasp the formative elements of history."

"Giuseppe, I'm not interested in another philosophical discussion with you."

"Nor am I," he replied. "But just listen for a moment. Every one of us is a composite of the things that happen in our past—good and bad. If you want to know who I am, wake your memory and recall when we were in our twenties. I did not fully comprehend what was happening to me in Boston. I was young. But I know now that I was in love with Jackson. It was not some mere obsession or desire. Sexual feelings are often quite transient. Love is not. I tried to put him out of my mind, to suppress my feelings for him, but they never really left me."

"Why are you telling me this?" I asked.

"Because I want you to know that I loved Jackson."

"I don't really believe you, Giuseppe. I also don't trust you. But even if what you say is true, it doesn't explain the trail of death you've left. People don't kill for love."

"Jesus, Giovanni, what world do you live in? People have been killing for love for centuries."

I hated being manipulated by my brother. I didn't call to listen to his nonsense and I was beginning to grow angry. There was no vindicating the choices he had made. He was responsible for killing ten people. And he certainly did not do it out of love.

"Suppose you're right. Put history aside for a moment. You say you loved Jackson. Then why did you have him killed?" I asked.

"Search your own soul for the answer to that question. In our last conversation you opened my eyes and in so doing you sealed his fate. After you hung up I realized that he was the weak link in my defense, just as you said. That link had to be eliminated. And that one cost me dearly."

"I'm not responsible for Jackson's death, Giuseppe. That's all on you. But this is disturbing. Do you feel any anguish, regret, anything at all?"

"I already told you that I loved him. Since you don't believe me you won't understand anything else I say."

This conversation was not even close to what I had anticipated, and even with the energy of the morning sun I was beginning to feel drained. But I was on a mission and wanted him to fully appreciate what was about to come.

"This is a courtesy call, Giuseppe. And although you don't deserve warning, I'm calling a press conference for Monday afternoon. You might want to watch."

"And why is that?" he asked.

For all the differences between us there were still strong similarities. I couldn't help being drawn into his world of gamesmanship and wanted him to know that this time I held the high hand.

"Giuseppe, how well do you know your Shakespeare?"

"Well enough to know that I am not a king and you are not holding a dagger."

"Not a physical one, but words can be just as deadly. I happen to agree with Brutus. The debt of your ambition is about to be paid. Except I won't be knifing you in the back."

He remained cool and calm, his response indicating no alarm.

"I suppose you're going to say something about me on Monday," he said.

"You like playing memory games, Sep." *Goddammit*, I thought to myself. I hated the familiarity of that nickname. Nonetheless I continued, hoping he would not comment on my use of it. "Think back to last Saturday when I promised I would bring you down. That's exactly what I intend to do at the press conference."

He suddenly became dismissive again. "I'm not really worried, Gio. You think you know me. But don't forget. I know you, too. Growing up I always thought you were more intelligent than I. When we became adults I learned that you were also weaker. You can't make the hard calls. You're not going to betray your faith."

"I don't think I need to," I answered. "I will simply state that I know you had your family killed. Why shouldn't people believe me? We're not opponents in a race, we're not competing for a prize. We're twin brothers. If I make such a bold claim, there must be a reason. I'll leave people to surmise their own conclusions. It should be enough to bring your career to an end."

"You're a good speaker, Giovanni, and I've always admired your talents. But there is a big difference between preaching to a captive congregation and speaking before the press. In church you're trying to persuade people to believe something they are already disposed to accept. Convincing a very skeptical media of something that sounds utterly ridiculous and incredible and unprovable is entirely different. Do you really think you possess the eloquence to succeed, to 'bring me down' as you say?"

If nothing else, he would take his hauteur attitude to the grave. For a long time I had wanted to believe that there was still some good in him. Yet every time we spoke he peeled off another veneer of hope.

"Giovanni, I did not get where I am by being outwitted," he said. "I will not be so easy for you to defeat."

He may have been correct about that. Emily had already raised suspicion in her writings and he would probably eventually lose in the court of public opinion. What contribution could I add? But then I thought about the ten people who had died because of him, four of whom I deeply loved. I thought about Tom whose career ended because of Giuseppe. How could I linger in the shadows? Should I not put as much on the line as Tom had?

"Giuseppe, you have tried to shroud your actions. But to me you've become transparent, your world made of glass."

"Perhaps," he replied. "But one advantage of living in a glass house is being able to see who else lives in one. You don't have what it takes to follow through on this threat."

"For God's sake, Giuseppe, you're not a Sith Lord," I replied. "You may grow closer to your desires with every death, but you do not grow more powerful and you are not invincible. In fact, considering that your career was built on the graves of your wife and children, and now your lover, you must be in a constant state of unease. You can't be as sure, as confident, as you pretend. And I'd be willing to bet you're not really happy."

"Giovanni," he replied, "please don't waste your mind tricks on me. Save them for Monday and good luck trying to convince the press."

His tone of voice had changed again. He no longer sounded merely arrogant. He was defiant. I offered one last thought.

"My suggestion is that you watch the press conference with a few close friends—if you have any left. You'll need their support." I didn't even bother to say goodbye. I just hung up.

I put music on the stereo, poured another cup of coffee and then sat down and began to think. I was uncomfortable and it was not just the whole saga of murder and revenge that had so consumed me these last years. Nor was it my impending encounter with the media.

I had been unable to forgive my brother and unwilling to try. I put all my effort into hating him. And in that I was quite successful. But the vortex of my faith kept drawing me deeper and deeper into confrontation with God. Unlike Giuseppe I would not be called to account for heinous acts of murder. Yet within me resided something just as dark and even more profound. I was in contempt of conscience.

I had regularly preached about reconciliation and forgiveness. Initially, my thoughts were premised on theological constructs. What is at once the most succinct and profound definition of God occurs in the First Letter of John, "God is love." From that it follows that reconciliation and healing are intrinsic to the divine. They are based not on the merits of the offender but on the nature of God who loves everyone and forgives even those who do not ask it. Without forgiveness—universal and unconditional—God is diminished to, at best, a super-human being and probably a capricious one at that.

The words, the ideas, all made sense. However, implementing them in my personal life was something different. Hate had come so easily. With the exception of Tom and Emily no one knew what I was experiencing. I realized that refusing to accept the call of God left my preaching hollow. I knew that love is not a feeling. It is a decision. I knew that I had been asked to love my brother. I simply didn't want to. I was not prepared to stand face to face with God.

Priest or not, I was unready to surrender myself to these particular demands of faith. I sought refuge in a world where my soul was insignificant, a world where God could wait. A more immediate task was at hand. I could not let Giuseppe pursue the presidency unchallenged. People had a right to know the truth and I reasoned that telling them would bring me a measure of peace.

As if all that were not vexing enough, something even more troubling was gnawing at my resolve. To halt my brother's rise to power, to achieve justice for those martyred before his ego, I was going to have to do more than I had threatened.

CHAPTER 26

I spent the rest of Thursday in a self-imposed seclusion, except for Tom and Emily. I agreed to have dinner at their home that evening and fill them in on my conversation with Giuseppe. My other friends had offered unwavering support over the previous three years, and while certainly capable of understanding, they knew nothing of who my brother was or what I was about to do. Tom and Emily did. But they were in the dark about one aspect.

In my years of seminary training I occasionally questioned rules of the Catholic Church, but never the principles of the sacraments. The seal of confession is not a rule, anyway. It is intrinsic to the church's ministry, to its ability to provide peace and elicit change in people's lives. Since we are all sinners it is easy to comprehend the confidentiality that accompanies the Sacrament of Reconciliation. It surpasses every form of secrecy whether the affection and trust of a great friendship or the certainty of attorney-client privilege. The seal is of such extreme magnitude that it admits no exceptions. It is not a rule. The consequence for violating it is.

Giuseppe had counted on that from the beginning at least from the day he first admitted to having his family killed. It was as if he had been playing a macabre game of chess but there was nothing noble or legendary about his moves. I had to acknowledge that his outmaneuvering Tom was ingenious. On the other hand, the way he chose to silence me was pure evil. The principle underlying every game is to play within the rules, not to manipulate them. His abuse of the sacrament had effectively reduced me from a bishop to a rook. With no diagonal means of putting him in check, he was free to roam about. This, of course was no game. But in life as in chess, if someone knows every move you're going to make, you need to do something out of the ordinary, something unanticipated.

• • •

Emily suspected that I might need comfort food that evening, which, of course, means carbohydrates. She prepared a fresh Caesar salad, homemade garlic bread, and a spectacular lasagna. She did not bother with a dessert since Tom and I as frequently as not took ours out of a bottle. I arrived just in time for dinner and we sat right down to eat. I could tell that they were both a little anxious about my morning call with Giuseppe. We wasted no time getting to the discussion.

"You're the one with all the information tonight," Tom said. "What happened?"

My first few words could have been the beginning of a song.

"Have I told you lately that I hate my brother?"

"Once or twice," Tom replied. He was trying to start the conversation off nice and easy, to prevent me from casting a pall over our meal. But I didn't smile. I was barely able to manage a slight curl on one side of my mouth.

"I began by telling him that I knew about Jackson. At first he didn't respond. I took his silence as an avowal. He went on to admit their relationship but claimed they were truly in love."

I leaned back, tilted my head up, closed my eyes, and sighed. I had done precious little during the day, but I was exhausted. Emily reached over and placed her hand on my arm.

"Gio," she said, "we don't have to talk about this tonight if you don't want to."

"Thanks, Em, but it's all right. I've been alone all day and I probably should talk to someone if only to maintain a little sanity."

"Did he say why he had Jackson killed?" Tom inquired.

"He blamed me for it."

"What?" Tom asked.

"Yeah. When I saw him last Saturday I suggested that Jackson would be his undoing. Although I didn't have proof that they were actually involved, I threatened to get Jackson to admit the affair. Apparently that pushed him over the edge."

Neither Tom nor Emily had a vocal reaction. Despite what all three of us had been through together I don't think either of them knew how to respond to that. After a brief silence I continued.

"Jackson was the latest sacrificial gift, one that Giuseppe offered to himself."

"Gio, in spite of what your brother says, you didn't cause this," Emily assured me.

"Oh, I know that, Em. As I listened to him on the phone the experience was even worse than when I saw him in person last weekend."

"What do you mean?" Tom asked.

"When I told him about the press conference he didn't seem concerned."

"Maybe he thought you were bluffing," Emily suggested. "Before you went to Washington that's what you called it."

"It was more than that. Sometimes I think he has the emotions of an adolescent who thinks himself invincible. But then I don't think he has any emotions at all. He has a black hole where his heart should be and it just sucks in everything. Like those unseen spaces in the universe nothing escapes—no light, no truth, no feelings."

"You really have been alone all day, haven't you!" Tom exclaimed.

"Tom," Emily cautioned.

"It's OK, Emily," I interjected. "Maybe I've been overthinking this. It has consumed my entire day." I looked at both of them and sighed. "I'm just so tired. I want all this to be over. But I really need to tell you something else tonight and it's not up for discussion."

I rarely spoke like that, at least not to the two of them, and I did not intend to sound so rude or abrupt. But neither of them objected. They just waited.

"I realized something while I was talking to Giuseppe this morning. Actually, I think I've been aware of it for a long time. I certainly knew it was a possibility." I paused and took a drink of wine. I had been so stressed out during the day that even the Charles Shaw Cabernet, while not a bad wine, tasted better than it was. I continued, "At the news conference on Monday I have to state how I know that Giuseppe had his family killed. I have to tell the press and the nation that he confessed."

Emily didn't respond. She sat silently as if some font of wisdom enabled her to foresee this turn of events. Tom on the other hand was quick to reply.

"You can't do that, Gio," he objected.

"What difference does it make to you?" I asked, maybe a little too dismissively. "You don't go to church anymore and refer to yourself as an agnostic."

"That's true. But you're my friend. And I remember what we learned in school. If you do this, your life as a priest is over."

"I know that, Tom. That's one of the things that makes this so difficult. That, and the fact that I still believe in the sacrament. But I'm not being impulsive. I told Cardinal Mahony three weeks ago that this might happen."

"How did he react?" Emily asked.

"About like your husband," I replied nodding toward Tom. "But he said more and reminded me of my obligation to the larger church. He also prayed with me."

"You never told us about that," she observed.

"I couldn't. I had also hoped to avoid sharing it tonight. But Giuseppe forced my hand. He is such an enigma."

"How so?" Tom asked.

"You mean other than the fact that the three of us grew up together, that we shared most of our lives together, that neither of us knew he was capable of killing ten people, that he has not even the slightest remorse? Or were you thinking of something else?"

That was not the first time that I regretted speaking words the instant they slipped my lips. But this was different. This was raw emotion surfacing unchecked, powering words unfiltered. The list I rattled off sounded pedantic and patronizing. He started to respond but Emily quickly caught his eye and silenced him. I hung my head for a moment ashamed of myself.

"I'm sorry, Tom," I said. "You don't deserve that. I have no right to take my frustrations out on you. Giuseppe is the source of my anger. I apologize."

I think Tom had been taken aback, maybe even hurt by my sarcasm. But he remained gracious.

"Forget it, Gio. When I was on the force there were times when I needed to blow off steam. We all do. And we need some place safe to do that venting. For you that place is here with me—and Emily. You and I have stood by each other for a long time, we've entrusted each other with feelings and secrets that we shared with no one else. I have always been there for you; I am here now and I will always be here for you."

Tom's tone and demeanor were such a contrast to my own. 'Music may have charms to soothe the savage breast,' as William Congreve once reflected. It is the reason sounds of Haydn, Mozart, Beethoven, and Schubert so frequently stream from my stereo. But there is another, equally powerful source of comfort and consolation. It is not the inspiration of the human spirit. It is the tenderness of the human heart expressed in loving and compassionate speech.

Consoled by Tom's words I realized that he, too, was an enigma, of a much different type from my brother. Fair or not, police have a near-universal reputation for being tough, unbending, even heartless. When he began his career Tom could have evolved into just such a cop. I give credit to Emily for saving him from that fate. He was a good, committed officer and an accomplished detective. What set him apart from others, certainly men like Jack Gorman, was Tom's empathy. It was on display in his response to my outburst.

I suppose I'm an enigma, also. Maybe we all are. Maybe nobody is normal, whatever that means. I had often been told that I was different from other priests. That was probably due less to my personality than to my intellectual orientation. The vast majority of priests are simply not as liberal as I am. In my conceit I consigned them to three categories: those who were ambitious for power and prestige, those who feared authority, and most cruelly of all, those who lacked vision. Perhaps it was too kind to call myself an enigma. But I was about to become even more so.

As they had throughout the entire ordeal, Tom and Emily proved my most valuable set of friends and greatest source of strength. Then again, they were the only ones who knew the truth. But I also had other friends, a core support group of twenty years. Although they did not know about my brother, they deserved to be notified of my plan. I called all the members together: Sr. Barbara Nixon; Brian and Judy Henderson; and the four priests, Perry Leiker, Bill Messenger, Tim McGowan, and Gilbert Cruz. I asked them to meet on Friday evening, not at the Henderson home, our usual gathering place, but at St. Catherine Parish. There was a common area in the rectory large enough for entertaining a group that size.

At first I did not open the bar or offer drinks, leaving all to wonder just how serious the evening would be. I also did not begin with prayer, not that it wouldn't have been valuable, but I did not need God's assistance for what I was about to say. I would need it at the end, when my friends had gone and I was left alone. And by the close of the evening any one of them would be more than willing to invoke the Holy Spirit upon me. Not to mention that we would probably all need a drink at that point.

When everyone was seated I prepared to speak. I momentarily found myself silent as if standing on the edge of some bottomless glacial crevice, gathering final thoughts and courage before leaping into the abyss.

"I know this was not a regularly scheduled gathering and I'm very grateful all of you were able to be here. As I said when I called, this is urgent. We've all read Emily's articles in the *Times* over the last few weeks. They have reawakened the entire city to my family's tragedy. Resurrecting this story, however, was not something Emily accomplished on her own or out of the blue. The idea was hatched some months ago and there was a specific intent.

"Contrary to what people think they know, the murders are not entirely unsolved. I guess I should more accurately say that Lt. Tom Moran knows for certain who was responsible, but it is not something that will hold up in a court of law. That is what caused the investigation to stall in the first place.

"Over the last several months Tom and I both worked with Emily to help her put all the information together. The three of us were aware that running the series in the *Los Angeles Times* carried certain risks. For one thing, success was not guaranteed. Nothing new would actually emerge in Emily's writing except to inform the public of evidence the police had withheld. But we hoped that maybe in an effort to further cover his tracks, the murderer might make a mistake that could be used against him. Of great concern was the possibility that Emily would be in danger. Still, we pressed forward.

"Unfortunately, our plan did not work. Emily has remained safe, but far from forcing an error, I think we have only emboldened the killer, making him feel even more invincible. Our attempts to unmask him resulted in yet another death. It's obvious now that the *Los Angeles Times* was not a sufficient weapon. Something more needs to be done and that's why you're all here tonight."

This must have been sounding quite ominous. I did not want them to think that I was forming some kind of posse. I also did not want to keep them in the dark for long. I had adequately set the stage.

"Let me first tell you about Tom Moran. Much of his investigation proceeded on the assumption that my brother was being blackmailed and the death of his lawyer, as Emily noted in the *Times,* gave some credence to that theory. But as Tom continued to pursue a variety of leads he eventually found himself face to face with the actual murderer and in that moment successfully solicited an admission of guilt. It was, unfortunately, offered in such a way that it does not constitute evidence or even justify an arrest. But the story gets better, or I should say worse.

"Because I am Giuseppe's brother, and Tom is a childhood friend, the killer realized that Tom would share any information he received with me and made a stunning, calculated decision to speak with me about the murders. Setting aside the actual deaths of my family, this may be the most evil element of the story. The murderer, realizing that I did not yet know who he was, confessed to me in the Sacrament of Reconciliation."

I paused to let that revelation sink in. Each person in that room immediately grasped the significance and import of what I said. These were people deeply committed to their faith who held respected positions of leadership in the church. They did not need much time to understand why my emotions had been so erratic over the past three years. Each understood my dilemma and intuitively suspected what I had in mind. I looked around the room and wondered where I would find support.

My hopes rested primarily with Brian Henderson and Bill Messenger. They were the two most iconoclastic members of the group. In our twenty years of supporting one other, they were the ones who intellectually gnawed at the rough edges of Catholic teaching, occasionally taking a hammer and chisel to the silly stuff.

I remember one meeting when we were discussing Catholic funeral rites. The church expects its members to be buried in Catholic cemeteries—sacred, consecrated ground. Brian rightly ridiculed the idea that a bishop could stand at one edge of a piece of ground, say a prayer, and the blessing he cast would stop at the fence on the other side. Bill added the comment that no blessing was needed to make the ground sacred. Quoting the poet Allen Ginsberg, he noted that everything is holy. But that night not even Brian or Bill was quick to jump to my defense.

"Please tell me," Bill said, "that you are not planning to do what I think you are."

"I am," I replied.

No one was aghast, but I had the distinct impression that I was standing alone, an invisible, but impenetrable divide separating me from my friends. I continued, "This is a very difficult decision and something I've contemplated for some time. I'm not being cavalier about it."

"Maybe not," Judy said. "But you're trampling a fundamental principle of our faith. The secrecy of the sacrament can't be broken."

Of everyone in the room, Barbara was probably the least appropriately named at birth. There was nothing foreign about her, as her moniker would suggest. She exuded a calm temperament more associated with Sophia. Barbara was truly a wise woman. She certainly was not going to agree with my choice, but took pains not to overreact.

"Wait a minute, everybody," she said. "Let's not be too quick to judge. This can't be easy for Gio. Let's hear him out."

"Thanks, Barbara," I replied. "Look, I already said that I'm not rushing into this. In fact, I discussed it with Cardinal Mahony about a month ago."

"What did he say?" Perry asked.

"What do you think?" I answered. "He used one of his favorite words, reminding me that it would not be 'helpful.' But I didn't go there to ask his advice or permission. This is bigger than me, and if I move forward he'll be questioned by the press. I thought I owed him a heads up. That's also the reason you're all here tonight. We've been through a lot over the last twenty years and I wouldn't be much of a friend if I didn't forewarn you."

Tim had always been a movie buff. When he spoke it was within that context. "Gio, even in fiction, the seal of the confessional has always been sacred. I can't think of one time that it has been broken. By contrast there are several movies in which priests suffer physical and psychological harm to preserve the secrecy of the sacrament."

"Tim's right," Perry added. "There's simply no precedent for breaking the seal."

"But this is different from a normal confession," I insisted. "This person was not looking for healing or forgiveness. There was no repentance, merely an attempt to pervert the sacrament. In fact, the only intentionality was abuse."

"That sounds more like a rationalization than a justification," Bill said.

I knew I had done the right thing by telling everyone, but I was really feeling isolated. I turned to Brian and said, "You're a doctor. You know about secrecy, about life and death. Can't you back me up?"

"I don't think so, Gio," he replied. "There's no comparison between our worlds when it comes to this. I certainly have issues with some of the church's teachings, but not this one. I will say, though, that I don't think the murderer's intention changes anything."

Barbara agreed. "It's not really a question of intention, Gio. You're being way too subtle. Even if people could make that distinction the integrity of the sacrament is based on perception. If there is reason to believe that a confession took place, whether or not it was genuine, then revealing what was said is what causes the damage."

"You should let God decide what's true and what isn't," Tim suggested. "Your obligation is to preserve the sacrament."

Not only was I isolated and alone on this issue, this was turning into a lecture and I was growing irritated.

Gilbert always kept things at their most basic and his question was simple: "Why do you have to do this anyway? Why not just stay quiet? It's not your job to bring the killer to justice. Besides, no one is pressuring you to say anything. I think it's all in your mind."

Judy, Gilbert's female counterpart, chimed in, "Are you sure you're not just looking for some kind of revenge?"

I was really feeling frustrated. I was sitting with seven trusted friends, had not made myself clear, and could get no one to agree with me. Maybe I should not have tried to speak to so many people at one time.

"This is not a question of justice or revenge," I insisted. "Of course, I'd like to see the murderer of my family pay for his crime. But there is something more going on. The killing continues. I already told you another person died since the *Times* started publishing Emily's articles. I have an opportunity to end this carnage."

"You don't know that," Perry said. "But even if you're right, is the cost worth it?"

"If you mean excommunication, I know that follows immediately and automatically upon breaking the seal."

"And you're willing to accept that?" Tim asked.

I took a good look at everyone before I answered. I had already asked myself that question. Excommunication is a big issue in any church. But it cannot separate someone from the love of God, or the love of friends. I was more concerned about being removed from ministry. After all, I had given my entire life in service to God and his church. I didn't know where I'd be without that, but I knew the answer to Tim's question.

"The short answer, Tim, is yes." Then I glanced at everyone in the room. "You all make it sound as if I'm being naive. Believe me, I've done the soul searching, my spirit split in two. My whole life I have believed and accepted, never needing to know how God would wield evil into a force for good. I just trusted that there was a higher plan at work. Until now that faith has sufficed.

"Today I am confronted by an evil I could have never fathomed. I see only two choices before me. I am falling helplessly but faith has not come to my rescue. Real lives are at risk. If my decision is wrong, then I trust God to wield it into a force for good. But this is the best I can do. So, yes, I am willing to accept excommunication."

"Then I don't see what more needs to be said," Brian observed. "I can't agree with your decision, Gio, but I can support you. As has always been the case, you have a room in our house any time you need it."

I looked at both him and Judy and simply said, "Thanks."

Once again I looked around at my friends. Then I said, "You've all made your positions clear, and to be honest I wasn't trying to change your minds. Nor was I expecting you to change mine. It just wouldn't have been right if you found about this like everyone else. I called a press conference for Monday afternoon and we'll see what happens after that."

"Do you want any of us to be there?" Perry asked.

"I don't think so. I appreciate the offer, but Tom and Emily will be there. And we're the ones who set this whole thing in motion."

"Why don't we take a moment to pray?" Barbara suggested.

To be honest, I was more interested in a drink. Still, I couldn't argue with her. These friends of mine were people of faith, and they were concerned about me. For them, prayer was not an artificial crutch. It was a source of strength and wisdom, two things I would need regardless of Monday's outcome.

Barbara's prayer tapped into our rich heritage, not just as people of faith, but as friends who had supported and encouraged one another through many of life's crises. When she finished praying I offered a variety of drinks. Despite our years of friendship mundane conversation did not come easily that evening. I treasured all of them but was grateful when the last person had left. I was exhausted and wanted only to sleep.

CHAPTER 27

It is the nature of youth to be rash, whether jumping to anger over a trivial slight or being rushed into love by superficial beauty. I had been no different from anyone else while growing up. But by forty-nine I had long abandoned reckless actions and impetuous decisions. Saturday I took stock of the distances I had traveled and the major events of my life. Two stood out as delineating the biggest transitions.

First there was the physical. Like most teenagers, although confused, puberty opened a whole new world, one that is more separated from childhood than adulthood is from adolescence. Parents rarely prepare their children and mine were no exception. And despite what turned out to be only the "street knowledge" of classmates, I quickly discovered what everyone does: that my friends were wrong. I was convinced that my experience was unique. What was happening to me had never happened to anyone else, at least not in the same way. Still, the rapid succession of visible changes allows most people to adjust to that powerful transformation quickly. The same cannot be said of the spiritual.

This second transformation is a drawn out process, requiring a maturity of thought. Unlike puberty which will take its course no matter what intervenes, developing one's connection with the divine does not occur without strong personal investment.

My faith drew me to the seminary at an early age. During those years it deepened beyond my expectations. I grew up in a strong Catholic family and had always believed in the basic tenets of our faith. Preparing for ministry convinced me not just of truth but also of presence. Not only is Jesus the fulfillment of God's promises to ancient Israel, he *is* God and he lives among us, in each of us. At my ordination, when Cardinal Timothy Manning placed his hands on my head and called down the power of the Holy Spirit, I was changed—changed by a love I was still coming to know and appreciate. That experience opened another whole new world.

In the intervening years I was on a modest trajectory, with no great ambitions and not suffering from delusions of grandeur. I was simply a priest doing what I always wanted, what I believed I was called to do. Though far from perfect, I was liked by many a parishioner. And while there were setbacks and failures, I was mostly happy. Until December 27, 2000, when my brother confessed to me that he had his wife and children murdered.

As catastrophic as that was it did not usher in a new transition. I continued to fulfill my priestly responsibilities. I just did it from within a whirlwind of confusion and bouts of depression. It all led up to this long Saturday of examination. I planned out the events of the next two days. Sunday would be difficult—turbulent for me and bewildering to the parishioners of St. Catherine Parish. But Monday? That was harder to prepare for, at least emotionally. Many lives would be upended that day unless I kept silent. Then again, in the long run many more lives would be upended if Giuseppe continued to operate at full rein. Emily's skillful writing would not be the end of him. Somehow he would survive her ignominious implications. Breaking my silence would enflesh the story written in the *Los Angeles Times*. Breaking my silence was the only thing that would make my brother bleed.

On Saturday afternoon I took one last trip through my history from childhood to the present, noting transitions big and small, and realized that Monday would be the great watershed of my life.

• • •

I awoke Sunday morning, November 23, at five o'clock and went outside to retrieve the paper and bring it inside. The outside temperature was a brisk 41 degrees, the house a more comfortable 68. But I shivered as if I were freezing. I knew it was only nerves, but that knowledge did not warm me up. The headline in the *Los Angeles Times* read **"LOZANO MURDER INVESTIGATION NEARS CONCLUSION."** A subtitle proclaimed,

250

"News Conference Tomorrow Afternoon." Emily recapped the entire saga. She only needed to maintain interest until Monday afternoon. As such she promised a resolution, guaranteeing that the entire city would be a captive audience the next day.

On Friday I had informed the other priests that I would proclaim the Gospel and preach at all Sunday Masses. For practical reasons I opted not to co-opt the Saturday evening service. Just taking over on Sunday was quite unusual, especially given that this was the Feast of Christ the King, the last Sunday of the liturgical calendar. November 30 would begin the season of Advent and the church's four week preparation for Christmas. I was grateful that none of the priests pressed me regarding the reason for this change and I'm sure I surprised them when I stood up and proclaimed a different Gospel passage from the one assigned.

Gospel Reading
John 8:31–36
Then Jesus said to the Jews who had believed in him, "If you continue in my word, you are truly my disciples; and you will know the truth, and the truth will make you free." They answered him, "We are descendants of Abraham and have never been slaves to anyone. What do you mean by saying, 'You will be made free'?" Jesus answered them, "Very truly, I tell you, everyone who commits sin is a slave to sin. The slave does not have a permanent place in the household; the son has a place there forever. So if the Son makes you free, you will be free indeed."

Final Homily

"In each Sunday bulletin we cite the scripture readings for the following weekend and I know that many of you regularly reflect on those passages before coming to church. You will notice that the Gospel I just proclaimed is not the one assigned for today. I had a serious reason for changing it, especially since the Feast of Christ the King is a major solemnity.

"What you are about to hear might be troubling. I assure you it is far more difficult for me to say. This is my last day at St. Catherine parish and I owe you an explanation. I do not want to seem too cryptic, but at the moment I cannot fully disclose what is going on. What I would like to do now is set the foundation for this unexpected news.

"For over twenty years I have given my life in service to God, embracing the mission of Jesus and his church. It has been a fulfilling experience beyond my dreams because of people like yourselves who have enriched me beyond measure. You have shared with me hopes and passions, joys and sorrows. We have laughed together at births, baptisms, weddings; we have cried together in hospitals and cemeteries. You have humbled me by your openness and generosity of spirit. For all that, I am a better person and will forever be grateful.

"In turn I have tried to answer God's call, to bring his love to all people. In this parish we have worked together and built a community of openness and acceptance, of compassion, healing, and forgiveness. We have worked hard to break through the barriers of discrimination and prejudice, to welcome everyone. Like the USC Catholic Center down the street, people who are not Catholic come to worship here, some occasionally, some regularly. And never have they experienced any pressure to convert to the Catholic Church.

"We embrace people of every race and ethnicity; we receive and pass no judgment on people of various sexual orientations. In all of this we live up to the moniker of "catholic" whether spelled upper case or lower. We are not perfect and have more to do. But St. Catherine's is a church where people can truly find the presence of Jesus, and it is a parish where I would have been content to spend the rest of my priesthood. So why am I leaving?

"Most of you know that the last three years have been particularly difficult for me and my family. There are no words to express the feelings following the murders of my sister-in-law and her children. Many of you offered condolences in both word and action. That certainly helped ease the pain. But during that time I became privy to information I have been unable to share and watched silently as more atrocities, more murders were committed. It is that knowledge that caused me to change the Sunday Gospel. As I read this particular passage the other day I was struck by the ideas of truth and freedom.

"In John's Gospel "Truth" has a particularly poignant meaning. It refers to Jesus, himself. It is a word that cycles throughout the fourth Gospel like a spiral, drawing us ever deeper into the person of Jesus, who is ultimate Truth. When he was brought before Pilate, just before his crucifixion, Jesus said that he came into the world to testify to the truth. The absurdity of the governor's question, "What is truth?" lies in two facts: The first being that he was not seeking an answer, he was fully uninterested and the question expressed his irritation as he brought their discussion to an end; the second fact being that Pilate, in his frustration, unintentionally asked the right question but was too blinded to recognize that the answer was the very person standing before him.

"Freedom is intimately bound up with truth, for as we hear in today's reading, Jesus possesses the power to free people from sin. Christians, although we frequently stumble, are lifted up, supported, and driven forward by the belief that the truth—Jesus—will make us free.

"Over my years as a priest I have tried to faithfully proclaim and teach the Word of God. And although humility is not one of my strengths, I have steadfastly refrained from disagreeing with what we hear from Jesus in the four Gospels. However, today I am struck by the word *truth*. I do not want to suggest that Jesus was wrong, nor do I wish to equivocate, but the reality is that truth has multiple meanings in our lives. If we were truly pure of heart we might be able to stop with the statement as it appears in today's Gospel and leave here freed by that truth. But we are usually not so innocent. Maybe it is a further indication of our penchant for sin and deception, but the truth does not always set us free. Sometimes it binds us just as tightly as sin itself. We know things we should not, or we know things that we dare not share. Such truth is twisted by the reality of sin and it does not make us free.

"It is my belief that Jesus tries to enter our sinful lives and wrench us from the clutches of evil. For most of us, most of the time, he is successful and, at least for a few moments we experience the powerful but gentle embrace of God. For others the descent into darkness is so deep that it obscures the light— for themselves and for others. That is my situation. I have lived the last three years in a twilight that has increasingly trapped me in its gloom, allowing neither the evening moon nor the morning sun to break through. If it is a foreshadowing of some perpetual darkness I wish it upon no one. For myself I cannot continue to live in this dusk. Like the prisoner who digs a tunnel under his jail cell, I have found an escape. But it comes at great cost. I am unable to offer a full explanation today, but all will be revealed tomorrow.

"For today I want to reassure everyone of my faith in God and my love of priesthood and my love for this parish. Whatever befalls me in the days to come, I will always be grateful for the opportunity to serve, and will always keep you in my prayers, which is all I ask of you."

Following each of the Sunday Masses I deliberately made myself unavailable to greet anyone. There was one exception. I had asked my sister, Bianca, to bring her family and my mother to the last Mass. Afterward, I invited them into the house, but we went to my office rather than the living room. I had neither the desire nor the energy to engage in a social visit. Besides, I would not be able to explain anything I said in church, and my family being thoroughly Italian does not easily accept no for an answer. The more formal setting of the office would bolster my resolve.

"Mom, Bianca, Edward, I asked each of you to come to Mass today because I owe you more than I do the parishioners. And yet there is little I can add to what has already been said. My words today were deliberately shrouded in mystery. The reason will be clear tomorrow. And tomorrow is what I am concerned about—for myself, for all of our family, but most of all for you.

"I know you have been following Emily's articles in the *Times* and that they have made for very painful reading. I worked with Tom and Emily to prepare the materials in the hopes that publishing the series would bring closure to our family tragedy. Despite her skill, there is a piece of the puzzle missing that only I can supply and it cannot be done in a newspaper article.

"I have scheduled a news conference for tomorrow afternoon at one o'clock. I do not want you to be present, but I want you to be together to watch it on television. Bianca and Edward, you both need to take off work and be with Mom."

"What about your brother?" Mom asked. "Does he know?"

My mother had always been true to herself. It was not just the fact that she was Italian. I imagine any mother would have had a similar concern, but Latin-blooded peoples seem to be particularly emotional. I revealed nothing in either expression or speech. I was honest, but a little evasive.

"Yes, Mom. Giuseppe knows. He will not be able to be here tomorrow, but he will watch from Washington. Nothing I say tomorrow will be easy to hear. I don't want to sound any more mysterious than I already have. I can only assure that it will be difficult and you will need each other for support.

Since Giuseppe cannot be in Los Angeles I suggested that he watch the conference with some close friends."

I looked over at Bianca. She was as easy to read as a picture book. Just in case my eyes did not sufficiently communicate, I spoke. "Please, Bianca. Don't ask me any questions. There is nothing more that I can say until tomorrow, except that I love each of you very much."

I suspect those last words sounded more ominous than comforting, but they were the best I could muster and at least they were true. My family left more confused than when they arrived.

Over the years Tom and I had come to appreciate the great legends and heroes of history. One that we both admired was Julius Caesar. I headed back into the rectory. But as my family drove away I turned around to look at them and realized that I was standing on the other side of the Rubicon.

CHAPTER 28

Monday morning I awoke in a world I had never truly envisioned possible. Needing extended time for meditation and prayer I had cleared my calendar. Over the years I have frequently turned to the great composers to reflect and sometimes even to alter my moods. This day I was in need of something profoundly powerful and did what I always do in moments of deep darkness and despair. I sought salvation in Franz Schubert's String Quintet. In attempts to claw my way out of depression no work has ever rescued me as successfully. A masterpiece of sublime inspiration, the second movement alone is a transcendent stroll through empyreal paradise, hand in hand with the Almighty. Written at thirty-one, only two months before his death, I have often marveled at how someone of such a tender age could have so fully surrendered to the divine. But on Monday morning I was grateful he had.

Tom and Emily, who had invested so much of their own lives in pursuing the sordid mystery of power, arrogance, love, and death, were the only two friends I asked to be present for the news conference. They arrived at the rectory at noon and we spoke one last time about my impending statement. In rather unusual fashion, I did not offer any drinks. I would be under great scrutiny in an hour and could not risk raising unnecessary questions, suggestions, or hints about my sobriety.

The three of us talked for a while and Tom and Emily voiced a few last-minute concerns that were undoubtedly driven by jitters. If I followed through on this decision I would never be able to retract it. But they each knew that my resolve was unwavering and final. Still, I felt a need to express my gratitude for all they had done and the support they had provided.

"I know that the two of you are still uncertain about this course of action. I have my own misgivings, also. But Giuseppe has grown into such an evil that my greatest concern is protecting others. And it's not as if I don't know what I'm getting into. When I step before the media I will speak only truth. Then when the last camera is turned off, when the final word written, I will be at peace—for the first time in three years."

"I don't think that's true, Gio," Emily replied. "At least not completely. You will certainly feel some relief at unburdening yourself. But it will be some time before you find any real peace."

She was, of course, right. She was always right. But the time for discussion was over. I had made my decision.

At 12:30 p.m. the news media began to gather outside the church. Such was the interest generated by Emily's articles in the *Los Angeles Times,* that camera crews for the network affiliates as well as local television stations were all represented, as were print and radio reporters from every part of Southern California. At one o"clock I exited the rectory, walked over to the steps of the church, and took my place before the press. Despite my determination I was frightened, overwhelmed, and empowered all at the same time.

．　．．　．

"I want to thank all of you for coming out this afternoon. But I have to admit that it is with difficulty and trepidation that I stand before you. Like Schubert, the great nineteenth century composer, I feel torn between the greatest love and the greatest sorrow. I called this news conference to make an important announcement about the articles that have recently appeared in the *Los Angeles Times* and the murders they detail. Permit me a few moments to share the context in which that announcement is made.

"We do not live in a time of myth and legend. Gods are not battling among themselves for control of the heavens or the earth. I suppose it was easier in ancient times when all the world's problems could be blamed on the capriciousness of deities. But we know that is not the case. In my tradition there is but one God and he seeks neither power nor control. We alone are responsible and accountable for the good and the evil that consume us.

"I am a Catholic priest and I believe in Jesus. In my heart I know him to be that same God so many of us worship in so many different ways. When he entered the world, he did so as we all do: weak, humble, and vulnerable. He grew into an adult as we all do. And as an adult he taught us to use power for service, not glory. He taught us to conquer evil with good, to overcome violence with love. Sadly, these are lessons all too rarely learned.

"He taught us something else, too. That victory comes through sacrifice, and that sacrifice is not always easy. Today I make a very difficult choice. One that most non-Catholics may not fully comprehend, one that many of my colleagues in the church will certainly disagree with, one that I nonetheless find necessary.

"Three years ago four innocent people—my sister-in-law, Yolanda, and her children, Carmen, Gina, and Leonardo—were gunned down in their home in Hancock Park. That crime has so far gone unsolved. But over the last couple of weeks, thanks to the dedicated journalism of Emily Moran, the city's attention has been refocused on those murders and we can now lay them to rest.

"The series in the paper reported many previously unknown facts, and was filled with innuendo, but nothing that would bring the criminal to justice. The purpose of Ms. Moran's work was to flush out the murderer, possibly causing a misstep that would allow the justice system to apprehend him and bring the case to a close. There is, however, a deeper truth and reality to these murders that I wish to address today.

"For the last three years, two people have known the identity of the killer, or more accurately, the person who ordered the murders. One of those people is Lt. Tom Moran, the other is myself. Unfortunately, the manner in which we each came to possess this knowledge prevented us from using it in any public forum.

"The murderer first admitted his crime to me, but he did so as a confession, perverting a hallowed sacramental act. He knew, as do most people, that a priest is prevented from divulging anything he hears in the confessional. The Catholic Church considers this so sacred an obligation that a priest who violates the integrity and secrecy of the sacrament is automatically and immediately excommunicated. Thus the killer deliberately burdened me with a knowledge that has upended my life for the last three years. I not only had to live with the violent murder of people I loved, but as a priest I could reveal the identity of the killer to no one, not even to the detective in charge of the investigation.

"Having successfully silenced me, the killer next admitted his guilt to Lt. Tom Moran. In a face-to-face meeting the lieutenant used a hidden microphone and recorder while eliciting the truth. Whereas the killer's confession to me was an exercise in evil, his revelation to Lt. Moran was fiendishly clever. A sophisticated anti-surveillance system had been activated that prevented the recording of any conversation. This left the lieutenant without any verifiable proof and no grounds for arrest. Had Lt. Moran said anything three years ago it would have been only hearsay and of no evidentiary value.

"When I was ordained a priest I accepted that part of my ministry was the preservation of every secret heard in the confessional. Until now I never envisioned myself violating that sacred responsibility. Unfortunately, the articles in the *Times* did not have the desired effect. Not only is the murderer still at large, but last week another person was killed in an effort to extend the shadow of secrecy. In total, this person has been responsible for the deaths of ten people. There is every reason to believe that the killing will continue and I can no longer allow that to happen.

"The person who ordered the murder of my sister-in-law and her children; who was indirectly responsible for the death of one of the assassins; who arranged the killing of a Los Angeles attorney; who orchestrated the murders of three men in Belgium, and last week a man in Boston; the person who confessed his crime to me; and the person who was behind all these murders is my brother, Senator Giuseppe Lozano.

Cameras began clicking at such speed that the sound of the shutters became a single whir. After a few moments of stunned silence, the reporters began firing questions. I did not have the energy to field their queries. I was not even sure my legs would continue to support me. I thought back to Emily's comment a few hours before. She was right. I did not experience any peace. But I was free.

* * *

Washington, D.C., had been abuzz with talk about the press conference. Giuseppe arranged to address the media from the steps of the capitol immediately after I finished speaking in Los Angeles. At 3:00 p.m. eastern time, he made an excuse to leave his office, and promised to return at four o'clock in time to hear me speak. Not surprisingly he did not heed my advice. He chose to watch with neither staff nor friends.

He had no idea what I would say and I suspect that for the first time he actually felt events spinning out of control. He wanted to be left alone. Only by himself could he figure out how to respond to any allegations I might make.

He drove to Georgetown and quietly entered his house unnoticed and undisturbed. He walked through the house taking stock of all that had transpired over the previous three years. He even paused to look at a picture of himself with Jackson enjoying dinner at a Maryland restaurant. At 3:55 he turned on the television and sat down to watch.

Just as I began to address the media the doorbell rang. He was fairly certain that no one saw him return home and he did not want to be disturbed. At the same time he knew that his staff would be worried and it stood to reason that his secretary or campaign manager was checking up on him. They, however, did not have a key. For Giuseppe carefully guarded his privacy. The only person he had ever entrusted with a key was Jackson.

He went to the door and just as he opened it he heard the quiet "thuup" of a silenced revolver. A moment later he lay dead on the porch, one bullet through his heart, a Glock 9mm pistol beside him.

CHAPTER 29

As the four o'clock hour drew near, heralding the beginning of my press conference, Giuseppe had still not returned to his office. He was known for punctuality, so there was some reason for concern. On the other hand, he was also a private person. Not even his closest associates knew his deepest thoughts and feelings. His campaign manager, Bill Morgan, assured the staff that all was well and that Giuseppe, overwhelmed with the *Times's* renewed interest in his family's murders, wanted some time alone and would return in due course. Secretly, even Morgan began to worry. The Washington press corps would be expecting a response from the senator immediately after my press conference. He called Giuseppe's mobile and home telephone numbers but received no reply. He waited in the office and switched on the television as I began speaking to the media.

From the day Giuseppe entered politics Morgan had been at his side and knew him as well as anyone, or as well as anyone could. As I rolled through the elements of my speech, Morgan began to worry. He knew about the electronic device known as the Silencer and when I detailed Giuseppe's admission to Tom, he shuddered in fear. Even before I reached the point of accusation he picked up the phone, called the D.C. police, informed them that my brother was in danger, and asked for an immediate dispatch to Giuseppe's home.

The moment that I accused Senator Lozano of multiple murders, chaos and confusion darted through the Washington establishment. The press and members of Congress were all in a state of disarray. In three short years Giuseppe had become a savvy and popular member of the senate—his star rising, his future undimmed. While he was not expected to win the presidential nomination in 2004, his brash challenge of a sitting president coupled with his moderate and peace-oriented policies positioned him as the leading candidate for 2008. Through the combined magic of radio and television, his luster suddenly faded and he was felled from the firmament by an accuser standing three thousand miles away.

When the police arrived at my brother's home in Georgetown they were greeted by the same crime scene that had confounded the authorities in Los Angeles, Brussels, and Boston.

Having opted against answering questions, I stepped away from the cameras at the conclusion of my statement. The rectory was adjacent to the church and Tom and Emily walked with me, each of us aware that I was entering it for the last time as my home. Media and police phones were already ringing around the country. In a silver screen movie from the 1940s there would have been at most a half-dozen reporters present who would have scrambled to find telephones in order to report back to their newspapers. Now everyone had a mobile phone at the ready. We had not even reached the front steps when Tom's phone rang. As he answered I looked back and saw the members of the press rushing toward the house. Tom insisted we enter immediately. He practically pushed me through the door then closed it.

"What's wrong, Tom?" I asked.

"Let's go upstairs," he said. The three of us went into the living room and sat down.

"Gio, Giuseppe's dead."

I was so stunned I could not even muster a question. I sat in a ghostly state of disbelief unable even to bring my vision into focus.

Emily asked, "What happened?"

"The police found his body on the front porch of his house. You can guess the M.O. He was shot dead with one bullet through the heart and a Glock handgun was left at the scene."

Beginning to return to reality I was able to ask, "How is this possible? He was the one who ordered the other killings. Who would have ordered his?"

"All I can give you is speculation, Gio. But there was one murder your brother was never directly involved with."

"Bass," Emily suggested.

"Exactly," Tom answered. "We know that Yolanda and the children were killed by two people. Bass made a mistake that night—only one. His foot slipped and left an imprint in the flowerbed but it was enough for us to track him down. The other assassin, however, made no mistakes. Bass was our only link to the murders. If we had been able to arrest him, the other killer would have been compromised. That's why he was murdered."

"And Giuseppe?" I asked.

"He was the only other link to the assassin. On four different occasions Giuseppe hired him to kill, one of those on a different continent. Whoever this guy is, he's a professional. My guess is that your brother had become a liability."

Admittedly, this case had consumed Tom for three years. Nonetheless, listening to him so quickly process information and weave together a compelling narrative was amazing. As we sat there his analysis reaffirmed my belief that the LAPD lost a great detective when Tom resigned.

•　　•　　•

Tom and Emily stayed with me for a couple of hours. During that time I began putting my affairs in order. First I called Cardinal Mahony. He attempted to be compassionate but was not convincing. To be fair, his own feelings were a bit raw. Despite the advance notice I had given him, he really expected me to preserve the seal of the confessional. Although he conveyed a hint of understanding, his disappointment and anger were unmistakable. I had put him in a difficult situation. But he could take care of himself. He always displayed masterful skill in front of the media. He would be just fine.

After Tom and Emily left I began to remember. When we were kids I could get so angry at Giuseppe. But we were brothers and eventually we would make up. I recalled the title words to a Kenny Rogers song, "I Wish That I Could Hurt That Way Again." Three years before I had shed all my tears for Yolanda, Carmen, Gina, and Leonardo. I had nothing left for my brother. I didn't feel hurt or anger or any other emotion. I felt nothing.

After lingering with those empty feelings for a while I went over to my sister's house. This would be terribly complex for my family.

263

The air of depression in the house was similar to the night Yolanda and the children were killed. It wasn't just the news conference. It wasn't just Giuseppe's guilt. It was his death. My mom took it the hardest. I'm not sure she fully understood what was happening. My father had only been dead for a month and now she lost one of her two sons. I figured there would be time enough in the future to help her piece everything together.

My sister on the other hand understood completely. But she did not know how to respond. She had known for three years that Giuseppe and I had grown far apart. Each time she broached the subject I deflected. At those times I was in no position to explain the truth. That night she grasped it all. Not unlike my support group she could not believe that I had betrayed the sacrament. In her mind that decision was the proximate cause of our brother's death. It would take her some time to get over that belief even though she now knew the depth of his depravity.

•   •   •

Mahony had graciously given me the rest of the week to move out of St. Catherine Parish, during which time I was to have minimal contact with parishioners. That was not a problem. I had no desire to subject myself to relentless questioning and possible condemnation. I was content to leave the next pastor to assuage their concerns regarding the security of their sacramental secrets. For the next several days I hardly left my room. One exception was Tuesday, my usual day off—that is, until that week when every day became a day off.

I was not in the mood for a casual conversation with friends at a cozy Mexican restaurant where we were well-known patrons. Nor did I wish to escape to the darkness of a movie theatre or while away the hours in a record store. My mind was murky, my thoughts obscure. My friends knew I should not be inundated but they also knew I should not be alone. Perry suggested a change of routine, a simple lunch, just the two of us.

He picked me up at St. Catherine, then we drove to Malibu and had lunch at Gladstone's restaurant. Located on the Pacific Coast Highway, it had been a popular landmark since the early 1980s. After our meal we walked for a long time along the beach speaking not a word. We listened to the waves rhythmically breaking upon the shore and watched pelicans gracefully gliding across the water. The silence of our stroll reminded me of a scene in A. J. Cronin's novel, *The Citadel.*

Dr. Andrew Manson, who had traded his principles for fortune, lost his wife in a tragic accident just as he was pulling his life together and recovering the idealism of his youth. A friend of his, Dr. Philip Denny, dragged him off to a deserted abbey in southeast Wales. Each day they went for progressively longer walks. After more than a month of this convention, mental and physical healing broke through and the two men made plans for opening a new medical practice.

But I was not a character in a novel and there was no new ministry in my future. I appreciated Perry's efforts that day, but in the evening I returned to a room that was no longer home. As I continued to pack my belongings I looked around and realized that I had become a stranger, discarded by and unwelcome in the church I had served for twenty years. It was a repercussion of my own actions, or as some might more critically assess, my hubris. My only comfort came in the knowledge that the church is not the institution. It is the people. Although I would undoubtedly be spurned by many, there were a handful of others, including my family, who would never reject me.

On Wednesday evening I had dinner with Tom and Emily, a meal of fried chicken, creamed corn, and French fries. My press conference and Giuseppe's death had become the topics of conversation at many a dinner table. That night I had the benefit of being with the only people who knew the details as intimately as I. We were exhausted from endless discussions and were each looking for a respite. But such is the pull of extraordinary drama that even we could not escape talking about the week's events. All of our futures were tied to a past that had just exploded. It seemed as if the three of us had braved the fires of hell and barely survived. At least in their company I was able to give voice to questions and uncertainties that I had previously ignored.

"I understand why people pray," I said. "There is a need for balance in our world. We see evil that we cannot control, so we believe that someone else can. And we pray. With our beliefs, regardless the religion, come rules. We expect those rules to free us. Instead they end up binding us. And so we pray some more. But contrary to what religious leaders say, God does not always answer."

My friends sat silent for a moment wondering if there were any other revelations pent up inside of me. Then Emily spoke.

"Gio, I've never heard such fatalism from you. More than any person I've ever met, you know how complex life is. I don't think you really believe what you just said."

Maybe she was right—again. Perhaps I was just taking advantage of being in a safe environment with no need to cushion my remarks. Certainly I was feeling guilty. That much was obvious. I had betrayed my principles and at least indirectly caused my brother's death. And although I paid lip service to my culpability, there was something that did not seem just about my situation. Faithfulness should not be measured in black and white. It exists on a spectrum. And I had been, through most of my priesthood, mostly faithful.

"You want to talk about the complexity of life?" I asked. "Look at where Tom and I are today. How much does either of us deserve this?"

There was an unintended petulance underlying my question as if I were a teenager complaining about life not being fair. Even so, Emily was not ruffled. She was probably the most gentle, even-tempered, and wise person I knew.

"Gio," Emily said lovingly, "I don't sit in judgment on the two of you. But there are consequences to every choice we make, good or bad. It's not a question of whether or not you deserve this. In fact, I happen to think you don't. It's just an aftermath none of us can control. You need to avoid the risk of falling prey to illusion."

"Meaning what?" I asked.

"We all want to be more than we really are," she answered. "No group of people is what it pretends to be—not the country, not the media, not the LAPD, not the church. The church is not as forgiving, the LAPD not as just, the media not as honest, and the country not as free. To some extent all life is an illusion. You did your part to change that. You lifted the veil. But the world is not going to thank you for it."

There was no point in continuing to beat that conversation. Emily had the upper hand and the clearer head. So I moved on. Maybe it was the transition unfolding before me, but I felt as if something was unfinished and wondered aloud, "What about the assassin?"

"Does it matter?" Tom asked. "He was not the person we were pursuing. He was just a hired gun, nameless and faceless. If not him, it would have been someone else. As far as I'm concerned we got the real killer. I don't want to sound heartless, but justice was served."

"Tom," Emily started to caution him. But I stopped her.

"It's OK, Em. I know Giuseppe was my brother, but on some level I think we all feel the same way."

"He was my brother, too," Tom insisted. "The two of you were the only brothers I ever had. For me that all changed three years ago when he murdered four people I loved. As for the hired killer, I'm through with this case. I've given copies of everything I have to the departments in Los Angeles, Brussels, Boston, and Washington. They also have Emily's articles from the *Times*. If they want to chase a phantom, they can have at it. But they'll never find him."

"What are you going to do now, Gio?" Emily asked.

"I don't know. I'm going to stay with my mom for a while. She'll need someone to watch her. And it'll take some of the stress off Bianca who has her own kids to take care of."

"You're an excellent counselor," she said. "Why not go back to school and get another degree or at least a certification?"

"I won't rule it out," I replied. "But I'm not ready to make that kind of a commitment. I need to recoup and reenergize. What I really want to do is sleep. I think I could set a record of sixteen hours straight! But I know everything would be the same when I woke up."

I really was feeling tired. I went back to the rectory earlier and more sober than usual. I still had some packing to do.

•   •   •

I was ready to leave the parish by Thursday afternoon and Tom agreed to help me move. I took only the items that were mine, leaving behind the furniture as well as anything I deemed unnecessary. That part of the experience was not unpleasant. I realized how easily material things had cluttered my life. To chart a future I would really need only my computer, my books, and my music. I had rented a small truck large enough to hold everything I needed. We loaded my possessions, then I said goodbye to the staff.

Tom and I drove to my mom's house where we proceeded to unload all the same items. I put them in the room I called mine as a child. The only thing I removed from the boxes was a twenty-five-year-old bottle of Glenfarclas scotch. I took two glasses from the kitchen and Tom and I went outside to have a drink.

Glasses in hand we leaned back against the truck, surveying our old neighborhood. Most of the families that had moved in over the years had children our age. Tom and I recalled many a childhood adventure and the sometimes dangerous games concocted in our imaginations. I started to laugh when I remembered the day he fell from the top of the house. Fortunately, he broke no bones and we swore every child present to secrecy. Parents tend to frown on kids playing on the roof.

Tom's mother and father still lived a couple of houses away, but many of the other families had long since moved. The street was quieter now and seemed much smaller than either of us remembered. We continued challenging each other's memories. Which of us could recall the most names of our neighbors? Who moved in and when? What cars did everyone drive? Occasionally one of us would successfully retell an event the other had forgotten. We alternated all these various recollections with moments of silence. As we drank I realized that I would not really want to return to my childhood. But it was a much simpler time. Of course reveling in the past did not liberate us from the present.

"Tom, I was thinking about what you said at dinner last night about the assassin, that he would never be caught. Do you really believe that?"

"Think about it, Gio. Including Giuseppe there were eleven people killed. And there is not a shred of evidence pointing to the person who pulled the trigger."

"So then, there is such a thing as a perfect murder?" I asked.

"Not in this case. Giuseppe was identified and brought to justice. He was the real killer. I don't think there's ever a perfect murder. But we may have encountered the perfect murder-*er*."

"That's cute," I said.

Tom could tell that I was still bothered and knew that I would be for a long time. He tried again to mollify my feelings and emphatically stated, "This is not your fault, Gio."

"Then why do I still feel as if it is?"

"Because you're a good person. And you think everyone else is, too. At least you think everybody can be redeemed. That's why you tried so hard to reach Giuseppe. Even after I told you there was nothing to save, you still tried. This is all on him. You're never going to find peace until you accept that. You've got to let it go, Gio. If there is a God, as you say, then Giuseppe is in his hands now."

I was so tired. I had spent my entire life talking, trying to share profound truths. I often found myself foiled not by ideas, but by the failure of language. In our world so many words have simply lost their meaning. These days people refer to one another as friends the day after meeting them. Maybe that says something about our need to be accepted or to feel connected. For despite our crowded streets and the density of our cities, we are really alone, alienated from one another. Instant friends allow us to believe that our lives—that *we*— matter. But it cheapens the value and essence of true friendship. The majority of people we know are, at best, associates, buddies, or comrades. I was standing with a friend.

"Tom, when I look at the last three years I know that you understand better than anyone what I have gone through. I don't just mean the tragedy of murder or confronting a narcissistic brother. In the words that have gone unspoken between us, I have come to understand and appreciate what Ralph Waldo Emerson meant when he wrote, 'A friend may well be reckoned the masterpiece of nature.' In truth, we don't make many good friends in a lifetime and I can count mine with ease. You, Tom, are my friend. And for that I am eternally grateful."

After he left that night I took stock of our lives. I was once again in the home where Giuseppe, Tom, and I played as children, in the room my brother and I had shared through adolescence. The unbreakable bond the three of us formed as children had been shattered by a cruel combination of greed, power, and lust. This was far from the world we envisioned in our youth.

That night I finally slept. Not for the sixteen hours I desired, but long enough to wake refreshed. In the morning I found that nothing had changed. Tom was no longer a cop, I was a "priest forever" with no place to minister, and Giuseppe was still dead. I was not really free but for the first time in a long time I did not feel as if everything depended on me. I was not yet at peace but I believed it was achievable. I had no idea where my future would take me, but for the first time in three years I could embrace it with hope.

Purchase other Black Rose Writing titles at www.blackrosewriting.com/books

and use promo code PRINT to receive a 20% discount.

BLACK ROSE writing™